To all boarding school alumni
especially the Feddy Girls and Boys:
"Hold your heads high. Pro Unitate!"

Chapter 1

Expelled!

Carlotta fingered the crudely rolled joint and marveled at its texture.

The lanky boy by her side watched with dead fish eyes, his greasy long hair limp and damp against the sides of his face, giving him the look of a homeless shaggy dog.

"Are you sure about this?" Carlotta asked.

The boy's eyes shifted. He leaned toward her, his voice dropping to a knowing whisper. "It's the best herb in town. Cost me a lot of dough, too."

Carlotta hesitated. The boy sounded like he was half-asleep or stoned out of his mind.

"Cigarettes are one thing, but I don't know about weed." She considered what she was about to do and her heart pounded.

Am I gonna get busted? She really didn't care, but since the shifty-eyed boy had smoked so much more dope, she wanted his opinion on how to handle unexpected occurrences.

She licked her lips. "What happens if we get busted? I mean, my parents don't even, like, know I totally smoke cigarettes—" she pinned the boy with a quizzical expression.

He was the notorious Sam Makiovich, nicknamed *Slinky Sam.*

He grunted. "Yeah, right... We only toke during recess and whenever we can cut classes—there's no harm in that." Slinky Sam fixed Carlotta with an amused stare for a second. His eyes

5

went blank again as he lifted one lazy shoulder. "Cigarettes are for sissies—who needs that stuff? *Wanna* go on a good ride? This joint here is all *ya* need."

Carlotta grinned.

Slinky Sam was a perpetual sixth grader with a moth-nibbled beard, who had enough of a bad reputation to buy a lifetime's worth of notoriety. At the same time, his nefarious actions never seemed to land him in any serious trouble with the school authorities. He was reputed to have the best connection for drugs in the school, and he had a knack for choosing the right students to whom he marketed his illegal wares.

He must so have a bumming-radar or something. How did he know I needed something more tripping than just cigs today? To Carlotta, Slinky was the best answer to an unspoken need for escape from her miserable life. She hated school and wanted out, but her parents wouldn't dream of letting her drop out of seventh grade.

It will totally serve them right if I, like, get busted.

They were behind the school dumpster, sandwiched between the wrought iron spikes of the school fence and the huge bin. Several boys sat a few feet away with their backs against the black metal surface of the bin. They were either in the seventh or eighth grade, Carlotta wasn't sure. One of them inhaled deeply on his joint, threw his head back, and let out a series of perfect smoke rings. The others giggled.

Watching the floating white circles distort and dissipate into thin air a few inches above her head, Carlotta smiled in wonder. She had never managed to blow a perfect smoke ring. Shrugging, she reached into her jeans pocket, pulled out a ten-dollar bill, and handed it to the shifty-eyed boy at her side.

Slinky tore it from her fingers and made it disappear at once. He immediately produced a cigarette lighter from nowhere and snapped on a flame.

Carlotta placed the joint between her lips and leaned close to the flame, moving her wavy brown stresses away from her face with her left hand. Her eyes perked. She raised her brows in expectation. Her heart pounded with excitement.

How totally wasted will marijuana make me? She sucked in a deep breath, her lips taut around the rough end of the joint. She could hear her heart beating wildly, *thump-thump!*

I so need to get wasted; my life sucks and my parents are total jerks. She watched the reefer glow red at one end then closed her eyes for a second and inhaled. The warm smoke sailed down her windpipe and into her lungs. She waited for the promised buzz.

It feels like—

"Hold it right there, all of you!" The voice was masculine. Harsh. Deep. Angry.

Carlotta flipped her eyes open in consternation, the spent smoke curling its way out through her nose and mouth.

Slinky Sam was gone.

Approaching was the gym teacher, a beefy mountain of a man with a pudgy face that was now rigid with disapproval.

Quickly, Carlotta threw down the smoking joint and clamped her hands over her face in a desperate attempt to hide the obvious. At the same time, she stamped her foot repeatedly over the joint on the ground, crushing it beneath her heel.

Busted! She braced herself for what was to come.

The four seventh-graders also stamped-out their joints; their eyes glazed with the confused sounds of their giggles. It wouldn't take more than a dumb teacher to tell they were already high and sailing.

But Carlotta wasn't high, and she certainly wasn't amused. The gym teacher was a drag; he always poked his nose where it wasn't wanted. He had cost her ten bucks and she would make him pay—*one way or another.*

Carlotta looked around again for Slinky Sam. The boy had an uncanny way of getting himself out of sticky situations, leaving his not so clever customers to extricate themselves as well as they could. As usual, he'd melted away from the scene before he could be identified. How he always managed his escape,

7

nobody knew. One minute he was right there with them, the next, he wasn't.

In four long strides, the gym teacher closed the distance between himself and the wayward students. He landed a heavy hand on Carlotta's shoulder. "What were you doing? Were you smoking—"?

"Let go of me," Carlotta screeched, and struggled. The next thing she knew, she was being dragged to the principal's office. The four boys apprehended with her came on their own accord, not minding that they'd been busted for dope smoking in school. They staggered along with deadpan expressions and let out an occasional giggle or sigh for the benefit of no one in particular.

Carlotta knew their type—they were the lucky ones. *They'll be so glad to totally get suspended. Finally, they can quit school without anyone making a fuss.*

"How on earth did you come about *this*?" Mrs. McWatters, the principal of the middle school, demanded in her office, the loose flesh on her neck wiggling as she spoke.

Carlotta glanced around and stalled for time. She knew it wouldn't be cool to rat out Slinky Sam, so she struggled to come up with some other kind of explanation. *Quick! Say something.*

The gym teacher moved off to one side and started describing what he had discovered in a high-minded voice.

"I had it at home last night," Carlotta cut-in, her eyes narrowing in defiance. She flashed a scathing look at the gym teacher who immediately fell silent and backed away.

"I want to know who supplied you with— With this stuff," the principal demanded. "Don't you dare turn your back on me, young lady!" she added, yanking on Carlotta's arm to prevent her from walking away.

"It's called marijuana and I brought it to school with me, all right?" Carlotta snapped. "Jeez! Leave me alone." She struggled to pry Mrs. McWatters' clamp-like fingers off her arm. "Let go of me," she screamed. "I hate you and your stupid school!"

But when the principal's fingers wouldn't budge, Carlotta

planted her teeth around the woman's wrist and clamped her jaw shut with all her might.

Startled, Mrs. McWatters yelped like a puppy and released her prey immediately. Cradling her injured arm to her chest, she stepped back to her desk and picked up the phone.

"Get Dr. Ikedi on the line for me at once!" She slammed down the receiver.

* * *

Dr. Shelley Ikedi was at her office, in the middle of a conversation with two of her graduate students when the phone rang with a shrill insistent sound.

She reached for it. "English Language Department, Dr. Ikedi speaking."

Shelley raised a forefinger to her students, silently requesting their indulgence for a minute. She listened for a moment then abruptly sat up straight, her face draining of color.

"Oh God, not again," she groaned, and crumpled. She pinched the bridge of her nose with her fingers, took a deep breath, and listened some more to the voice on the other end of the line.

"Yes, yes, thank you," she said in a shaky voice. "I, I will be right there." She hung up and got to her feet.

"I am so sorry, students, but there is an emergency I need to deal with right away. Shall we continue with our discussion later?" Shelley reached for her handbag and picked up her keys, upsetting a few paper files in the process.

The files hit the floor with a muffled thump, spewing their contents at her feet.

She stepped over the scattered papers, bustled the students out of her office, and slammed the door. She rushed at once to the exit at the end of the hall, the two graduate students striving to keep up with her.

"Maybe we can drop by this afternoon?" one of the students asked.

"It is likely I will be away for the rest of the day," Shelley replied. "Tomorrow morning might be a more convenient arrangement." She rounded the hallway and bounded down the stairs.

Once outside the building, she headed toward the faculty parking lot, her thoughts flying in every direction. She had just been informed that her daughter, Carlotta, was in discord with the school again. Mrs. McWatters' restrained voice over the phone had made her uneasy.

"Your daughter has landed herself in a lot of trouble…"

There was no telling what kind of mess Carlotta was in this time.

Shelley approached her car and felt for the remote button attached to her key chain. Her hands shook so badly she dropped the keys twice before managing to get the door open. She dumped herself behind the wheel of the blue Honda, and flung her handbag down on the front passenger seat.

"Goddamn it," she blurted, mentally kicking herself for being so wrangled with nerves.

Just one swallow—heaven knows I need it.

Shelley glanced suspiciously around. Certain no one was watching, she reached down and removed a small, liquor bottle wrapped in a creased, brown paper bag from underneath the front passenger seat. She uncapped the bottle, ducked, and took a long pull of the clear, fiery liquid, then replaced the bottle, making sure it was well-hidden from curious eyes.

She waited a few seconds for the shaking in her hands to subside then turned on the car ignition and backed out of the parking spot.

Twenty minutes later, when Shelley arrived at Carlotta's school, a straight-faced and swollen-handed Mrs. McWatters informed her that Carlotta was expelled indefinitely from school because of the use and possession of marijuana.

"You are in so much trouble, young lady," Shelley raged as she drove Carlotta home. "What on earth were you thinking?"

"Just leave me alone, all right?" Carlotta snapped.

"You will not speak to me like that—"

"Screw you!"

"You do not dare swear at me!" Shelley's temper rose like steam from a boiling kettle. In her anger, she lost control of the car and it skidded.

Shelley panicked.

Oh God! She swerved. Then swerved again, managing to keep from wrapping the car around a lamppost. She struggled to regain control of the vehicle by turning the steering wheel—first one way, then the next—within the space of a few seconds. Drivers around them quickly switched lanes in a bid to avoid a disastrous collision. A silver sports car let out a series of sharp beeps and zipped by.

In a desperate attempt to regain control of both her car and composure, Shelley gripped the wheel so hard her hands lost all color and appeared to be made of wax. Adrenaline raced through her veins. Her eyes darted from the road to the rear view mirror.

Carlotta pretended not to react. She remained stubbornly tightlipped, and watched with indifference as her livid mother fought to control the car and her temper. She rolled her eyes and faked a yawn.

Finally, Shelley pulled over to the side of the road. "Your cell phone," she demanded, drawing in a ragged breath. "Hand over your cell phone right now."

"What?" Carlotta exclaimed in disbelief.

"You heard me!"

"Oh no, you can't—"

Shelley yanked the phone out of Carlotta's hand and threw it behind her on the back seat. She took a few steadying breaths then re-started the engine. "It is high time someone taught you a big lesson, you strong-willed little fool," she fumed, nosing the Honda back on the road. "Just wait until your father learns what you have done." *You just wait.*

As soon as the car pulled into the garage, Carlotta jumped out without waiting for her mother to kill the engine. She stuck her head back in. "I don't care what you tell Dad. I hate you both, and I wish I was never born." She turned and ran into the house, slamming the door.

Shelley rushed inside and was only in time to hear the bedroom door slam. She winced and watched the stairs for a minute.

God help me with this kid.

Like a broken rag doll, Shelley walked to the laundry room and pulled out a well-hidden bottle of vodka.

❋ ❋ ❋

Thirty minutes from the local university where his wife worked as an English professor, Dr. Richard Ikedi was in the medical examination room consulting with an obese patient.

"My feet hurt when I walk, Doc," the patient whined.

Richard scrawled something on a clipboard. "Lay off the cheeseburgers and fried chicken, Bruno. Then maybe we can work on getting your feet to be like that of a ballerina." He looked at Bruno and hid his irritation behind a mask of professionalism. *You look like an elephant, for Christ's sake.*

Richard wasn't happy that Bruno had weighed-in at three hundred and fifty-six pounds and carried the bulk of that weight around his middle. *Diabetes is certainly in your future.*

"Doc, how long do *ya* figure I should lay off them cheeseburgers?"

"For as long as possible, Bruno," Richard replied without looking up from the clipboard. *That is, if heart disease doesn't kill you first.*

Bruno's heart was a ticking bomb. Judging from how much weight he had put on since his last visit, he was lucky to still be able to move.

The doctor warned again, "For as long as you wish to live." *The major arteries to and from your freaking heart are probably going to explode. Soon, chronic atherosclerosis will be battling with advanced metabolic syndrome for immediate attention.*

Bruno's beaded eyes narrowed and he asked in a deathly quiet voice, "Burgers I can handle, but how about some help with the old Family, Doc?"

Richard stiffened. His mouth tightened. His heart skipped a beat then began to thud insistently in his chest.

Help with The Family? Oh, hell no!

His connection with the Palorizzi Family in Las Vegas was a subject that wasn't open for discussion, and as far as Richard was concerned, Bruno was overstepping his boundaries by bringing it up.

Richard ran his fingers through his hair. He was saved from having to provide an immediate answer, for Maria Ryczek, his new personal assistant, poked her head through the door.

"Doctor, your wife is on line two. She says it's an emergency."

"Thank you, Maria," Richard replied. "We're almost finished here." He put down the clipboard and peeled the surgical gloves off his hands.

Maria smiled and left.

"She's very pretty, ain't she?"

"Excuse me?" Richard turned defensive eyes on his patient.

Bruno grinned, his fat face resembling a lump of pizza dough punched with a baby's fist to create his eyes. The ruddy lips of his leering mouth contrasted sharply with the wide monstrosity of his sunken nose. "You dig her, Doc?"

Richard ignored the jibe. "Take care of that old heart of yours," he said, and dropped the rubber gloves in the hazardous waste bin. "Remember to stick to your diet routine—eat plenty of fruits and vegetables." He stood and washed his hands at the sink, then dried them with paper towels.

"Stuff the *heart* talk," Bruno grunted, "why *don'tcha*? I don't need no doctor tellin' me *howta* look after myself."

Richard shrugged. "Honestly, Bruno, a few minutes of physical exercise every now and then would do you a lot more good than harm." He paused and regarded the patient coolly for a while. "And about your earlier question, the answer is *no*. I have no intention of resurrecting my connections with The Family, and I want nothing to do with your lot. See you around, old pal."

"Big mistake, Doc."

Richard walked out of the examination room. There was no way he would consider Bruno's proposal to get involved with the Palorizzi Family again. He was rid of organized crime and wished to remain that way.

Back in his office, he snatched up the phone and punched the blinking red light before raising the receiver to his ear. He raked a hand through his short curly hair and sighed. Shelley never called him at work with good news.

"Shelley? You there?" Richard asked. He listened to his wife's babbles with growing irritation. She sounded like a breathless eight-year-old bent on reciting a particularly bad poem. "Honey, I can't make out what you're saying." He mussed his hair again.

Many guys, when bothered, slam their fists into their palms or tap their feet. Some crack their knuckles or strum out a rhythm with their fingers. Richard raked his hair. And gritted his teeth.

"*Itsh* Carr— Carlotta," Shelley's voice sailed over the phone.

"What?" Richard demanded. It seemed Shelley had hit the bottle.

"She got *exshperrled* from *shchool* this morning."

Richard's face slowly turned into a dark formidable mask. "I'll kill that little punk," he swore. "I will bash her stupid head right in!"

"But—" Shelley hiccupped. "But you have not *hearrd* what she did."

"I don't care," Richard thundered. "Where is she?" His blood boiled. His daughter Carlotta was a damned force to be reckoned with. She excelled at nothing but getting herself into grave trouble. *Her last freaking expulsion was because she—*

"I got her from *sshchool* and brought her *shtraight* home."

"You stay right there," Richard instructed through gritted teeth. "I'm on my way."

Shelley hung-up. Richard continued to hold the receiver against his ear, his hands tightening around it with so much force his knuckles turned white. "I swear, I'll kill that little punk this time!"

Maria sauntered in. "Doctor," she drawled, "you have a patient that wants to come in for an annual physical this afternoon. Would you like to take the appointment?" Her large eyes smiled at him.

Richard groaned. "No, not this afternoon." He put down the phone and brushed the back of his hand across his forehead. "I have a family emergency. Please reassign my other appointments for today, or reschedule." He tugged the stethoscope from around his neck, tossed it on his desk, and picked up his car keys.

"Sure, Doctor." Maria winked. "Have a great afternoon." She retrieved the stethoscope and hung it up then sashayed out.

Yeah, right. Some great day it's turning out to be. Richard sighed and shrugged off his lab coat. He flung the white garment across his chair and strode out, letting the office door bang shut behind him.

✳ ✳ ✳

"What on earth are we going to do with Carlotta?" Shelley wailed. She longed for a drink but wouldn't dare take one with her husband standing just a few feet away. Even though she suspected that he already knew she was drinking again, she didn't want him to catch her in the act.

"You are asking me what we are to do? I'm going to do away with the silly kid, that's what," Richard replied. "What the hell kind of a child smokes marijuana in middle school?" He grabbed a bottle of water and slammed the refrigerator shut.

"We need to figure this out," Shelley told him. She managed to keep the shaking out of her voice. "And you need to clean up your language, Richard. It would not do well for a physician to speak the way you do."

Richard slammed the bottle down on the kitchen counter. The force of the impact caused a generous portion of water to slosh out the bottle's open top. He turned to face his wife.

"Who the hell cares about the way I talk?" His breath hissed through clenched teeth as he stared his wife down. Then his jaw slackened and he took a deep breath. "No need to make this more complicated than necessary. The little pothead upstairs is the problem—let's deal with that." *And you need to lay off the vodka.* Shelley couldn't fool him, or anyone else for that matter. It would be very devastating if the faculty at the local college threw her out because of her drinking problem. She had obtained the faculty position a few days before they left San Francisco, and had only been with the English Department for a little less than a year.

Shelley was an alcoholic, but had managed to stay on the water wagon for seventeen years. Now she had slipped again. Nobody would want a drunken professor to teach his or her kids, no matter how pretty the professor turned out to be.

"This is the second time Carlotta has been expelled from school," Shelley said, and without warning, slapped her hands to her face and began to sob. "Oh God, where did we go wrong with her?"

"It's okay, it will be okay," Richard consoled roughly. He hated it when she got emotional, crying and blaming herself for their daughter's lack of good judgment. *More like an abundance of bad judgment.* "It's not your fault, Shelley." He figured his wife was probably just beating herself up for picking up the bottle again. Maybe she thought of herself as a bad mother for depending on alcohol to get her through tough situations. *I wish you would just admit the real problem and talk to me about it so I can get you some professional help.*

"What do you mean by *it is not my fault?*" Shelley turned to face her husband. She curled her shaking hands tight into balls. "Are you somehow implying that it is indeed *my* fault?"

Richard put his hands up in exasperation. "What the hell are you talking about?" He watched her with narrowed eyes, a look of irritation clouding his face.

Shelley advanced a few steps, her blue eyes narrowing in anger. "Oh, so you *are* trying to blame *me* for this, too, like you did the first time Carlotta was expelled from school?"

Richard quickly put the kitchen counter between them. He ran a hand through his hair. "I am not blaming anyone for what Carlotta has done." He decided it would be a good idea to add a few more feet to the already existing distance. Shelley looked furious and could start hurling dangerous objects at any time. He wouldn't put it past her to throw a kitchen knife straight at his heart. *Alcohol can do that to people, especially to her.*

"You know the reason Carlotta became a bully in the middle school back in San Francisco," Shelley accused. "You read the report from the doctors and teachers explaining what prompted that incident?" She folded her arms under her breasts and lifted her chin.

"Christ, woman, give me a break!" Richard gauged the distance between them and deemed himself safe. *What doctors? They all are a bunch of stupid charlatans posing as psychiatrists!*

Shelley did not back down. "You *did* read the report, Richard, did you not?" It had been his fault. She had suspected he was seeing someone else, but he had denied it and refused to talk about it. They had grown apart. Carlotta had acted out because of her frustration with her parents' failing marriage. They had then sold their home in San Francisco, California and moved to Owasso, Oklahoma more as a means to salvage their pride than to teach Carlotta a lesson. *Better to blame the consequences of your lecherous habits on your defenseless daughter, right? How typical!*

Richard now worked as a general family practitioner with a major hospital in Tulsa, while Shelley had accepted a faculty position to teach English at a local college about twenty miles from where they lived. As for Carlotta and her bad educational record, they had called in every favor they were owed and even donated handsomely toward the school library before Mrs. McWatters had agreed to admit her to the school.

Richard moved back to the counter and picked-up his bottle of water. "I can't justify why anyone should blame me for my daughter's decision to beat up two kids almost half her age and land them in the emergency room with several fractured ribs." He drank from the bottle.

"You cannot now, can you?" Piercing blue eyes challenged him.

"Of course not." He wiped the moisture off his lips. "I had nothing to do with Carlotta's outburst in school."

"Yeah, right. The rumors were unfounded."

"What are you getting at, Shelley?" Richard tipped his head back to take another gulp but changed his mind and set the bottle on the counter with more force than necessary. "Just what's the freaking problem?"

Shelley's voice shook. "You very well know to what I am referring." She placed one hand over her mouth as if to hide the sobs that were threatening to erupt. Her husband was a very handsome and passionate man, equipped with the kind of angular features that made middle-aged men seem distinguished.

At an age when many men go bald, Richard's head was chock-full of dark, curly hairs that outlined his prominent fore-head in the most sensual way then began again after the vivid outline of his clavicle—enrobing his broad, masculine chest in a velvet cushion. He had muscles of steel, the type that makes men over six feet appear lithe and powerful.

He was an arrogant python of a man. The only problem with husbands like Richard is young women always fall without invitation at their feet. And they never learned to say *no*.

Richard regarded his wife with narrowed eyes. She still possessed much of the milky, blonde-fairy-princess beauty that had attracted him to her almost twenty years ago. Then, she had been a dropout graduate student and a raving drunk. When they met, he had helped her get on the wagon and encouraged her to return to college and fulfill her degree requirements. Four years later, after she graduated with a Ph.D. in English, he had proposed and married her. Three years after that, baby Carlotta had come along. And his blonde princess had slowly turned into a shrew.

"That is fine. I do not quite expect you to own up to your actions," Shelley sneered. She straightened her back, blinked, and squeezed her lips together to keep them from quivering. *If only you would come clean and discuss what made you seek solace in the arms of a younger woman, maybe our marriage will get back on track.* He hadn't admitted her suspicions were right. He didn't deny them either. He just would not discuss it. It was driving her crazy, and that was why she had started drinking again. She had to stop. She knew she had to.

"Carlotta needs to be seriously disciplined," Richard volunteered, deliberately changing the subject and getting them back to the problem at hand. He knew better than to allow himself be goaded into a verbal fight with his wife. "I don't think grounding her, taking away her cell phone privileges, or moving to a more remote area than where we are right now will cut it this time." He picked up his water, swallowed several mouthfuls and capped the bottle, placing it back in the refrigerator.

"So, what do you suggest?" Shelley asked. She noticed her husband ignored the spilled water on the counter. Sometimes, she swore he purposely did things like that to drive her crazy. She reached for a dishtowel and began to mop up the spill.

"Boarding school," Richard said.

Shelley stopped. "Boarding school? Are you poking fun at me?" She sounded incredulous. "You want to send Carlotta to a boarding school? Where we will not be able to keep an eye on her?" She shook her head. "No. Carlotta would only get *worse.*"

"No, she won't. Not if we send her to a school where discipline is valued as much as education. She will not only learn moral values, but gain a decent education in the process." Richard nodded in satisfaction. He had an ulterior motive for wanting to send Carlotta away to boarding school but wasn't about to admit it to his wife—or himself. It was just easier to maintain Carlotta's insubordination as the ultimate reason. *This way, Bruno can't get to her.*

Shelley stared at her husband for a moment and recognized the smug look on his face. "So, what is the idea? Where is this altruistic school you speak of?" She spread her arms wide; her demeanor indicating schools like that couldn't possibly exist outside military grounds. And military school was out of the question.

Richard smiled. His voice took on a faraway quality. "There is only one environment I know that can instill discipline into our darling daughter. Nigeria!"

Shelley's jaw dropped. "Nigeria? Do not be ridiculous."

"On the contrary, I'm dead serious. It's our only hope right now," Richard said with conviction. Then he added, "Hey, it worked for me, remember? How do you figure I came to be the person I am today?"

Shelley stopped short. She opened her mouth to say something, but closed it again. She shook her head and leaned back against the sink.

Richard watched his wife. He saw her eyes slowly widen and knew she was considering the possibility. He also knew it was now safe to approach her. He closed the distance between them and began to explain exactly what he had in mind.

Chapter 2
Lagos, Nigeria

Lagos!
The center of excellence—or so it is called.
The heartbeat of Nigeria; a place where everything happens.
The good, the bad, the ugly, and the very ugly.
A safe place and then again, a not so safe a place.

Moving from Ajegunle to Ojuelegba, from Oshodi to Alakpere;
The 'Area Boys' rule, they are the best in their trade!
Their trade you say?
Oh yes! For you cannot outwit their ability;
To snatch your bags, pick your pockets, and rob your cars.
And sometimes, they ask nicely!

The bus conductors with their grave voices;
Yelling their destination amidst the crowd of waiting passengers:
"Sanfield! Yaba! Costain! Ojota! Ketu! Mushin!"
The list is endless.

The numerous hawkers crowding the streets;
Pushing their wares to your face.
"Sister, buy this! Brother, this is good!" they holler.

In Lagos, everyone learns to be tough;
Yet, we know where and how to have fun.
The joints, beer parlors, restaurants, eateries, and best of all
—the Bukas;
Where we get the best of the local food:
Amala and Ewedu, Pounded-yam and Vegetable, Eba and Egusi.

21

Lagos!
A city for the famous and rich, A city for the poor;
A city of the black and white, A city for the young and old;
A city for everyone!

The city with the busiest roads!
Ah! The endless traffic, the yellow buses and taxis;
The numerous cars that crowd the road.
The molues, trailers, and best of all, the dangerous yet necessary okadas;
All honking their way through, from dusk till dawn.

It's amazing how people get around in Lagos!
The bridges crossing from one town to another;
The endless stretch of sand covering the beaches that surround the city;
The beautiful sky-scrappers of Marina and Broad Street;
The high-rising apartments of Victoria Island and Ikoyi.
And the awesome estates of Lekki;
The fish farmers' huts on the shores of the sea;
The one-room flats of Ajegunle, and the low cost houses of Gbagada.

Everything and everyone make up the beauty of Lagos!
It's no wonder everyone wants to come to Lagos.
A true mix of different people of different nationals:
Different traits, tribes, races, and languages;
The Igbos, Yorubas, and Hausas.

This is the mystery of Lagos;
A city we call home.
Eko for sure!
Eko for life!
Eko o ni baje!

–Debbie Anaga, 2008

Carlotta bit her lip and squinted at the beaming girl in front of her. The girl's teeth gleamed under the yellowish tint of the bedroom light, and her right hand was extended in a friendly bid for a handshake.

Carlotta noticed the girl was watching her with a patient smile and quickly averted her eyes. Under her cordial scrutiny, Carlotta felt like a tortoise caught outside its shell. She offered her hand for a handshake and bit her lip.

"Welcome to Lagos, Nigeria," the girl said, shaking Carlotta's hand in a sincere and hearty manner. "I'm so happy to see you again. I hope you like it here." She moved forward and gave Carlotta a brief hug.

Carlotta's cheeks turned a bright shade of pink. The girl was Ada, her second cousin, whom she had met only once before, a long time ago, back in San Francisco. Ada's father, Daniel, was Carlotta's dad's cousin.

Ada had visited Carlotta's home when she was eight, with her parents and two-year-old brother, Somto. Then, Carlotta had been three years old.

Carlotta gave a weak nod and tried to smile. She'd been looking forward to seeing her cousin again, but somehow, now that she was actually here in Lagos, things felt a little awkward. Ada had matured since the last time Carlotta saw her—she was now a beaming eighteen year old, quite unrecognizable.

Carlotta hesitated.

Ada definitely looked different. Ten years ago, she had been an energetic and babbling little girl. Now, she was tall, dark, and skinny. Her features were soft and feminine, her skin looked flaw-less. She sounded different, too.

"You've grown a lot. The last time I saw you, you were very little," Ada said. She let go of Carlotta's hand and deposited herself on the large bed in the middle of the room. "I don't even know if you still remember me."

"Of course I remember you," Carlotta replied, scratching her arm. "It's really nice to see you again." *How can I forget? I totally worshiped you—tagging along and trying to get you to play with my toys.*

Since Carlotta was an only child, she had been pleased to have her cousins around for a few weeks. Right now, though, she didn't know how to react. Ada seemed like a stranger. A pretty, dark-skinned stranger.

Carlotta scratched her arm again and was infuriated to notice that tiny red welts had erupted on her skin, revealing the exact spots where mosquitoes had viciously bitten her. She grimaced.

"So, what's going on in America?" Ada asked, smiling and shaking her head in expectation. The large, loop earrings hanging from her ears dangled and reflected the light in the room.

"Um, nothing much," Carlotta said, and shrugged. "We don't live in San Francisco anymore; we moved out to the country last year." Carlotta shrugged again. "I don't have any friends in Oklahoma, so..." She didn't know what else to say and let her voice trail away.

Scowling, Carlotta swatted her smarting arm with the palm of her hand.

Ada giggled.

Carlotta spared her a furious look. Obviously, the mosquito bites weren't a big deal to Ada—*her dark skin wouldn't show any bumps anyway.*

Carlotta's eyes traveled around the bedroom. It was neat and tidy. Window screens peeked from behind the thick, colorful drapes. An overhead fan churned and rotated the air in the room with a lazy *whump-whump-whump!* The atmosphere wasn't warm, but it wasn't cool, either. Bed looked large enough for two; wooden dresser bore the weight of all kinds of cosmetics and make-up; large vanity mirror loomed precariously over the dresser.

"You don't care that I will be sharing your room?" Carlotta asked, peering at her cousin. She bunched her mouth to one side and shrugged one delicate shoulder. "I'm only *gonna* be here for two weeks, I guess."

"Oh, no problem," Ada said. "I'm actually glad you will be here with me, 'cause we have a lot of catching-up to do."

Carlotta had just arrived at her cousins' house, in Ikoyi, Lagos State, Nigeria. Daniel and his wife, Nkem, had met Carlotta and her mother at the international airport in Ikeja and driven them back to their home. This was Carlotta's first visit to Nigeria, and so far, the cruel mosquitoes weren't making it any easier for her to appreciate her new surroundings.

Stupid mosquitoes! Jeez! I'm so glad the screen on the window is totally doing a good job of keeping the evil insects from having me for dinner.

Carlotta sat beside Ada on the bed. "What's something fun to do around here?"

"A lot!" Ada's eyes shone. "It's going to be very exciting showing you around Lagos. My mother said you will be leaving for school very soon, so I've planned for us to—"

"Wait. Hold on—" Carlotta interrupted. "What do you mean by *leaving for school?*" she asked, quite forgetting about her jetlag and the mosquito bites she had suffered.

Ada looked perplexed. "School. You know, the girls' boarding school—"

But again, Carlotta did not let her finish.

"What?" she yelled, bounding to her feet. "What boarding school?"

"I don't know—stop shouting." Ada put her hands over her ears, attempting to protect her eardrums from Carlotta's ringing voice.

An icy cold hand wrapped itself around Carlotta's heart.

"Wait, I don't understand. You mean I was brought here to be sent to a boarding school?" Carlotta demanded in a voice that resonated around the room. "My mom said we were only visiting for a couple of weeks." She stopped and glared, her hands curling into fists in her anger.

But Ada looked very confused.

"Oh my God!" Carlotta ran straight out of the room in search of her mom, leaving behind a surprised Ada to stare after her in open-mouthed wonder.

※ ※ ※

*A*fter dinner the next day, Shelley sat quietly in the sitting room of her cousin-in-law's house. The big-screen TV in the corner sparkled with glaring scenes of a local movie. She paid no attention and was absorbed in her own thoughts and worries.

Daniel and his wife, on the other hand, were staring at the screen, easily drinking in the scenes. Daniel was a successful branch manager of the Royal Bank in Ikoyi, while Nkem worked as an accountant in a different bank located in Illupeju. He had his arm around his wife's shoulders. She had her feet tucked underneath her on the sofa and was leaning against the solid wall of her husband's massive chest.

Shelley gazed wistfully at them and envied their closeness. She couldn't remember the last time she'd been that close to Richard. *That would probably be a few years after Carlotta started primary school,* she thought ruefully, and sighed.

Shelley's mind was in turmoil. There were so many problems to deal with.

There was Carlotta.

Shelley wasn't exactly proud of the means by which she had manipulated her daughter into coming to Nigeria. Back in Owasso, she had enticed Carlotta to come with her to Lagos for a two-week visit. She had made no mention of boarding school.

"Honey, the experience will do you a lot of good, and give you a different perspective on life. In addition, you will be able to spend time with your cousins," she'd coaxed. She knew Carlotta wanted to see her second cousins, Ada and Somto, again. Daniel and Nkem's youngest son, Junior, who had been born the only time they'd visited in San Francisco, was ten years old now.

Carlotta had loved Junior as a baby, and ached to meet the ten-year-old boy. So, she'd trusted her mother and agreed to come to Nigeria. Now they were in Lagos and she'd learned she would not be returning to the United States, Carlotta first raised a tantrum then started to sulk.

Then there was her failing marriage. Shelley shut that out of her mind.

"Where exactly is this boarding school Carlotta will be attending?" Shelley asked Daniel. She had only visited Nigeria once, and hadn't exactly toured the whole country during that visit.

"It's located in Uddah, a small town in Anambra State. It's about eighty kilometers from Onitsha," Daniel answered. He looked at his wife, who nodded at him, then smiled at Shelley.

"I remember Onitsha but I do not recall this town, Uddah. Is it close to your hometown?" Shelley pronounced it as 'You-dare.'

"No, no," Daniel laughed. "Uddah is on a different road out of Onitsha from our hometown, Edeh. Let's just say that Edeh is on one side of Onitsha, while Uddah is on the opposite end," he explained to Shelley.

"All right." Shelley nodded. She really had no idea what he was talking about.

"You remember that we go from Asaba, over the Niger Bridge, to get to Onitsha?" Daniel asked. He expantiated, gesticulating with his hands, "So, from Onitsha, instead of heading to Edeh, we go in the opposite direction using the road to Aguleri. Uddah is a small town in that area."

"Well, so long as You-dare is not as rowdy as Onitsha, I suppose it is all right then," Shelley said. She had visited Onitsha the only time she was in Nigeria. The city was a hellhole.

"Uddah is a small town, a little backward, maybe, but peaceful," Nkem reassured.

Shelley studied her. Nkem was a small, soft-spoken woman with a kind disposition and an empathic face.

"Peaceful is good," Shelley affirmed.

"Yes, that's right." Nkem glanced briefly at her husband as if to confirm her words then turned back to Shelley and continued, "The boarding school there in Uddah is very prestigious. It is one of the best girls' boarding schools in Anambra State. The quality of education in that school is equal to that of the private colleges." She beamed. "Ada attended that school for six years and just graduated recently."

"The students there are better behaved than the students in the public schools here in Lagos," Daniel added. He shook his head and said in a sad voice, "Lagos has a way of influencing people, especially children. It's like a bad infection."

"Tell me about it," Shelley said. She recalled the sight of principal McWatters berating Carlotta for smoking marijuana in school. "The boarding school environment is not anything like what you have here in Lagos, am I correct?" she asked, looking expectantly at Daniel.

"No way," Daniel asserted. "I don't think there is any city in Nigeria that is worse than Lagos."

"Not all parts of Lagos are that bad," Nkem chided, looking slightly amused. "I mean, Victoria Island, Maryland, Ikoyi, Ikeja, Festac, Bariga, and places like that are okay. It's just that the bad areas out-number the good ones. Districts like Maroko, Orile, Oshodi, Apapa, Alaba, Agege, and Mushin, for example, are very notorious for all sorts of crimes."

Nkem shook her head and looked meaningfully at Shelley then sighed and continued, "You know how bad you thought the Marina area was, when we went there to see the Monterey Bay Aquarium? Well, you need to go to Oshodi, Ebutte-Metta, or Iyani-Ipaja. Those places will definitely give you something to worry about."

Shelley nodded and didn't argue the point. She would take Nkem's word for it. Marina, Lagos hadn't exactly been Miami, Florida. Marina was on the coastline of Lagos State and was awash with ocean liners, cranes, and beautiful skyscrapers. However, it also thronged with scores of people jostling one another on the streets, screaming motorists, street hawkers, and no traffic rules.

Just to drive from their home to the Monterey Bay Aquarium and back had been a great ordeal. The traffic was horrible at best. There were no red lights or overhead signs to direct motorists. All the major routes had been jammed with traffic—cars and trucks blaring their horns with infuriating impatience. Drivers yelled obscenities, motorcyclists weaved through traffic in whichever way they pleased, while roadside vendors harassed motorists and passengers with pleas to buy their wares which ranged anywhere from cell phones and electronics to shoes and clothing accessories, and from household equipment to food and water.

It seemed, though, that the sights of the Marina were the best Lagos could offer. Shelley would have to admit the place had changed quite a bit since she had last visited, which was the year after she and Richard had been married.

Now that they were safely tucked into her cousin-in-law's house in Lagos, Shelley knew that the crazy Lagos journey was just about to begin; they would have to go shopping to equip Carlotta with the stuff she would need for boarding school.

Shopping in Lagos was not something Shelley yearned to repeat. The last time she went shopping with Nkem, she'd been informed the local markets had better quality items that couldn't be obtained in the modern shopping malls. Shelley would have been content to shop at the various modern stores conveniently situated in Ikoyi, close to where they lived, but Nkem would not hear of it. She had dragged Shelley all over Lagos State—to the Tejuosho Market located in Yaba, to Balogun Market in Lagos Island, and to some strange market in Lagos Mainland. As a result, Shelley had sported a splitting headache for days after the crazy ordeal that was supposed to pass for a shopping excursion.

The farmers market in Tulsa, Oklahoma was a piece of cake in comparison to any of the grocery markets in Lagos State or Anambra State. Shelley shuddered just thinking about it. One only had to experience shopping at the Balogun Market in Lagos Island, or the Main Market in Onitsha, to understand what it was like to be a survivor.

Shelley thought that shopping in Lagos was an unusual experience no tourist in his or her right mind would crave to repeat. But, who said a mother's sacrifice wasn't the greatest gift on earth? She would go through the death-defying experience again for Carlotta's sake.

Fortunately, this time around, Nkem was planning for them to stick to the new shopping malls in Lagos like the Silverbird Galleria and The Palms Shopping Mall. Though the Tejuosho Market hadn't offered a pleasant shopping experience ten years earlier, Shelley was sorry to learn the market had been torn down quite recently. However, she was looking forward to shopping in the more modern stores.

Shelley leaned back and settled herself more comfortably in the overstuffed armchair. Overall, she was glad to be away from her husband and the hassle of dealing with college students for a while. She was going to utilize this opportunity to clear her thoughts. There was a little more than a week before she was due back at the university. Students would soon be returning to campus for the fall semester, and she still had some book manuscripts on her desk that needed attention.

As soon as Carlotta was safely off to school, Shelley planned on returning straight home and clearing things up with Richard. She would not stand by and watch her marriage hit the rocks, even if it meant publicly admitting to her drinking problem, or physically fighting to win back his devotion.

Shelley blinked back the tears in her eyes and swallowed the emotion that threatened to engulf her. Right now, she needed to deal with Carlotta's case and pray that her own problems would be solved in the end. Leaving her only child behind in a foreign country was proving to be a very tough row to hoe. But Shelley knew she needed to remain strong for Carlotta's sake.

There was no other option. The girl was so headstrong and obnoxious that Shelley was determined to clutch at the faintest hopes of turning her daughter into a responsible human being. She had watched Carlotta grow from a sweet little girl into a conceited and flashy pre-teen, and that was not the worst of it.

Shelley hadn't known that Carlotta had picked up the disgusting habit of cigarette smoking.

That not withstanding, she had thought that beating up two six-year-olds and smoking marijuana in school was the worst kind of trouble Carlotta could get herself into by the tender age of thirteen.

That was until she discovered birth-control pills and condoms in the top drawer of Carlotta's dresser a few days after her second expulsion from school. It was at that shocking moment she had agreed whole-heartedly to her husband's suggestion to send their only child away to a boarding school.

She hoped for Carlotta's sake that staying in Nigeria would work the magic that Richard claimed it would.

For the sole purpose of salvaging her daughter's future, Shelley prayed with all her heart the all-girls Federal school in Uddah, Anambra State, Nigeria, would clip Carlotta's wings and transform her from an ugly duckling into a beautiful swan.

✳ ✳ ✳

Richard watched in fascination as the tip of Maria's tongue traveled the length of her luscious lips. She gazed at him with large, hazel eyes and smiled.

He could tell what was on her mind—it was quite obvious. The way she had been holding his gaze for a second longer than necessary when she speaks to him in the hospital about something trivial; the casual way she places her hand on his arm when she bends over to explain something in a patient's file; even the way she laughs and winks when he says something she thinks is funny.

Hell, the girl is like a virus in my blood, driving me crazy with subtle come-ons.

Richard couldn't help staring at Maria's pretty face. *You really do want me, don't you? Every woman does.*

Maria was now smiling and running one delicate finger over the rim of her glass.

Richard's pulse raced. He took a sip of wine and crossed his legs.

"What item on the menu particularly strikes your fancy?" He asked in a voice he hoped hid his sexual interest.

"Oh, let's see," she replied. "How about the grilled lamb chops, steamed vegetables with French Hollandaise sauce, and rice pilaf on the side?" Her eyes caught his and she smiled again.

"Sounds lovely," Richard admitted. Swirling his glass of wine, he signaled for the waiter to come take their order. Then leaned back and studied Maria.

After a long workday at the hospital, and an even longer emotional battle, Richard had invited her out to dinner. She'd accepted quite readily and he'd been thrilled. He suspected Maria was attracted to him and was hoping the dinner would ease her up enough to make the next move. He watched from under his lashes and sipped his wine.

She stared back, eyes bold and unflinching. She was beautiful, sophisticated, and obviously cultured. Not the type of woman you'd expect to see working as a personal assistant—especially not at a hospital in Tulsa, Oklahoma.

Bruno had insisted he hire her, and after taking one look at the tall, sleek body she possessed, Richard had readily acquiesced. She had no previous medical experience, though her phony credentials showed otherwise. However, she was a quick learner and a great assistant with a face to die for and a killer body to boot.

Bruno is right, she's a real catch and I'm lucky to have her as an assistant. Boy, she belongs on the cover of 'Playboy.'

"How was the conference in New York?" Maria asked with laughter in her eyes, pulling Richard out of his reverie.

He gave a sly smile. "Just the usual boring medical symposiums. You don't want me to lecture you on any of that, not during dinner at any rate." He shifted and raked a hand through his hair. "I don't know about you but talking about malignant cells and virulent organisms has a way of spoiling my appetite." His light laughter took the sting out of the words.

"Very well, Doctor. I'm with you on that one." Maria chuckled and winked at him.

"You should laugh more often, it suits you."

"Are you trying to charm me, Doctor?" She sounded coy. One slim finger reached up to twirl a lock of straight, shiny jet-black hair.

"Absolutely."

She raised a delicate eyebrow. "So, what part of Africa exactly is your wife visiting?" she asked, changing the subject.

Richard didn't care to be reminded of the fact that he was married, but Maria seemed genuinely interested, so he said, "West Africa, Nigeria to be exact. Have you ever been to any country in Africa?"

"Oh, no," Maria replied, laughing. "I'm not much of a traveler. I've never left the United States since I arrived here from Denmark six years ago." She nodded slowly as she added, "Africa sounds interesting, though."

"You should visit someday. You might enjoy it."

"What's it like in Africa?" Her eyes shone.

"I can only tell you about Nigeria. My father was one of the people and lived there until he immigrated to New York in the late sixties. Shortly after that, he met and married my mother, who was white and from New Jersey, and lived here in the United States since."

Maria shook her head. "I didn't know your dad was Nigerian. Is he still living in New York? Are your parents still together?"

"No. I lost them both the year I started medical school— him to cardiac arrest, her to cancer. They went within a few months of each other." He remained silent for a moment then added in a voice that was barely above a whisper, "They were a remarkable couple."

"I'm sorry for your loss," Maria sympathized. The chinking of cutlery on expensive china drummed out a melancholic tune, as if in agreement to her sympathy at the loss of his parents.

"That's all right, it's been a while now." Richard didn't want Maria to feel sorry for him. "I lived in Nigeria a few years myself; you know, high school and that sort of thing."

"Oh really? You went to school in Nigeria?" Maria leaned forward and placed both arms on the table, supporting herself with her elbows. "Any particular reason?"

"Well, let's just say my parents thought it was a good idea." A rueful smile marred his face. He liked it when her eyes widened in surprise. "I will admit they turned out to be right, though."

Their food arrived and they began to eat. Richard watched as Maria speared a steamed baby carrot with her fork.

"Is it true what they say?" She closed her mouth over the carrot and chewed thoughtfully.

"What do they say?"

"Once you go black, you never go back?" She laughed. Her laughter was contagious.

Richard chuckled. "You've been indulging in a lot of 'Mind of Mencia' reruns, huh?" He swatted at her playfully with his napkin. "How about you find out for yourself?" His eyes teased. When Maria looked up, he winked.

"I admit it was a stupid joke, Doctor. Please, forget I mentioned it." She popped a piece of lamb in her mouth and dabbed at her lips with a napkin. She watched him with speculative eyes.

"Rick," Richard said. His eyes followed her every movement. Maria swallowed. "Sorry?"

"Call me Rick, Maria," he drawled. He took her hand and held her gaze for a few moments, his dark eyes boring into hers. A hesitant smile formed on her face and his heart almost missed a beat. She neither withdrew her hand, nor her eyes. After a few electrifying seconds, he released her.

Maria picked up her fork and jabbed at a piece of asparagus. The fork shook. She glued her eyes to her plate and concentrated on eating her dinner.

Richard just picked at his food. He wasn't hungry anymore.

"What's she really like?"

Richard sighed. His jaw tightened. He bowed his head to hide his countenance. After a moment, he said in a low voice, "Remember Bree Van de Kamp of 'Desperate Housewives'?

Maria raised an eyebrow.

"There! You've met Shelley."

"When will she be back?" she asked, not looking at him.

"Next weekend," he replied in a tone that was low and husky. "Exactly nine days from today," he added, and smiled to himself. *It is a long haul back from Nigeria after all.*

✳ ✳ ✳

Carlotta lay wide-awake in bed listening to the sound of Ada's heavy breathing. It was early Thursday morning. The clock on the tiny table beside the bed showed the time to be seven minutes past three. She couldn't sleep and had spent the last several hours staring at the ceiling, horrified at the thought of leaving for boarding school in two days.

Carlotta was still mad at her mom for tricking her into coming to Nigeria. Although she wasn't sorry she had come, after all she had really wanted to see Ada and her brothers again; she hated the idea of being tricked into attending a boarding school. Visiting Nigeria for two weeks sounded fun and exciting, she thought, but having to go to boarding school in Nigeria for six years? *Now, that's a totally different ball game.*

Her experience in her uncle's house, so far, was different from what she'd ever known.

There was no central air conditioning unit in the house; the living room had a window unit, but that was about it.

The power went off at any time of the day or night without warning and the blackouts lasted for hours on end. To make matters worse, the portable generator her uncle owned was temporarily out of order and the power had gone out six times in the past five days. The last episode, which took place that afternoon, had been unpleasant. It had become so warm in the house that Ada suggested they go out on the veranda. But the sting of the mosquitoes had forced them back indoors to endure the stifling heat instead.

What a convenient time the generator chose to go bad. If I didn't know better, I'll totally swear the stupid thing is plotting with the heat and the mosquitoes to purposely make my life miserable.

The cruel bugs weren't the worst of it, Carlotta decided.

The ethnic food alone required a different level of endurance. On her first morning, Carlotta's aunt had happily placed before her a plate of something that looked like fritters and a small bowl of white, pasty stuff that resembled plain yogurt. Nkem had poured some evaporated milk on the white substance and dumped-in two or three cubes of sugar then smiled indulgently at her. Carlotta hadn't known what to do with the strange looking food. She had picked up a fritter and nibbled at it, then realized immediately that it wasn't breaded fried-chicken.

"Hey, what's this?" she'd queried her aunt, an unmistakable look of wariness etched on her face.

"*Akara,*" Nkem had replied. "It's made from beans. Try it, you'll like it," she had added with another smile.

Carlotta had nibbled at the fritter again but wasn't able to swallow. It reminded her of Mexican food, which she disliked. At her Aunt's urging, she'd spooned a little bit of the white paste that was called *pap*, raised it to her lips, and touched her tongue tentatively to it. The pap at least was bland in taste. She had managed to eat a few spoonfuls before giving up entirely.

That breakfast had been much better than what was served later for lunch. The smell of that meal alone…

Ugh!

As soon as she had gotten a whiff of the steamy scent wafting off her plate in cloudy, smoky tendrils, Carlotta had gagged and made a beeline for the bathroom to involuntarily empty the contents of her starved stomach. The offensive odor of Limburger cheese came nowhere near the smell of that dish.

Carlotta had thought she was going to suffocate. When her mom had asked what type of food it was, she'd been informed it was bitter-leaf soup. When prodded further, Nkem had revealed the ingredient responsible for the distinctive aroma was some type of locally fermented beans.

Gross!

The stench of that dish had permeated through the whole house and hung heavily in the air for several hours afterward. Shelley had been excited since she loved everything to do with food and sensory experiences. But Carlotta had been plain disgusted—and hungry. Luckily, Ada understood and had taken her out to a fast food joint, where she indulged in a burger and fried chicken.

Among other bizarre foods Carlotta came across since then were yams—a kind of white starchy food that looked and tasted like boiled potatoes; red stew—this wasn't bad at all if one liked hot peppers and spices; plantains—nice and sweet and tastes like bananas; *moin-moin*—made out of steamed bean paste; some strange soups and sauces; and, of course, the recognizable staples of bread, eggs, and rice.

There weren't snacks or frivolous foods of any sort, like cookies, chocolates, cakes, candy, pizza, corn or potato chips, ice cream, or peanut butter in the whole house. Usually, they only ate at meal times and food was served with plain, cold water. Beverages such as sodas, juice, and alcohol were reserved and served as refreshments to visitors. Eating in-between meals was unheard of unless, perhaps, one went out and spent money on fast food, which was very expensive.

Apart from the food, Carlotta also noticed a difference in the way her cousins communicated with their parents. They always stood and listened attentively when their parents addressed them. Worse still, Carlotta's cousins also answered their parents' calls respectfully, with the tag "daddy" or "mommy" at the end of each answer.

For instance, when her dad calls for her, Ada would reply, "yes, Daddy," whereas any American kid in the same situation would just say, "yeah." And that was if they were in a good mood.

If caught at a bad time—usually when on the phone or playing a video game—the average American kid would just scream, "what?" when called for by their parents.

Carlotta thought her cousins were really funny. *Imagine saying "yes, sir!" to my dad after being yelled at. Uh-uh, not cool!*

Carlotta rolled over on the bed and her mind went back to the problem at hand.

How can I totally avoid going to boarding school?

She considered running away. She would need to get out of the house without being seen, find her way to the airport in a very dangerous city in the early hours of the morning, and then get herself aboard a flight headed for the United States.

That plan would work, she thought, sitting up in the dark, her eyes shining like tiny stars on a moonless night. *Why didn't I totally think of it before? First, I need to go grab my passport and some cash.*

The clock read a quarter till four.

Carlotta slowly got out of bed, being careful not to wake Ada. She tiptoed to the closet and eased it open. The creaking sound of the door hinges was not loud enough to disturb her oblivious cousin. Gingerly, she felt through some odds and ends in the closet until she found her backpack, which she quietly withdrew and shouldered.

Carlotta decided there was no need to pack a bag, since she had a whole closet full of clothes at home in Oklahoma. She grabbed the clothes she wore the day before, and picked up her shoes. Tiptoeing into the bathroom, she changed out of her nightshirt into jeans and a tee shirt. She slipped into sneakers and did up the laces.

Carlotta stuffed her nightgown into the backpack, left the bathroom, and snaked out of the bedroom. Ada did not stir.

Not daring to breathe, Carlotta closed the door. She crept along the dark hallway, inching along with her hands on the wall, all the while hoping she wouldn't bump into something and make a noise.

Once in the living room, she flipped on the light switch and was startled by the sudden brightness that flooded the room. Instinctively, she shielded her eyes against the harsh light of the overhead florescent bulbs.

Carlotta scouted around for the desk lamp and turned it on, then cut off the overhead light. The sitting room became bathed in a soft, yellow glow. She looked around for the house keys, remembering seeing her uncle place them atop the cabinets. A few seconds later, her fingertips found the keys. She placed them inside her backpack then dropped the bag near the door.

Next, she needed to find her mother's purse.

Carlotta headed for the bedroom where her mother was staying. It was two doors down the hall, on the right. She edged to the door and eased it open. She held her breath and listened, her heart beating hard against her ribs. Shelley's soft breathing signaled she was dead to the world.

Carlotta snuck into the room, hunched, and waited for her eyes to adjust to the darkness. After a few moments, the eerie outline of objects in the room became discernible. She crawled to her mother's big black bag, and grabbed it—clutching it under her arm. Then Carlotta retreated from the room, careful not to make a peep.

By the time she returned to the sitting room, Carlotta's heart was pumping furiously. She opened the purse and searched for the small booklets she knew should be there.

But, she couldn't find the passports.

They have to be in here.

Agitated, she dumped the contents of the purse on the floor and riffled through the pile. Finally, her fingers located some booklets and she peered at them. They were dark blue in color.

Thanks goodness!

She opened the first booklet. Her mother's name stared back at her in bold, stylish letters. She shoved that one back into the purse and stuffed the other one in her hip pocket. She then picked up her mother's wallet and transferred all the cash into her back pocket.

Her pulse raced.

She crammed the other items back and dropped the purse on the chair near the desk lamp. She tiptoed to the door, picked up her backpack, and headed for the stairs.

A few minutes later, Carlotta unlocked the compound gate and pushed against the heavy steel.

It wouldn't budge.

She braced herself against the gate and pushed hard, her knees straining with the effort. Just as her feet threatened to give way and loose their grip on the ground, the gate moved. The jarring sound of metal scraping gravel filled the air.

Carlotta froze.

Cringing, she surveyed the house, her brain pounding against her ears.

Nothing happened. No one moved. Silhouetted forms remained still.

Carlotta breathed out a sigh of relief and pushed the gate ajar with tiny jerky movements. Her heart was positively thumping now, drumming out all senses of caution and inhibition. Quickly, she dropped the padlock with the keys still attached, stepped outside, and forced the gate shut with all her might.

The grating noise came again.

This time, Carlotta ignored it. She didn't wait around to see who would wake up and catch her running away. She just turned and bolted down the deserted street, into the dark depths of the new day.

After what seemed like an eternity, Carlotta stumbled onto the side of a main road perpendicular to the street her uncle lived in.

She stopped and started searching for a cab.

✳ ✳ ✳

*C*car stopped and honked. It was a pitiful-looking sedan of an unrecognizable make and model. The weather-beaten surface of the car was painted a dirty yellow with a pair of black stripes running across the sides. The bulb from a smashed headlight hung limply from its socket by a thin wire, while a nasty crack spider-webbed across the windshield. The car really was worse for wear.

The driver poked his head out the window and beckoned.

Carlotta stared. She didn't think people could get any darker. The man was too dark, even for a black guy, and his face gave the impression that a large cat had run its claws down the length of his cheeks, leaving the scars to heal into deep, distinct furrows.

"You need taxi?" the driver asked in a gruff voice.

"Um, yeah, I suppose," she replied.

He got out and threw open the rear passenger side door. As soon as she scrambled in, the driver forced the door shut with a sickening clank, slid behind the wheel, and took off.

The whole vehicle reverberated with the clattering sound of loose parts smashing against metal.

Carlotta's breath caught in her throat.

The stench in the cab was unbelievable. Stale sweat oozed from every soft surface and mingled with the smell of the driver's unwashed body.

It felt impossible to breathe.

Carlotta stuck her nose out of the window, taking in gulps of the cleaner air, not unwary of the closeness of the cars whizzing past her face.

"Where you *dey* go?" the driver asked.

"Sorry? What was that?"

"To where?" the man asked again before leaning out the window to scream obscenities at a passing car.

"The airport. Take me to the airport. And please hurry," Carlotta announced with great urgency. Sweat trickled down the sides of her face. Her eyes widened. Her heart drummed out a staccato rhythm. She dried her chin with the back of her hand.

"To go Ikeja *na* one thousand."

Carlotta did not reply. She hadn't caught any of the words the man said, and didn't care. Her only concern was to get to the airport as fast as possible. She leaned back on the dirty-smelling seat and let the cab driver whisk her away.

Without warning, the taxi cut hard and almost careened into several cars coming from the opposite direction. Horns blared. Tires screeched. People yelled. The smell of burnt rubber filled the cab.

Carlotta was flung sideways across the back seat with the force of the swerve. She covered her head with her arms, clenched her teeth, and shut her eyes tightly in expectation of the imminent crash.

Oh my God!

No crash came.

Wary, she peeked through her fingers, then sat up and looked around in a daze.

The cab hadn't crashed or toppled over.

That was close.

Then she realized what had happened. The unconcerned cab driver had only made a U-turn.

The other drivers yelled something that certainly sounded like obscenities and the cabby bellowed back at them. Finally, he straightened the cab and barged into the traffic going in the opposite direction.

"You *dey* craze!" the taxi man shouted at one guy in particular who dared shake a fist at him. He yelled something else in a strange language and, with the horns blaring, suddenly changed lanes.

The vehicle shot forward.

Carlotta was terrified.

Quite forgetting about the nasty smell in the vehicle, she opened her mouth and breathed rapidly several times, desperately trying to calm her wrecked nerves. The traffic continued to flow as if nothing had happened. Apparently, in Lagos, it was acceptable for drivers to make U-turns in the middle of the road and drive like demons from hell.

No big deal.

The taxi coughed and sputtered. Carlotta's eyes snapped open. She'd dozed off without realizing it. The taxi coughed again then shuddered to a complete stop.

The driver leaned back and threw the passenger door open.

"*Oya,* make you come down now," he said, looking at Carlotta with bloodshot eyes.

"Are we at the airport?" Carlotta asked. She didn't see any sign or marker to show they were anywhere close to an airport.

"We never reach airport but fuel *don* finish for my tank. Make you come down now," the man insisted. He looked impatient.

"I don't understand. I thought you were taking me to the airport." Panic rose within Carlotta like soapsuds in a hot tub.

"I no get fuel. *Wetin* you *wan* make I do?" the driver hollered. He looked at Carlotta, then said in a stilted voice, "The thing be say, we *dey* halfway reach Ikeja, but my fuel *don* finish. I fit stop you another taxi, or *okada,* or I fit show you where you go enter motor *wey dey* go Ikeja."

Carlotta listened intently as the man spoke. She only understood enough to know it was officially okay for her to panic. She was stranded in the early hours of the morning, in the middle of nowhere, with nobody but a cab driver who hardly spoke English for company. *I'm totally screwed.*

"Okay," she said in a shaky voice. "What do I do now?"

"First, you pay me."

"All right, how much do I owe you?" Carlotta glanced around; there was no meter anywhere in the cab.

"Seven-fifty."

Seven-dollars-and-fifty-cents? Not too bad for something that definitely felt like a fifteen-minute ride in a four-wheeled garbage can. She pulled out the wad of bills from her pocket. They were all hundreds.

"Do you have change for a hundred?" Carlotta asked the man who was now glaring.

"I say seven hundred and fifty naira!" He rattled off something in a language that sounded really weird and creepy.

Carlotta looked aghast. "What? Naira? But I only have dollars. Will you accept them?"

"*Oya,* make you give me one hundred dollar." The man was brusque. He held out a hand blackened with soot.

Carlotta peeled off a hundred-dollar-bill.

The taxi driver snatched it and stuffed it down his drab robes. Then he got out of the cab and she followed suit.

They stood at the side of the road for several minutes.

No empty taxis came by.

No available commercial bikes.

Finally, the cab driver grew impatient.

"Make you go that way," he instructed, pointing to his right. "You go see Motor Park. Tell them say you *dey* go Ikeja. As *dem* carry you *dey* go, when *dem* call 'Airport!' make you come down." The taxi driver looked at Carlotta. "You hear?"

Carlotta thought it would be wise to shake her head. The man had a strange way of speaking and she hadn't grasped a word.

"*Kai, wetin dey* carry you *oyibo* people come Lagos *sef?*" he asked as he locked the taxi doors. "*Oya* come," he said to her. "I go *waka* you reach park."

Having said that, the man turned and walked off at a rapid pace, leaving Carlotta struggling to keep up.

✳ ✳ ✳

*A*fter a short walk, they approached the park.

The man stopped and pointed ahead. "*Na* Motor Park be *dat.* Tell them say you *dey* go Ikeja. You hear me? I say *Ikeja.*"

Carlotta nodded. "*Eek-kay-jar*," she repeated.

The taxi driver shook his head derisively and walked away, muttering something under his breath.

Carlotta walked into the park. She looked around and immediately became apprehensive.

The so-called park was in semi-darkness, the rising sun just below the horizon. It brimmed with mini-buses painted in the same manner as the taxi she had ridden and were in as bad of a physical condition as well.

Total chaos reigned.

People were all over the place, shouting and screaming, chatting and laughing, pushing carts, and running with wheelbarrows. It was proving to be a very hectic morning for indigenes who probably hadn't gotten much sleep the night before.

Everywhere she looked, Carlotta saw wooden tables piled high with all sorts of goods for sale. Crude lamps constructed out of small metal cans and oiled rags lit the tables, which looked ready to buckle under their heavy burden. Hawkers, stationed by each table, bantered and haggled with potential customers.

Several vendors also had open fires on which they were cooking or grilling various types of food for breakfast.

The smell of oranges, bananas, peanuts, frying oil, and wood smoke saturated the sultry air.

The food aroma, however, did nothing to disguise the underlying noisome odor of the park. The stench was that of vehicle exhaust fumes tinged with the odor of burnt engine oil, accompanied by the pungent smell of human urine topped with a mixture of garbage and feces.

Carlotta pinched her nose and almost vomited. Her stomach rumbled and broiled. She waited for the nauseous feeling to subside. Biting her lip and still clenching her nose against the noisome odor, she approached one of the mini-buses.

"Where you *dey* go?" a rough-looking boy standing by the side of the bus asked. He couldn't have been any older than fourteen.

Carlotta understood he wanted to know her destination. She opened her mouth to answer but closed it again. With a feeling of dismay, she realized she had forgotten the name of the place she was told to ask for. She stared at the boy in confusion and her eyes stung with tears.

A portly woman carrying a large basket approached the bus.

"Masha—Lawanson," the boy announced in a singsong voice, his eyes zeroing in on the would-be passenger.

"Where be last stop?" the woman asked.

"Market," the boy replied, staring back intently.

The woman turned and walked away, supporting her basket against her ample stomach.

The boy hissed at the departing woman. Raising his leg, he slapped a dog-eared rubber flip-flop against the rear tire of the bus to dislodge some sticky mess then scrapped the rest of the stuff off by rubbing the footwear over the rough ground.

He stamped his foot several times, shuffled, and stamped some more.

Satisfied, he repositioned his foot correctly into the slipper and looked at Carlotta. "You *dey* go Lawanson?"

Carlotta shook her head. "Airport," she replied. "I need to get to the airport."

"Airport?" the boy repeated. "We no *dey* go Airport. Make you go enter *dat* motor *wey dey* call CMS—Mile2—Airport Road." He motioned to a bus on the far right.

Carlotta managed a feeble "thanks" and approached the bus he pointed out.

"Airport?" she asked, when she got near enough to the other bus boy, this one bare-chested and a little older than the first.

"Enter!" the boy instructed, hooking a thumb over his shoulder at the open door of the bus.

Carlotta hesitated for a moment then shrugged and climbed in.

"Airport Road, fifty naira. Hol' your change o!" the boy called as Carlotta squeezed in beside a drooling, old man and a thin, wiry woman in the first row.

The bus was almost full. People of all possible sizes were packed on flimsy benches that served as seats.

Carlotta placed her backpack in her lap and held on tightly. Even hotdogs couldn't be packed any tighter, she thought, trying not to elbow the old man in the ribs.

The boy tapped on the side of the bus and the engine groaned and whined to life. The bus driver turned and shouted something in a foreign language to the boy, who placed one foot in the bus and hung on. They rolled forward a few feet then stopped abruptly, the passengers rocking back and forth with the sudden stall in momentum.

The driver honked at a woman with a large bundle of clothes balanced precariously on her head, then poked his head through the window and shouted words that sounded like profanities.

The woman cursed back and moved quickly aside, managing to keep her load from toppling over.

The bus gathered speed. It joined the busy traffic on the main road and roared down the highway. The boy still hung from the open door, more than half his body dangling in thin air.

The vehicle growled, rattled, and puffed as it sped along.

Carlotta gritted her teeth and clutched her backpack tightly against her chest.

The boy finally pulled himself inside and took a seat, then commenced collecting the bus fare from the passengers. Here again, Carlotta ran into the same problem she had with the taxi driver. She had only dollars, no naira. After a brief consultation with the driver, the boy, whom she now understood was the bus conductor, handed her four five-hundred naira notes as change for a hundred dollar bill, minus her bus fare.

Carlotta placed the notes in her backpack. *If one hundred dollars equals a little more than two thousand naira,* she imagined, *that means seven hundred and fifty naira should have been less than fifty dollars! The slimy taxi driver had taken a hundred dollar bill from me and hadn't given any change for it.*

Carlotta was not well versed with dollar to naira conversions, but instincts indicated the taxi driver had cheated her big time. Unknown to her, the taxi driver had taken twenty times his actual fee, while the bus conductor had retained two-hundred-and-sixty times the correct fee for her bus fare, as well.

The conductor kept banging against the side of the bus to signal the driver to drop off passengers or pick-up new ones on the side of the road.

There are no official bus stops, Carlotta decided, and kept listening for when the boy would call 'Airport!'

When the bus huffed to a stop after what felt like forty-five minutes, the conductor slammed his fist against the side panel and announced in a loud voice, "Airport Road. Final stop."

The rest of the passengers dismounted.

Carlotta sat where she was. She did not move an inch.

"Oyibo, oya make you come down now, *na* final stop be *dis,"* the conductor prodded.

"It doesn't look like we're at any airport," Carlotta declared. "I need to get to the airport immediately." She took one look at her surrounding and added in an urgent voice, "Please, you gotta take me to the airport."

"Wetin? Airport?" the boy asked with an air of indifference. "We no *dey* reach airport gate. You *wan* make mopol catch us? *Na* final stop be *dis.* Airport Road. *Abeg,* come down *joor."*

Carlotta remained seated and looked really worried.

The boy eyed her insolently and added as he reached in to pull her down, "You must to come down oh. *Abi* you think say because you be *Oyibo,* you fit do *wetin* you like? *Abeg* come down *joor!"* His hand closed on Carlotta's upper arm and he yanked.

Carlotta's heart sank into her stomach. She tumbled out the bus, legs shaking so badly she lost her balance and crashed to the ground, scraping her knees and elbows.

The bus shot off.

Carlotta looked around. Apart from a few early risers and a few scurrying rodents, the place was totally deserted. Old dilapidated buildings and a scruffy landscape met her eyes everywhere she looked.

A creepy feeling began to gnaw at her insides.

Mustering up courage, Carlotta shouldered her backpack and stomped to the main road, in search of a cab or anybody who could tell her how to get directly to the airport.

✳ ✳ ✳

$\mathcal{S}$helley woke with a start. Nkem was standing over her, looking worried. She knew instinctively that something was very wrong and snapped herself upright, her mind flashing immediately to Carlotta.

"What is it? What has happened? Is everyone okay?" she asked, all traces of sleep gone from her voice.

"It's Carlotta," Nkem said in a grave voice. "We don't know where she is."

"What? I do not understand." Shelley quickly got out of bed. "What happened?" A glance at the bedside clock informed her it was nearly six in the morning.

"I think she ran away," Nkem explained in an anxious voice. She fidgeted and couldn't stand still. "Daniel has gone to look for her."

"What do you mean? How could Carlotta run away? Where would she go? She does not know how to find her way around here. Why would she do something so foolish?" Shelley headed out the door, her thoughts racing. She went into the living room.

Nkem followed.

Ada stood in the middle of the room, in tears. Her brother Somto sat on the sofa, staring at his feet.

"What happened?" Shelley asked Ada.

"I woke up one hour ago and Carlotta was not in bed. I thought maybe she was in the bathroom." Ada sniffed and wiped her eyes with the neck of her nightgown. She continued, "After a while, when she did not come out, I went into the bathroom

49

and she wasn't there. So, I came out and looked here, then in the kitchen and on the veranda. When I went to check the parlor downstairs, I found that the front door was open. So I went outside and checked. Then I noticed the gate was open and the keys and padlock were on the ground. I then came back inside and woke my parents." She started to sob again.

"It's okay, Ada," Nkem consoled. "I'm sure Carlotta is fine."

But Ada sobbed even harder.

"It is ten past six," Shelley said. "Carlotta must have been gone for several hours." *She probably headed for the airport in hopes of sneaking back to the United States. The little idiot! What made her think Lagos was a safe city to wander about alone, especially at night?*

To go to the airport, Shelley suspected Carlotta would have swiped her passport. She decided to confirm her suspicion.

As Shelley was leaving the sitting room, something caught her eye. She turned and saw her black purse sitting on the chair where Carlotta had left it. She immediately knew she was right—the girl had decided to run away to the airport. Just to make sure, Shelley opened the purse and dumped its contents on the chair.

Carlotta's passport was definitely missing and so was all the cash in her wallet.

"Carlotta must have gone to the airport," Shelley announced. "Her passport is missing."

Nkem rushed over to Shelley's side. "If she went to the airport, she should be safe until we get there," she said with obvious relief, but the worry lines were still etched in her face. She snapped open her cell phone and dialed. "I will inform Daniel so he can go there and look for her. Thank God. I was really beginning to worry. Lagos is a bad place for one so young to be wondering around alone."

Shelley put the contents of her purse back where they belonged and sat in a chair. There was nothing they could do now but wait and hear from Daniel. She hoped fervently that Carlotta was at the airport. The idea of her daughter running around alone somewhere in the middle of Lagos made her cringe. She was surprised Carlotta had even tried to run away.

The girl is impossible. What human being in their right mind would attempt a thing like this in a country or city they had only been in for a few days?

Owasso or Tulsa was one thing. Lagos was something else. This is a city where beheaded human bodies turn up in the streets every day, their heads having been collected for nefarious purposes.

Shelley's hands shook. She was badly in need of a drink.

Lagos was as bad as cities came. There was hardly any law and order enforced anywhere. Dismemberment of strangers and unsuspecting victims with machetes was a common occult practice. The kidnapping of foreigners was not uncommon.

Shelley had heard and read many frightening stories about Lagos on the news and in newspapers. She prayed her daughter would be spared from the sharp jaws of the city.

Carlotta needs to be locked away somewhere safe. For her own good, she deserves to be safely tucked away in a boarding school.

Shelley checked the time again. It was almost eight-thirty. She had called and notified the United States Embassy of Carlotta's disappearance. They promised they'd check and see if Carlotta had purchased an US-bound ticket, and take the necessary actions to find her.

Nkem called Daniel several times.

There was no good news.

Her shoulders sagging with the weight of uncertainty, a grief-stricken Shelley covered her face with trembling hands and wept.

❄ ❄ ❄

Carlotta stood on one side of the Airport Road looking for a cab, ignoring the people glancing curiously at her as they passed. They looked quite unfriendly and she couldn't summon the nerve to approach any of them and ask for directions. She decided to wait for a taxi instead.

And just like that, everyone started running.

Carlotta was perplexed. She looked to her right and saw people running toward her. She shrank back a few steps and out of their way.

"Run! Run for your life," one man yelled as he sprinted past Carlotta.

Chants filled the air. *"Na Gbomo-gbomo! Na Gbomo-gbomo!"* Kidnappers! Murderers!

People on the street ran as if a mad bull was after them.

Carlotta couldn't tell what had gone wrong. Her eyes widened into huge saucers, her heart hammered into her ribs. She wanted to run, too—her mind screamed for her legs to kick into action, but she couldn't move. She stood there, paralyzed with fear.

Shit! Everyone is running! I oughta run like hell!

But Carlotta remained nailed to the ground. Off to her right, sinister looking men in black hoods came down the road. They strode menacingly, their hooded figures stark and defined against the shadows of the dimly lit street. In their hands were huge black sacks. And glinting blades.

The men advanced.

"Oyibo, make you run o! *Gbomo-gbomo* go catch you o!" someone yelled insistently at Carlotta and knocked past her with an elbow.

The blow caught Carlotta on the side of the mouth and pain sliced, like a hot searing knife, into her brain. Suddenly, thanks to the pain, Carlotta's mind engaged and she bolted.

The men were only a few feet behind.

Carlotta flew blindly down the street, dodging out of side lanes and into main roads, running, and running, even after she was certain the men weren't coming after her.

She alighted on a street where a crowd was shouting and screaming, and stopped. She drew nearer, wondering why the crowd was raising such a racket.

When she was close enough, she noticed that the people were pelting stones at a clearing in their midst and yelling obscenities, their voices carrying far in the early morning air.

She inched nearer.

Oh my God! Carlotta was shocked by what she saw.

Two men were held captive in the clearing, cowering, arms around their heads. The first sported an ugly split on his forehead and was bleeding profusely. The other's hand hung limply over his head, the positioning of the elbow at an angle one would not expect.

The screaming crowd knew no mercy. "You be thief!"

"Abeg, we *dey* take God beg *una,"* the captured men pleaded.

"*Dem* go teach you big lesson today! *Ole!*" Robbers!

"Abeg, abeg, we no go thief again," the captured men implored. They looked really desperate.

"Na from your mama you for go thief!" There was no stopping the crowd. They kept hurling stones and other solid objects at the thieves.

"Abeg, we *dey* sorry, make *una* no vex." The men's eyes were wide with fright, their tones fearful as they pleaded in vain with the furious mob.

"God punish your mouth there! Thunder fire your head well-well! *Barawo!*" Thief!

The men understood their fate.

Their voices reeked of sheer terror.

All it took was someone to throw the first punch to make the crowd descend on the two men—pummeling and clawing at every inch of flesh.

Carlotta watched in horror as the men were subjected to blow after severe blow of beating.

The enraged people howled and became frenzied with their demand for blood.

The only thing that stopped the two men from being beaten to death, right there and then by the crowd, was the timely arrival of several mobile policemen equipped with flashlights and wooden clubs. The uniformed men surged into the crowd and began to hammer, restrain, and arrest everyone in sight.

"Mopol *don* come oh!" one woman yelled, and scuttled away.

The mob abandoned their quest for blood and started in confusion.

Panic broke out.

People ran and collided with one another, screaming and pushing down anything and anyone in their way. Several fistfights erupted. Stray blows flew every which way as the crowd resisted arrest and fought the uniformed men.

Carlotta sustained one painful hit and several rude pushes before she had the presence of mind to run from the scene. Nauseated, she ran, thrashing blindly into unknown streets, feet pounding wildly on the ground, breath wheezing out of her over-worked lungs, heart threatening to burst with the strain of the whole ordeal.

Blinded by tears and the sheer force of her terror, Carlotta crashed into piles of garbage and fell into gutters filled with stagnant water bioactive with all kinds of micro creatures.

Dawn was approaching and it was growing lighter by the second.

Carlotta's legs weakened.

She staggered on until she came to a street that had a large building. The elegant sign in front indicated the building was the Royal Bank of Nigeria, Ikeja. A high cement wall with an imposing metal gate enclosed most of the building from public view.

Carlotta stopped running and moved close to the gate. She knew her uncle worked as a manager in a Royal Bank—Ada had taken her for a visit to his office.

Exhausted, she supported herself against the wall, struggling to catch her breath. Her long, curly hair, now wild and damp from her mad dash across the streets of Ikeja, hung limply against the sides of her face. Her shoes were wet and muddy. The lower part of her jeans had dark-greenish splatters from where she had fallen into the shallow gutters.

Carlotta shuddered in fright.

Fortunately, she was not badly hurt. But the roll of cash in her back pocket was gone—someone in the mad crowd had probably picked her pocket.

Without taking off her backpack, she sat on the ground with her back against the side of the fence. She began to wish she had never run away and were back in her uncle's house, where she would at least be safe.

She recalled the bloodied sight of the thieves and cowered.

Those guys will totally not survive the serious beating they received. If they do, I'm positive that neither will steal as much as a pin again for the rest of their lives.

Carlotta knew she would never take Lagos for granted again. She couldn't shake the horrors of what she had seen and knew memories of it would haunt her forever.

Already, the side of her face where she'd been struck had swollen to three-times its normal size. It felt raw and painful.

Drawing her knees up to her chin, her arms wrapped around her legs, Carlotta sandwiched her head between her knees and began to cry.

Chapter 3
Federal Government Girls' College, Uddah

ichard unlocked the front door and pushed it open. He stepped aside for Maria to precede him into the hallway.

"The bathroom is to your left," he called, shutting the door. He shook off his jacket and loosened his tie, flexing the sinewy muscles lining his back. He'd taken Maria out for Saturday dinner, and since his family was still away in Nigeria, he invited her into the house for a nightcap.

He plunked his muscular frame down on the comfortable sofa in the living room and waited for Maria to reappear. When she returned, she carefully deposited herself in the armchair opposite him and crossed her legs. She seemed to be on edge.

"Would you like something to drink? Coffee maybe?" Richard asked.

"It's kind of late for a strong drink. I'll have orange juice, thank you." Maria did not meet his eye.

"Fine by me." Grinning, Richard strode to the kitchen and poured a tall glass of orange juice. He also grabbed a can of sparkling water and returned to the living room. He placed the glass of juice on the coffee table beside Maria and cracked his can open. His eyes held hers for a moment then raising the can in a silent toast, he tipped his head back and gulped.

Maria acknowledged the toast and sipped her juice.

She's deliberately not looking at me. Richard put down the water and knelt beside her.

Reaching out, he touched the tips of his fingers to her chin and lifted her face slowly upward so she was gazing back at him. Her hazel eyes stared out from a smoky background, the lashes dark and moist.

"Are you okay?" Richard's voice was very low. He barely heard himself speak.

"Yes, I'm fine, Doctor," Maria replied. He traced the outline of her lips with his thumb. The skin underneath was soft and yielding. She trembled.

"Call me Rick, Maria," Richard invited, breathing heavily against her neck. The tip of his tongue traced the shape of her ear, his left hand sneaking underneath her hair and rubbing the back of her neck. He moved to cup her chin, and brushed his thumb against her cheek. Warm, passionate blood coursed through his veins.

"You're so beautiful," he murmured, and leaned closer. His nose barely touched her ear and her flowery scent reminded him of the early bloom of spring flowers. He groaned and buried his face in her hair, his ears pounding with the force of his arousal.

Maria shifted. "It's getting late. I ought to be on my way now, Doctor," she said, refusing the open invitation to use his name.

Richard relished the feel of her shoulder crushed against his chest. His eyes bored into hers, noticing her eyelids flutter. He heard her suck in a breath. *She's definitely attracted to me.* "Are you absolutely certain you have to leave right this minute?" He moved the hand he had under her hair against the nape of her neck, tracing the curve of her shoulder all the way down her chest, and cupped her left breast. *Things are just beginning to get interesting.*

Maria let the hand linger for a few seconds then pushed it away and shook her head. "It's late and I need to get on home to bed. I have a busy day ahead of me." She drained the rest of her juice and rose to her feet.

Sighing, Richard mussed his hair. He stood and walked her to the door. He reached for his car keys.

She placed a halting hand on his arm. "It's fine," she said, her voice shaky. "I can manage on my own. Thanks for the gesture."

"You don't have to be so damn independent when you're with me, Maria." Richard took a deep breath. He braced his hands on either side of her, caging her in.

Maria laughed and shook her head. "What are you anyway? A romantic hero?" She tried to push him away.

Richard's hands caught hold of her shoulders and he drew her close. "Let me be your hero," he whispered, pulling her delicate form into a tight embrace. She did not struggle. Instead, her arms reached out and wrapped themselves around his neck.

Richard's heart raced.

Maria pressed herself closer.

He felt himself harden, his heart beating widely to an unknown music. With a groan from somewhere deep within, he bent his head and covered her mouth with his. Her lips parted and she kissed him back, her moist tongue yielding to his insistent thrust.

Without warning, Maria stiffened and pushed him away. He straightened, hands reluctantly dropping from her waist. It took him a great deal of self-control to keep from pulling her roughly back into his arms. His face tensed with the force of his need.

"I have to go now, Doctor," Maria said in a breathless voice. "Thanks for the drink." She inclined her head. "And the lovely dinner."

Before Richard could collect his thoughts, she turned and sashayed out the front door, disappearing into the blackness of the night.

"Damn it, my name is Richard," he almost yelled after her, but she was gone. *I'm gonna get you yet, you little tease!*

✳ ✳ ✳

Carlotta sighed and fidgeted in her seat. Her chest felt constricted and a feeling of despondency gnawed at her insides.

She knew her situation was hopeless, and couldn't think of any good way to get out of it.

Feeling stifled, she lifted a shaky hand to the car door and tried to lower the back-seat window. Though the automatic button buzzed, the windowpane did not budge. That was not surprising since the inside of the car was missing a door panel. And that wasn't the worst of it—the car lacked functioning seat-belts.

With annoyance, Carlotta turned her attention to fanning herself with the outdated *Seventeen* magazine she'd been reading for the past hour. She soon gave up fanning, and put down the magazine. Wiping the sweat from her brow, she thought it was unbelievable how hot and humid the atmosphere was. *And the air conditioner has been running at full capacity for two hours. Talk about sluggishness!*

Carlotta felt faint. Aside from her discomfort, she was at a loss on how to change her mother's mind about boarding school. Shelley was relentless. Though Carlotta had promised to behave and swore never to touch drugs again, her mother remained adamant.

It's so not fair. I already said I'd be good. What more does she want from me?

Carlotta glanced at the back of her uncle's head and sighed. Her uncle had offered to drive them to the school. They had departed the previous day, Saturday, from Daniel's residence in Lagos, and headed east for the better part of nine hours. They'd stopped for the night in a city known as Onitsha, setting off again after breakfast for the final stretch.

The city of Onitsha was behind them, for they were now crawling through a dry, desolate area. Daniel was careful in maneuvering the SUV through a bumpy stretch of unpaved road.

Moving at a snail's pace, they skirted around several large potholes, which caused them to buck from side to side. Carlotta couldn't remember being on a road that bad in her entire life.

Biting her lip and feeling increasingly desperate, Carlotta glanced at her mother.

Shelley was reading a newspaper and seemed not to mind the heat. Every now and then, she'd look up and question Daniel about something she read in the paper and they would discuss the topic for a while. She certainly looked calm and oblivious of the oppressing heat, the dismal scenery, and of her daughter's misery.

Carlotta didn't understand how her mother could be tolerant of the nonexistent scenery. *Jeez! The hellhole I got lost in two nights ago is so better than this.*

Since they left Onitsha, they hadn't driven past a single Mr. Bigg's, Tantalizer's, Tastee Fried Chicken, or Sweet Sensations. Carlotta hated the road trip and fumed inwardly. *We could have just flown or something, and not totally riding around in this hillbilly car.* But no, her uncle wanted to drive for twelve hours in the oppressing heat and give them a tour of the uninspiring countryside.

Totally uncool.

What she wouldn't give to see a gas station, red light, road sign, or any infrastructure that hinted at the barest level of civilization? *How can people, like, even live here? It's totally worse than a nightmare!*

What seemed like ten slow minutes ticked by. Carlotta gave an exaggerated sigh. She made to wipe her brow again. Her shiny polish flashed with the movement of her hand and she paused to examine her nails. She'd carefully buffed and polished them two nights before and was a little miffed to notice a chip on the little finger of her right hand.

"Great," she muttered, simultaneously rolling her eyes and smirking. "All that lost sleep for nothing."

"Are you all right, honey?" Shelley asked, eyes glued to the paper.

Carlotta ignored her, and with a casual display of nonchalance, switched on her iPod. She connected her headphones to the iPod and clamped them firmly over her ears. Scowling, she turned to stare out the window. She'd refused every attempt by her mother and uncle to draw her into a conversation. She resented the idea of boarding school and wasn't going to pretend otherwise. And she wanted her mother to know it by all means.

My dad hadn't even bothered to come along for the ride, Carlotta reflected with distaste.

Richard had conveniently needed to travel to New York for a medical conference the same night as his daughter's departure. They had all driven together to the Tulsa International airport that fateful night. He bade them farewell at the gate before hurrying off to another terminal, where he was due to catch a belated flight to New York. As if seeing his only daughter off to a foreign country wasn't important enough for his attention.

If my dad couldn't even spare the time from his precious schedule to come with us, I don't see why I should be forced to go to school here.

It's so not fair.

The SUV was now plodding through a treeless landscape.

The hot sun blazed relentlessly from the sky, its rays determined to scorch every living thing off the face of that part of the earth. Except for a few pedestrians, the dusty roads were deserted because of the heat.

Every now and then they drove past a few people walking along the side of the road. Carlotta gazed absentmindedly at them. The women had what Carlotta thought were tablecloths wrapped around their mid sections into which a matching blouse was tucked in an ill-fitting fashion. A few had on flowing robes that fitted worse than the tablecloth attire. The robed women resembled round tents as they warbled along the dusty road. They all had scarves, woven in a turban-like manner, around the top of their heads. Many of the turban-clad heads supported large wooden trays balancing various kinds of produce bound together with crude ropes.

Carlotta shook her head and glanced irritably at the dismal scenery. *At least there are no street vendors running after us with their wares, like in Lagos and Onitsha.* She wasn't exactly used to the idea of hawkers pursuing moving cars with their goods, yelling for attention at the top of their lungs.

"Buy Gala!"

"Fanta! Coke!"

"Okpa!"

"Pure water! Yogurt!"

"Phone card! Charger! CD!"

On her first night in Nigeria, she'd had a shocking experience after leaving the Murtala Mohammed International Airport and headed toward her uncle's residence in Ikoyi. Daniel had slowed down the car, while Nkem rolled down the side window, pushed her head through and yelled, "Bread!"

At once, several vendors had shoved large loaves of bread in Nkem's face. Others, who hadn't been able to get their loaves through the window, pressed them against the windshield. The amazing thing was, the vendors had actually been running after the moving car and keeping pace with it as they shoved and jostled one another for a more advantageous position.

Great. Carlotta's lips curled into a derisive smile and she tried to shut the memory out of her mind.

Worse was the fear she experienced when she tried to runaway from her uncle's house to the airport. Somehow she'd ended up in a place just a few meters from the airport entrance, robbed and beaten, lost, and terrified out of her mind. With no idea how to proceed, she'd been forced to camp outside a bank building till the sun came up and the streets became awash with people.

Had it not been for the helpful workers at that bank, Carlotta didn't dare think what would have become of her. When she was discovered, she was a nervous wreck, sobbing hysterically and begging to be taken home to her mother. She had neither Daniel's address nor phone number. She hadn't even been able to remember the simple word *Ikoyi*, which was the city where her uncle lived.

What had saved Carlotta that morning was that Daniel worked for a different branch of the same bank. When she mentioned it, one of the accountants had retrieved Daniel's records, tracked him down on his mobile phone, and informed him of his niece's whereabouts.

An enraged uncle had come to pick Carlotta up. By 10:30 AM, she was back in his home, feeling very foolish indeed.

Shelley had been really furious. "You could have been kidnapped or killed!" Carlotta was advised several times that day. The adults kept expressing their horror at what she had done, so much so she cringed each time anyone said "Imagine!" even if they weren't referring to her in that instance.

Carlotta shuddered. She'd learned a great lesson. *I'll never try to run away in Lagos again.*

Carlotta stared out the car window and tried to concentrate on the passing scenery. Small mounds of fresh earth on both sides of the road extended as far out as the eyes could see. Poles stuck out of each mound, with plant tendrils curled around them. Green leaves, extending from the tendrils in all directions, were unmoving in the hot, windless weather of the early August afternoon.

Over the sound of her iPod, Carlotta heard Daniel informing Shelley that those were yam mounds. Judging from the number of mounds they passed, she guessed yam must be a subsistence crop for the villagers in that area. She didn't particularly like boiled yam—*it's so loaded with carbohydrates and tastes like boiled potatoes. Yuck!*

There were a few clear areas devoid of yam mounds that contained small houses made out of mud and sticks. One of the little houses had an ancient looking bicycle leaning against its front wall. Wooden vases hung off the bicycle handlebars and were suspended by rough brown ropes. Stained and tattered laundry was secured to wires connecting one dismal window of each house to another. Several odds and ends littered the bushes within the immediate environs of the houses.

This place is officially creepy. The car dragged by several more houses of the same fashion. *Who in their right mind would want to live here?*

Carlotta sighed. She flitted hair away from her face and shook her head from side to side in an attempt to allow her pretty curls settle in a more comfortable manner. She selected a track from Hannah Montana's latest on her iPod and settled back in her the hot, clammy seat; willing herself to remain calm.

She was mad that her mom tricked her into coming to Nigeria. Although she was now enrolled in an all-girls Federal school situated in the eastern part of the country—an area inhabited mainly by the race of people called Igbos—she couldn't believe her mother would actually leave her there to survive by herself. Or rather, she wished her mom would not. *Let's hope she's just bluffing.*

"Anambra State," Shelley had said in a stern voice while admonishing Carlotta for running away. "If any school environment can instill some discipline into you, it should be a boarding school located there. And it would serve you right, too."

While Shelley berated Carlotta, Daniel had paced the entire length of the living room—his very silence more ominous than Shelley's anger.

Carlotta had gaped in frustration at the turn of events. Back in Oklahoma, she'd assumed she would be grounded for a whole month, at the very worst, as punishment. What she hadn't imagined was boarding school, and Shelley's acquiescence to it.

Nigeria, West Africa of all places. Jeez! Why me?

And now that she'd failed in her attempt to run away, Carlotta was dismayed to discover that her mother seemed pretty convinced boarding school was exactly what was needed to whip her into shape.

"You can't make me go!" Carlotta had yelled at her mother before running upstairs to the bedroom she shared with Ada, howling at the top of her voice, slamming the door in a rage.

Born and raised in San Francisco, Carlotta had led a pampered life, never leaving the sheltering shores of the United States, not even for Canada or Mexico. When she got expelled from school the first time, her parents had panicked, then up and moved from San Francisco to Owasso, where the only places within a four-hour radius that resembled a city were Oklahoma City and Tulsa. As if living in Oklahoma wasn't bad enough, her parents had now decided to send her to a boarding school as punishment for getting herself expelled again—this time for smoking marijuana.

I only tried the freaking reefer once. It's not like I totally stashed loads of it in my school locker, or got a gun and popped a cap in my classmate's ass like some kid did in New York. Not that they wouldn't totally deserve it if I did.

"Here we are!" Daniel suddenly exclaimed with undisguised enthusiasm, and swerved the black SUV through a wide, wrought iron gate.

To Carlotta, what Daniel said sounded more like, *hiyaah we aah*, because of his heavy accent. She snapped out of her inner turmoil and tried to take an interest in their surroundings.

Carlotta's grandfather was a Nigerian who had immigrated to the United States and married a white woman from New Jersey. His only brother, however, had remained in Nigeria and married an Igbo lady. Daniel, their only son out of seven children, had never left Nigeria except for one visit to the United States several years before, during which he had spent a few weeks with his younger cousin's family. Therefore, while Richard was of mixed American and Nigerian decent, Daniel, on the other hand, was a hundred percent Nigerian.

"Finally, we have arrived," Shelley said with an audible sigh of relief. She folded away the newspaper she had been reading and took off her dark glasses. "Sweetie, this is exciting, is it not?"

she asked in a forced cheery voice, glancing over her shoulder at Carlotta.

Carlotta met her mother's gaze but did not reply. She snatched off her earphones and switched off her iPod. She figured if she sulked long enough, Shelley would realize how stupid the whole boarding school idea was and take her back home. So far, she had succeeded in not letting herself be drawn into any conversation—no matter how hard her mother baited. As for getting Shelley to change her mind, Carlotta didn't think it was going to be that easy.

But I'm so gonna try.

She remained silent as they drove through the school gate. The driveway was wide enough to hold three normal sized cars side-by-side. They got to the end and waited for the blue Benz in front to pull into the large clearing serving as a parking lot.

Daniel brought the SUV to a final stop between a gray Toyota and a black Ford. The driver of the Toyota, a black man in his mid-forties, was seated with one foot planted firmly on the ground. As her uncle parked the car, Carlotta caught the man peering at them in awe.

She glared. *Stop staring at me!*

The man shook his head and leaned over into the back seat of his car. She kept watching as he grabbed a brown manila envelope from his back seat, got out of his car, and slammed the door. She saw him throw a peculiar glance her way before hurrying off to a large white building that was in full view of the parking lot.

A big, white banner that read: *Welcome To Federal Government Girls' College, Uddah* in large, black letters was displayed against the wall of the building.

"*Hiyaah* we *aah*," Daniel repeated. "FGGC Uddah." He exited the car; his protruding belly preceding him, then stretched, and cracked his knuckles.

From her seat, Shelley looked around the parking lot. "All right, we sure do stand out," she said without seeming to move her lips at all.

It gave Carlotta a little satisfaction to realize Shelley was reluctant to exit the car. Not that she would blame her mother, though. There were people at every nook and corner. All were black—each and every one of them.

Carlotta's heart sank. *What exactly was I expecting? After all, we are in Nigeria.* Turning back to address her mother, she said, "Mom, you don't have to do this. I know I messed up and everything, and you and Dad have totally made your point but…" she began, wiping her sweaty palms on her pants. She tried to blink away the hot tears that stung her eyes.

Shelley pinned her daughter with cautious, unwavering eyes. The stiff smile on her thin lips vanished. "Your father and I have made our decision and we are standing by it. The sooner you come to terms with this, the better it will be for you." She sounded harsh.

Carlotta pushed on in a stricken voice. "Mom, please, you can't actually leave me here all by myself." Tears rolled down her cheeks. She took a deep breath, deliberately neglecting to wipe-off the tears. "Mom, all my friends are back in California. I don't know anyone here, and I don't want to go to school here." She leaned forward and let the tears flow freely for her mother's benefit.

Shelley said nothing.

Carlotta tried again. "If I couldn't make friends in my last school, how on earth am I supposed to make friends here?" She gestured with her hands as if to say, "Hello, look around you."

"We have been through this before," Shelley said. She took a deep breath and sighed. "Your father and I think this is exactly what you need. We are doing this to help you. Honey, we are really doing this for your own good." She rubbed her temples with the tips of her fingers. "I am sure you will make many friends here in no time at all."

Shelley planted both feet firmly on the ground and got out of the car. Keeping her spine straight and holding her head high, she forced a pleasant note into her voice. "Besides, you need the discipline." Eyebrows slightly raised, she shot Carlotta a pointed look. "Right?"

"Mom! You can't do this," Carlotta retorted, all traces of her attempt to be Miss Goody-two-shoes gone. "I said I was sorry, all right? I wasn't the only one who got busted for smoking in school. Why should I be the one who totally gets dumped in Nigeria?" Had she been standing, she would have stamped her foot as she always did whenever conversations with her parents weren't going exactly the way she wanted. She was used to always having her way and couldn't understand why her parents needed to do something this drastic.

Impervious to her daughter's brewing tantrum, Shelley turned and strode off. She joined Daniel behind the SUV and surveyed the crowd of people bustling about in the parking lot.

Carlotta closed her eyes and took a deep, steadying breath. Her hands shook. She tried to calm herself by cupping the palm of one hand around the balled fist of the other. She steeled her muscles.

How on earth can anyone expect me to survive alone in a place like this? This must be some kind of bad joke, or a very bad dream.

But wish it as she may for the situation to be unreal, Carlotta knew she wasn't dreaming and suspected her mother wasn't joking, either.

Carlotta's eyes became shiny with tears. The feeling of trepidation that had been nagging at her all morning deepened. She was beginning to sense that no matter how much she pleaded, her mom wasn't going to back down. This made her even more desperate and fueled her decision to keep trying.

Reaching down with defiance, she stuffed her iPod and head-phones into her pink purse. Then she jerked open the car door and stormed out. The white, strappy, wedge summer-sandals she had on immediately sank a quarter inch into the red dust covering the ground.

A feeling that hovered somewhere between fear and hope-lessness washed over Carlotta. Blinking rapidly several times, she swallowed the lump in her throat and willed herself not to break-down and cry like a silly two year old. She felt both her mother's and uncle's eyes on her and strengthened her resolution to not give in so easily. She still had a little time. She sniffed and wiped her eyes and cheeks, then ventured another look around.

Girls littered the parking lot, dressed in the same uniform of stiff-collared, white shirts tucked into knee-length, straight black skirts. Their feet were encased in white socks and brown sandals. The girls were talking with their parents and guardians, striding toward the entrance of the white building, or standing beside their vehicles.

Carlotta guessed they were new, too. There was something that wasn't quite right about their appearance. Before she could pinpoint what it was, she heard her mom call for her to come help with the luggage.

Feeling utterly gruff, Carlotta slammed the car door and stomped to the rear of the SUV where her mom and uncle were already placing her gear on the ground.

Daniel locked up. He hoisted Carlotta's suitcase and a travel bag, while Shelley lifted two other bags.

Carlotta, still clutching her pink purse, swung her backpack over her shoulders, picked up her green duffel bag and a blue plastic bucket that had a plastic water container nestled in it.

The trio made their way to the entrance of the big building, where other groups were headed. As they passed through, Carlotta saw her mother say something to her uncle, who nodded something back in reply. She wondered for a second why they were talking in hushed tones, but thought nothing of it. The next moment, they emerged in a large reception hall awash with people and buzzing with conversation.

Suddenly, there was a lull in the noise. A few seconds later, the entire room became very still. All eyes were on Carlotta and her guardians. Some of the people in the crowded room stared with their mouths open.

Carlotta tried to make herself a little less visible by moving slightly to her left, so she was partially concealed by her uncle's massive form.

The crowd was obviously surprised to have a white woman and her daughter in their midst. They continued to stare, unabashedly, until a stern voice in the crowd chided, "What are you looking at? Haven't you seen *Oyibo* people before?"

Apparently, many of the people in the room had never seen a Westerner, let alone been this close to one. Just as suddenly, the conversations resumed and everyone went about their business, a few still sneaking a peek at the two white ladies every now and then.

Carlotta wasn't technically *white*. She had a white-American mother and a dad of mixed race, so she was three-quarters white. Her eyes were ice-blue like Shelley's, but her skin was only a shade or two away from her mother's milky-white skin. Carlotta also had thick and wavy brown hair cascading halfway down her back, while Shelley's straight blonde hair was clipped to shoulder length.

Carlotta's eyes roamed the reception hall. Several tables were arranged along the length of the room. A big sign displayed on the wall directed new students to check-in at one of the tables. At each check-in station was seated a matron-like woman and two students, who although older and more mature than the new students, had on the same uniform of white shirt and black skirt. A queue of new students, with their escorts, formed before each table and waited to be checked-in.

As they crossed the room and joined the queue in front of the fourth table, Carlotta's face reddened in embarrassment. Her tight-fitting outfit of low-hung blue jeans and pink, halter-neck half-top stood out as much as her light skin did. She closed her eyes and gave a tiny shrug. *Yeah, yeah, you all can stare at my outfit all you want. How was I supposed to know to dress in that drab uniform? I don't plan on staying behind anyway, so, there!*

One of the students beside the matron held a clipboard and read items off a list, while the matron and the other student went through the luggage of the new girls. Occasionally, they'd stop rifling through the student's belongings and look up to the parents or guardians to ask for an item they couldn't find. Twice, Carlotta heard the matron admonish a parent about an item that hadn't been accounted for, while the new student cowered in fear.

Soon, it was Carlotta's turn to be checked in.

"Good afternoon, sir. Good afternoon, madam," the matron and students said in unison.

Shelley and Daniel acknowledged the greeting and placed Carlotta's luggage on the table.

The matron chiseled out a frozen smile, and launched into a welcoming speech that went on, and on, and on.

Carlotta barely listened. The matron had a heavy accent that rendered the speech indecipherable. She was wondering if her mom was fairing any better with the matron's rambles, when one of the students addressed her.

"Your name please?" the student asked.

To Carlotta, it sounded like the student had said, *yoh name pleez.*

"Carlotta Ikedi," Carlotta replied in a small voice. She pronounced her name in the American way, *Cahlorda Eye-key-dye.*

The student glanced up from the clipboard and squinted at Carlotta. "*Pah-done? Pleez* repeat *yoh* name."

"*Cahlorda Eye-key-dye,*" Carlotta repeated, a little louder this time.

An awkward silence followed.

"Hello, my dear. I am Dr. Ikedi," Shelley volunteered in a crisp tone, addressing the clipboard student. "This is my brother-in-law Daniel, and my daughter, Carlotta. I am sorry my husband couldn't be here." She gave a self-conscious chuckle. "He had to attend a medical conference at the last minute. How do you do?"

The student who'd been staring at Carlotta's mom during this little speech, and who clearly looked muffled now, shifted her gaze to the matron, as if hoping to receive an interpretation of what the white woman had just said. When it was clear no help was forthcoming from the matron, the student glanced down at her clipboard, then up again at Carlotta's mother. Obviously, she hadn't understood a word of what Shelley, who had a California accent, had just said. And neither did the matron.

"I, I, please, what—? I mean, what?" The student looked at her feet and chewed on her lip. She needed the whole statement repeated but was too embarrassed to request it.

Mercifully, Daniel intervened and supplied Carlotta's name.

This time, the girl smiled and repeated, "You are Carlotta Ikedi." She said the name exactly like Daniel did. Then she added with a relieved smile, "*Yoh* name *ees Car-lot-tah Eek-kay-dee.* Okay, now I understand."

"*Duh!*" Carlotta smirked.

At once, everyone following the exchange cackled. Some of the parents made humorous remarks in a language Carlotta felt quite sure wasn't English. A bulky man in the queue next to them said something indecipherable to Daniel, who gave him a strange reply, smiled and shook his head.

Shelley appeared not to notice the giggling crowd.

She's probably used to embarrassing situations like this—being married to my dad, and having to attend all those Nigerian functions back in 'Frisco. Carlotta rolled her eyes. *Yeah, it must be so hard for her.*

The matron and the other student exchanged knowing looks, and continued with their search through Carlotta's luggage, while the clipboard student proceeded to read the required items off her list.

Carlotta put her backpack and duffel bag down and reached into her pink purse for some strawberry-flavored lip-gloss. She glanced around again at the other new students. Then it hit. She suddenly realized why the students looked funny. They all had short hair! Most of the girls had their hair cropped so closely to their skulls their scalps were visible.

Almost as if the matron had taken a cue from Carlotta's thoughts, she said to Shelley, "Your daughter will have to cut her hair. We don't allow junior students to wear long hair in this school." The matron waited for a reply.

Carlotta understood enough. She looked up and saw her mother nod her assent to the matron. She couldn't believe it.

"What?" Carlotta shrieked. "No way, Mom. No freaking way!" She was genuinely shocked.

"Honey, it is all right," Shelley replied, and patted Carlotta on the shoulder. "All the other new girls have short hair, too."

Carlotta backed away a few steps and collided with an ample woman waiting to check-in her equally ample daughter. She lost her balance and almost fell. The woman steadied and released her then tugged her dislodged shoulder bag back onto the crook of her elbow. She surveyed Carlotta with mild interest then mumbled something intelligible.

Carlotta started sobbing. She buried her face in her hands, quite forgetting to thank the woman for saving her from a nasty fall. The woman said something that sounded rude, hissed, and made a clucking sound with her tongue then looked the other way.

At this point, everyone was staring at Carlotta. Some were gesticulating and clapping their hands in a way that made Carlotta think they weren't sorry for her at all. Others had pity in their eyes.

"I'm so not going to let anyone touch my hair," Carlotta wailed.

"It will be fine, sweetie," Shelley tried to console her distraught daughter. "You will be fine—"

"No, I won't. I totally won't be the same, and my whole life will be so over. Mom, you can't do this to me. It's so not fair!"

Carlotta considered her hair to be her best physical attribute. Everyone had always told her how pretty her hair was. Sometimes she spent a great deal of effort grooming it in front of the mirror. She'd always gone to the hairdresser's twice a week, since she was six years old. She couldn't come to terms with the fact that she was being told it would have to go. Just like that!

"It's so not fair," Carlotta blurted. She then became aware of the staring crowd. She wiped her eyes and glared at them, daring anyone to smirk or smile at her misery.

The room became eerily quiet again. Carlotta felt as if all the happiness had been sucked out of her being. She resented the academic environment her parents had chosen. She didn't want to be in Africa. She didn't want to be in Nigeria. She definitely didn't want to be in boarding school with a bunch of stupid girls wearing close-cropped hair. Most of all, Carlotta didn't want to cut her hair.

"Stupid boarding school! I hope you totally blow up and burn to the ground," she raged. She turned and marched toward the hall exit without another word.

✳ ✳ ✳

It was Sunday afternoon and Richard was seated in his living room, glad he was not on call. He needed the lazy day to take things easy and think about Maria. There was something about her that tugged at his heartstrings and his loins. But for some inexplicable reason, she was reluctant to end up in bed with him. Last night had been a perfect setting for some stolen romance, Richard reflected. He ran a hand through his hair.

My wife and daughter were not even in the country, for heaven's sake.

He couldn't remember the last time he had wanted a woman so badly. It was such a pity that Maria was playing hard to get, but he had confidence.

He vowed to get her.

Eventually.

He was willing to woo her until she gave in to him entirely. His wife was not due back from Nigeria for another week or so. There was still time.

Leaning back, he cracked open another can of beer. Alcohol wasn't allowed in the house because of Shelley's drinking problem, but since she was thousands of miles away, he didn't see any harm in indulging in a six-pack right in his own home.

He let his mind wander.

He saw himself wrapped around Maria's slender frame, his hands traveling all over her sleek body. Her long tapered fingers traced his eyebrows then traveled to his ears. Her tongue soon replaced her fingers.

He stirred.

Her nails raked his shoulders, leaving behind long, fiery trails of passion. He massaged her slim neck, and kneaded her shoulders.

Her blouse melted away. Her bra undid itself and waved goodbye. He loaned her a centerfold's rack.

He became taut.

She reached for him. He took in a deep breath and waited.

You are so handsome, she whispered.

He let out his breath. *Yes, baby. I can be all that and some more for you. Just for you.*

I want you, she cooed in his ear.

I know. He took her mouth in his.

You're so huge…

Damn right, I am. Richard glowed with male pride. His hand trailed to his belt buckle. His other hand applied pressure on her neck, pushing her head down.

Oh my! Get a load of you, Maria exclaimed, tongue flicking.

Richard groaned, and shifted to give her more room. He sought for her to—

The doorbell rang.

"Damn!" Richard muttered, snapping out of his daydream. He poured himself back into his pants and got up to see who was at the door.

Who knows? It might be Maria. She'd probably changed her mind and come to seek him out, he thought, to finally bring his fantasies to reality. He recalled the long legs. The luscious lips. The bobbing rack.

He hardened.

"Oh baby, what I would do to you," he moaned as he yanked open the door—

It was a little girl in pigtails selling Girl Scout Cookies.

Chapter 4
Sapphire House

Shelley kept her composure after Carlotta's earlier outburst at the school's hair policy for junior students. She regarded her rebellious daughter in silence.

Carlotta leaned against the side of Daniel's car, her back to her mom, looking very furious. Every now and then, she kicked out at the front wheel of the vehicle and stamped her foot in frustration. Shelley reached out to put a consoling hand on her daughter's shoulder but Carlotta avoided her and turned around.

"Mom, you're totally not planning on leaving me here, are you? You really wouldn't return to the United States without me, right?" Carlotta's shoulders heaved and tears welled up in her eyes.

"I am so sorry, honey—" Shelley began.

But Carlotta didn't want to hear her mother's apologies. She cut in, "Mom, please, I'm sorry I was kicked out of school. But it's so not fair to leave me here, in the middle of nowhere. Please, take me back home." Carlotta was weeping now, her shoulders shaking so much she could hardly get her words out.

"I promise to be good this time. Honestly, I do. Please, don't punish me by leaving me here. It's not fair. It's totally *not fair*." She gave a particularly heartbreaking sob and buried her face in her mother's bosom.

Carlotta cried.

After a few moments, she stepped back and looked up.

Shelley's eyes were closed. When she opened them, they were wet with tears. She took a deep breath and slowly let it out. Several drops escaped her eyes. She turned away and wiped them off.

A feeling of elation surged through Carlotta's mind. *Finally! I've won. My mom will give in and take me back home. Hurray!*

Shelley said, "Honey, why not stay here and work very hard on your grades? And if you make a significant improvement by the end of the school year, I will persuade your dad to let you return home. Agreed?"

Carlotta's last bit of hope dashed to the ground. She suddenly stopped crying, her eyes taking on a look of defiance. "Mom! I can't stay here," she yelled. "I don't speak the language, I don't even understand half what they say when they speak English. I'll be so miserable and I definitely won't fit in. How am I supposed to, like, survive for one year in this place?"

Her hands hurt from being curled so tightly into fists. She didn't know what else to do to make Shelley relent. Nothing seemed like it was working this time. Carlotta deeply regretted ever getting on the plane that brought her to Nigeria in the first place. *I know I should never have come here.* She stamped her foot.

"Honey, this is the best I can do," Shelley said, trying to placate her distraught daughter. "You go ahead and spend one year here and work really hard. Then, we will see how much you can be trusted with responsibility and gaining a decent education. If you prove you can handle all that, I will persuade your father to bring you home at the end of the school year. Do we have an understanding?"

Carlotta saw her mother wasn't doing a good job of hiding her distress. She realized it wasn't as easy for her mom to let her only child go off to boarding school in a foreign country, as she had believed. *My mother doesn't really want to leave me here. I can tell.*

"Well, I need to know, Mom. If it wasn't for Dad, would you have done this?" Carlotta looked Shelley straight in the eye.

Shelley remained silent for a long time. Then she said in a hard voice, "Honey, listen to me. Your dad is a good father. He only wants what is best for you and I must say I agree with him. The decision to send you here was made by the both of us, and although I have offered to bring you home after one school year, I will not do so without his consent. However, this offer stands only if you put an exceptional amount of hard work into your studies."

Carlotta read the pain in her mother's eyes. But far from pain was the expression of futile helplessness she saw reflected in the blue eyes that mirrored her own.

Shelley took a deep breath before continuing, "So far, you have shown nothing but contempt and a bad attitude toward your academics. But, I know you have it in you to be a better person."

Shelley placed both her hands on Carlotta's shoulders and added, "I sided with your father on this unusual idea because I know there is still a very good chance of turning you around into a responsible and disciplined young woman. I refuse to let you continue living a life like you have done so far in the United States."

Shelley's eyes bored into Carlotta's as she said, "Maybe it is the different environment or the deep-rooted cultural practices of the people, but your father believes schooling here will help you evolve into a responsible person, and I am with him on that idea."

Her voice shook as she continued, "Honey, you stay here and work very hard, then after a year goes by, you may come back home, but not one day before." She looked like she was going to say something else but thought better of it. She nodded toward the white building, her hands dropping from Carlotta's shoulders.

Carlotta looked up and saw Daniel walking back to the car, several students following in his wake. One of the students appeared older and taller than the others, her long dark hair woven in cornrows, a look of importance carved on her face.

Carlotta knew that she must be a senior student because of her long hair. The other students were carrying her luggage.

Upon their approach, the senior student greeted Shelley and smiled at Carlotta.

Carlotta nodded in acknowledgement. She turned and relieved one of the students of her backpack and swung it over her shoulder. She mouthed a word of thanks to the student who nodded, but didn't say anything in reply.

The senior student introduced herself as Lola Ajayi, the senior boarding house prefect, and explained she would see Carlotta to the dormitories and get her settled in.

Shelley thanked her profusely and then got into the car beside Daniel, who was already seated behind the wheel. They bade Carlotta farewell, and drove off amidst promises to stay in touch.

A weird feeling came over Carlotta. In an instant, she realized she was homesick and already missed her mother.

"What is your name?" Lola asked.

Carlotta supplied her name in a shaky voice. She felt so small and scared in her new environment.

Lola smiled.

Carlotta figured Lola had asked the question more as a means to help her relax than to learn her name, which she probably already knew.

Lola said in a gentle voice, "Welcome to FGGC Uddah. I'll see you to your dormitory." She led the way out of the crowded parking lot. The junior students carrying Carlotta's things marched ahead of them.

"There are two groups of girls here—the senior girls, and the junior girls," Lola explained as they walked. "The junior classes progress from JS1 to JS3," she continued, smiling indulgently at Carlotta's puzzled look, "while the senior classes range from SS1 to SS3. These students helping with your luggage are all in JS2."

"Right…" Carlotta said in a non-committal tone. She had her eyes fixed on the JS2 students, who were whispering gaily to one another as they conveyed her luggage along. She noticed they all had short hair, like the new students she'd seen in the parking lot, and her heart sank.

As Lola continued to speak, Carlotta toyed silently with the idea of running away. She had no knowledge of exactly where she was, and had no idea of where she would go, but she was confident she would fare better this time than she did in Lagos.

But Carlotta was terrified of getting lost again.

The neighborhood outside the school doesn't seem too dangerous and I don't remember seeing any guards at the gate when we drove in. It should totally be a piece of cake.

Then Carlotta remembered the nine plus hours it had taken her uncle to drive them from Lagos to the hotel in Onitsha, and her hopes sank. She would never be able to pull it off. *Oh brother! I didn't even see any bus or train stations during the nine-hour journey.*

"Maybe I can get a cab or something, there must be an airport around here," Carlotta thought aloud without realizing it.

"The closest airport is in Enugu State," Lola said brightly. "Why do you ask?"

"Oh, er, never mind. Totally not important," Carlotta replied. She looked around in search for a sign that would promptly point her to a taxi stand.

Her heartbeat accelerated. *I only need to find a way to the airport—any airport at all.*

Suddenly, Carlotta remembered, to her dismay, her mother had her passport.

Shit! I still should try and get to the airport anyway. Maybe someone there would, like, help me out. My mom may still be around by the time I get there. Anything is better than being here and having them totally cut my hair.

They approached several white, rectangular buildings arranged in a straight, long row extending far out to the right.

"Classroom blocks," Lola pointed out, gesturing at the buildings with a sweep of her arm.

"The farthest one over there is the JS1 Block, the one next to it is the JS2 Block, then there is the JS3 Block, followed by the SS1 Block, and the SS2 Block." She pointed to the building closest to them. "*This* is the SS3 Block."

Carlotta glanced through the windows of the SS3 Block and saw empty classrooms containing desks and chairs arranged in neat rows. Large blackboards were attached to the walls facing the desks.

As they made their way past the other buildings, Lola pointed out the technical workshops, laboratories, staff building, business center, library, and the dispensary. Although the buildings were shaped with modern artistic angles, they looked just as severe and imposing as the classroom blocks.

The landscape beyond the buildings sloped gently downward and away toward another group of buildings in the distance.

Carlotta guessed the distant buildings must be the dormitories. All around them, and everywhere she looked, the grounds were covered with short carpet grass that glistened a bright green under the brilliant rays of the afternoon sun.

A major pathway was carved into the grassy landscape, leading from the front of the classroom blocks to the dormitories. The pathway meandered in a gentle fashion down the slope, giving the impression of a huge lazy snake warming itself in the sunlight.

Smaller pathways, originating directly from the front of each building, curved their way into the major pathway. The paths were covered in gravel, and contained a sprinkling of mica, which sparkled in the sun like many twinkling little stars.

Several small shrubs lined the edges of the pathways, demarcating them from the green grass. Clusters of trees stood at strategic positions along the curved areas formed by the meandering pathways. The tree branches splayed out gracefully from their trunks, providing an umbrella of shade on the ground beneath them. The beginnings of white and yellow flowers interspersed with the dark green leaves that crowned the trees.

The total effect of the view was stunning and beautiful, and in spite of her surly attitude, Carlotta was impressed. She listened for a while to the clunking sound the heels of her sandals made as she walked beside the prefect. The meandering pathway reminded her of the legendary 'Yellow Brick Road' featured in 'The Wizard of Oz.'

Follow the yellow brick road, follow the yellow brick road, Carlotta chanted to herself and smirked. She might as well be Dorothy, after all she was in a strange land, and the prefect beside her would do well as the Tin-Man. Maybe the JS2 students carrying her things could pass for the Munchkins, she thought. *All we need now is a cowardly lion and a wicked witch then we'll be good to go.*

The JS2 students were far ahead of them by now.

Carlotta saw several other new girls being escorted to the dormitories in a similar fashion. The groups looked like small clusters of soldier ants marching mindlessly to their predetermined destinations.

As they approached, Carlotta counted six large buildings—square in shape, painted in different colors, and arranged in such a way that their façades formed a large circle. The path they'd been following looped around the circle and formed a large ring. Wide walkways extended from the loop to the front entrance of each of the buildings.

"Those are the six houses," Lola explained. "And over there is the dining hall." She pointed to a white building—standing off to the right of the dormitories—which was almost twice as large as each of the houses.

Carlotta nodded.

"That mango tree standing over there is mysterious. It's supposed to be as old and fruitful as the school itself." Lola chuckled. "Nobody knows who planted it or how it came to be. Students call it the Mystical Mangy, and it goes with legend that the tree is alive, breathing, and listening to the gossips of students. If only trees could talk, what secrets we would learn."

"Mysterious and fruitful, huh?" Carlotta wasn't very enthusiastic about the alleged mystical tree.

The Mystical Mangy stood majestically in the middle of the ring. Its branches extended so far out it nearly crossed beyond the boundaries of the loop, the tips straining to touch the rooftops of each house. Patches of sunrays danced within the shade provided by the tree's large branches. Sturdy cement blocks formed a small circle on the ground around the tree's trunk, as if marking out the territory that brooked no trespassing from students. Large fibrous roots originating from the foot of the tree criss-crossed viciously above the earth and disappeared underneath the restraining circle of the cement blocks. A few wooden seats stood within the shade under the tree.

Although deserted at the moment, it was obvious the cover provided by the giant Mystical Mangy often served as a gathering spot for students.

They turned into the pathway leading to the entrance of the first building on their right. The building was painted a rich blue. A stairway as wide as the building's façade led up to the landing adjoining the front wall. The JS2 students lolled around on the landing, Carlotta's luggage on the floor around their feet.

Lola walked up to a tall and slender student standing in front of the entrance and said something to her. The student looked up and beckoned to Carlotta to come forward. Like Lola, the student was dark-skinned and pretty, but had an unmistakable air of arrogance. Something about her demeanor commanded instant respect and—fear.

"Your name is Carlotta Ikedi?" the prefect inquired. Without waiting for confirmation, she continued in a businesslike manner, "Welcome to Sapphire House. I'm Senior Chidi Anayo, the Sapphire House prefect."

Chidi consulted the list she had in one hand and added, "You are in Sapphire-Six. Your dormitory prefect will take you to your dormitory and show you to your assigned bed." She poked her head through the doorway behind her and called, "Anita! There is another new student for your dorm!" Then she turned back and looked Carlotta straight in the eye.

Carlotta shuddered.

"How old are you?" Chidi asked.

"I just turned thirteen two months ago," Carlotta replied.

"Aren't you a little too old to be in JS1?" There was no warmth, or trace of a smile, anywhere in the house prefect's grating voice.

At Chidi's rebuke, hot distaste filled Carlotta's eyes. She opened her mouth to retort but closed it again. Chidi, she realized, had turned away and was now saying something to Lola. She'd obviously meant the question as rhetoric and not necessarily a direct attack on Carlotta's person.

Carlotta disliked the house prefect instantly and knew the feeling was mutual. She bit her lip and struggled to regain her composure.

Who gave this prefect the idea that I want to be in JS1, or whatever, in the first place?

Carlotta detested being at FGGC Uddah, and suspected her dad's ruling was the sole reason for her predicament. She knew for a fact it had been her dad's decision to relocate her family from San Francisco to Owasso. He'd talked her mother into it, just as he'd also talked her mom into sending her to boarding school.

And this cheeky prefect has the nerve to totally suggest—

A voice interrupted Carlotta's thoughts.

"Ah, we have us a Feddie Girl here," the voice observed.

Carlotta looked behind Chidi. The owner of the voice was another tall and slender student.

Maybe they were all manufactured from some kind of 'Eve doll' factory or something.

It wasn't helping Carlotta's case that the students were all very pretty. She wanted them fat and ugly, or to look like monsters. That way, she would have another good reason behind her decision to run away.

"Anita, this is Carlotta," Chidi said by way of introduction, "the third new student for your dorm."

Turning to Carlotta, Anita said with amusement, "I'm Senior Anita Desouza, Sapphire-Six dorm prefect. Please follow me." She started to lead Carlotta away. "So, I have a Feddie Girl in my dorm this year, my dorm girls are going to have themselves a ball." She laughed and led the way through the entrance door.

Carlotta nodded to Lola, ignored Chidi, and tailed Anita through the building entrance to the hallway beyond. The JS2 students helping with her luggage promptly followed.

The long hallway had three doors on each side and one large door at the end. The six side-doors each had the letters 'S' and a number from one to six engraved on them. They went through the third door on the right engraved with S-6, and emerged in a large room.

Metallic double-bunks stood along the length of the room, four bunks on each side. The bunks were painted a shiny black and stood in strategic positions, looking large and sedentary against the backdrop of the room.

Wooden lockers, about four feet high, stood on one side of each bunk, while smaller versions protruded outwards from the wall above the bunks. The smaller lockers were positioned about three feet above the top beds in such a way that they could be reached from the bed if one stood or knelt.

Carlotta was shown to the top bed of the first bunk on the right row. Anita directed the JS2 students to put Carlotta's luggage down beside the bunk. They gladly obeyed and left the dormitory at once.

Carlotta surveyed the room. All the beds were neatly made. The two other new girls were on the other side of the dormitory, slowly unpacking their belongings, and generally giving the impression they were timid and unsure of what they were doing.

Anita introduced the girls to Carlotta as Uche Ijeogu and Sandra Uzor. The two girls smiled and went back to unpacking.

Carlotta shrugged one delicate shoulder, wondering where the rest of the students were. *Maybe I can sneak away, unobserved.*

Anita's voice broke into her thoughts.

"Your bunkmate is Senior Zika Makanna, an SS2 student. The rest of the dorm girls are in the dining hall at the moment but will be back soon," Anita announced. It was like she had read Carlotta's mind and was trying to stave-off her escape.

Then Anita addressed the students together. "Lunch will be provided to you in about an hour, so that should give you time to settle down a bit. Your bunkmates will soon be here to help you." She said to Carlotta, "I hope you brought your school uniforms. You need to change out of your street clothes and put on your dormitory uniform." Then she pointed to the farthest bunk on the left row, and said, "That is my bed. If you have any problems, please come and see me for help." She smiled and strode through the door.

Carlotta sighed; it had been a long morning. She placed her purse down, took her backpack off her shoulders and placed it beside the purse. She yawned and hunched down to open her suitcase, her arched spine visible underneath the fair skin of her partially exposed back. She smoothed back her curls from her damp forehead, and let out a resigned breath. *I need to get out of here!*

The ripping sound made as Carlotta unzipped the large suitcase was like a desperate cry for help in the eerily quiet dorm. She observed Sandra climb sluggishly up her bunk, reaching out to place something in her overhead locker. The girl was doing this very quietly, as if afraid to disturb the dead stillness of the room.

Carlotta rolled her eyes and shrugged. Gently, she went through the contents of her neatly organized suitcase, courtesy of her mother who had repacked all her stuff the night before they set out from Lagos. Carlotta, who hadn't been keen on leaving for boarding school, had initially thrown the newly purchased items pell-mell into suitcases and bags that already held the things she brought with her from the United States.

When the tips of her fingers found the rough material she sought, she closed her hand around it and pulled gently, taking.

care not to upset the rest of the neatly folded clothes. Still hunched, and balancing the rest of her weight on her feet, she unfolded the black school skirt she'd unearthed and studied it ruefully. The skirt had the unmistakable fresh smell that all her clothes had after her aunt did the laundry.

A wave of nostalgia went through Carlotta and her lips trembled. *I'd totally give anything to be back in Uncle Daniel's house.* She put the skirt down, fished out the white shirt that completed the uniform, and made to heave herself to her feet.

Immediately, a hand bell rang.

Startled, Carlotta toppled over backward and ended up in a sitting position on the ground, her hunched knees striking her chin.

Sandra and Uche, who were also surprised by the bell, jumped and shrieked. Eyes wide with panic, poor Uche put a hand to the left side of her chest, as if attempting to hold her racing heart in place.

Carlotta recovered quickly and dropped her garments unceremoniously into the open suitcase. She scrambled to pick herself up, an action made difficult by the wedge sandals on her feet.

The sound filled the dorm and seemed as though it was coming directly from the other side of the wall, behind the three girls now heaving sighs of relief to calm their high-strung nerves.

The girls looked at one another and giggled, apparently embarrassed by their reaction to the *ring-ring* sound of the bell. It felt like they were lone survivors of a ship wrecked at sea, seemingly grateful for one another's company.

As Carlotta braced her left hand on the ground and straightened her elbow to push herself back into a hunching position, the dormitory door burst open and a dozen girls poured in, talking loudly and cackling as they bustled to their beds.

From her position, Carlotta made out many pairs of feet, all encased in folded down white socks and brown, rubber sandals of different sizes, striding purposely from the door to their owner's destination.

One of the pairs of feet halted abruptly in front of Carlotta's open suitcase.

Warm blood rushing to her ears and flooding her neck, Carlotta let the lid of her suitcase fall back in place. She braced an arm on the bed beside her and pushed herself up to her full height of five feet four inches. One look at the face poised a few inches higher than hers, made her heart leap.

It was another 'Eve doll.'

Carlotta parted her suddenly dry mouth in what she hoped wasn't a grimace. Her tongue peeked out and nervously moistened her lips. She smiled.

The student leaning against the bunk and regarding Carlotta with interest was a dark beauty. Her large, black eyes gazed from lids softly lined with coal. One natural shaped eyebrow was partially concealed beneath the tips of her long, black hair, which was woven in cornrows. Her narrow forehead and high cheekbones accentuated her face as much as her beautifully shaped, full-lipped mouth did.

Carlotta caught the faint scent a flowery body spray, and watched with fascination as the girl's long, tapered fingers reached up and tucked the tips of her woven hair behind one delicate ear. Tiny, gold earrings gleamed from each ear lobe.

"You must be Carlotta. I'm Zika, your bunkmate," the girl said.

Wow! She's cute. Carlotta gulped and glanced from Zika's face down the rest of her body.

She gawked.

As suggested by her exquisitely chiseled face, Zika also possessed an exotic body.

Carlotta moistened her lips again. In her young and conceited life, she had never thought that some other girl could be better looking than she was.

Everything about Carlotta, from the roots of her long, curly, full hair, to the delicate tips of her pink-coated toenails, was very pretty. Though she had just turned thirteen, Carlotta sported an evenly distributed one-hundred-and-five pound body and appeared mature for her age. Her appearance necessitated admiration and more than a second look. She was the perfect queen-bee.

Zika's exotic beauty, on the other hand, commanded a different kind of attention. Full bust narrowed into a flat stomach. Slim waist, accentuated by the tight band of her school skirt, flared out slightly to outline her slender hips, while long, well-shaped legs tapered into the white socks and brown sandals that completed the school uniform.

White, perfectly shaped teeth peeked out as Zika smiled and put out her right hand.

Carlotta adjusted the strap of her halter-neck top and tossed back her brown curls. Her nervousness totally forgotten, she flashed what she considered her most winning smile and shook Zika's proffered hand.

"Hi, *Zicker*," Carlotta batted her long, dark lashes and smiled again. "I'm Carlotta, so pleased to meet you." She exhaled. She hadn't even been aware she was holding her breath. "I'm totally sorry about my stuff being all over the place. I just got in and haven't had a chance to unpack yet. Here, let me make room for you."

A few students were now standing behind Zika and were regarding Carlotta with pleasant curiosity.

"You girls, we have a Feddie Girl in this dorm! Zika's new bunkie is a Feddie Girl!" one of the girls behind Zika exclaimed.

Later, Carlotta would understand that though everyone who passed through a Nigerian Federal school was automatically a Feddy student, the term 'Feddie Girl' was the nickname used by the students of FGGC Uddah to indicate girls of mixed race and non-Nigerian students.

At once, a voice from the general direction of Carlotta's left, shrieked, "Are you serious? A Feddie Girl! Where is she from?"

"What is her name?" another voice quipped. The owner of the voice materialized and poked her head over Zika's shoulder, straining to get a closer look at Carlotta.

"Zika, what country is the Feddie Girl from?" a deep voice asked.

Carlotta turned a few degrees to her right. She located the owner of the deep voice. A round face, thick spectacles balanced firmly on the bridge of its stubby nose, beamed back at her. The senior girl stood by the bunk next to Zika's. Her head barely made it above the mattress on the top bunk. Her round chin was balanced on splayed-out fingers that were sunken into the soft mattress underneath. The full, round face and short, stubby fingers promised a rotund body. Carlotta wasn't disappointed.

So they're not all pretty. Relieved, she looked away from the bespectacled beaming face. *For some reason, the students here seem totally delighted to see me. And I like it.*

Before long, the rest of the students were gathered around Zika's bunk. The three new students were made to sit on Zika's bed, seven senior girls crowding around them and bombarding them with questions about themselves, their families, and their backgrounds. Junior girls sprawled on Carlotta's bed and the one next to it, observing the scene with keen interest.

Unlike Sandra and Uche, who were slightly embarrassed by all the attention, Carlotta reveled in it. She was used to being the center of attraction and had been the leader of her girls clique in middle school.

Wow! They make me feel just like London Tipton from 'The Suite Life of Zack and Cody.' Yay me!

Carlotta's eyes danced as she regaled the students around her with interesting stories of her family and childhood, basking in their admiration. The girls listened in awe and sighed wistfully as they riddled her with questions about her life in America. They wanted to know about the weather, food, people, clothing, music, snow, celebrities, environment, and any other topic they could conceive. A few of them tried to mimic her Californian accent to the loud guffaws and amusement of others.

Quite forgetting about her decision to run away, Carlotta happily gave herself up to the attention bestowed upon her by her fellow dorm girls. She actually began to think she liked being in boarding school. She also imagined she would fit in nicely with the adoring students in her dormitory.

With that thought warming her insides, she launched into a recount of how she spent her last Christmas holiday. She obliged the gushing girls around her with tall tales of places she visited with her family and the things they did to make the holidays so special.

Carlotta felt really happy, and started to relax. That was, until lunch arrived.

"*Eeuw,* what is that?" Carlotta blurted out before she could stop herself. She'd seen Anita hand Sandra a plate of something she couldn't identify.

Anita, who had walked into the dormitory in the middle of Carlotta's animated tale about how fantastic San Francisco was during the winter, was laden with a small silver tray on which she deftly balanced three plates of food. On each plate was a tiny piece of something that looked like boiled beef atop a small heap of white rice coated with a thin, yellow liquid. Chunks of stewed tomatoes and onions, filtered-out by the rice grains, lay limply on the surface of the heap.

"This," Anita said bitingly, holding out a plate of the food to Carlotta, "is supposed to be your lunch."

Carlotta looked doubtfully at the plate being offered and made no move to relieve Anita of it. She wrinkled her nose and shook her head, wondering what sort of people could bear to eat food that consisted primarily of cooked starch and promised a bad gustatory experience just from the looks of it.

"Hmm," Anita remarked, one eyebrow raised. "I can see you are not hungry." She placed the plate back on her tray and offered the other one to Uche, who received it with shaky hands and mumbled a feeble word of thanks to her supposed benefactor.

"Nnenna, collect the plates when they have finished eating and return them to the kitchen," Anita said stiffly to a JS3 student poised on Carlotta's bed. With a rueful shake of her head, she strode out of the dormitory, the rejected plate of food still balanced on the silver tray.

"Allow the Feddie Girl not to want your precious Sunday lunch," a senior student, who Carlotta understood to be Sandra's bunkmate, threw after Anita in a high singsong voice. Fortunately, her words didn't make it past the door, which Anita had promptly closed upon her exit.

"Nneka, please spare us your crooked voice," another girl admonished. "It's not Anita's fault that we eat rice, garnished with weevils and stones, for Sunday lunch." She rolled her eyes. "The *pomo* self is tougher than Hausa leather!"

At this juncture, all the girls except the three new students rolled around in laughter. Sandra and Uche looked down with dismay at the plates in their hands, and then looked up at the girls around them, apparently at a loss of what to do with the food.

Listening to the chuckles of the older students, Carlotta thanked her lucky stars she'd had the presence of mind to refuse the meal.

"You girls, don't mind her," the bespectacled senior girl consoled Sandra and Uche in her unusually deep voice. "There are no weevils in the rice—maybe a little chaff and some small stones—but nothing to be worried about."

"Er, yes. Do you want the girls to die of hunger before you provide them with forks?" Zika admonished the junior girls sitting on Carlotta's bed. Then looking at Carlotta, she added, "So, what are you going to eat? You know, we don't have chicken and chips here."

"Oh, it's okay." Carlotta flipped a dismissive hand. "I'll be totally fine with some soda. Diet Coke should be perfect, thanks." She smiled and added, "May I have extra ice in the Coke? It's *kinda* warm in here." She glanced up at the two overhead fans rotating sluggishly from the ceiling. "And could someone turn those up? We could do with a little more air, right?"

The girls burst out laughing.

Two or three of them were actually bent over from their sitting position, laughing their hearts out.

An SS1 student placed a hand over her mouth as she heaved with mirth, tears seeping from her closed eyes down her cheeks.

"What did she say? Please tell us what she said," a few girls who hadn't really understood what Carlotta said, owing to the staccato way at which the words tumbled out of her mouth, asked their mates.

But, the girls were too busy laughing to oblige.

"She said ice. She said she wants ice—" Bisi, the only SS3 student of Sapphire-Six besides Anita, started to explain but couldn't finish as a fresh bout of mirth hit her. Carlotta later learned the girl's name was pronounced *Bee-see*.

At that point, Zika, who had regained some semblance of control, took hold of the situation. "Okay girls, the gist is over. Everyone go back to your corners." Then she added sternly to the junior students, "*Oya* find your square-roots."

Reluctantly, the girls stood and shuffled back to their respective bunks. Sandra and Uche, who had barely touched the food on their plates, followed their bunkmates back to their own beds across the room. A few girls were still laughing, but otherwise, the dormitory was relatively calm.

Zika called out to a JS2 student, "Joke, please fetch my bunkie's water." Zika had pronounced the name as *Jaw-care*. She handed the student Carlotta's blue plastic bucket with the water container still nestled within.

Joke took the bucket from Zika without a word and placed it on top of a pile of three plastic buckets she had gathered from under her own bunk, and left the dormitory.

Carlotta shook her head in wonder. *Really! She just accepted some work without demanding a fee. Loser! I would have totally given her ten bucks for her trouble.*

"Bunkie," Zika said to Carlotta, "let's get you unpacked and settled in. You also need to change into your dormitory uniform."

She poured a cup of warm coke from the jumbo bottle she removed from her locker and handed the cup of frothing, dark liquid to Carlotta, who took it and raised it gingerly to her lips.

Carlotta felt tiny, jumping droplets from the warm, hissing liquid make contact with the tip of the nose. She took a tentative sip, then a long draught, which nearly emptied the cup. Seconds later, the carbon dioxide made its way back up her esophagus at an alarming rate. The next thing she knew, the invisible gas was pouring out of her nose, and water was streaming down her eyes. She wiped her upper lip and stabbed at her eyes with her palms.

Carlotta emptied the cup and put it down. She bent over and untied her summer sandals. She slipped her feet into the new pair of flip-flops Zika fished from one of her bags.

Carlotta couldn't remember packing the flip-flops. She figured her mom put them in the bag when she did the repacking. She changed into her dormitory uniform of blue, short-sleeved blouse and plain-black, pleated skirt.

Zika explained that each of the six houses in the school had a signature color that corresponds to the color their building was painted, as well as the color of their dormitory uniform. "Normally, we wear our day uniform during weekends but since today is the arrival day of new students, we had to wear our correct school uniform. We also wear correct uniforms for Visiting Days."

Whatever! Carlotta plunked herself down on Zika's bed with a resigned sigh and reluctantly helped with putting her things away. She already sensed that the term *bunkie* was a pet name for *bunkmate*. Zika kept addressing her in that fashion, as she sorted through her stuff, deciding where each item should go.

While they went through the luggage, Zika explained certain pertinent facts about boarding life to her new bunkmate, who was obviously clueless about what life at FGGC Uddah entailed.

※ ※ ※

On their way back to Onitsha after depositing Carlotta at FGGC Uddah, Shelley felt like a huge chunk of her heart had been yanked out of her chest. She was desolate. As they crawled along the road, she prayed she'd done the right thing by leaving her only daughter at the mercy of a boarding school in a strange environment. Her eyes watered and she closed them, a lone droplet escaping down her left cheek.

"She'll be all right," Daniel said to Shelley. "I felt bad, too, the first time I left Ada behind at the school."

"I sincerely hope you are right." Shelley fell silent and offered up a long solitary prayer for Carlotta's welfare.

Chapter 5
School Rules And Regulations

"Y ou girls, stop disturbing!" someone screamed. "We can't hear her!"

The crowd in Sapphire-Six dormitory quieted down. There were still a few excited whispers, but one could now hear the sweet voice emanating from the middle of the crowd.

Carlotta was in the middle of reciting the song 'That's How You Know' from the Disney movie 'Enchanted.' She pranced about like a little pony, perfectly coordinating her movements to the imaginary beat that only she could hear, as she strung out the well known lyrics from the depth of her being. To the eyes of her spectators, she was Giselle, the fairy princess to be, searching for her one true love.

The dormitory was filled to capacity. More students arrived to see the performance in response to the cries of "You girls, the Feddie Girl in Sapphire-Six is giving a balm show." This call was all it took to make scores of students drop whatever they were doing and rush down to Sapphire-Six to see for themselves what was going on.

Girls from the other five houses were also present, all identifiable by the color of their blouses. While the Sapphire House students had on blue blouses, the Emerald House students were in green; Crystal House students in cream; Gold House students, yellow; Ruby House, red; Pearl, pink.

Apparently, the news that a Feddie Girl was giving a performance had spread beyond the walls of Sapphire House, and nobody, it seemed, wanted to miss out on the fun.

Someone in the crowd thoughtfully provided a multi-colored bed sheet, pulled off a junior girl's bed, for use as a cape. Carlotta had the sheet wrapped delicately around her shoulders. Her pulse beat to the tempo of her melody. She imagined herself free from gravity as she launched into the final lyrics of the song.

The crowd applauded.

Carlotta lost all senses of inhibition. She felt as light as cotton.

At the end of the performance, Carlotta curtsied and bowed several times before the jubilating crowd. The cheering students gleefully yelled encouragement and adulation.

The applause was deafening.

Carlotta reveled in it.

Abruptly, the bell rang. It was time for dinner.

The noise stopped at once. The girls sighed for they wished to see Carlotta perform songs from 'High School Musical,' 'Hannah Montana,' and 'The Cheetah Girls.' But at FGGC Uddah, the school bell brooked no argument and had to be obeyed.

Hopeful pleas for another performance at a more convenient time came from all sides, as the students scurried out of Sapphire-Six and headed to the dining hall for their last meal of the day.

✳ ✳ ✳

*A*fter dinner, the new students waited behind for an address by the school prefects. They sat together in one corner of the dining hall and stared timidly at the group of prefects smiling down at them. Each prefect stood and waved to the students as she was introduced, and offered a few words of wisdom or advice before taking her seat again.

"You are expected to obey all school rules and regulations without exception," Marietta Adams, the head girl, announced after the last school prefect had been introduced.

Carlotta was not listening. She regarded her fellow new students with curiosity. Many of them were really small, too small to be a day older than eleven, she decided. Only three of them didn't have the cropped hairstyle of the others.

"You should always be in your uniform at all times. Correct school uniforms should be worn during school hours, and dormitory uniforms after school hours," Marietta advised in a stern voice. "You should always respect the SS1 to SS3 students," she admonished. "And use the prefix *senior* each time you refer to them by name, whether directly or indirectly." She looked down at her notes, then at the students, and gave the universally understood first-finger indication that what she was about to say next was of prime importance.

Carlotta wasn't paying the head girl more than the barest attention. She was busy inspecting her short and recently cleaned nails, resenting Anita for forcing her to cut and wipe them free of polish before leaving the dormitory for the dining hall. Zika, bless her heart, had stayed back and helped her with the job.

"You should always obey the school bell and all instructions from prefects," Marietta warned, looking very solemn. She then went on to list the other school rules, informing the students of the type of dress accessories allowed and the electronic gadgets that were out of bounds.

Carlotta yawned. It had been a long day and she was tired.

Next, Marietta read out the school regulations. These accounted for the whole twenty-four hours of a typical school day. It began with the rising bell at 5:00 AM and ended with the final lights-out at 11:00 PM. The predetermined activities were portioned out in thirty-minute increments with the ringing of the school bell signaling the end of one activity and the beginning of the next.

"A copy of the school rules and regulations will be posted on the notice boards in your house lobbies." Marietta stopped and smiled.

Who cares? Carlotta thought. *Enough with the boring talk already; we're about to fall asleep.*

But all the other new students were wide-eyed.

Marietta continued, "It is your responsibility to familiarize yourself with these rules and regulations." She paused and nodded, as if waiting for the importance of what she'd said to sink in. "Failure to be at the right place at the right time will earn you a punishment from your presiding dormitory prefect, or from any school prefect who apprehends you," Marietta cautioned.

The rest of the new students were visibly white-faced now. Carlotta, on the other hand, was just bored and eager to get back to the dormitory and into bed.

"Manual Labor is on the first Saturday of every month, while Visiting Day is on the first Sunday. No boycotting of Manual Labor shall be tolerated. You are also expected to dress in your correct school uniforms for Visiting Days.

"Friday morning assembly is mandatory, for the principal addresses the school then." Marietta paused to collect her thoughts. "No unauthorized absence, or zapping of any kind, shall be tolerated during school activities."

A buzz of amusement went through the group of prefects and the new students looked at one another in puzzlement. The head girl had obviously thrown them with the term, *zapping*.

Okay, Carlotta thought, with immense relief. *It's like we're almost done here.*

But Marietta waited for the disturbance to die down and instructed, "You will be required to assemble at the school hall tomorrow morning, where you shall be assigned to your class-rooms and provided with books for the school year."

Finally, the head girl turned to the other prefects and inquired if any of them had anything else to add. At the negative shake of their heads, Marietta turned back to the new students and concluded, "Welcome to FGGC Uddah. We wish you a very happy school year. You are dismissed."

The new students shuffled to their feet, their eyes wide and round. Mindful not to make any more noise than necessary, they picked their way out of the dining hall and headed straight for their respective houses, their trembling voices and timid footsteps belying their brave attempts at small talk.

※ ※ ※

"We have just one hour before lights-out," Zika instructed Carlotta. "So you should go take a bath now and get ready for bed." She pulled Carlotta's thick, fluffy, yellow bath towel off its hanging position by the bunk. "Change into this," Zika said, and reached under the bunk to retrieve Carlotta's bucket, which thanks to Joke, was now filled with water.

Zika emptied half the bucket's contents into a smaller plastic container then dropped Carlotta's new bath sponge into it. The sponge landed on the water—*swoosh*—and sank beneath the surface.

Carlotta stripped and wrapped the yellow bath towel around her person. The towel, which featured a grinning Mickey Mouse amidst a backdrop of other Disney characters, came halfway to her knees. She felt self-conscious. Never had she taken off her clothes in a room full of people.

But no one paid Carlotta's towel-clad form any undue attention.

Still, Carlotta hugged the top of the towel close to her bosom and placed a concealing arm over her breasts. *Gosh! Why am I so shy? The other girls are walking about in their bra and panties, for Pete's sake.*

At Zika's instruction, Carlotta took her soap dish and picked up the bucket of water. Following Joke and some other junior girls out of the dormitory to the Sapphire House bathrooms, she wondered why they needed a bucket of water if they were only going to shower.

At the first sight of the lavatory, Carlotta gasped. "What?" she blurted. "Don't tell me this is the bathroom?" She hadn't expected to be so rudely shocked.

"Yes now," Joke replied. "But this is the junior section." She glanced at Carlotta. "Why are you asking?"

"Er, what the hell—?" Carlotta was dumbfounded. There were no bathtubs anywhere in sight, and definitely no luxurious showers of any kind. She stared in horror at the individual small stalls, which amassed to rows of rectangular spaces demarcated by shoulder-length walls. Bare water pipes, originally meant to convey running water, hung dryly over each stall. The bath spaces were so narrow Carlotta believed her shoulders wouldn't fit cross-wise within.

"It's a good thing you guys have mostly thin girls in this school, huh?" Carlotta smirked, eyeing Joke's skeletal frame.

"Pardon?" Joke frowned. She peeled-off her towel in one movement and stood naked before Carlotta. "What did you say?"

Carlotta averted her eyes. "Oh, never mind." She brushed the question aside. *The girl just doesn't get it, and she certainly isn't shy.* She observed Joke and the others climb into stalls with their buckets of water. They didn't bother with the doors. They just hung their towels over the walls, positioned their buckets in front, and splashed bowls of water on themselves.

Carlotta stared down at her towel. She placed a hand on the knot she had tied. She hesitated. *It's not such a big deal. Take the towel off already!*

Back in San Francisco, Carlotta's best friend, Sasha, had told appalling stories about what life had been like in summer camp. Watching the girls lather themselves, Carlotta felt sure that Sasha's horrid descriptions were nothing in comparison to what she would have to endure in boarding school.

Though Carlotta had used communal gym bathrooms in her former schools, that experience hadn't prepared her for the zero privacy boarding school entailed. She watched to see how the other girls managed to bathe out of a bucket of water in a too-small bathroom stall.

Finally, Carlotta rid herself of her towel and hung it up, just like the other girls had done. She threw bowls of water on her shoulders, and worked up a good lather with her soap and sponge before commencing to scrub herself down. She felt cramped and constricted in the narrow stall, and somehow managed to get soapsuds in her hair and eyes.

Carlotta's eyes smarted and she bit her lip to prevent herself from crying out. She dropped the soap and reached out blindly for her bucket of water. Her hand connected with the bucket and sent it toppling over on its side. She felt currents of water flow over her feet as the bucket emptied its contents.

"Damn it!" Carlotta stamped her foot in a fury. But that, too, was a mistake, for her foot came down hard on the wet soap lying on the floor. She slipped and lost her balance, sending the empty bucket flying out of the stall in a jumble of thumps and clatter.

Smarting eyes still tightly shut; Carlotta struggled in vain to regain her balance. Her legs gave way entirely and the next thing she knew she was airborne, following the trajectory course mapped out by the bucket. She put out her arms to brace herself then felt her backside connect with the cold wet floor.

"Shoot!" Carlotta pried her eyes open. The stinging pain immediately forced her to close them again. "Oh shoot! Screw this place."

"Are you all right?" someone asked.

Carlotta imagined it was Joke. "Sure. I just thought it would be fun to sail butt-naked across the bathroom floor. Nothing wrong with that."

"Did you fall? These floors can be very slippery when wet."

Carlotta controlled the urge to open her eyes. "*Duh*! I'm sitting here—naked. Hello? A little help?"

"Let me help you," Joke offered, grasping Carlotta's arm. "Hold my hand." She heaved Carlotta back to her feet and presented her with a towel.

Carlotta wiped the soap off her eyes. "That's better," she said, blinking tentatively. The sting felt bearable so she looked around. Except for Joke and herself, the bathroom was empty. The others had long since finished and departed.

"Thanks," Carlotta said in a small voice.

"Don't mention," Joke replied. "I think I'll go and get you some more water. You have soap all over your body." She picked up Carlotta's empty bucket and turned to leave.

"Hey—"

Joke turned around.

"I'm sorry I snapped at you."

"It's okay. I'll come back soon." Joke hurried out of the bathroom.

Carlotta wrapped her arms about herself and crawled back into the narrow stall, cursing silently and shaking her head in frustration. She picked up the offending soap and slapped it back in its dish. Fortunately, she hadn't sustained any serious injury, but she checked to be sure her hipbone was still intact.

When Joke returned, Carlotta gratefully rinsed the soap off her body, her skin reacting to the cool water.

Thirty minutes later, a soap-free but exhausted Carlotta tumbled into bed, her damp curls splayed out on the single pillow underneath her head.

"G'night," she said to Zika who was getting ready to go take a bath. "Thanks for making me feel welcome here," she added at Zika's nodded reply. "And, be careful not to slip in the bathroom."

"Don't worry, we're used to it," Zika replied with an amused smile. The look in her eyes indicated Joke had already spilled the beans on the little mishap in the bathroom. Carlotta became self-defensive, but was too tired to pursue the matter any further. She watched with half-closed eyes as Zika left the dorm with

Nneka—Sandra's bunkmate; and Uche's bunkmate, Shade—
pronounced *Shah-day*.

Already, Carlotta had learned that out of the sixteen students
in her dormitory, two—namely Anita and Bisi, were in SS3;
three—Zika, Nneka, and Shade were in SS2; another three—the
bespectacled student and two others were in SS1. The remaining
eight students were junior girls, three of which were in JS3;
another two—Joke and Grace—in JS2; leaving Uche, Sandra,
and herself in JS1.

Carlotta turned onto her stomach and yawned. *Not bad for
my first day in boarding school, the girls here aren't too bad.* She
stifled another yawn. *And despite the warm soda, sluggish fans, lack
of running showers, and slippery bathroom floors, dormitory life
doesn't seem bad, either.* Her eyelashes hugged her cheeks, and
within seconds, she was asleep. She barely heard Zika and the
others return from the bathroom minutes later.

By the time Anita, the Sapphire-Six dormitory prefect,
announced "its lights-out! You girls, jump into your beds now!"
Carlotta was dead to the world.

❋ ❋ ❋

Shelley was unhappy. It had been ten days since she left the
United States for Nigeria, and contrary to her hopes, things
had taken a turn for the worse. Richard hadn't called to ask how
she was doing or how Carlotta took to boarding school. It was as
if he didn't care.

Even before Shelley departed for Nigeria, things had been
bad enough. Gone was their little bedroom intimacy—she'd even
had to wheedle a goodbye kiss from him right before she left.

The night before her departure, Shelley had tried to put
things right and had arranged an impromptu romantic dinner
just for the two of them, with hopes that the gesture would spark
a light back into their strayed marriage.

Then she'd called Richard at the hospital to inform him of the arrangement and inquire what time he would be home. To her utter astonishment, he'd told her, quite flippantly, that he'd be home whenever he felt like it.

She'd put Carlotta to bed and ended up sitting alone at their dining room table for three straight hours, watching the dinner grow cold. She'd sat there, by herself, until the candles burned low and flickered out. Then with tears of anger and frustration coursing down her cheeks, she'd stuffed the ruined dinner in the refrigerator and gone on up to bed. She'd been too hurt to eat.

When Richard finally made an appearance at 3:00 AM, reeking of sweat and cigarette smoke, she'd pretended to be fast asleep.

❋ ❋ ❋

*R*ing-ring! *Ring-ring! Ring-ring!* The rising bell went off at exactly 5:00 AM the next morning.

Carlotta woke with a start and, for a moment, wondered where she was. The un-risen sun was still hidden beyond the dark blanket of the night sky, and the morning air was cool and crisp. She had never been required to get up early.

The room was full of movement as students got out of bed and made preparations for the first week of the new school year.

Carlotta remained in bed for a few extra moments, listening to the sounds of movement. Then she clumsily climbed out of bed and down her bunk to the floor. She slipped into flip-flops, stretched, and yawned. She imagined she could hear her tired bones creaking in protest as she extended her arms high above her head and arched her back. She wasn't used to climbing up and down bunks or sleeping on a thin foam mattress supported by metal springs. She felt the beginnings of a dull pain in her neck and lower back.

What's this place anyway—some kind of military school? Carlotta stretched again, touching the tips of her fingers to her toes. She straightened and observed the others for a while. Zika and all the senior students were still in bed, sound asleep. *Why do we have to get up if they don't?*

The junior students moved about quietly, loath to disturb their sleeping bunkmates. Joke and Grace, Carlotta noticed, were already done with brushing their teeth. They grabbed their towels, obviously getting ready for baths. Some of the other junior students were also leaving the dormitory to go brush their teeth at the sinks located in the bathrooms.

Carlotta decided to start the day by brushing her teeth, too. She recalled that her toothbrush and toothpaste were in the overhead locker that now held her toiletries and personal effects. She climbed onto her bed. Lifting her pillow, she grabbed her 'Bart Simpson' key-holder.

Carlotta knelt and positioned herself directly within reach of the overhead locker. She inserted one of the keys into the padlock and turned it. She removed her toothbrush and toothpaste and placed them on the bed. Then she secured the locker and climbed down carefully.

Once down, Carlotta tore-off the paper package, uncapped the tube, and squeezed a line of paste on her brush. She then placed the open tube on the top of Zika's locker, slipped back into flip-flops and went on her way to the bathroom sinks.

Halfway to the door, Carlotta realized she'd forgotten to get a cup of water with which to rinse her mouth, since there was no running water in the bathrooms.

She returned with resignation to her corner and placed the toothbrush next to the toothpaste on her bunkmate's locker. She kicked off her flip-flops and climbed back on her bed to retrieve a cup.

This time, as she climbed down, Carlotta lost her footing and fell against Zika's locker, the open toothpaste taking a harsh blow from her elbow.

Cup in hand, Carlotta regarded the mess she had made. *Great! Now I'll have to clean all this up.*

The tube had disgorged nearly half its contents onto the flat surface of the locker and the blue wall beyond. The sticky, white mess was making its way down the wall in big, fat globs, just as peanut butter or jelly does after a food fight in a school cafeteria. Carlotta's toothbrush lay meekly on its side, as if it were glad to be rid of the heavy burden it had been carrying.

Carlotta almost swore to herself. Aghast, she put the empty cup down on her bed, and wished her mom were there to take care of the messy situation.

Carlotta stared at the scene for a while, willing it to vanish into thin air and save her the stress of having to do some major clean up. *How cool it would be to have a magic wand like the students in 'Harry Potter' did.*

Carlotta reluctantly made her way up the bunk a third time to retrieve a roll of bath tissue. *Just one flick with the wand, and a muttered spell, this whole mess would vanish.*

This time, Carlotta was careful not to lose her footing. She jumped off and landed squarely on her feet, bath tissue in hand. She unrolled the tissue and began to clean up the sticky mess.

By the time Carlotta was done wiping the toothpaste from her bunkmate's locker, the wall, and her elbow and fingers; Joke, Grace, and the rest of the junior students, including Sandra and Uche, were already bathed and dressed. Senior students were beginning to stir their sleepy selves out of bed.

Zika sat up and was immediately confronted with the sight of her bunkmate still clad in her nightshirt, struggling to squeeze a fresh line of toothpaste from a sticky looking tube on an equally sticky looking brush.

"Bunkie, you haven't had your bath!" Zika shrieked in dismay. She took one look at the mess on her locker and asked, "What happened?"

Carlotta could not find her voice. She had used almost the whole roll of bath tissue.

Zika took the items form Carlotta and wiped them clean with a moistened face towel. She squeezed the tube with a practiced hand and deposited the right amount of toothpaste on the toothbrush, which she handed back to Carlotta with a flourish.

Zika retrieved the cup from Carlotta's bed and filled it with water from the plastic can under the bunk. She then handed the filled cup to Carlotta who took it gratefully and went off to brush her teeth.

When she returned ten minutes later, Carlotta noticed that Zika had already capped and returned the toothpaste to its position in the overhead locker. Taking the cup and wet toothbrush from Carlotta, Zika instructed her bunkmate to go bathe.

Carlotta wondered how possible it would be to have warm water for her bath that morning but didn't dare ask. She'd endured an uncomfortable cold bath the night before. It wasn't an experience she hoped to repeat. A bucket of cold water with her fluffy sponge in it was already waiting outside the corner, beside the bunk. Apparently, there were no hot-bathwater indulgences at FGGC Uddah.

Fat chance!

Quickly, Carlotta changed into her bath towel as instructed and, biting her lips in chagrin, carried the bucket of water out of the dormitory. Zika called after her to hurry back and get dressed. Carlotta honestly had every intention of doing just that but the bathrooms were crowded with girls in towels, each of them with a bucket of water in tow, waiting to use the bath stalls.

Carlotta had no choice but to wait her turn. When she returned to her corner thirty minutes later, she was the only towel-clad student in Sapphire Six.

"Hurry!" Zika conveyed a sense of urgency.

Carlotta was surprised that Zika was already bathed and dressed, and was now tucking her school shirt into her skirt.

How'd she get through the bathroom so quickly?

"Get dressed immediately!" Zika instructed, pulling on her socks and sandals. "It will soon be time for morning duty. All students are required to leave the dormitory then."

Carlotta put away her bucket and hurried to dress. Zika's insistent urging had hit its mark. Her legs shook as she stepped into her school skirt and she almost toppled over. Zika reached out to steady her. Carlotta just wasn't used to getting dressed in a hurry. She grabbed her school blouse and shoved her arm into it.

"Shoot," she cursed. "Some of the buttons are still done up." She withdrew her arm and undid the buttons with shaking fingers. She didn't have the faintest idea what would happen if she failed to leave the dormitory at the appointed time, but Zika was close to a panic and the feeling was contagious.

As promised, the bell rang. It was time for morning duty.

"Uh, oh," Zika wailed. "Now we are done for!"

Carlotta's heart leaped. She was still half dressed.

"Leave the dormitory!" Anita the Sapphire-Six dormitory prefect, ordered.

Immediately, students, armed with wet towels and school bags, filed out the door.

"New students, you are to go directly to the house lobby and meet with Chidi Anayo, the house prefect. She will assign you to your places of duty," Anita announced.

Sandra and Uche nodded and trotted out of the dormitory.

Carlotta bit her lip.

"Junior girls, proceed to your places of morning duty!" Anita ordered.

"Hurry! Hurry!" Zika urged. She hustled Carlotta into her white school blouse and lifted her full curls out of the way to straighten the shirt collar.

"Thanks," Carlotta whispered in a shaky voice as she buttoned up the shirt. She really wasn't quite sure what all the fuss was about. *What does it matter how long it takes me to get dressed anyway?* She tucked the tail of her shirt into the stiff band of the skirt around her waist. She could not help thinking that her mother had never complained about how much time she took to get ready for school. *My mom always lays out my clothes for me every morning before I get up.*

Carlotta had always depended on her mother for everything. She had never bothered to do her own laundry or tidy her room. She never did the dishes, took out the trash, or helped clean the house. She left all the cleaning and housework to her parents. *Apparently, things are so gonna be different in boarding school,* she speculated, while zipping up her skirt and fastening the waistband. *Everybody seems to be in a rush all the time.*

"Senior students, you have exactly five minutes to complete whatever you are doing and leave the dormitory. Junior girls, just disappear, I don't want to see any of you in the dorm right now." Anita inspected each corner, going from one end of the dormitory to the other, ordering tardy junior students out, and taking note of improperly made beds.

She approached Zika's corner.

"Please excuse my bunkie," Zika implored. "She's new." Flashing Anita an apologetic smile, Zika conspired in a low voice, "Carlotta is not used to dormitory life yet."

"That's no excuse," Anita intoned, her voice dripping with derision. She made notes on a sheet of paper. "If the other new students were able to manage," the hand holding her pen motioned around the dormitory, indicating that Sandra and Uche had both left the dormitory, "then, Zika, your bunkmate really has no good excuse. However, I'll pardon her but just for today." She eyed Carlotta for a second and then moved on.

Carlotta watched as the dormitory prefect marched to the next bunk and ordered Ursula, a JS3 student, out of the dormitory. Like Carlotta, Ursula who wasn't completely dressed, either, hesitated for a moment and stepped into her school sandals.

Through lips tightly drawn together to make her mouth appear like two perfect lines, Anita repeated, "I said you should leave the dormitory, Ursula. Right now!"

Ursula appeared desperate. She tried to grab her school bag with one hand, while throwing a towel over her shoulder with the other. "I am leaving—" she pleaded. "Let me just—"

Ursula never got the chance to finish her sentence.

"Just get down on your knees," Anita interrupted in a harsh voice. "Kneel down right there, away from your bunk. And fly your hands."

The JS3 student grudgingly obeyed. She dropped her school bag and towel, knelt, and extended her arms out on either side of her—at ninety-degree angles.

Anita noted something on paper. "You should know better than to remain in the dormitory during morning duty." She moved to the next bunk.

Ursula rolled her eyes but said nothing. Luckily, Anita did not notice the gesture.

Carlotta paused while putting on her socks. She stared white-faced as Anita marched on with her nose in the air.

Carlotta couldn't believe her eyes. She hadn't observed anyone being physically punished before. In the schools she had attended in the United States, unruly students were usually punished with detentions. She had never even imagined that one could be ordered to kneel down as a form of punishment, let alone complying with the order, *and from a fellow student at that. Hah!*

"Hurry up with that!" Zika instructed as she handed Carlotta her school sandals. Carlotta folded down the ends of her white socks, took the sandals from Zika and struggled to put them on. Unlike the cheap rubber pair Zika had on, Carlotta's sandals were made of leather—chic, with cute straps and buckles. Her mom had purchased them, along with her backpack, from a department store in Lagos.

She finished with the buckles, and picked up her hairbrush.

When Carlotta was done brushing out her long curls, Zika suggested she make her bed.

Carlotta, who had never made a bed in her life, not even her own bed at home, wasn't sure what to do. *My mom makes the beds at home.* She pulled and tugged at the sheets. She had no idea what she was doing, and did such a bad job of it that Zika came to her aid.

"Before leaving the dorm in the morning, you have to make your bed properly, just like I am doing right now. Otherwise you will be punished," Zika cautioned. "Also, make sure you don't leave your towel, keys, or school bag behind, because, once you leave the dorm, you can't come back in until after lunch." Zika plumped Carlotta's pillow and repositioned it. "If you make the mistake of leaving your wet towel in the dorm, it will be confiscated and you'll have to serve a punishment and pay a fine to get it back."

Finished, Zika picked up her school bag and gave her own bed a final straightening tug. "If you come with me," she said to Carlotta, while she arranged the tips of her plaited hair away from her eyes, "I will show you to the clothes lines, where you should air out your towel every morning. After that, I will take you to the house lobby where the other new students are waiting."

"Sure thing. Thanks." Carlotta exhaled in relief and tossed back her hair. She picked up her backpack and followed Zika out of the dormitory, pausing at the door to give the still kneeling Ursula a final sympathetic glance. As she closed the door, she heard Anita sternly direct the students whose duties it were to sweep and tidy the dormitory, on what to do.

Carlotta hurried after her bunkmate, wondering if she would have undergone the same fate as Ursula had Zika not interceded on her behalf.

As these thoughts ran through her mind, a feeling of nostalgia washed over Carlotta. She bit her trembling lips, wiped tears off her eyes, and wished to be safely home in Oklahoma with her parents.

* * *

Carlotta walked into the Sapphire House lobby and the room suddenly became silent. Twenty pairs of eyes turned to stare. She bit her lip and looked around at the eager faces deposited everywhere in the room. The faces belonged to students milling around comfortable armchairs arranged to face a wide screen television mounted on the wall.

Sandra waved. She stood at a corner with Uche and two other students.

Carlotta waved back and walked to them.

Sandra was thin and shriveled-looking with a large, squat nose dominating most of her facial features. She was dark-skinned and sported the kind of face that appeared rough and full of pores—almost like, if scrubbed hard with a damp cloth, a new layer of smoother skin would be successfully revealed.

Uche, on the other hand, was chubby and jolly, and equipped with a kind face and subtle eyes.

"Hi, girls," Carlotta said. She looked at the other two girls and couldn't place them. "Hey. I'm Carlotta."

"This is Yvonne," Sandra introduced a mousy looking girl. "And this is Emeh," she finished, indicating the thin girl beside Uche. "They are both in Sapphire-Five."

"*Bonjour,*" Emeh said, smiling. "How are you this morning?"

Carlotta nodded. She wasn't sure the meaning of the first word Emeh had spoken. "I'm good, thanks." She smiled back.

"You must be the Feddie Girl the girls in my dorm were talking about last night," Yvonne squeaked. "They said your parents live in America." In addition to her appearance, Yvonne possessed a mousy voice.

"Tell me something I don't already know." Carlotta shrugged and rolled her eyes.

"Is it true your mother is white? I mean she's really white, *n'est elle pas?*" Emeh asked, her wide eyes staring at Carlotta as if she were something from out of space. "Pardon my French," she quickly added when she noticed Carlotta's irritated look. "I can't help myself."

Emeh had two large front teeth, Carlotta noticed, that kept poking out of her mouth as she spoke. Her appearance reminded Carlotta of a stuffed Easter Bunny she had seen in a toy store somewhere.

"Well, although my mom's totally a white-American, being born in California and all, I really can't tell you her skin's white in color if that's what you *wanna* know." Carlotta's mouth showed the hint of a smile. "She's more of a light-tan, you know," she said, and winked.

The girls laughed.

Carlotta ran her hands through her hair, tossed back her curls and asked, "So, what actually is the deal here? Why are we waiting?"

"We're waiting for Senior Chidi," Uche apprised. "She is supposed to assign us our morning duties."

Carlotta noticed Uche held an object that looked suspiciously like the brooms she had seen her cousin and aunt use to sweep floors clean back in their home in Lagos State. It resembled a witch's broomstick but without the long handle—basically a bunch of thin flexible sticks tied up together at one end. "Why do you need that?" she asked, indicating the broom. Glancing around the lobby, she realized that almost every girl had one, too.

"I don't know," Uche's voice was doubtful. "My bunkie thought I might be assigned a place to sweep for my morning duty."

"You must be kidding me. You don't mean to tell me we are actually expected to work? I mean, really work? Like janitors?" Carlotta asked in an unbelieving tone. "How much are we *gonna* be paid?"

"*Ah non,*" Emeh remarked. Oh no. "You don't get paid for doing your morning duty."

"Oh, *puhleease*, give me a break," Carlotta scoffed, rolling her eyes. The girl and her French were beginning to get on her nerves. "Why should we work if we aren't *gonna* get paid? I totally don't get it." She tossed back her hair. "I mean, even if we *are gonna* be paid, I don't want any janitor's job."

"Morning duty," Sandra corrected.

"Whatever. I still don't want any part of it."

"Ah, you don't understand," Yvonne wailed. "You have no choice. It's just like the chores you do at home. You don't expect payment for them, do you?"

"Really? No choice, huh?" Carlotta gave Yvonne a daring look. "We'll see about that." She sniffed. "And as for chores, don't tell me you guys work at home, too?"

The four girls just stared. They tried to make Carlotta understand that *morning duty* meant mandatory work that has to be done every morning, and without reward. They asserted that the school head girl said as much when she addressed the new students the night before.

Carlotta, who wasn't used to boarding schools in Nigeria and hadn't paid much attention during the speech, had obviously missed that part. She wondered what other unpleasant surprises lay ahead.

Just then, the Sapphire House prefect Chidi Anayo, flanked by two dormitory prefects, paraded into the room and stood before the students.

Even with the harsh light in the lobby, Carlotta saw Chidi looked as imposing as ever. She also noticed that the house prefect had the same pompous air like she had the day before, when she'd ridiculed Carlotta about her age.

Watching her strut to the front of the room like a majestic peacock, Carlotta instantly felt an intense dislike for the house prefect. She stood still and watched as one of the flanking prefects read names off a list, while Chidi assigned each girl to a duty as her name was called.

Soon, Carlotta heard her name. Donning a charming attitude, she sauntered up to the prefects. "Hi. It's a great morning, right?" she volunteered with a bright smile. She looked meaningfully at Chidi but the house prefect pretended not to notice.

"Sapphire-One windows." Chidi's tone was clipped. She dismissed Carlotta with an abrupt wave of her hand.

Carlotta's face burned. "Stupid bitch," she muttered, and made to leave. If there were two things she despised, they would be—being ridiculed, and being ignored.

"Come back here," a voice commanded.

Carlotta stopped. She turned.

Chidi was glaring.

The chattering in the room stopped. The air became electrified. The rest of the new students held their breath and turned to watch.

Carlotta hesitated.

Chidi's lips tightened against her teeth. "I said you should come back here," she repeated, this time spitting the words out, one by one, like fiery bullets out of a pistol. There was no mistaking the meaning behind the words.

Carlotta took a deep breath and returned to face the prefects. Her heartbeat accelerated to a new level. She tried hard to swallow her hatred and retain her composure.

"What did you say?" Chidi's voice was low but distinct. Her lips barely moved.

Carlotta rolled her eyes and shrugged.

"Don't you dare roll your eyes at us," one of the flanking prefects yelled.

Carlotta eyed her with distaste.

Quick as lightening, the prefect's hand struck out.

Carlotta ducked. The sailing hand missed her head by a mere inch. But Chidi's palm followed and caught Carlotta at the top of the head. *Smack!*

Carlotta reeled back. She had never been struck.

Oh no! You just didn't!

Warm blood flooded her neck and face. She felt like screaming and striking back, but instincts told her it was best to remain silent and bide her time.

You stupid bitch! You're so gonna pay for that.

"What did you say?" Chidi demanded in an ominous voice. Her eyes were hot black coals.

"I didn't say anything," Carlotta supplied in a voice that was thick with suppressed rage. Her breath came in short spurts. Her heart pumped furiously.

"Are you sure?" Chidi sneered. "I most definitely heard you say something."

Carlotta ignored the hammering in her chest and continued to stare into the unblinking coals that were Chidi's eyes.

Yeah, that's right. I called you a bitch. Carlotta was a coiled dangerous snake, ready to strike at the next slightest provocation. She imagined the satisfying crunch the bone of Chidi's jaw would make when her fist finally connected and a sense of satisfaction trickled down her spine. The prefect was her archenemy. And the jig was up.

The black eyes narrowed. "Don't you ever, never ever again," Chidi hissed. "Now, get lost."

Carlotta uncoiled, then turned her back to the prefects and strode to the door. When she emerged on the other side, she realized her hands were shaking.

Chapter 6
Classes Begin

Richard walked into his office. His eyes immediately fell on Maria's butt. She had on a tight-fitting pair of pants that molded her backside into twin provocative muffins—the type one would itch to take a bite out of, no matter how big a breakfast one had.

"Good morning, Doctor," Maria called, her voice vibrant.

Richard's breath caught in his throat. He felt the material around his crotch begin to tighten.

Maria licked her lush, red lips and smiled.

Richard wasn't sure if his personal assistant was as oblivious to his discomfort as she appeared. He grunted a quick reply to her greeting and dove into the men's room. He remained in one of the stalls until the hardness between his legs subsided and he deemed himself suitable for company again.

Richard emerged from the stall determined and focused, ready to tackle another long day with his patients. For him, the difficult part about his time at the hospital was keeping his hands off his utterly hot personal assistant. He was not a very patient man—he liked having what he desired when he desired it.

Getting Maria is just a matter of time, Richard told himself as he ran warm water over his hands and scrubbed them with soap. *One of these days, I'll make her want me so much she'll beg me to take her—the whole of her.*

The fantasy image of a sultry Maria, naked and squirming under him, almost sent Richard back into the stall.

He grinned and pushed the thought out of his mind. Fantasies would have to wait for later. *Right now, I have patients to see.*

Giving his tie a final tug, Richard walked out of the men's room, a large self-assured smile stamped on his handsome face.

✻ ✻ ✻

Carlotta contemplated the books on her desk and ran the tips of her fingers around their crisp edges. They looked like little mountains of decorations and added a splash of color to the otherwise dismal classroom.

Carlotta was seated in the very heart of the room, in the middle row of the middle column. All around, her classmates packed their new books into lockers that closed to form their classroom desks. She began to stow her new items as the other students were doing.

"Ahah! Settle down please," Mr. Dubem instructed the class, motioning for them to stop talking.

They had just returned from the school hall where all the JS1 students had assembled that morning. There were about a hundred and twenty new students, their names divided into four lists of JS1 classes designated from A to D. Each class amounted to about thirty students. Mr. Dubem, the JS1D form master, had shepherded his charges from the school hall to their classroom.

It was the first day of class.

Mr. Dubem clapped his hands several times in an attempt to gain the attention of the students. "Be quiet please! Stop whatever you are doing and settle down!"

The class ignored him. The noise went up a notch.

Carlotta stopped and studied the form master. He stood helplessly in front of the classroom, watching with growing irritation as lockers were opened, banged shut, and opened again.

The sound of lids connecting with wooden frames created a roar amidst the thudding sounds of heavy books being dropped into storage cavities.

As Carlotta watched, Mr. Dubem pinched a piece of white chalk from the flat panel lining the bottom edge of the large blackboard and scrawled his name on the board. Then he slammed his fists against the board to gain the students' awareness. "Settle down!"

This time, he managed to get some attention from the class. He thudded on the board again. The students groaned and protested, some visibly wincing from the harsh noise.

A few seconds later, the class was completely silent.

Mr. Dubem addressed the students. "Ahah! We need to introduce ourselves to one another." He paced the front of the class.

Whenever he said *ahah* he would suddenly face the students, forefinger in the air, eyes wide open, looking like he'd just discovered a scientific breakthrough.

The classroom lockers were joined together in pairs, creating a desk seating two students each. Wooden, straight-backed chairs accompanied the lockers. Desks and chairs were anchored to the floor, in perfectly straight and immobile columns of three and rows of five, reminding Carlotta of a small squad of soldiers assembled for routine drill. The teacher's table and chair were stationed to the side of the room, facing the class.

Mr. Dubem deposited himself on the teacher's table. "Ahah! Let's start from the front," he said, indicating the girls seated at the desk closest to the door. "Stand up and tell us your names."

The students introduced themselves in turns.

Carlotta learned her seat neighbor was called Ossie something or the other. She was unable to repeat the girl's last name and promptly forgot what it sounded like.

Ossie, though plain looking, was quite friendly. She took it upon herself to explain everything the form master said, to Carlotta, who still had difficulty understanding English spoken with a Nigerian accent.

"Ahah! I will appoint two students to act as the class monitor and assistant." Mr. Dubem pointed to a girl seated in the front row. "Stand up and face the class."

The girl slowly rose from her seat.

"Tell the class your name again," Mr. Dubem prompted.

"Rosemary Beluchi," the girl replied in an uncertain voice.

"Ahah! Rosemary will be your acting class monitor," Mr. Dubem announced, forefinger in the air, eyes widened as usual. "She will be responsible for reminding your teachers to come for their lessons, and keeping the classroom in order." He pulled himself to his feet and walked to the back of the class. The students followed him with their eyes, many shifting in their seats to avoid breaking their necks.

"What is your name again?" Mr. Dubem asked a girl seated in the back row.

"Bukola Adenike," the girl replied, getting to her feet without being asked. She towered above the form master.

"Ahah! Bukola will act as the assistant class monitor." Mr. Dubem moved away, using distance to diminish the striking difference in height between them. "It will be Bukola's duty to collect chalk for the teachers, and make sure the board is wiped clean after every lesson," he announced.

Bukola put her right hand up in a mock salute. The class cheered. A few hailed.

"Ahah! You can sit down now, thank you," Mr. Dubem said to Bukola and wove his way back to the front of the class.

The assistant class prefect gave an exaggerated bow and sat down, a satisfied grin plastered on her face.

The class sniggered.

"Settle down, please! Settle down!" Mr. Dubem's voice hinted anger.

The chitter-chatter gradually abated and soon gave way to complete silence.

"Ahah! I am going to hand out your class time-table," the form master said when he finally had the full attention of the students. He waved a sheaf of papers back and forth, over his head, like a heap of football paper flags. He walked to the desk closest to the classroom door and deposited some of the papers on it.

"Pass them down," he instructed the two students seated at the front desk, and went to the middle column to do the same, his oversized shoes making soft squelching sounds as he walked.

"The time-table shows your lesson schedule for the entire school year." He handed the rest of the papers to a student seated in the third column, and thumbed down his black moustache.

Soon, every student had received a copy of the class timetable.

"Ahah! You will be taught a total of fifteen compulsory subjects." The form master fiddled with his belt buckle. "The textbooks for all the subjects have already been provided for you," he said, indicating the lockers into which all the new books had disappeared.

"You have been given six long-note books meant for the subjects that require a lot of note-taking." He returned to the blackboard and scribbled: mathematics, integrated science, social studies, home economics, agriculture, and introductory technology.

He cleared his throat. "Ahah! You will be taught a total of four different languages."

The girls proclaimed their disapproval by lamenting in shrill tones.

"Quiet! Quiet please!"

Carlotta glanced at her timetable and noted there were indeed fifteen subjects listed down one side of the page. Each subject had the name of the responsible teacher beside it in block letters. She scanned quickly through the list for the four languages.

English language was at the top of the list. *That's sort of expected.* Halfway down, she came upon French language. *French? Who needs to learn French?* In her former school, she'd been required to learn Spanish. "As if anyone in their right mind would actually consider moving to Mexico," Carlotta had grumbled. Then her eyes caught the last two subjects in the list: beginner's language, and native language. "What the—?"

"Quiet!" Mr. Dubem was positively fuming. "If you need to speak, you should indicate by raising your hand."

Several hands shot up at once.

"You." Mr. Dubem pointed to a student.

"My name is Nelly Ezeka," the girl said, bounding to her feet. "I want to ask what languages we should study as the beginner's and native."

"Ahah! Good question." Mr. Dubem nodded, approaching the students. "You should study a language that is not your native tongue as your beginner's language," he explained, "and study your native tongue as your native language. Is that clear?"

"No, sir! No, sir! No, sir!" the class chorused.

"Yes, it is clear," several girls answered, but were drowned out by the chorus.

"We don't understand!" A shrill voice rose above the din.

"I don't speak Ibo!" another complained.

"I am from Benue State," one girl shrieked.

"Shut up all of you," the form master yelled. The class became orderly again. He regarded the students sternly for a few seconds. "If you need to say something, you should indicate by raising up your hand." He demonstrated by putting his right hand up in the air.

Several hands went up.

Mr. Dubem ignored them. "I will not tell you this again. I will punish the next person who opens her large mouth without permission."

Several more hands shot up to join the ones already hanging in the air.

But Nelly was still standing. "Excuse me, sir, I am from Enugu State," she insisted, "but I live in Lagos, and I don't speak Ibo. Which languages am I to take then?" Her tone was underlined with mischief.

A round of applause greeted Nelly's question as nearly all the girls showed their support.

"What a very useless question," a dry voice exclaimed.

Carlotta studied the student who'd spoken. The girl was tiny, couldn't be any older than ten. However, what she lacked in physical maturity, she made up for in head girth. Her eyes bulged from a head that appeared almost twice the size of a normal human skull. The girl was glaring at Nelly.

Nelly scowled back.

Mr. Dubem overlooked the animosity brewing between Nelly and the bigheaded student. "In that case, you should take Igbo as a native language and choose either Yoruba or Hausa for your beginner's language," he said smoothly.

The class unrest started up again. Carlotta didn't understand the reason for the altercation. Ossie dutifully filled her in.

Carlotta put up her hand.

"Ahah! *Oyibo*," Mr. Dubem called.

Carlotta remained in her seat, her right hand still shooting upward.

"It's you," Ossie whispered, and nudged Carlotta in the ribs.

"Oh," Carlotta said, suddenly noticing that all eyes were on her. She rose and said, "Hey, I'm Carlotta Ikedi. I'm an American and, well, I don't speak or understand any of the languages spoken in this country. Actually, I speak only English. So, is it okay for me to just take English as both the beginner and whatever other language that's studied here? I mean, like, English is totally the only language I speak, so it will make more sense if I just stick to studying it, right?" Carlotta glanced at her fellow classmates, expecting to get at least a few nods of support.

Everyone just stared in quiet consternation. The form master absently stroked his thick moustache as he zeroed in on Carlotta.

The giggling started. Carlotta's ears singed.

"Come here," Mr. Dubem signaled, curling a forefinger in Carlotta's direction.

Carlotta walked over to the teacher. The giggles got louder. She stared at her feet. *Why didn't I just keep my stupid trap shut?*

"What did you say your name was?" Mr. Dubem asked.

Carlotta looked up. *Huh?*

Up close, Mr. Dubem's moustache appeared thicker than from afar. He owned mismatched, unruly eyebrows that arched roughly over his deeply lined eyes, black pupils trapped in bulging, yellowish eyeballs. These pupils were now staring away from Carlotta's face, fixated at a point above her right shoulder.

Carlotta turned. She couldn't tell the subject of the form master's fascination. She faced him again and waited.

"I asked you to repeat your name," Mr. Dubem prodded.

Carlotta looked into the form master's eyes. She noticed the tiny, red veins that criss-crossed the yellow eyeballs in a haphazard fashion. The eyes were still staring above her right shoulder.

Carlotta looked back. Again, there was nothing. She became a little confused.

The class was laughing.

"I am talking to you," Mr. Dubem said. He parked a heavy hand on Carlotta's shoulder and shook her slightly.

"Are you referring to me?" Carlotta asked. She was still unsure whether the form master, who was staring doggedly away from her face, was addressing her. She glanced back once more, just to make sure.

Then Carlotta realized what the problem was. *Oh, he has a lazy eye!* A sickly kid in her neighborhood in San Francisco suffered from the same condition.

The class roared with laughter.

Carlotta felt like laughing, too, but she dared not.

"I am asking you your name!" Mr. Dubem, who had a severe case of strabismus, snapped.

"Okay, okay," Carlotta retorted, backing away. "My name's Carlotta Ikedi, all right? I didn't realize you were talking to me just then."

"Write your name on the board," Mr. Dubem instructed. He held out a piece of chalk.

Carlotta took the chalk and wrote her name in the careful cursive handwriting of most American students.

"Ahah! Now, how do you pronounce what you have written?"

"*Cahlorda Eye-key-dye!*" the class thundered, and resumed laughing and cheering. They'd pronounced the name exactly the way Carlotta does.

The form master, who had his hands over his ears to save his eardrums from splitting, waited for the noise to subside before announcing, "Ahah! *Callorra*, or whatever you choose to call yourself. To pass the JS1 class, you are expected to study two Nigerian languages—one as a beginner, and the other as a native." As always, the forefinger and widened eyes accompanied the *ahah!*

Mr. Dubem adjusted the band of his brown pants, cleared his throat—more for dramatic effect than to dislodge whatever might be stuck in there—and continued, "There are only three Nigerian languages offered as subjects in this school." He turned to face the class and counted the languages off his stubby fingers. "Igbo. Yoruba. Hausa. So, whether you are from London, America, or Russia, you are mandated to get a passing grade in two of these languages before you move on to JS2. Is that clear?"

"Yes, sir!" the class responded.

The bell rang. Time to change lessons.

Squeaking sounds of opening lockers promptly filled the room. The form master and Carlotta were forgotten as the students rummaged for their textbooks, getting ready for the next lesson.

"So, my American friend, you can wipe your name off the board now and go back to your seat," Mr. Dubem said, handing the blackboard duster to Carlotta, who took it and did as instructed.

Carlotta watched as Mr. Dubem retrieved the bulky manila folder he had brought with him and strode out of the classroom, his back rigid beneath the outline of his starched blue shirt.

Carlotta sighed. Thus went her first classroom experience in FGGC Uddah.

✳ ✳ ✳

*A*s Carlotta made her way back to her seat, the bigheaded student who was seated in the second row accosted her.

"Was that an Igbo name you were pronouncing like that?" Carlotta ignored the sneer and walked on.

Nelly was not as complacent. "Mind your own business, you fatheaded, little rat," she threw back at the tiny student.

Another girl backed Carlotta up and challenged Miss Big-head. "You should tell us your own name before you open your mouth to ask someone else about hers." She jumped to her feet. The girl was quite tall for her age.

"If you must know, my name is Ndidi Onah," the tiny student snapped. She scrambled to her feet and was immediately dwarfed by the girl standing before her. That not withstanding, she placed her hands on her waist—elbows out, and reared up for a verbal showdown. "Are you looking for my trouble?"

"What is your business with the way Carlotta pronounces her name? She's American. What else do you expect?" the tall girl demanded.

"It's a lie," Ndidi retorted. "My bunkie said her father is Igbo, so that makes her a *Feddie Girl*." She climbed onto her locker to gain a height advantage over her opponent. "You that you're talking, you haven't told us your name." Ndidi balanced herself on the desk and was ready to do battle.

"I am Joyce Obum," the tall student said, and moved forward to face Ndidi. "And just like Nelly, my parents are Ibo but we live in Lagos. I don't speak or understand Ibo at all. So, what does that make me?" she demanded.

"What is *Feddie Girl*?" someone asked.

Nelly ignored the question. "Carlotta's father is not a hundred percent Ibo, he's a half-caste. And by the way," she taunted Ndidi, "do you expect everyone to speak in the same Igbotic fashion like you?"

"At least I can pronounce my own name correctly," Ndidi yelled from the top of her locker where she was still perched.

"Igbo major!"

"You send?" Ndidi bit back. "*Ezi* Bida!" Bida Pig!

"*Aje pako!*" Rugged human being!

The whole class joined in the argument. Several girls climbed onto their lockers in a parody of Ndidi and started yelling at the top of their voices. A few others sided with Nelly and Joyce. One girl demanded to be enlightened on the meaning of *Feddie Girl*. Bukola began shrieking for the students to be quiet. Rosemary started thumping on her desk to gain everyone's attention.

The classroom became a war zone. Books went flying from all corners. Sandals became missiles. Voices cheered as particular missiles found their intended targets.

It was a battle for domination, where winners ruled and losers were subdued.

Carlotta whipped her head sideways just in time to avoid a flying notebook. In a split second, a pocket dictionary rocketed its way past her face, missed her nose by a hair's breadth, and landed with a resounding slap on Ossie's cheek. *Splat!*

Ossie shrieked and laid low.

Carlotta ducked beneath her desk.

The classroom turned into a battleground—one either joined in the melee, or stayed out of the way.

More girls joined in the fight. Before long, Nelly's team gained the upper hand. Ndidi's team began to suffer.

*T*he next morning dawned bright and clear, but Carlotta was apprehensive in the presence of her new classmates.

Attending a girls' boarding school in a foreign country wasn't detestable. What Carlotta loathed was the deafening and head-splitting quarrels her classmates indulged in when there was no teacher in the classroom.

It was only 8:45 AM and, already, the JS1D students were at it again. This time, they were bickering and fighting one another about what cities and towns in Nigeria had the best residential areas. When words weren't enough, they resorted to throwing missiles in the form of books, combs, and school sandals.

As if anyone cares where others grew up, Carlotta thought, feeling miserable. She'd lived her whole life in the United States and couldn't do a thing about parents' decision to have her enrolled in a boarding school in Nigeria.

The noise was making her head hurt. Carlotta depressed her vibrating eyeballs with her knuckles, hoping to keep them from shooting out of their sockets. She was wondering how the girls were able to keep up such a racket, when a particularly loud bang surprised her into snapping her eyes open.

A furious-looking male teacher stood at the classroom door.

The fighting stopped at once. The screeching was cut off from the throats of two students—like a raging fire abruptly doused with water. One final sandal arched high over the heads of the students and landed squarely in the middle of the blackboard with a loud thud, then skidded mournfully down to the ground. Several girls scuttled back to their seats. Ndidi and her cohorts scrambled down from their lockers.

When all was calm, the class stared sheepishly at the dark male teacher leaning against the doorframe.

The teacher considered them for a while, his handsome face devoid of expression. Without much show of annoyance, he strolled into the classroom and stood before the students.

"I am not going to inquire into the cause of the noise," he declared. "But, this is a classroom, and it is time for my lesson." He strolled over to the blackboard and picked up the lone sandal. "Who lost this?" he asked in a scathing tone, holding the rubber footwear aloft by the tips of his forefinger and thumb, dangling it like an offending rodent for the whole class to see.

A chubby girl walked up to him like one would to a dangerous dog. "Please sir, it's mine," she breathed, and held out her hand for the shoe.

The teacher cast her a wary eye, snorted, and dropped the sandal in her hand.

The girl clutched the shoe and scurried back to her seat.

The teacher sneered then turned abruptly and picked up the duster. With a swift swipe of his left hand, he wiped the board clean. His right hand moved with lightening speed as he wrote the word *mathematics* on the board with a piece of white chalk. He whirled around in one fluid motion and began to teach.

The teacher's mannerisms were mesmerizing: teaching—effortless, movement—electrifying, voice—spellbinding.

There was not a peep from the class during the entire lesson. The students were caught in the fast-paced style of his teaching. They watched in fascination as he stabbed and slashed at the blackboard with the chalk, whipping-up seemingly intoxicating mathematical symbols and equations from thin air.

The math teacher was the performer; the mesmerized class his spectator.

Not until the bell rang did Carlotta realize she hadn't grasped a thing from the lesson.

The math teacher had raced through his lesson in a well-meaning tactic to revise the basic skills he believed the class had already acquired. He'd breezed through even and odd numbers, and the rules of addition and subtraction. After those came multiplication and division. Then types of fractions. Simple proportions. Percentages. Finally, it had come to algebra and the real lesson had commenced.

The math teacher sauntered out of the class as soon as the bell rang, leaving an awed class behind him. He didn't even bother to introduce himself.

A stunned silence followed the teacher's departure until someone broke the spell by saying, "Please, what was his name?"

"Mr. Wesley Iorshimbe-Ngongngong," another offered.

"Mr. Wesley what?" a different girl quipped.

"Wesley Snipes!" Joyce snapped at the girl. "*Kai*, are you deaf?"

The student gave Joyce a reproachful look. "Please allow me oh, the man's name has k-leg, *abeg*."

Another admonished Joyce. "Yes oh, allow her. I'm sure that even you can't pronounce the name *sef.*"

Nelly laughed and shook her head. "Come to think of it, that mathematics teacher is a real Snipes." She jumped to her feet, her eyes shinning with mischief. She couldn't stop laughing. "Wait oh, he even looks like the real Wesley Snipes." She stopped to catch her breath.

Several girls laughed, too.

That opened the floodgates. In excited tones, the students compared the math teacher's movements to that of Wesley Snipes' ingenious stunts in the 'Blade' movies.

They got so wrapped-up in their stories they lost track of time, until Rosemary, the class prefect, announced in dismay, "You girls, it's time for integrated science, and it says here on the time-table that we are supposed to go to the biology lab for the lesson."

They were already six minutes late. Lockers were opened and banged as the students reached for their science texts and note-books. In a flash, most of them were out the door.

"Biology lab, Carlotta. Let's go," Ossie apprised. She scooped up her books, shut her desk with a bang, and ran for the door.

"Hey, wait up!" Carlotta called to Ossie, "I *dunno* where to find the biology lab!" In a rush, she grabbed a heavy textbook she assumed was for integrated science, and bolted out the door after her classmates.

※ ※ ※

The JS1D students sat in the biology laboratory, on high, wooden stools, around several large, Formica-topped work-benches.

Carlotta scrutinized the room. A strong scent assailed her nostrils. *Mothballs! Eeuw!*

Big shelves, on one side of the room, held strange specimens. Large, capped jars atop a long shelf at the back of the room harbored animal facial parts floating in a yellowish liquid. One of the jars, Carlotta thought, confined what she swore was a graying animal tongue. *Gross!*

The integrated science teacher, Mr. Ndubuisi, strode in and seated himself behind the instructor's desk located on a dais in front of the room. The newly polished blackboard gleamed behind him. He surveyed the students, his mouth stretching into a grimace serving as a smile. Seated, his elbows hardly made it above the top of the desk, suggesting he was on the short side.

"Morning Class," Mr. Ndubuisi barked. His voice was surprisingly deep for a man of his stature. He waved away the student's nervous attempts to return his greeting with an abrupt movement of his small hands. His beady eyes bored into each girl in turn, seemingly missing nothing.

"Open your textbooks! Chapter one!"

The students jumped. The lab was suddenly filled with rifling noises as they turned over the pages of their books in haste.

"Quiet!"

The class froze.

One girl shrieked and fell off her stool.

Carlotta's heart constricted. She imagined a hand closing around her throat. The hand squeezed. Her pulse slowed, then escalated. Pressure built in her head. She was suddenly thirsty.

"We shall begin with *matter*," Mr. Ndubuisi growled, stroking his beard. The facial hair gave him the uncanny resemblance to a billy goat. "You!" He pointed to a cringing student seated on Nelly's right. "What is matter?"

The girl whose name happened to be Chikodili quickly glanced around, hoping the teacher was pointing to someone else. When it became clear that she indeed was the subject of the teacher's unwavering attention, she rose from her seat.

"Stand up straight!" Mr. Ndubuisi snapped. "Tell us what matter is."

"Matter is, matter is—" Chikodili began, twisting her fingers. It was obvious she didn't know what matter was. "It is a, it is a, an—" She was now staring into the faces of her classmates, silently pleading for a helping hand.

Caught in the tension of what was going on, it didn't occur to the rest of the class to quickly look up the meaning of the term. The definition was clearly outlined in their open science textbooks, right on the first page of chapter one, under their very noses.

Mr. Ndubuisi scanned the class again, the tip of his tongue moving over his lower lip in a silent snarl.

"You!" he suddenly called out, this time pointing directly at a fat student called Doorshima. "What is matter?"

Doorshima jerked to her feet, upsetting her stool. "Sir, I don't know what matter is," she admitted in a shaky voice.

"You don't what?" Mr. Ndubuisi barked.

The class flinched. Someone let out an involuntary gasp.

"The two of you, come here!" The science teacher scrambled down from his position on the dais and signaled for Doorshima and the still cowering Chikodili to come forward. "Stupid students! Stand up straight! With your backs against the wall! Tell the class your names!"

"My name is Chikor," Chikodili said in a whimper, providing the class with the short form of her name.

"Did you say your name is *Nchikor?*" Mr. Ndubuisi queried. He'd wrongly concluded that the girl had called herself a crab, for *Nchikor* translated to *crab* in the Igbo language.

The class tittered. One girl choked and began coughing.

"Oh! Oh! You are laughing! How dare you laugh during my lesson?" Mr. Ndubuisi spun to face the class. His expression turned into an ugly scowl.

Abruptly, the tittering stopped. No one dared breathe.

Carlotta trembled. *I hope he doesn't call me next.* Her tongue felt glued to the roof of her mouth, and she badly needed a drink of water. *I don't think I can take this!*

Mr. Ndubuisi's eyes roamed the class. He left the two girls standing against the wall, and climbed back to his seat.

"You! White girl," he bellowed, looking directly at Carlotta. "Read aloud the definition of matter from your textbook."

Damn! Carlotta's heart sank. She looked down at her textbook, and opened her mouth to read. But no words came. Instead, she stared at her book in dismay.

"Stand up!" Mr. Ndubuisi snapped.

Carlotta shot to her feet. Her eyes widened in fear. Three long seconds ticked by with the *thump-thump-thump* sound of her heart. A dry croak escaped her open mouth before she had the presence of mind to shut it. The pressure in her head increased.

Oh God! Carlotta swallowed. The open book before her was solemnly introducing her to the subject of technology. *I must have grabbed the wrong textbook!* She knew it. Just to make sure, she turned to the book cover and yes, there it was: *Introduction to Technology! Shoot!*

Carlotta ventured a look at the teacher.

His gnarled fingers produced impatient tapping sounds. "Start reading!"

She looked at her classmates.

The students stared back in confusion.

"I'm sorry—" Carlotta stopped and swallowed. "I, I think I have the, the wrong textbook." She bit her lip, squeezed her eyes shut, and braced herself for the outburst.

"What do you mean you don't have your textbook?" Mr. Ndubuisi thundered, springing up from his perch. He needn't have bothered—the action did little to improve his height.

Carlotta avoided gazing at the teacher. "I, I was in, in a hurry, and I, I didn't realize I—"

Mr. Ndubuisi interrupted, "You stupid idiot! I don't allow students without books in my class!"

"But I only grabbed the wrong—" Carlotta began, aghast at how her simple mistake was being interpreted. But again, she wasn't allowed to finish her sentence.

"Out of my class! Get out," Mr. Ndubuisi roared. "Don't you ever step foot in my class without your correct textbooks!" he added, for the benefit of the other students.

Carlotta's neck burned. She grabbed her books and ran to the door, almost tripping over Doorshima's upset stool. She felt her classmates staring after her, and imagined their eyes were wide with terror.

Carlotta's throat constricted. Her eyes smarted. Her ears seared. Without a backward glance, she zipped through the biology lab door and ran all the way back to her classroom.

✽ ✽ ✽

*A*ngry tears coursed down Carlotta's cheeks as she marched into her classroom and slammed the door. She took two steps into the room—and froze.

Thirty pairs of eyes stared back in astonishment, mouths agape.

A scathing male voice belonging to a teacher poised by the blackboard, said something Carlotta couldn't decipher.

Then Carlotta realized what she had done. Blinded by her rage, she'd run into the wrong building and walked into the wrong classroom. *A senior classroom, too, from the looks of it!*

Carlotta unfroze, whirled around, flung the door open, and tried to escape. She tripped over the doorframe. Her books went flying.

The senior students laughed.

Carlotta yanked herself up, dived for her books, and made a beeline for the building exit. She could still hear the senior students' laughter ringing in her ears as she fled down the long corridor of the SS1 building.

"That was totally dumb," she admonished herself with trembling lips while darting down to the JS1 block and to her classroom. This time, when she opened the door, an empty room greeted her. She marched in and jammed the door shut, leaning against it to catch her breath. Tears rolled from her eyes and her head hung with shame. She shuddered and kicked at the door.

"This sucks!" Carlotta vented. She hurled her books at the blackboard. "Screw this stupid school." Her head felt stuffed and heavy.

I hate this place! Without warning, she flung herself against the door and pummeled its wooden frame. She kicked till her toes felt sore. Then she broke down completely and wept.

Several minutes later, her heart returned to its normal rhythm. Carlotta dried her eyes, and picked up her books. *I've totally made a fool of myself. So, what now?* She went to her seat and stared sightlessly at the empty desks.

She decided to cut the science lesson altogether.

It was a stupid class anyway; Carlotta rationalized, and leaned back in her seat. She closed her eyes and tried to recall instances when she had made mistakes like these in her former schools— taking the wrong books to class, handing in the wrong homework, even forgetting to do her homework altogether. But, no matter how hard she tried; she couldn't recall ever being ordered out of class.

After a few moments, Carlotta opened her eyes, sat up, and looked at the round clock on the wall above the blackboard. It was barely past 9:30 AM. She lifted the top of her desk, and pulled out her integrated science textbook. Her eyes went to the clock again. *It will be another thirty minutes before they return from the science class.*

Carlotta turned the pages of the textbook to chapter one. Then, with a determined expression, she leaned her elbows on the desk and began to read about *matter*.

✳ ✳ ✳

Though her marriage was falling apart, Shelley decided to keep trying. She had no choice. She so desperately wanted to save her family.

That night, close to 2:30 AM, when Richard tumbled into bed beside her, Shelley turned her back to him, curled herself into a ball and waited. She'd deliberately shed her nightclothes before sliding under the sheets hours ago. Richard's cold hands drew her closer and moved up her stomach to cup her breasts.

Heartened, Shelley molded her naked form to his. She felt the telltale hardness against her butt and sighed with relief and pleasure.

He still wants me. In that moment, Shelley was ready to forgive Richard anything—anything at all.

Chapter 7

Feddie Girl!

The JS1D students returned from another tension-filled science lesson looking subdued and weary. Fortunately, they had a fifteen-minute break before the next lesson was due. It was as if whoever designed the class schedules had known for a fact Mr. Ndubuisi's students needed time to wind down before facing another teacher. The science course had progressed from matter to plants, then animals. The students, after faithfully enduring barks and snarls for three weeks, came to the conclusion that since they weren't dead from all the stress, they would probably make it through the rest of the term alive.

"What is even wrong with Mr. Ndubuisi?" Nelly asked a rhetoric question. "When he points, he expects you to jump to attention like a soldier and answer immediately." She drew herself to her five-feet-seven frame, one hand raised to her forehead in perfect imitation of a soldier saluting a senior officer. "Primates are animals with backbones that can stand on two legs and grasp things with their hands," she spewed without emotion. "Please, who talks like that?"

"Ask me oh," someone agreed.

"It wasn't even funny the way he kept asking us to kneel down," Joyce said, pouring a cup of water from a small plastic container.

"Oh yes, that part was funny," Nelly declared, eyes shinning with mischief, voice dripping with malice. "Did you girls see Ndidi kneeling down? Even the lab stool was higher than she was at that position!"

"Better mind your mouth there, you Iroko tree!" Ndidi was on her feet in a flash, whirling around to face Nelly who was seated two rows behind.

Iroko was the symbolic king of trees in Igbo land. Its trunk was easily ten times the height of a single story building, making other types of mature trees look like shrubs. Ndidi's likening of Nelly to the tree signified, in no uncertain way, she considered her archenemy too tall. In fact, overgrown.

"What's your own?" Joyce challenged Ndidi. "Is it not true? Or don't you realize you are as short as a rat?" She would not let any arrow directed at her friend go without retribution.

"What? Who are you calling a rat?" Ndidi began, reacting to the barb about her height, or lack thereof, and advanced several steps toward Joyce, hands on hips in the legendary stance of one readying for a verbal showdown. "Just who do you think you are, you *Longitude*? You think you can just open your mouth and say—"

"Shut up and go back to your seat," Bukola interrupted in a heavy, Yoruba accent. "And you, Joyce, stop looking for trouble or I will report both of you to the form master."

"See this one oh!" Joyce stared Bukola down, the expression on her face indicating she was temporarily at a loss of befitting words to efficiently depict her dislike for the assistant class prefect.

"*Biko,* from which angle of elevation did you arrive?" A different student prompted.

"Yes oh," Nelly sneered. "Bukola, you've only been the assistant monitor for three weeks and you already want to report somebody. *Na wa* for you oh."

"*Abeg,* spare us!" Chikodili's shrill tone was discernible from the ensuing uproar. "You are not even the main class monitor," she yelled, waving her hand in Bukola's direction.

"*Yeh*, see me see trouble!" Bukola could almost not believe her eyes. "Look at this one who was shaking in science lesson. So now you've learnt how to talk, *ehn*? What was it you called yourself the other day? Crab?" She flipped a dismissive hand at Chikodili. "*Shioor*," she hissed, turning back to the matter at hand.

Chikodili opened her mouth to bite back, but no words came forth. Carlotta almost felt sorry for her. The unfortunate mishap in science class on the second day of school had left Chikodili with a stigma. The JS1D students had nicknamed her 'crab' and, like any other group of students, were always ready to taunt her about the incident irrespective of how the nickname might hurt her feelings.

Poor Cheek-or-daily, the crab girl!

"You that you're calling someone a crab, didn't the science teacher call you a stupid goat?" Nelly was quick to defend Chikodili from Bukola. Next to Ndidi, she disliked the Yoruba-speaking assistant class prefect less.

"What about you?" Ndidi quipped, looking at Nelly with glee. "Last week, Mr. Ndubuisi called you a blind giraffe!"

"*Ehn?* What did you just say?" As far as Nelly was concerned, Ndidi was about to overstep her boundaries.

"You are a blind giraffe!" Ndidi boldly repeated. "What can you do?"

Nelly charged. Joyce seconded.

Ndidi bravely met them head-on.

Everyone was now yelling, each trying to be heard above the others. Rosemary was banging on her locker, trying in vain to restore order. Bukola, who had given up the attempt to placate her classmates, joined in the melee, switching from English to Yoruba as she directed her malediction at everyone and no one in particular.

Many girls cheered Nelly's group, egging them on with verbal support.

Others jeered, clearly in league with the tiny, bigheaded Ndidi who was brazenly taking on the verbal abuse of more than a dozen girls on her own, slashing at them with both tongue and arms.

As was the case with such classroom altercations, the students were subconsciously divided into three groups: Nelly and her cohorts; Ndidi and her supporters; the classroom slackers.

The war raged on.

Suddenly, Carlotta could take no more. "Stop it, all of you," she yelled at the top of her voice. "Just stop it already!"

Silence greeted Carlotta at once.

"I can't believe you guys! Seriously? You only met less than a month ago and you're already on the verge of killing each another!" Carlotta continued to yell, in a rage, not realizing the class had suddenly gone quiet. "Go on, rip your throats out and see if anyone cares! Trust me, it will probably be worth the fun!" She leaped to her feet. "You are all acting out like a bunch of stupid losers! And honestly, it totally sucks!" She stormed out of the classroom, leaving twenty-nine perplexed students behind.

"She's right," Ossie said after a few moments. "You should all be ashamed of yourselves. *Na wa* for all of you!" She went after Carlotta.

"*Biko,* what's even the Feddie Girl's problem?" one girl asked.

"See me oh," another girl replied.

"And why is her neighbor supporting her?"

"*Abi o!*"

The spell was broken. The girls resumed chattering.

The noise filtered through the open windows to the surrounding pavement where Carlotta hunched with Ossie, face in hands, temples throbbing.

Soon the bell rang and the break was over. It was time for double period of English literature. Carlotta and Ossie returned to the classroom in the wake of a young female teacher and took their seats.

The teacher, Ms. Nora McKenzie, looked more like a fashion magazine editor off the streets of New York than a schoolteacher. High heels clicked as she made her way to the teacher's table, flowery perfume lingering behind and permeating the classroom. She placed her handbag on the table and pushed her sunglasses into her hair. On the first day of class, she'd instructed the students to address her as Ms. Nora. "I don't want any *aunty, me!* nonsense," she'd warned.

"Class, how are we today?" she greeted merrily.

"We're fine, thank you," the students chorused haphazardly. As always, they were fascinated by her chic appearance. Carlotta thought the literature teacher looked a little like Halle Berry.

"Good. Today, we shall continue with the various types of literature." Ms. Nora sashayed to the board, high-heels tapping, and chalked down the subject heading. Pirouetting to face the students, she wiped the chalk stain from the tips of her fingers by rubbing her hands together. Her nails were painted a bright red—they matched the color of her lipstick.

"Literature can be said to be the art of the written word," Ms. Nora said to the class and returned to the board to write it down. Several girls opened their notebooks and copied down what she had written. The others just continued to stare—mesmerized. That always happened. The literature teacher had a feminine presence that was so intriguing it was commanding.

"Let's review what we've learned so far. Who can tell us the major types of literature?" Ms. Nora surveyed the class. Only one hand was up.

"Yes?" Ms. Nora invited, looking at a shy and studious-looking student. "What are the three major types of literature?"

"Poetry, drama, and prose," Ndidi supplied without hesitation before the shy girl had a chance to open her mouth.

"Hmm, very good," the teacher said, fixing Ndidi with a pointed look. "Next time, please put up your hand if you wish to answer a question, and wait to be called before you answer."

Nelly sneered. "Little rat, did you hear that?"

145

Ndidi eyed her.

Joyce harrumphed. "Over *sabi-sabi* house wife."

"You're just laughing at your own stupidity," Ndidi replied. She produced a sound with her lips pursed and slightly parted. *Mscheew!*

"Poetry, drama, prose," Ms. Nora said, wagging a *no-no* finger at Ndidi. "We discussed each of them last week, starting with poetry." She turned and faced the rest of the class. "What is poetry? Does anyone remember?" She clicked her way back to the board and scribbled the three major types of literature in white chalk. On cue, the efficient students copied that down, too.

The class briefly reviewed poetry and gave famous examples. They reviewed prose. Then drama.

"Have any of you actually been in a play before?" Ms. Nora asked, hands hidden behind her back. She walked around the classroom, surveying the students. White slacks hugged rounded hips and outlined shapely thighs as she moved. "Any play at all?"

No hands went up. The class was deathly still.

Carlotta sized-up Ms. Nora's outfit and awarded her a nine-and-half out of ten. *The lady is obviously loaded. That outfit totally cost a lot of dough.* She had seen pants like that in a department store the year before, the last time she went shopping with Sasha, and they'd been priced at a whopping $199.99 after the sale mark-down. Handbag was definitely a Prada; shoes looked like Manolo's; scarf was obviously Hermès. The sunglasses? *Well, anyone totally worth their salt can recognize the bold and stylish, silver-rimmed signature of Ray-Ban.* The only glitch, Carlotta thought, was the polka-dotted, baby-doll top. She couldn't place it. *Saks, perhaps, or—?*

"Any kind of play at all?" Ms. Nora prodded, staring expectantly at the class. "Anyone?"

Reluctantly, Carlotta put up her hand. Heads turned. Eyes gawked.

"Good," Ms. Nora encouraged. "Please, stand so we can all see you."

"Feddie Girl! Feddie Girl! Feddie Girl!" the class chanted.

"Quiet please," the teacher cautioned, and turned back to Carlotta.

Carlotta stood. *Please don't stare at me.*

"Come up to the front of the class, Carlotta," Ms. Nora instructed. "Tell everyone what kind of play you've been in."

Carlotta walked to the front of the class on shaky legs and announced in a small voice, "I was in 'Romeo and Juliet' last spring." She bit her lip. "It was really just a school play organized for charity—" She stopped and looked at her feet.

"Wonderful," Ms. Nora beamed, her red lips forming a wide reassuring smile. "What part did you play?"

"Juliet," Carlotta answered, fidgeting with the waistband of her school skirt.

"Can you remember some parts of the play?" Ms. Nora's smile was still in place.

"Um, yeah, I guess…" Carlotta said, slowly nodding.

"Now, I want you to perform a scene from any act for us," Ms. Nora suggested, striding to the teacher's table, leaving a stricken Carlotta standing alone in front of the class. "You can do that, can't you?"

"Please, ma'am, I'd rather not," Carlotta mumbled. "I might have forgotten some of the words." She was nervous. Performing at a charity organization back in San Francisco was one thing, having to simulate that act in class with dozens of critical eyes watching was a different scenario. *Not that I can't remember the dialogue, but still—*

"It's all right, just give it a try," Ms. Nora encouraged. "You can go out the door and walk in as Juliet." She pointed to a girl in the front row and instructed, "Come out and stand here. You shall be Romeo."

The girl shuffled to the front of the class and stood where she was told.

Carlotta left the room and tried to calm her nerves. When she returned, a few seconds later, the nervousness was gone. She was Juliet.

"It is, it is: hence, be gone, away!" she said, floating into the room—graceful as a swan, eyes upon the form of her lover.

"It is the lark that sings so out of tune," she continued, her face surreal as she implored Romeo to stay a while longer.

She joined her hands together and closed the distance between them with dainty steps. *"Straining harsh discords and unpleasing sharps."*

Looking into his face with all sincerity, she said in a soft voice: *"Some say the lark makes sweet division."* She reached for his hands and angled her head, fluttering her lids in a delicate way.

"This doth not so," she whispered, dropping his hands and taking a few steps away from him, *"for she divideth us."*

She came close again, and gazed into his eyes, a look of longing etched on her face. *"Some say the lark and loathed toad change eyes."*

She took his right hand in both her hands, caressing it like one would a fragile object. *"O, now I would they had changed voices, too!"*

She placed the hand gently against her cheek. *"Since arm from arm that voice doth us affray."*

Her voice dropped to a murmur. *"Hunting thee hence with hunt's—up to the day."* She closed her eyes and savored the feel of his skin against her face. She remained like that for a moment.

Then her eyes flew open in alarm.

"O, now be gone, Romeo," she urged, sweeping him to the door. *"More light and light it grows!"*

Juliet stopped and waited for Romeo to acknowledge the rapidly dawning day. Instead, thunderous applause reached her ears and chants of "Feddie Girl! Feddie Girl! Feddie Girl!" rendered the air.

In an instant, Juliet was gone and Carlotta crashed back into her shoes. Beaming at the applauding students, she gave a theatrical bow.

"Feddie Girl! Feddie Girl! Feddie Girl!" the class cheered.

This time, Ms. Nora did not stop them. "Marvelous performance," she said. "Simply wonderful, Carlotta. Simply wonderful!"

Carlotta was very pleased. She returned to her seat feeling all bubbly and happy. At that moment, she really believed she could fly.

"That was very good," Ossie said, and clapped Carlotta on the back.

The teacher raised her hand and the class became quiet again. Smiling, she addressed the girls, "I'm glad you appreciate the brilliance of Carlotta's performance, for I shall expect no less from the rest of you by the end of the school year."

She strolled to the teacher's table and picked up a book. "In preparation for the next time we meet, I want you all to read scenes one and two of the play 'Wedlock of the Gods' by Zulu Sofola." She held up the book for the class to see. After a few seconds, she continued, "In addition, I expect you to be able to recite by heart the poem given in the prologue." She put down the book, looked at the clock on the wall, and said, "We are halfway through the first period. Please take out your notebooks and write these down." She started dictating at a rapid pace and the class hastened to scribble her words down.

Carlotta wasn't a fast writer, and found it hard to keep up. She contented herself with copying from Ossie's notes.

Periodically, the teacher would stop and explain a few points to the students. Then she would say, "Students, you may continue writing," before she would launch back into rapid dictation.

Finally the bell rang. The lesson was over.

"We shall stop here for today," Ms. Nora announced, as if she had a choice. "I will see you next lesson." She picked up her books and handbag. "Class monitor, please wipe the board clean."

Replacing the sunglasses over her eyes, the literature teacher sashayed out of the classroom, her heels clicking merrily on the concrete floor.

❋ ❋ ❋

$\mathcal{S}$ helley finished with the buttons of her pink, sleeveless blouse and shrugged on a black jacket. Studying her reflection in the mirror, she decided on a string of pearls, which she strung around her neck before reaching for the matching earrings.

The pattering sound her husband's bare feet made on the bathroom floor floated out as he exited the shower. Hot, steamy air emanated from the bathroom when Richard opened the door. He stepped into the bedroom.

"I need a ride to school," Shelley said, turning around to face her husband. His wet, dark curls were plastered to his skull, a white, terry cloth robe wrapped around his person. "The Honda has a flat tire, and I do not have the time to get it fixed before classes this morning." She clipped-on the earrings and adjusted her hair. Then she picked up a light-pink lipstick and began to coat her lips.

"All right," Richard grunted. "We'll need to leave in twenty minutes though." He threw off the robe and walked to his closet. *Why does she always insist on talking like that? No one said English professors shouldn't use contractions in their speech. She's probably doing this to piss me off. She only started talking like this a few years ago.*

"Fine, I will meet you downstairs then." Staring at Richard's naked body, Shelley was reminded again why she'd decided to remain with him, despite his proven inability to keep his hands off other women. "Do you want a cup of coffee before we leave?" She made for the bedroom door.

"No, I'll get some at the hospital. Thanks, anyway." Richard selected a necktie and looped it around his neck. He was one of those men who considered it a priority to knot their ties before stepping into their pants. "On second thought," he called, when he was satisfied he had the perfect knot, "I think I'll have that cup of coffee before we leave."

Shelley was already out of earshot.

Richard shrugged.

He was getting tired of the polite conversation. They were hiding their true feelings behind a wall of plain civility. She'd been home from Nigeria for several weeks and things still hadn't improved. Their routine was same as it had been for the past three years—cool politeness and blind eyes to potential problems, sporadic moments of intimacy in the dark that gets forgotten by daylight.

He strung a black, leather belt through the loops of his pants. Lately, the sporadic moments happened in wider intervals. *Twice since she'd been home from Nigeria. And what—another two or three times in the four months before the trip?*

"Shit!" *What kind of an able-bodied guy lives like this?*

He finished buckling the belt and went into the bathroom for a comb. *And it's not like I'm not well endowed.*

He rubbed a dry patch onto the steam-coated mirror and stared glumly at his reflection. *She's the problem, she and her prim-and-proper attitude! She lacks the right kind of enthusiasm, never willing to experiment, and the "Do not use dirty diction, darling."*

He shut his eyes for a second. *Maria, on the other hand, would—*

Richard refused to let his mind go there.

He sighed. And attacked his damp hair with the comb.

Now that Carlotta was no longer in the house, one would expect their relationship to improve. But no, things were still as drab as ever. They wake up in the morning and go their separate ways to work. They return in the evening and have dinner together, while talking about mundane happenings of the day. Afterward, they go to bed and fall asleep, only to wake up the next day and repeat the whole boring cycle.

Gone was the passion and excitement that served as the corner stone in their marriage. Their love life was over, they both knew it, but neither was willing to be the first to broach the subject.

Returning to his closet, Richard drew out a pair of black, leather shoes and folded his six-feet-two-inches frame on the bed.

He had barely slipped his stocking-clad feet into the three-hundred-and-fifty-dollar leather encasements when Shelley came bursting into the room, her blue eyes spitting fire.

Looking enraged, Shelley held something up. "What is this?" she demanded in a voice that could cut through ice.

"What is *what*?" Richard asked, looking wary. He glanced at the object in Shelley's hand—it was a hairbrush. He didn't know what the big deal was about the common object. He shook his head and bent back to his shoelaces. *Just like you to make a fuss about nothing. Women!*

Shelley's arm arched. The brush sailed through the air.

Richard's eye caught the movement and he dodged, narrowly missing being pelted badly on the forehead. "What the hell did you do that for?"

Shelley was unrepentant. "I suggest you take a look first and ask questions later."

Irritated, Richard retrieved the brush. It was of the feminine variety and contained long straight-strands of black hair intertwined between its bristles. He stared at it with narrowed eyes. Shelley's ragged breathing filtered through his ears and pounded on his brain. He couldn't figure out what was so upsetting to his wife. He looked up. "It's a hairbrush. So *what*?"

"You bastard!"

Suddenly, Richard understood. There was no way the long, black strands on the brush could be mistaken for his wife's shoulder-length blonde hair or his daughter's curly brown hair. There was only one person he knew that could possibly be the source of the offending strands.

Maria! Oh God. His heart sank. He was in for it.

Oh boy!

Maria had used the guest bathroom downstairs the one night he'd invited her into the house for a nightcap. That occasion had been the only time she'd ever set foot in the house.

How could she have been so careless to leave traces of her presence here?

The fact that Shelley didn't discover the hairbrush earlier was nothing short of a miracle.

Richard's pulse raced. *Hopefully, she wouldn't make the connection—no one knows I've been seeing Maria. I've been careful.*

But Shelley's next words chilled him to the bone.

"You have been seeing someone else. How dare you bring your little whore into my home?" Her lips curled in an ugly fashion, showing she was furious and half-drunk.

Richard knew he couldn't risk lying to her, for to provoke her further would be a big mistake. He knew that Shelley, while angry and under the influence of alcohol, would hurl anything and everything within her reach at her adversary. Once, she had nailed him with a bottle of perfume, which required him getting stitches in his head. He still had the scar to remind him of that particular incident when she caught him trying to weasel his way out of a compromising situation.

I can't possibly tell her about Maria—nothing really happened!

"I know nothing of this," Richard attempted, brandishing the hairbrush. He gritted his teeth and tried hard to think of a suitable explanation.

"You lying son of a bitch!" Shelley's eyes darted around the room for something to wield as a missile. Her hand closed around a picture frame.

"Hey! Aren't you just overreacting a little?"

"I am *now* overreacting?" Shelley hurled the frame.

Richard inched to one side. The projectile struck the headboard and rained glass splinters on the pillows.

"You are obviously jumping to the wrong conclusions!" Richard sounded stricken. "You only saw a freaking hairbrush for goodness sake!"

"I see. Now I know you will never change, Richard." Shelley calmly reached down and removed one of her shoes.

Richard stalled. His wife's quiet was more deadly than her tantrums—he knew that from experience.

"You will always be the promiscuous, self-centered, and sorry excuse for a husband that you are." Shelley armed herself with the shoe—sharp, four-and-a-half-inch heel protruding outward like the blade of a pickaxe.

Richard took several steps back. He hit the bedroom wall. *Someone please call the ER.* He hunched and scouted around for something to use as a shield. His eyes strayed longingly to one of the king-sized pillows on the bed before Shelley bounded down on him.

"Right now, I want you to get out." Her voice was steel.

Shocked, Richard was on his feet in an instant. "*What?* You can't be—"

Shelley flung the shoe.

He jerked; howled. The shoe had caught him squarely in the groin, the pointed heel striking against his soft spot.

Richard doubled over in pain. "You bitch," he managed in a strangled voice. "You mean, frigid bitch."

Shelley strode up to him and bent over so her face was level with his. The smell of alcohol on her breath was unmistakable.

"I want you to get out and never come back. If I come home and find you here, God help me, I will first break your balls then saddle you with a nasty divorce suit that will make your whole career come crashing at your feet. I have had enough of your lies and infidelity." She spoke in a slow, measured tone. "Just remove yourself from this house and stay out of my life." Ice-blue eyes stared right through him.

Shelley straightened, turned, and limped out of the bedroom, one bare foot supporting half her weight.

Stunned, Richard stared helplessly after his wife. *Good grief, she's finally snapped!*

✳ ✳ ✳

The week after Carlotta's marvelous performance as Juliet, the JS1D students were seated in their classroom recovering from another spellbinding math lesson from Mr. Snipes when the bell rang.

"Class prefect, what lesson do we have next?" one girl asked.

"Look in your time-table and see for yourself," another retorted.

"We have French now," Rosemary replied. Her head was partially concealed by the cloud of white dust ensuing from the board she was wiping clean. As usual, Snipes had used every inch of the blackboard for his mathematical symbols and equations.

The French teacher, Madame Alimi, a portly lady with twinkling eyes, ambled into the classroom a few moments later.

"Bon après-midi, la classe!" she greeted in a singsong voice. Good afternoon class! Her twinkling eyes roamed the students. *"Bon. Aujourd'hui, nous allons commencer avec les verbes français. Ouvrez vos manuels à la leçon quatre."* Good. Today we'll begin with French verbs. Open your textbooks to lesson four.

The class stared at her. They didn't move a muscle.

Carlotta could not fathom why the French teacher deemed it beneficial to always address the class in French when, obviously, no one understands what she says. *Several weeks of teaching this class should have taught her better.*

"Excuse me, Madam," Rosemary volunteered, speaking-up for the class. "We don't understand French."

"Pendant ma classe, nous parlons seulement le français," Madame Alimi admonished in a patient voice. During my class, we speak only French. *"Comprenez-vous?"* she asked the class. Do you understand?

The class just sat there. She could have been speaking Greek instead of French for all they understood.

"Ah non! Ce n'est pas bon! Où sont vos manuels français?" Oh no! This is not good! Where are your French textbooks? Finally, Madame Alimi was beginning to show a trace of annoyance at the silence that greeted each of her statements.

"Excuse moi, Madame," one girl answered in a timid voice. Excuse me, Madam. *"Nous avons nos livres ici, dans nos bureaux."* We have our books in our desks.

"Ehen! Mrs. French has started again," someone remarked snidely under her breath.

"You girls, hold on. We're about to be *Frenchrized*," Nelly whispered, a little loudly.

Several girls giggled. A few snorted. The student who had spoken in French put her hands over her mouth and managed to look contrite for speaking up for the class.

"*Ah bon.*" Oh good. Madame Alimi ignored the quips. "*Parlez-vous français?*" she asked, approaching the girl, her face full of hope. You speak French?

"*Oui Madame,*" the girl replied, staring at her desk. Yes Madam. "*Je parle un peu français.*" I speak a little French.

"*Ah, c'est très bon,*" Madame Alimi clapped her hands with glee. Very good. "*Bien, recevez vos manuels de vos bureaux.*" Take your textbooks out of your desks.

The girl lifted the lid of her desk and retrieved her French textbook. Giving her looks that would slam the brakes on a whizzing bullet, the rest of the class followed suit and fished their books out of their desks.

Madame Alimi returned to the front of the class and commenced teaching most of the lesson in French, as usual, only reverting to English to clarify certain difficult points.

The French teacher drilled the class on word translations of common objects. She conjugated the verbs *avoir*, *être*, and *aller* on the board and made the girls repeat them after her, several times, until she was satisfied. She gave instances of how each verb is used, and insisted they practice incorporating them into simple sentences of their own.

When the bell rang half an hour later, Carlotta thought her head had been run through with a chain saw.

After Madame Alimi came the fine arts teacher—a small, spidery woman with a crackling voice. She instructed on the origin of fine and applied arts, and discussed the various types of crafts indigenous to Nigerian cultures.

After that was thirty minutes of a much-needed break, then double period of Religion. The non-Christians went to a different location for Islamic instruction.

The Christian religion teacher was an albino with a high-pitched voice, who was afflicted with sorry-looking freckles on his face, neck, and arms. He wore a pair of thick glasses and kept shading his eyes with his palms as he read passages from the Bible. As if these flaws weren't enough, he also stuttered.

Carlotta was very much reminded of pink guinea pigs as she watched the instructor and listened to his teachings against sibling rivalry and treachery.

After what felt like an eternity with Cain and Abel in the Old Testament, the bell went off and classes were done.

The students were relieved. It had been a long school day. They put their books away and prepared to leave the classroom.

"What house are you in?" Ossie asked, replacing her religion notebook in her desk.

"That would be Sapphire House," Carlotta replied, coating her lips with strawberry-flavored lip-gloss. She wiped off the excess with the tip of her fingers and put the little mirror and tube of gloss back in her school bag. "And you?" she asked, removing a hairbrush from the bag. It was amazing how they'd been class neighbors for several weeks and hadn't really spoken at length to each other about matters not concerning academics.

"I'm in Crystal House. Ndidi and Bukola are also in my house." Ossie said. "Oh yes, and Joyce, too," she added, nodding toward Joyce, who was chatting animatedly with Nelly.

Ossie watched, fascinated, as Carlotta brushed out her long curls. "Did they really say you would have to cut your hair?" she asked.

"Yeah," Carlotta replied. "It will be done this Saturday. My one-month of grace is up. Sucks right?" She gave her hair a slow sweep with the brush. "I've never had my hair cut. Maybe a few trimmings at the hairdresser's, but that's about it."

Carlotta sighed and let the brush drop from her hand. It landed on the desk with a thump and flipped over. The dismal sound of the brush hitting the locker brought a formerly resigned

Carlotta to tears. She turned away from Ossie and dabbed at her eyes.

"It's not easy for us to cut our hair," Ossie empathized. "I had long hair, too, but my mother made me cut it a few days before I came here. I cried for two whole days," she confided, a wistful expression on her face. "My hair wasn't as long as yours *sha*." Reaching out to feel the texture of Carlotta's hair, she asked, "Can I brush it for you?"

"Sure," Carlotta replied, and turned her back to Ossie, who picked up the hairbrush and did a clumsy job of sweeping it through the thick, brown curls. She understood that Ossie was trying to be sympathetic and that made her feel a little better.

For a moment, Carlotta wondered if all the junior students with short hair once had long hair like Ossie had revealed she did. *They must have felt terrible to let it go. Yet, here they are, going about their business, as if it really didn't matter.* Tears stung her eyes and she wiped them off with the collar of her school shirt. She didn't want Ossie or any of her other classmates to think she would cry over having her hair hacked off.

Stemming the nostalgic emotions that suddenly took hold of her, Carlotta closed her eyes and concentrated all her thoughts on the sweeping action of Ossie's hand working the brush through her hair.

✸ ✸ ✸

Students were beginning to leave the classroom. Carlotta picked up her bag and left with Ossie. Three other girls came with them.

"Which house are you in?" Carlotta asked one of the girls.

"I'm in Sapphire-Five. *Je m'appelle Emeh.*" I'm called Emeh. The girl beamed at Carlotta. "I spoke to you in the bathrooms this morning, and in the house lobby on our first morning here, remember? My place of morning duty is right next to yours. I clean Sapphire-Three windows."

"Oh yeah, I remember. Sorry, sometimes faces just look alike to me, and I'm bad with names." Carlotta gave the girl an apologetic smile. She really had no idea who the girl was. She turned to the other two students walking with them. "Are you two also in Sapphire House?"

They both reacted at the same time, one nodding, and the other shaking her head.

"Okay, you go first," Carlotta referred to the dark girl walking to the right of Ossie.

"I'm in Crystal-Two and my name is Amanda," the girl said in one breath.

"Sapphire-One. Onyedikachukwu," the second girl said, kicking at gravels on the path with the toe of her brown rubber sandal. She was thin and nerdy looking, with sharp, piercing eyes visible behind thick glasses.

"I'll so not be able to pronounce your name," Carlotta said lightly.

There is something about you—

"Your name sounds like the end of the world." Carlotta recalled the girl had her nose in a textbook when the rest of the class had been in an uproar that afternoon. Come to think of it, the girl always had her nose in a book, she never said much in class. The spectacles made her appear studious and kind.

"Come on, Carlotta, just try and pronounce the name," Ossie prompted.

"Yes, try." Amanda implored. "The name is really not as difficult as it sounds."

But try as she may, Carlotta couldn't get past the second syllable of the nerd's name. The girls giggled at the way she pouted while trying to say *chukwu*.

"Call me Onyedi," the nerd said, taking pity on Carlotta.

"On-yeh-dee," Carlotta finally managed, after several trials, much to the girls' amusement. "I guess that's the best I can do." She couldn't reproduce the *ny* consonant of the Igbo alphabet; no matter how many corrections she received from the girls.

159

"You know, Onyedi's mother is a teacher here?" Amanda declared.

"Are you serious? What does she teach?" Ossie asked.

"SS2 chemistry," Onyedi said. She was not one for much elaboration.

"Cool! That must totally give you some kind of advantage in something, huh?" Carlotta asked. She wasn't sure what kind of subject chemistry was.

"I prefer mathematics," Onyedi said simply, her light-colored skin drawn tightly against her cheekbones. She had a way of making her words sound clipped, as if the act of speaking opposed her very nature.

She's so the exact opposite of Sasha, Carlotta thought. "Oh my God. Math? You like math? Are you kidding? I didn't, like, get anything the Snipes guy said in class this morning," she gushed. "It's totally awesome that you are good in math." Carlotta wished Onyedi would smile or something. "Snipes would *so* appreciate someone like you in his class."

"You mean Mr. Wesley?" Emeh corrected.

"Whatever," Carlotta said, flipping a nonchalant hand to dismiss the teacher's real name as unimportant. The class had taken to calling him Snipes since his last name was just impossible to remember.

"Well *sha*, his surname is difficult to pronounce," Ossie reasoned.

"And Nelly said he looks like Wesley Snipes, the Hollywood movie star," Amanda seconded.

"So, Snipes it is then." Carlotta shrugged and kept her eyes on Onyedi. The girl was staring elsewhere, a calm but disinterested look on her face. "The point is, I'm really bad in math, and I totally need help. Could you, like, go over some stuff with me later?" Something about Onyedi pulled at her heart. She wanted to see the girl smile.

"Yes," Onyedi replied, not glancing in Carlotta's direction.

"Really? That would be totally awesome. Thanks a bunch," Carlotta said. She felt a surge of warmth toward Onyedi and smiled. But Onyedi just resumed walking. She didn't seem to have anything else to say.

"Carlotta, why did you decide to come to school here?" Ossie asked.

"Yes oh," Amanda joined. "I've been meaning to ask you the same question."

Carlotta tore her eyes from the back of Onyedi's head. "Er, I—" she was at a loss for words. She didn't want to talk about that part of her past, and at the same time, she didn't want to appear snobbish to her new friends. She swallowed and took a deep breath. "My parents forced me to come here, all right? They dumped me here for something bad I did back home, and I so don't *wanna* talk about it."

The girls were taken aback.

"Well, you are probing into my private life!" Carlotta stopped and bit back her annoyance. "I'm so sorry. Can we just let this go?" she said finally, after a long pause.

"But how come? Couldn't you have gone to a boarding school in America?" Amanda asked in a quiet voice.

"What about missionary schools?" Ossie added.

What part of 'let this go' is so difficult to understand? Carlotta sighed. "It's a long story." She felt her ears begin to get warm. "A totally embarrassing long story."

Onyedi wasn't looking at Carlotta like the other girls were. It was almost like Onyedi didn't care and just wanted to be left alone.

Carlotta felt disappointed. "Honestly, I'd rather not get into the story of my past right now."

"Pourquoi?" Emeh probed. Why?

"Jeez!" Carlotta snapped. "What is it with you and the strange language? Why can't you just speak in English like the rest of us?"

"Yes oh! Why are you always talking like that?" Ossie asked.

Emeh whimpered. She looked like she was going to cry.

"Her mom speaks French," Onyedi informed them matter-of-factly without looking up.

"Oh, really? French, huh?" Carlotta mocked in a false voice. "Shouldn't you save your breath for a group of people who would understand what the hell you're talking about?"

Carlotta wasn't sure why she was lashing out at Emeh. Come to think of it, she recalled Emeh speaking like that in class most days. She had thought the girl was speaking a Nigerian language.

"We speak French all the time at home," Emeh wailed. *"C'est n'est pas ma foute!"* It's not my fault! The tears rolled down her eyes and she clamped her hands to her mouth.

"You girls didn't have to be so witchy to her," Amanda said under her breath. At FGGC Uddah, *witchy* was slang for being mean.

"Emeh, please sorry," Ossie said. "We didn't mean it like that."

"I'm totally sorry, too." Carlotta tried to make amends. "You are the girl who was totally bonding with the teacher during French class, right?" she asked Emeh, still keeping a wary eye on Onyedi and wondering why she was the only calm one in the group. She wished Onyedi would look in her direction—she longed to see her smile.

Emeh nodded. "My mother speaks French at home all the time." She dried her eyes. "I picked it up when I was little, and most times, I just speak the language unconsciously."

"*Heeyaah*, that is good," Ossie said. "I wish I could speak French, too."

"Does your mother teach French?" Amanda asked Emeh.

"Yes, but in a different school," Emeh replied. She still looked hurt.

"Okay, we understand why you do it, but take it easy, *biko*." Ossie soothed. Emeh gave her a sulky look.

Onyedi remained silent. It appeared it didn't matter to her what language Emeh chose to speak. She seemed the most condoning of the girls.

"Just try and stop it, *abeg*," Amanda advised.

Emeh sniffed and nodded.

The girl probably couldn't help herself, Carlotta decided. Who knows? Maybe she could express herself better in French than English. *How cool is that? Instead of pouncing on her, we should try to be a little more tolerant like On-yeh-dee.* She voiced out her opinion and the others agreed.

Soon, they approached the dormitories and were almost upon the walkway of Sapphire House. From where they stood, Carlotta noticed groups of girls hanging out under the Mystical Mangy.

The huge mango tree was a popular gossip spot for students, especially senior girls. They hoarded around it, right before meal times and during weekends, trading funny stories and gossip about school clubs, students, and teachers. Favorite pastime topics, discussed under the alleged mystical tree, included which student was overly friendly with whom, and which male teachers were considered hot, gay, or lecherous.

Carlotta and her friends stopped short of the Sapphire House walkway. They knew better than to approach the Mystical Mangy when it was tolling with chattering senior girls.

"I guess I'll see you all in class tomorrow, huh?" Carlotta said, curling tendrils of her hair around the tips of her fingers. She beamed in Onyedi's general direction, willing her to look up. "Can we meet up after lunch or something?" *Please look at me. Please look up, On-yeh-dee, just this once, for me, please!*

"During prep," Onyedi said. This time, she looked straight into Carlotta's eyes, held the gaze for a second, and smiled.

Carlotta felt her heart leap. Time seemed to slow down then stop completely. It seemed as if every other person was invisible. Nobody else mattered, nothing else existed, except Onyedi's really cute smile and her tiny teeth.

"Okay," Ossie said, "we'll meet-up during prep."

"Huh? Prep? What? When is that supposed—?" Carlotta started in confusion but was interrupted by the bell.

The girls raced to their dormitories to freshen-up before leaving for the dining hall.

✼ ✼ ✼

"It's time for lunch. Leave the dormitory!" Anita ordered, glaring at the few girls bustling about their corners.

Carlotta dropped her school bag and left the dormitory. She bumped into Sandra on her way out.

"Hi," Carlotta said, stepping aside. "Don't bother going in there, everyone is being asked to leave." She hooked a thumb at the door and inclined her head.

Sandra shrugged and followed Carlotta down the hallway of Sapphire House, amidst the other girls headed toward the relentless *ring-ring* of the bell coming from the dining hall.

"Hmm, Feddie Girl," Sandra remarked, when they were clear of the Sapphire House walkway. "It must be very difficult for you here."

Carlotta stopped in surprise. Sandra had never spoken to her like that. The ridicule behind the words was plain and obvious. She regarded Sandra briefly. "What do you mean?"

A smile slowly splayed itself on Sandra's face but stopped short of her eyes. "You know, being a foreigner here, it must be difficult for you to fit in." The ridicule was there again, only stronger.

"Oh, yeah?" Carlotta cocked her head and licked her lips. She sized Sandra up with cold eyes. "Most of the time, I don't get what people like you say when they speak English, the prefects totally suck, the food stinks, my classmates are so bent on killing one another, and the bathroom is a death trap." She explored the inside of her cheek with her tongue, her eyes boring into Sandra's skull. "Does that just about sum it up nicely for you?"

"I understand," Sandra leered. "My bunkie said your parents brought you here to make you turn away from your evil ways. I know about your family, and I know how you feel." Sandra smiled, but her eyes were like black marbles. "Poor you."

You must be kidding me. Carlotta's eyes narrowed in defiance. She couldn't believe the girl's cheekiness. "Don't you dare stand there and give me that pathetic attitude," she snapped. "What are you—a goddamned shrink? You can't possible understand me or pretend to know the way I feel. I don't care what bullshit your bunkie tells you or anybody else for that matter, and I don't especially give a damn about how you came by your stories."

Sandra sneered. "I know what I'm talking about."

Carlotta's temper rose and she struggled to keep it in check. "You don't even know me or what life was like for me in the United States. How can you totally know what it's like to be me?" She curled her hands into fists by her sides, the blood drumming insistently in her temples.

Now, Sandra looked offended. "Sorry oh, Madam America," she said, stepping back. "I was only trying to be your friend. My bunkie said that your mother wanted you to make friends here."

Carlotta eyed her. "You know what? You're so full of crap. Thanks, but no thanks. I don't need pathetic friends." Her temper started to rise again but she checked herself. "And I sure as hell don't need your sympathy."

"Okay, I've heard." Sandra's tone became defensive.

Carlotta stared into the girl's cold eyes. Her voice hardened. "Do me a favor, Miss Goody-goody, don't you ever say a word about my mom again. Just stay away from me and leave my family out of it." She turned on her heels and made to walk away.

Carlotta took a few steps, stopped, and looked over her shoulder.

Sandra was still standing where she was, a furious expression on her face.

Carlotta went back and leaned close to Sandra's ear. "Listen," she whispered in a harsh tone, "if I ever catch you telling tales about me again, I'll so twist your spine it will come out looking like a pretzel. Got that?" She turned and marched off.

As she walked away, Carlotta wished she had a cigarette to calm her racing heart. This was the first time she craved a smoke since she left the United States. She imagined she could just about deal with one of Slinky Sam's rolled joints.

Fortunately, the likes of Slinky Sam could not be found anywhere near FGGC Uddah. Carlotta wanted to stay clean of drugs and tobacco. And she'd been doing so well for the past several weeks, never even thinking about smoking. *It's surprising how the wrong people tend to rub you the wrong way. Screw Sandra for trying to trip me up.*

Gritting her teeth, Carlotta ran her fingers through her hair, and followed the other students into the dining hall.

❋ ❋ ❋

Seated at her table, several minutes later, Carlotta put Sandra and thoughts of bumming a cigarette from one of the school staff out of her mind. Hardly any of the school staff smoked. Those who did, would definitely not concede to letting a student do so. They'd probably report her to the school authorities and she'd be in serious trouble. Besides, Sandra wasn't worth her breaking the commitment to stay clean.

Carlotta turned her mind instead to wondering about what would be served for lunch. The day before, they had been served what she regarded as refried beans with pieces of fried plantains. She hadn't minded much and had consumed the sweet treat without a problem.

While fried plantains were fast becoming her best meal at FGGC Uddah, bean porridge was a different case. To Carlotta, it always appeared mushy and boring, and held no fascinating sensory appeal. She'd tried it once, during her first week in the school, and had never bothered to repeat the experience. She quickly decided she didn't like beans.

For breakfast, bread, with either tea or a spicy red sauce, was usually served. The sauce had made Carlotta splutter and cough the first time she tasted it, and reminded her of the meal she'd had with her parents in an Indian restaurant in San Francisco. She'd gradually learned to tolerate the heat in the sauce and, before long, had grown quite fond of it.

The dining hall held fifty tables, arranged in long columns of ten tables each. A plastic jug of water, stacked plastic cups, and a small plastic basket containing forks and spoons, resided squarely in the middle of each table. Two girls from every class level were seated at each table, making a total of twelve girls per table.

Carlotta was on Table-32. The other JS1 student assigned to her table was a pinch-faced girl from Ruby House named Vivian Gussoh. Carlotta didn't know what to make of her.

Vivian had an elder sister, Agnes, who was in SS3 and a dormitory prefect of Gold House. During breakfast that morning, Vivian had boasted to Carlotta that Agnes was responsible for overseeing the SS1 students whose morning duties it were to clean the Gold House bathrooms. Agnes had been displeased with the students' work that morning and had punished the whole lot, denying them breakfast.

Carlotta had shuddered at the obvious glee in Vivian's voice while she recounted the incident. *What kind of sick twisted mind took delight in the suffering of others?*

The hand bell stopped ringing and the students rose to say 'grace.' The dining hall prefect led the prayer, the students yelled, "Amen!" and sat down. The JS2 students from each table were called upon, column by column, to go collect food for their tables. They went through the side door leading from the dining hall into the kitchen, and each emerged with a metal tray containing six plates of food.

That afternoon, the students were served the only kind of dish at FGGC Uddah that Carlotta had not tried sampling.

"Please remind me, what is this called?" she whispered to Vivian as one of the JS2 girls on her table passed her a plate.

"It's eba and okro soup," Vivian replied, accepting the food.

"Okay, I get that, but what exactly is this *erber*? And the soup thingy you mentioned, what is that?" Carlotta asked, looking doubtfully at the small mound of rough, starchy, yellow meal on one side of her plate.

The yellow meal acted as a dam for the river of soup containing dark, greenish-looking ingredients Carlotta supposed were overcooked leafy veggies. She wondered what would happen if she poked the meal with her fork.

Carlotta nudged Sandra. "Seriously, what is this?"

"You girls, Feddie Girl, keep quiet!" a senior girl hissed. "If a prefect catches you talking, you will be punished like those girls over there." She inclined her fork at several junior girls kneeling a few feet away.

Carlotta knew better than to push her luck. She looked down at her plate and pursed her lips. Problem was, she didn't even know how to commence eating the food, assuming she were hungry enough to want to attempt it. Judging from her previous experience, she knew there was a technique to eating the meal but hadn't yet figured it out.

She looked at the other girls to see what they were doing. She observed one girl break-off a lump of the starchy meal with the side of her fork, then spear it with the fork prongs and immerse it into the soup.

When the girl lifted the lump that was now covered with the soup, a slimy, yellowish string followed suit and connected the fork to the plate in a slow, languid fashion that reminded Carlotta of drooling babies. The girl deftly twisted the fork with a sudden movement of her wrist and broke-off the slimy string. Quickly, she popped the loot into her mouth, withdrew the fork, and swallowed the whole thing in one noisy gulp without chewing.

Eeuw, gross! Yet Carlotta was unable to look away. All the girls around her were expertly attacking their food in a similar manner.

Carlotta imagined she could hear the slime-covered yellow lumps winding sloppily down their throats and ending at the bottom of their stomachs with a soft *plop!*

Eeuw! Carlotta almost gagged. *Totally gross!*

When the bell rang ten minutes later, Carlotta hadn't touched her food at all.

After 'thanks' was said for the food that was graciously provided, the students filed out of the dining hall to their dormitories.

Carlotta hoped she would have time to grab a quick glass of coke, and maybe wolf down some cookies before Anita made one of her "Jump into your beds!" announcements.

Unfortunately, by the time she stepped into Sapphire-Six, the bell signaling siesta time was already ringing and Anita was ordering students into bed.

Carlotta changed quickly into her nightshirt and climbed wearily into bed. Zika was already in bed, too. Carlotta had barely greeted her when Anita announced, "No talking during siesta!"

Her stomach rumbling furiously, Carlotta lay in bed thinking about the Snickers chocolate bars in the locker above her head. *Too bad I can't just get up and take one out.* She didn't want to be asked to kneel down like the junior girls in the dining hall.

Up until when she left her uncle's house, Carlotta had always done exactly as she wanted.

Not anymore.

She was beginning to understand that in an environment like FGGC Uddah, one had to abide by the rules or face the consequences. If the alternative meant kneeling on the hard, concrete floor, for heaven knows how long, Carlotta decided she would rather endure hunger.

I can always get the candy after siesta. It's not like I haven't totally skipped a meal before. I will just pretend I'm so on a diet.

Carlotta closed her eyes and tried to forget about being hungry. Minutes later, she was fast asleep.

Chapter 8
The Study Group

The roller coaster beckoned to them. They ran toward the long line of kids waiting to enjoy a thrilling ride on the huge, silver ribbon glinting merrily in the sun.

The excited cries of young children floated out as the little train with small boxy compartments first swooshed them down the steep side of one silver hill, then up the next. Up and down, up and down the train went, swooshing away, the kids within yelling at the top of their lungs—thrilled with the sensation of being undulated at high speed.

"The line should move on already," Sasha said, popping a piece of bubblegum in her mouth.

"Yeah, I can so not wait to be on that ride," Carlotta answered, blinking with expectation. "It's totally *gonna* be so much fun." She dislodged the mass of curls that had fallen over her eye with a toss of her head.

"Totally on point!" Sasha agreed, making an *I get you* gesture with her right hand.

They were at a theme park in San Francisco, waiting in line with dozens of other kids to get on the biggest roller coaster.

Sasha, a vivacious thirteen-year-old with peppermint-green eyes and numerous freckles dotting her up-turned nose, was Carlotta's neighbor and childhood friend. They grew up together in San Francisco and their mothers were friends, as well. They'd attended the same schools for eight years and were inseparable.

The line kept getting shorter. Finally, it was their turn to go for a spin. They scrambled into a compartment and strapped themselves in.

"Have fun, honey!" Carlotta's mom waved from the sidelines.

"Be careful, sweetheart, remember not to flail your arms while in motion!" Sasha's mom called.

"We'll be fine, Mom!" Sasha yelled back. She grinned at Carlotta. "As if we're ever *gonna* be intimidated by a roller coaster." She eyed the metal monstrosity. "It does *kinda* look awfully scary from here, though."

"Oh *puhleease.*" Carlotta rolled her eyes then leaned over and waved fervently at the two women still calling out instructions. It had taken her two whole minutes to convince her mother she could handle the scary thrills of the roller coaster and she didn't want anything to jeopardize her efforts. *I'll so not appreciate Sasha spoiling all my hard work.* It's not as if Carlotta ever doubted her mother will let her get on the ride, *it's just that it takes a lot of work these days to persuade my parents to let me do exactly as I want.*

The guard came over to confirm they were securely bolted in. Sasha stuck out her tongue at him.

She probably thinks he's cute, Carlotta thought, and giggled. He cast them a cursory look before moving on down the train, checking all compartments to make sure all safety latches were locked and all riders secure. He strode over to the controls and flicked some switches.

The little train vibrated. They were off.

"This is so cool," Sasha babbled. They made their way slowly up the first hill. "Nicole *shoulda* totally come with us."

"What's so the biggie with you and that bitch?" Carlotta wondered why Sasha would think of Nicole at the moment. *Sasha is such a wimp!*

Nicole had managed to steal Sasha's boyfriend, then persuaded the gullible girl to trade cell phones last summer, an action that had gotten Sasha in serious trouble with her folks. After a series of catfights, Carlotta had suggested that Sasha stop speaking to Nicole, which, as far as she was concerned, was what the conniving brat deserved.

Suddenly, they were hurtling downward. Carlotta opened her mouth but couldn't hear her own scream—the noise made by the others was deafening. The excitement built as the train rushed up the second hill. Her heart beat rapidly; the sensation that only high-speed motion brings wove through her stomach.

Down again the train went at full speed.

Carlotta's heart leaped into her mouth. Her brain felt like wool, her whole weight disappeared—leaving her with a floating sensation. The wind whipped past her face, streaming her hair and making it difficult to breathe. She knew she was screaming but she couldn't distinguish her voice from the other voices drumming against her ears. She held on tightly and closed her eyes against the wind.

The train swooshed up a big hill. She screamed.

The vibrating compartment stimulated Carlotta's senses. The excitement was intoxicating. She opened her mouth and yelled in reckless abandon, releasing some of the tension through her vocal cords. She became one with the train—feeling nothing but the vibration, the sensation, and the rush of wind against her skin.

They plummeted again and Carlotta screeched, closing her eyes, her hair a long sheet of curls suspended high above her head.

Soon the little train slowed and came to a grinding halt.

The ride was over.

The girls climbed out on shaky legs and stumbled to their moms, trying to catch their breath.

As Carlotta reached out to her mother, the theme park slowly faded out of sight and she found herself in a room. She looked around in bewilderment and soon recognized principal McWatters' office. Sasha was not beside her anymore, and neither was her mother. But a creepy feeling at the base of Carlotta's spine intuited she was not alone.

Carlotta looked around in trepidation, assuming she was trapped in some strange, time-space continuum.

Mrs. McWatters, the principal who had expelled Carlotta from the middle school in Oklahoma, suddenly loomed in the middle of the room, eyes piercing. Sharp-looking teeth hung from the sides of her mouth like a vampire's. An eerie look was etched on her face.

The gym teacher, who'd busted Carlotta for smoking marijuana, materialized in the shadows to the side of the principal's desk. He was explaining something in very agitated tones to the room at large and looking really scared. His eyes bulged from his face, making him look like he'd both seen and swallowed a ghost.

This is so weird. Am I dead or something? Carlotta's brain tried to come up with a rational explanation for the ensuing bizarreness. *I must have died in the theme park and been rocketed back here as a ghost.*

She considered asking the principal why she mutated into a vampire. But the woman's face darkened and her claw-like hands gripped Carlotta's shoulders and shook them in anger.

Oh my God! Now she's gonna sink her fangs into my neck and totally suck my blood, Carlotta screamed in her mind, sick with fear. *She's gonna feed on me right here in her office—whatever happened to vampires asking for permission first?*

The principal uttered something in a voice that had the hair on Carlotta's arms standing on end; a guttural voice—like running shoes crunching sand.

Oh no! Here it comes! Carlotta flinched. And braced herself.

"Wake up! Wake up, Carlotta!" the vampire commanded.

Leave me alone, you evil, bloodsucking vampire! Carlotta wanted to scream, but couldn't. Her hands flew up to protect her neck. Somehow, her voice was gone. She had lost it to yelling in the theme park.

Leave me the hell alone! You don't have my permission!

Carlotta opened her mouth to try again, and just then, Mrs. McWatters' ghastly face vanished and was replaced by a much darker and younger face. The gym teacher vanished, too.

"Wake up, wake up," the dark face said.

Carlotta recognized the face. It was Zika's.

What are you doing? Carlotta wanted to ask. The shaking on her shoulder got more insistent, and she realized her eyes were closed and opened them. She yelped and sat up.

She was not in the principal's office. Vampires didn't surround her. Instead, she was thousands of miles away from home, exiled in FGGC Uddah—an all-girls boarding school located somewhere in the depths of Nigeria, West Africa—lying on her bed in Sapphire-Six dormitory. Zika, her bunkmate, was trying to wake her up.

"Siesta is over." Zika's tone belied the urgency she was trying to hide. "We only have five minutes to get ready for afternoon prep. You need to get up at once or Anita will have your neck!"

Carlotta gasped. The unmasked fear and confusion displayed on her face almost had Zika laughing.

Carlotta realized how silly she must look and her ears burned with embarrassment. *It's so not my fault. I just had a weird vampire dream and you said, 'neck.' Only vampires love human necks.*

In that moment, Anita announced, "Get ready to leave the dorm for prep!"

Carlotta shuddered.

❋ ❋ ❋

When Shelley returned home that evening, she was relieved to notice Richard was gone. It had taken him three weeks to actually get around removing himself entirely from the house and not just relegating himself to the spare bedroom. His closet was completely empty—almost as if he had called in the cleaners. There was no trace of him anywhere in the house.

An inexplicable wave of loneliness washed over Shelley. She shivered, and rushed into the bathroom. His toothbrush and razor were no longer where they used to be.

Shelley felt sick. She braced herself against the white, marble countertop and took a few deep breaths. Upon feeling better, she mustered up courage and returned to the bedroom. The king-sized bed dominating the room now seemed too big—the whole bedroom appeared empty.

Shelley hadn't realized, until now, how much she'd depended on Richard's presence to fill the space around the house and the void around her life. Now he was gone. And he'd left a bottomless pit behind.

Have I acted too hastily by asking Richard to leave? Like any other woman who relapses into a state of self-doubt after making a difficult emotional decision, Shelley became desolate. *Is it really worth losing a husband over an alleged case of infidelity? Maybe two cases? All right, who am I deceiving—several cases?*

Shelley plodded to the bed and hunkered on one side. Propped against one of the king-sized pillows was the blue hair-brush that had caused all the altercations of the past few weeks. She picked it up with remorse, wondering what kind of hard-hearted woman would resort to helping a married man cheat on his wife. Lying on the pillow underneath the brush was a hand-written note. Shelley flipped the paper over.

I really did love you. What were you thinking?

—Richard

Tears escaped her eyes and trailed down her cheeks before Shelley realized she was crying. She sat there for a few moments, staring at the paper. Again, just like before, he hadn't denied he was seeing someone else.

He didn't even say he was sorry.

Not an ounce of regret.

No guilt.

Just nine little accusing words meant to play on her emotions and erode her resolve.

Shelley read the words aloud. "I really *did* love you—" *Did? Past tense?*

"No, not this time!" Shelley decided, her shaking fingers crushing the paper into a tiny, rough ball.

Not now. Not ever!

She wouldn't give him the opportunity to hurt her in that way again. She'd had enough.

"Bastard!" she yelled, and threw both the paper ball and hairbrush across the room. The hairbrush bounced off the wooden dresser and landed with a clatter into a vanity thrash can. The weightless ball landed only inches from Shelley's feet.

Sobbing, Shelley bent and picked up the crumpled note. Meticulously, she straightened out the kinks then tore the paper into several tiny pieces with slow, deliberate movements.

Wanting to shield her heart from the hurt and frustration, Shelley dashed into the bathroom and flushed Richard's pathetic apology down the toilet.

❋ ❋ ❋

On Sapphire-Six, girls bustled about—getting dressed, and making beds.

Shaking her head from side to side to clear it, Carlotta climbed down her bunk. The air was filled with the stifling smell of powder and body sprays as more than a dozen students raced to complete their mid-afternoon grooming in the little time allowed.

Carlotta hurriedly dressed in her day uniform of pleated, black skirt and sky-blue blouse. She smoothed the tail of the sleeveless blouse on top of the skirt that barely made it to her knees, then thrust her feet into flip-flops and picked up her school bag.

"I have to rush to class now for a physics lesson," Zika said, walking briskly to the door. "Be sure to come back to the dorm after recreation, so we can go fetch our water for tonight and tomorrow morning." She left without much more than a goodbye, the door banging shut in her wake.

The bell rang.

Just as Carlotta knew she would, Anita ordered students out of the dormitory in a raised voice.

"Leave the dormitory!"

Carlotta wasn't interested in waiting to see who would be punished for tardiness this time around. The day before, she'd been punished along with Grace and Uche, and today, she didn't relish the thought of fifteen minutes of kneeling on the hard, cold floor. She quickly brushed her hair, took one last look in the mirror—ignoring the zit that had sprung bright and pink on one side of her nose—and made for the door.

She was halfway down the winding path toward the classroom blocks when she realized she'd forgotten to take the much desired chocolate bar with her.

Carlotta's stomach rumbled. She sighed and considered going back for the candy. But the throng of girls pushing past her, aiming to get to their classrooms in time for prep, made it impossible to dash back to the dormitories.

Furthermore, the thought of being asked to kneel down and possibly raise or fly her hands quenched any desire for candy. *Balancing my weight of a hundred-and-five pounds on my knees is totally not worth it,* Carlotta rationalized, *even if the prize for my trouble is a full-sized Hershey's bar!*

Carlotta took one last longing look at the walkway back to Sapphire House, which was now bathed in the shadows of the Mystical Mangy, turned, and pushed on to the JS1 classroom block.

Once in the classroom, Carlotta ambled over to her desk and sank herself in the straight-backed platform that served as a seat. Ossie was already in place, searching through her locker for a book or something.

"Hi Ossie, what's up?" Carlotta stifled a yawn and wiped her teary eyes with her fingertips. She was so hungry she thought she'd collapse. And the enticing aroma of food her classmates brought with them wasn't helping.

Ossie withdrew her head from the locker long enough to smile and mumble something in reply. She promptly returned to her former position, part of her head submerged in the open desk.

The classroom became noisy as the last of the students arrived and filled their seats. Many were snacking while getting ready for the afternoon prep.

Carlotta thought the smells of oranges, bananas, and peanuts emanating from different points in the classroom were wrapping themselves around her head. Her stomach rumbled and she swallowed hungrily. She imagined that downing the lunch of eba and okro soup she had so flippantly passed up that afternoon, wouldn't have been such a bad idea after all.

Poor Carlotta was beginning to get the message—in boarding school, meal times were there for a reason. One should eat the provided meals at the appointed time, no matter how gross the food looked. Either that or have a dormitory locker full of edible goodies—and always remember to grab the snacks before leaving for class.

A few girls stood in a group in the front of the room. One of them—Carlotta could not recall her name exactly but believed it was unpronounceable anyway—was sharing out something that looked like raspberry juice.

Ndidi was busy peeling an orange with a pocketknife and chatting unconcernedly to her desk neighbor who was staring back with glazed eyes.

Joyce was talking loudly to Nelly.

At least two girls were eating breakfast cereal out of plastic cups.

Bukola was humming and nodding in beat to a song while stirring powdered milk, then sugar cubes, into a bowl of water. A small stack of crackers sat waiting their turn on her locker.

Rosemary was rummaging through her desk and popping peanuts into her mouth at the same time.

Doorshima was stuffing her face full of bananas.

Chikor was peeling an orange with her fingers.

Carlotta spotted Emeh and Amanda and nodded to them. They waved back enthusiastically.

Onyedi had her nose buried in a textbook as usual.

The students were all dressed in the knee-length, pleated skirts and sleeveless blouses that constituted the day uniform. The skirts were black in color, but the blouses were of different colors, each corresponding to the color of its owner's house.

Carlotta's stomach rumbled. She wished she had gone back for that Hershey's bar—punishment or not. She lifted the lid of her desk and stared at her books for a moment. A dull pain in the depths of her head was making its presence known.

Carlotta blinked and wiped tears from her eyes. She groaned and stifled a yawn. Her brain was tired and she was starving. There was no way she was going to be able to study. She gave up trying to focus and was about to let out a dejected sigh when she noticed someone standing in front of her desk. She let the lid drop, and looked up.

Onyedi stood there, thick glasses framing her eyes like twin halos. She held out a hand. In it was a thick slice of white bread smeared lavishly with margarine.

"For you," Onyedi said, the ghost of a smile tugging at her lips.

Carlotta's heartbeat quickened. She forgot all about being tired and straightened. "Are you sure?"

Onyedi confirmed.

Carlotta studied her benefactor. Onyedi had soft, dark eyes that shone behind the thick lenses of her glasses—they reminded Carlotta of twinkling little stars.

Onyedi inclined her head. Her gaze held. "Here," she said.

Carlotta needed no further prompting. She accepted the proffered gift and sank her teeth into it. "Thanks," she said, her mouth full.

But Onyedi was already striding back to her desk.

Awww... she doesn't say much. Munching on the bread, Carlotta quietly thanked her stars for the lifesaver in the form of Onyedi. *She's just so different.* She finished the slice and wiped her mouth with the back of her hand.

"Do you want some water to drink?" Ossie asked, watching Carlotta with amusement.

"That would be great. Thanks." Carlotta took the offered cup and drank. The water was warm and insipid but she couldn't have cared less. At that point, she was more concerned with quieting her stomach than indulging her culinary preferences.

"Thanks," she said again, and returned the empty cup to Ossie.

"Do you want more water?" Ossie indicated the plastic water container in one hand.

"Uh-uh, I'm good for now." Carlotta wiped her mouth and sighed. She thought the simple combination of bread with margarine was the best meal she'd had in a long time. She looked to the front of the class, trying to catch Onyedi's eye. No such luck. The nerd already had her nose buried in her book once more. *How did she know I was totally starving and desperately needed something to eat?*

"Neighbor, why didn't you tell me you are hungry?" Ossie asked. "Did you miss your food this afternoon?" She rummaged through her school bag and removed two unpeeled, greenish oranges. "I almost missed my food, too, but I was lucky. I got to the dining hall just in time." She offered the oranges. "You should have brought some of your provisions to class."

Accepting the gift with a gracious smile, Carlotta wanted to tell her desk neighbor how gross lunch had been that afternoon, and how she'd forgotten to bring a candy bar with her, but she didn't get the chance, for at that moment, the prep prefects entered the classroom.

The class quieted down. The JS1D students didn't mind having their two prep prefects around because they seemed quite harmless and never keen on punishing anyone.

"We are your prep prefects," one of them, the short fat one, had wheezed on the first day of prep by way of introduction. "I'm Senior Oge and this is Senior Patricia." They had walked to the teacher's table and deposited their books on it. The rolls of fat on Oge's sides had been discernible through the Ruby House blouse she wore on that day, and they were still visible now.

Rosemary gave five sharp taps on her desk. The students hid their food and stood to greet the prefects.

Oge positioned herself in front of the class like she always did, her large eyes scanning the faces of the students. "I hope everybody is present, for I expect each and every one of you to be on time for prep. If you're not yet here, it means you should see me later for your punishment."

The class tittered.

Oge pretended not to notice. "If you get detained, please get a written note from the prefect or teacher that detained you. If you fail to do so, you will be punished for coming late to prep. Please be quiet today." She pinned Joyce with a meaningful look. "No eating. No talking. No whispering. No coughing."

Oge's eyes roamed the entire class. The heavy bags of flesh around the eyes made it seem like she was peering through slits in her face. When she cleared her voice and swallowed, her jowls jiggled.

"You already know the rules. If you want to leave the classroom for any reason, you must first get permission from me or Senior Patricia." Oge indicated the other prep prefect who was already seated.

Patricia nodded and returned to her books.

Oge turned back to the students. "I'm sure you've all been hearing about the school clubs since you arrived here. In a few minutes, the representatives of the various school clubs will come here to talk to you about the merits of joining their clubs." She paused and looked to Patricia for confirmation.

Patricia, a tall, wiry, SS3 student with a face and neck that can only be likened to that of a vulture, nodded vigorously several times in total agreement to whatever her colleague had just said.

"And now, Senior Patricia will take the roll call. Please indicate by raising up your hand when you hear your name." Oge positioned herself beside her mate at the teacher's table. She laid her thick head down on her fleshy arms, which she arranged carefully on the desk. Her whole body sagged as she settled herself into a comfortable position. By the time the class roll call was halfway done, she was fast asleep, and snoring softly, much to the amusement of the students who were watching and giggling.

"*Whaddya* know?" Carlotta whispered to Ossie. "That never gets old." She shrugged and commenced working on her social studies assignment.

* * *

The senior student in front of the class summed up the merits of becoming a member of Hausa Club and continued to stare at her feet. Her voice sounded every bit as tiny as her appearance.

Carlotta hadn't understood a thing the club representative said, partly because the rep had been standing still like a broken twig and looking downward the whole time, but mostly because of the thick, Hausa accent that made one doubt she was speaking English.

"Does anybody want to ask Senior Habiba Kazeem a question, and does anybody want to join Hausa Club?" Patricia asked in a voice that insinuated she wasn't really expecting any reaction from the class but was just fulfilling her duties.

Actually, most of the students had long since decided to follow their fat, prep prefect's example and were nodding off to sleep.

The tiny Senior Habiba, who unfortunately was the Hausa club representative, thanked Patricia without looking up from the ground, and shuffled out of the class, her over-sized flip-flops tapping dourly against her heels.

Carlotta silently empathized. *They totally should have chosen a better speaker, or, at least, a cool-looking student to represent that club. No one wants to join a club for losers.*

Hausa Club not withstanding, Carlotta's mind rang with the interesting things she'd heard about some of the other school clubs.

There was Interact Club—for students who liked to network. Press Club—for the literary inclined students. Social Club—meant for students who were into modern dancing and socializing. JETS Club was for Junior Engineers, Technicians, and Scientists. Computer Club was obviously for nerds—*ugh!* There were clubs for the natives of the three major ethnic groups, Igbo, Yoruba, and Hausa. Senior Habiba's feeble way of delivering her speech had definitely given an adept insight into what the Hausa Club might entail. *Great!* There were also French Club, Music Club, and Sports Club; those were self-explanatory.

Amidst the ogling of her classmates, Carlotta was specially presented with a red-and-gold-trimmed, purple card by a senior student who looked Asian with long dark hair plaited down her back. The card requested that Carlotta join the Feddie Girls Club. Carlotta inferred it was an exclusive club, meant only for non-Nigerian and multi-national students of FGGC Uddah. *Obviously!*

Although all the students of FGGC Uddah were regarded as Feddy Girls, only the *Feddie Girls* were eligible to join the Feddie Girls Club. The club currently had seventeen members—thirteen of which were senior girls.

Carlotta eyed the gold-and-red-trimmed purple envelope the card had come in. *Okay, I'm a Feddie Girl so I'm totally expected to join the Feddie Girls Club by default? How stereotypical. Whatever happened to my freedom of choice?*

The club that had the most effect on Carlotta, however, was the Drama Club. Members of this club were aspiring actresses. There were many drama competitions handled by the club, and the members also got to meet Nollywood celebrities, movie directors, and talent scouts. *Awesome!*

Carlotta loved the theater and other performing arts, and had been a member of the drama society in her former school. She found the talent of certain Nollywood stars fascinating, especially that of Rita Dominic, Joke Silva, Omotola Jolade-Ekeinde, Genevieve Nnaji, and Chioma Chukwuka.

Despite her keen interest, however, Carlotta didn't sign-up to join the FGGC Uddah Drama Club. She knew extracurricular activities always ended up taking away most of one's free time. And her parents had made it clear she was to study hard and concentrate on getting her grades up. Good grades were her only ticket to returning to the United States at the end of the school year.

Since she obviously would need her free time to study, social activities were definitely out. Putting the issue of school clubs out of her mind for the moment, Carlotta completed her social studies assignment and started on Snipes' homework.

Ten minutes later, the bell rang.

Senior Oge's massive form immediately stirred itself to life and snapped "Prep over! Leave the classroom!" then settled back into its comfortable position and promptly went back to sleep.

The students couldn't hold back their giggles. Oge was just too funny to ignore. Even Patricia smiled and raised an eyebrow.

"Please leave the classroom now," Patricia advised, and returned to her books.

As the students filed out of the classroom, Emeh, Amanda, and Onyedi joined up with Carlotta and Ossie.

"You should try and join the Drama Club, Carlotta. You are very good in literature." Emeh's shinning eyes reflected the setting sun. Looking at her, Carlotta couldn't get past the vision of a stuffed Easter bunny.

Emeh had joined the French Club and Music Club, Ossie and Amanda had signed up to join Igbo Club and Interact Club, while Onyedi had joined JETS Club and Computer Club.

"No, *A-mer*, I'd rather not," Carlotta said, slowing her pace so Onyedi could catch up. "I doubt if I will be able to manage extra curricular activities with all the schoolwork." *In a few years, I so wanna be in a Disney movie like Vanessa Hudgens, Demi Lovato, and Ashley Tisdale.*

"The schoolwork is not that plenty," Ossie asserted. "Today, we were only given assignments in integrated science, maths, and social studies. And Mr. Onwuzor told us to read a passage in the Bible for religion."

"My point exactly!" Carlotta looked at Ossie. The girl featured a contemplative look, as if she were trying hard to remember something.

Ossie was only a half-inch shorter than Carlotta but her assertive presence made her appear much taller. The look on her face deepened.

"Hello? You still with us?" Carlotta asked, waving a hand in front of Ossie's eyes to catch her attention.

Ossie finally shook her head and shrugged her bony shoulders. Apparently, she had decided to dismiss whatever it was that she couldn't remember.

"French," Onyedi intoned.

"Ahah! I knew I was forgetting one assignment. *French!*" Ossie beamed, clapping her hands and jumping up and down with satisfaction.

"Ossie, you sound so much like the form master when you said the *ahah.*" Amanda laughed.

Carlotta frowned. "Yes, for our French assignment, we're supposed to categorize some common objects into masculine or feminine. *Le sac, la table*— I tried it earlier during school period. It's totally difficult," she wailed, flailing her arms in despair. "You have to memorize the words to determine if it's masculine or feminine."

"It's true oh!" Amanda shoved herself between Ossie and Carlotta.

"*Ah non, le français n'est pas difficile du tout,*" Emeh stated, struggling to maintain her position on Carlotta's other side. Oh no, French is not difficult at all. "*S'il vous plaît —*" If you please—

Amanda and Ossie shot Emeh a withering look and she fell silent.

"At least you understood what Madame Alimi was yapping about this morning. I totally didn't get anything out of that class. I was so lost I ended up day-dreaming the whole time." Carlotta sighed. "To make matters worse, I didn't even get much work done this afternoon. Not with the talks about school clubs and all."

Emeh caught Carlotta's eye. She moved in and rattled off a long sentence in French.

Carlotta could not believe her ears. She stared at Emeh. "Are you totally kidding me?"

Amanda rolled her eyes.

Ossie shook her head in exasperation.

Onyedi seemed unconcerned.

Emeh nodded enthusiastically.

"Yeah right. I totally understand, *A-mer*," Carlotta said in a sarcastic tone. "Thanks a bunch for the tip. And keep saying—" she reached up with her right hand and made a *shut-up* sign, "whatever it is you just said."

"Emeh, *biko* what's even wrong with you?" Amanda hissed, and shook her head.

"Which levels are you trying to feel, *abeg*?" Ossie asked, placing a hand on her hip in perfect parody of the *shakara-* stance—basically communicating to Emeh with her attitude that she was going too far with the French.

"What's your own?" Emeh challenged. "I was talking to Carlotta."

Ossie turned to Emeh. "Wait oh, you are just joking with us, *shey*?" she asked with irritation. "Okay oh, Mrs. French, you want us to beg you, *abi*? Come-on, interpret what you just said before I *konk* your head."

"Mrs. French *kor*, Mama French *ni*," Amanda retorted. "Emeh, just start translating now oh before I dis-*bambam* your face."

187

Ossie laughed.

Onyedi did not react.

"Okay, very easy," Emeh scoffed, making herself sound important. "What I said is that I will like to help Carlotta with French, if she wants." She turned to Carlotta. "There's no problem at all. French is very easy to learn, and I know you'll start liking it."

"You don't say? *A-mer,* can you teach us all?" Carlotta asked. Then she had an idea. "You know what?" she suggested. "Why don't we form a study group or something? *On-yeh-dee* can tutor us in math, *A-mer* can help with French, and you all can assist with the rest of the subjects, especially the native languages. I probably won't be of much help to you guys, though, except maybe in English grammar. But, trust me, you are already good in English." She looked expectantly at the four girls. "So? *Whaddya* say? Can we form a study group?"

The girls readily agreed. They arranged to meet in the Crystal House lobby to utilize the rest of the recreation time for their French assignment.

Once they were done, the Crystal House girls rushed off to go fetch water, while Carlotta, Onyedi, and Emeh headed toward Sapphire House.

"Thanks *A-mer,* that wasn't bad at all," Carlotta said as they walked around the Mystical Mangy. She kicked a pebble, feeling a little lighter than she felt earlier, now that the French homework was out of the way.

Emeh beamed. "It's my pleasure."

"Thanks," Onyedi said. She glanced briefly at Emeh then looked away.

"You are welcome," Emeh replied, smiling largely at Carlotta and avoiding looking at Onyedi. "Maybe we can revise the lesson Snipes taught in class today."

Carlotta noticed Emeh was gaping and smiling, as if fascinated by the shape of her nose or something. Blood rose to her cheeks. Quickly, she turned the other way and almost bumped into a group of JS3 students standing around the walkway of Sapphire House.

"Feddie Girl! Look where you're going. Or are you blind?" one of the JS3 girls snapped.

"*Gbe se!*" another remarked.

"Sorry," Emeh said quickly.

"*Ehwo!* See me see trouble oh!" the first JS3 student exclaimed, and eyed Emeh in an insolent manner. "Since when did you become her mouth piece?"

Emeh rushed on before Carlotta could throw in a word, "She didn't do it on purpose. Sorry." When the girl turned away, Emeh added under her breath so that only Carlotta and Onyedi could hear, "Maybe you should stop blocking the way. *Vous êtes très gros.*" You are very fat.

The older student heard. "*Excuse-moi?* Are you talking to me?" she challenged Emeh.

"No!"

They quickly moved out of reach of the JS3 students.

"*Yeh!* I almost entered trouble," Emeh said in a small voice.

"You got that right," Carlotta replied. "You shouldn't go picking on older students, *A-mer.*"

Emeh shrugged. "So, what about the maths revision?"

Carlotta studied Emeh's face. She realized Emeh was embarrassed to admit she wasn't good in math, and decided to save her further discomfort. "Tell you what?" she asked in a bright voice, "Why don't we all go fetch our water then meet in the house lobby before dinner? Since *Sleeping Beauty* won't let us have a group study session during night prep, we *oughta* get together sometime before then. Right?"

Onyedi nodded.

"*Sleeping Beauty?* That's very funny." Emeh laughed more from gratitude at Carlotta's tactfulness than from humor. "Onyedi, you're in Sapphire-One? Yes? Carlotta and I will call you when we are ready. Let me go and tell Ossie and Amanda, in case if they want to join us." Emeh turned around and skipped back the way they had come.

Carlotta watched Emeh disappear around the Mystical Mangy. It was rumored the leaves of the tree never fell off no matter how hard it rained or how windy it became. A chill ran down her spine. She recalled the stories about the fruit of the tree never turning yellow—they remained green all year round. When ingested, they were purported to cause minor hallucinations, much like what one would expect from smoking one of Slinky Sam's weed concoctions.

Won't my parents just love to know we don't need the likes of Slinky Sam to get high around here? Reefers made out of green mangoes—now, there's a huge joke.

Carlotta stared fixedly at the mysterious tree, wondering how it had survived for so long. The branches stood proud and tall, their bright green leaves glinting ominously in the evening sun. She shivered, and became mesmerized by the mysterious tree.

"Cold?"

Carlotta snapped out of her reverie and turned to face Onyedi. "No, I was just—" Suddenly, her mouth went dry. They were alone. *At last!*

Onyedi gazed directly into Carlotta's eyes.

Carlotta held the gaze—senses sharpening, spell of the Mystical Mangy forgotten. She noticed the way the bridge between Onyedi's eyes sloped to form her nose. She took in the twin arcs of her brows and the thin lines of her lips. She observed the way the black eyes hinted at a savvy brain and kind disposition.

Carlotta took a deep breath and swallowed.

Onyedi shrugged and continued on the way to Sapphire House.

Carlotta went after her.

❋ ❋ ❋

When Carlotta returned to Sapphire-Six fifteen minutes later, she realized Zika had already filled their buckets and plastic containers with water and was now on the other side of the dormitory, chatting and laughing with Nneka and Shade.

"Hi, girls!" Carlotta called to the SS2 students. "How's it going?"

"*Ehn?* See this Feddie Girl oh!" the bespectacled, SS1 student intoned in an incredulous voice, jumping to a sitting position on her bed. "She's getting quite *chumsy* with senior girls." She clapped her hands twice and announced to no one in particular, "Can you imagine her?"

"No-no, Maryanne, don't start with my bunkie," Zika warned.

"Oh... Hmm..." Maryanne said with eyebrows raised, dragging her words in a manner pregnant with meaning. "*Na wa* for some of us oh!"

Zika pretended not to notice. She called to Carlotta, "Bunkie, don't mind them *joor*. Just put down your bag and rest. There's Coke in my locker if you are thirsty. Later, you can gist me about what happened in class today."

Maryanne sneered and rolled her eyes. "Zika, *o kwa* serious bunkie pampering you're displaying to the whole dorm. Wonders shall never end!"

"Maryanne, please hold your own there!" Zika didn't sound too pleased.

"Hmm, *o di kwa* so risky." Nneka sided with the bespectacled Maryanne.

Carlotta ignored the taunts of the senior students. It irked them that she and Zika were quite close as bunkmates—a rare relationship between an SS2 student and a JS1 *newbie*. She put down her school bag and poured a cup of Coke.

Bless Senior Zicker's heart. Carlotta was relieved she didn't have to fetch and carry buckets of water up and down the long Sapphire House hallway. She sighed and checked her wristwatch. It was barely 6:45 PM. She climbed up her bunk, and took out five snack-size bars of chocolate and a box of chewy chocolate-chip cookies she planned to share with her study group members, from her locker. She felt Maryanne's eyes on her as she dumped the loot on Zika's bed.

"Would you like a cookie, Senior Maryanne?" Carlotta asked, offering the box of cookies.

"Thank you." Maryanne grabbed a cookie from the box. She examined it closely before plunging it into her mouth. She snatched two more.

Carlotta took the box over to the other side of the dormitory and offered some to Zika and the others. Zika declined with a slow shake of her head but Nneka and Shade accepted two cookies each.

"Where's Uche?" Carlotta asked, looking around the dormitory. "And Sandra?" she added, after making sure the girl was nowhere in sight. "They don't seem to be in here, anywhere."

Zika's eyes narrowed. She threw a cautioning glance at Carlotta.

"They're outside fetching water," Nneka replied carelessly. "At least, that's what they're supposed to be doing."

"Shouldn't you girls go find out if they need help?" Zika suggested. "Senior girls always monopolize the line at the taps and sometimes, junior girls don't get a chance to fetch their water. But I'm sure you already know that." The derision in her voice was discernible.

Shade batted her eyelids. "How else will my bunkie learn a common thing like fetching water if I have to do it by myself?"

"Please, tell me oh," Nneka agreed, and rolled her eyes. "Ju-girls *gats* to learn how to fetch *warrer*." She'd used the FGGC Uddah short term for junior girls—Ju-girls.

"Yes oh! They *berrer*," Shade agreed. "I *pirry* my bunkie's condition if she fails to return here with my buckets of *warrer*." She assumed a condescending tone. "She shall be so done for!"

"How come you girls don't have any heart?" Zika admonished. "You always expect your bunkies to serve you from head to toe, morning till night. Helping them fetch *your* own water is the least you can do to show gratitude for all their hard work."

Shade spewed forth something long and incomprehensible in reply—she sounded really pissed. Nneka was also on the defensive. But Zika wouldn't back down. Before long, Bisi, Anita, and two SS1 students including Maryanne, joined in the argument.

Carlotta did not stay to hear the rest of the banter, for just then, Emeh poked her head through the door.

Not bothering to say goodbye to the arguing senior girls, Carlotta just loaded her snacks into her backpack and left the dormitory, thankful that Zika was her bunkmate. *Had I been bunking Senior Necker or Senior Shah-day, I would really be in for it.*

In the Sapphire House Lobby, Carlotta was impressed by how Onyedi simplified the strategic steps to algebraic solutions that Snipes had introduced that morning. Despite her taciturn habits, the nerd actually proved to be an excellent math tutor. She guided the four girls through the practice sums in the textbook till they got the hang of it.

By the time the bell signaling suppertime rang, Carlotta was quite confident she could handle the first and second stages of algebra on her own.

❋ ❋ ❋

The next morning, while performing her morning duty, Carlotta had a minor altercation with the dormitory prefect of Sapphire-One over a windowpane she failed to shine to perfection. The louver looked like someone had poured a cup of white booze on it and maliciously left it to dry into a scaly crust.

At FGGC Uddah, *booze* was slang for a sweetened mixture of garri and water, prepared as a snack. When laced with a dash of milk, it became *white booze.*

Carlotta refused to tackle the mess, insisting that whoever was responsible for creating it should be the one to clean it up. The cheeky attitude had bought her twenty minutes of "Kneel down there and fly your hands" from the Sapphire-One dormitory prefect.

After all said and done, Carlotta was forced into cleaning-up the mess, and she also ended-up missing her breakfast. But the last straw came when the dormitory prefect said, "See Chidi Anayo, the house prefect, for your punishment this afternoon."

The injustice of it all! Carlotta fumed. She was truly beginning to learn just how much power the dormitory prefects wielded.

That afternoon, Carlotta forgot to report to Chidi.

❋ ❋ ❋

On her way out of the dining hall later in the evening, Carlotta felt a hand on her arm. She turned.

"She likes you," Onyedi said in a matter-of-fact way.

"Who?" Carlotta stopped walking. "What do you mean?" In the semi-darkness, she barely made out the expression on Onyedi's face. The sky above them was dark and deeply speckled with tiny white dots. The only light came from the dining hall behind them, and the houses in front of them. The last groups of girls to leave the dining hall were now walking ahead, their shadows gliding along like elongated black balloons.

They were alone. Carlotta's stomach flipped.

Onyedi did not say anything else at first. They moved away from the dining hall, aiming for Sapphire House.

"Emeh," Onyedi finally said. She stopped walking and stared at her feet. "She obviously likes you."

"Oh, come on." Carlotta jabbed a playful hand at Onyedi's shoulder. She hesitated, uncertain. The chirping of insects filled the lengthening silence. Finally, she said, "*A-mer* is just being nice. Besides, I'd rather be friends with someone else."

Onyedi looked up. There was a wary expression in her eyes. "I know."

"Really?" Carlotta teased. "Sometimes, I just toy with the idea of smacking you over the head or something, just to make you react."

Onyedi nodded and giggled.

Carlotta laughed, too. Onyedi had a nice way of laughing, she noticed. She also had dimples that graced her cheeks each time she smiled. *There's something about her that makes me feel warm and happy inside.*

They started walking again.

Carlotta felt like singing. She wanted to imitate the happy sounds of the night bugs going about their business in the dark grass. She wanted to soar high in the sky and spew forth her happiness.

Carlotta held out a hand. "Friends?" Her eyes searched Onyedi's face. Her heart beat wildly. "Best friends?"

Onyedi held Carlotta's gaze for a long moment. Then her tiny teeth flashed and she placed her fingers in Carlotta's open hand. "Best friends," she whispered.

Carlotta's chest tightened, and her throat constricted. She felt like nothing she'd ever done before mattered anymore. All she cared about now was being a good friend to Onyedi. A sob escaped her lips and tears rolled down her eyes. She remembered beating-up two little kids the year before and her heart melted with remorse. She was extremely sorry. Suddenly, she started to cry.

"It's okay," Onyedi whispered.

"Thanks," Carlotta wanted to say, but couldn't stop sobbing. She felt Onyedi's hand on her shoulder and tried to control herself. She wished she hadn't done all those cruel things. She regretted ever saying mean things to her parents. She was sorry for smoking cigarettes and marijuana, and for getting involved with Slinky Sam and the likes of him.

Carlotta felt so ashamed of herself, her past, and her questionable character and wished they would somehow vanish. She wanted the slate wiped clean so she could start over.

"Cheer up," Onyedi consoled, patting her on the back.

"There are some things you should know about me," Carlotta started in a voice that was wet with tears.

Onyedi reached out and wiped Carlotta's tears with her palms. She placed a finger on Carlotta's lips to silence her. "I already know," she said quietly.

"But that's not possible. You can't know much about me, not about my past, my family—" Carlotta stopped. She cast Onyedi a questioning look. "You mean you know? Everything?"

Onyedi's eyes were unblinking. She nodded, slowly, in a meaningful way. "My mother," she explained, still nodding.

"Oh—" Carlotta suddenly looked doubtful. Her shoulders sagged. She turned away. "In that case, I'll totally understand if you don't want to be friends anymore," she said in a small voice.

Onyedi bit her lip and stood still for a moment. Then she reached out and put her arms around Carlotta's neck. "Best friends, remember?"

Carlotta sighed, and hugged her. Tears rolled down her eyes and formed a wet patch against the side of Onyedi's face and neck. "Thanks," she said, her voice coming out in a grateful whisper. She was so full of sorrow and gratitude that she thought her heart would break in two. She closed her eyes and pushed the bad memories away as she hugged Onyedi tight.

"Thanks. Thank you, so much," Carlotta's voice shook with emotion. "I promise to— To be good, to be your best friend, for ever." Her heart drummed wildly in her chest. She was so sad and happy at the same time. Above all, she was relieved.

Finally, Carlotta had found someone who really cared about who she was, what she was, and what she made of her life. She didn't want to let go of Onyedi; she didn't want to be alone anymore. She looked into Onyedi's face.

Onyedi was crying, too. She hugged Carlotta tighter.

Time stood still for a moment.

Then they were rudely interrupted. "Feddie Girl! Come here!"

Carlotta started. She stepped back from Onyedi's arms.

Chidi Anayo was standing on the Sapphire House pavement, a sneering look on her face.

Holy shit! I was supposed to see her for a punishment this afternoon. I totally forgot! Carlotta imagined it was too late to pull off one of the zapping methods she'd learned from the JS2 students in her dormitory. They were standing a good distance away from the nearest shrub that looked like it could support full-body hiding. Besides, they just couldn't take-off and run. Chidi already knew who they were.

Oh, what the heck! Carlotta looked at Onyedi and said goodbye without using words. Wiping her eyes and draining her face of emotions, she steeled her nerves and went to find out what the Sapphire House prefect wanted.

"Bring your teddy bear with you," Chidi commanded.

Carlotta turned pale. She stopped and looked back. Onyedi was still standing where she left her, staring at her feet. Carlotta felt anger rise in her chest as she turned to face Chidi. Her eyes hardened, her jaw tightened.

"Leave her alone. It's me you want, right?" Carlotta darted up to Chidi. "She hasn't done anything to you. Please, just let her go."

Chidi ignored Carlotta and looked instead at Onyedi. "Come here," she snapped. "I know who you are, so don't bother zapping."

Carlotta watched as Onyedi walked over. She looked calm and her face was passive.

"Yes, Senior Chidi?" Onyedi asked in an even tone.

Chidi's lips curled maliciously upward, the expression in her eyes was unreadable. "What were you doing out there when you're supposed to be in class for prep?"

Onyedi shook her head. "Not prep time yet." Her voice was low and neutral.

"Please, just let her go," Carlotta insisted. "She hasn't done anything wrong."

Chidi turned black, coal-like eyes on Carlotta. Her face seemed to darken as she said, "Feddie Girl, you still have a lot to learn about this school. Most importantly, you need to learn how to address senior students and prefects. I will not tolerate students with your kind of attitude in my house." She eyed Carlotta, her eyes full of venom. "You failed to show-up for your punishment this afternoon. Go and wait for me in my corner. You are so done for."

Anger broiled with hatred in Carlotta's eyes. "And who the hell do you think you are?" She raised a fist and advanced on Chidi. "How dare—"

Carlotta felt a restricting hand on her arm and turned her head. Onyedi was looking at her, imploring without speaking. Carlotta's arm dropped to her side. She let out a heavy breath and took a step back.

"Glad to see that one of you have got brains in her thick skull." Chidi gave a ferocious chuckle and shook her head. "You!" she ordered Onyedi. "Go straight to your classroom. Start running!"

When Onyedi was beyond the Sapphire House walkway, and out of earshot, Chidi moved close to Carlotta and said in a low dangerous voice, "As for you, just go and take your position in my corner." Her black eyes bored into Carlotta's blue ones, wrathful and intimidating. "I will so deal with you. When I'm done, you will learn by force the meanings of respect and humility." She eyed Carlotta. "Because you are a Feddie Girl from America, you think you can behave the way you want here?"

"You wish," Carlotta hissed. Unflinching, she held Chidi's gaze and stood her ground. All the hatred and loathing she had for the house prefect solidified her eyes into dark-blue pebbles.

"I see you like being very disrespectful." Chidi sneered. "I hope you are also made of stone 'cause you will be kneeling down and flying your hands in my corner until senior prep-over."

Carlotta's fist itched to strike against Chidi's jaw, knock the domineering expression off her face, and probably dislodge one of her teeth in the process. But she remembered Onyedi's silent warning and stood still. She locked eyes with Chidi. *You may break my body, but you will never break my spirit.*

Finally, Carlotta tore her eyes away and marched past Chidi, making for the Sapphire House double doors. *Here's to all junior girls who find oppression in the hands of—*

Abruptly, Carlotta stopped and looked back. Then opened her mouth to ask.

"Sapphire-Three," Chidi supplied without turning her head. "Last corner on your right. Now, get lost!"

Chapter 9
Boarding Life At FGGC Uddah

ichard was surprised to discover he had no phone messages. He had tried calling Shelley countless times the week before, and had left a thousand voice messages requesting that she return his call so they could talk. She never took his calls. She didn't call him back.

He was getting impatient. He thought letting her have her space for one week would be sufficient to bring her back to her senses. So far, it wasn't working.

Richard decided to keep waiting. He needed Shelley back on his side so he could move back home. *A divorce at this time will completely ruin me.*

As each silent day went by, it began to dawn on him that Shelley really meant business.

Richard sighed. *I did nothing wrong. I merely invited my personal assistant home for an innocent nightcap. When did that become a crime?* How was he to know Maria would leave some kind of evidence behind—intentionally or not? How was he to know his wife would find the evidence and put two and two together? At least Shelley didn't know the hairbrush actually belonged to Maria. *Come to think of it, Shelley doesn't know I have a hot female for a personal assistant.*

Richard let himself into his hotel room while thinking he ought to give Shelley another week to come to terms with her unwarranted jealousy. If by the end of the week she did not make contact, he will throw in the towel and get himself an apartment or condo. *Then, I will file the papers for an official separation, something I should have done a long time ago. Soon Maria can have me all to herself.*

Sadly, Richard shook his head and ran a hand through his hair. He'd rather not have a divorce, but Shelley gave him no choice—his hands were tied.

✻ ✻ ✻

*O*t the end of her first month at FGGC Uddah, Carlotta sported an Italian hairstyle, as suggested by Zika, Nneka, and Shade who had accompanied her to the school's hair salon. Although Carlotta preferred long hair, she couldn't help but admit the short Italian style looked quite good on her. Her study group members thought it was very becoming.

Short hair not withstanding, Carlotta learned a lot about FGGC Uddah and the way the boarding school system functioned. She mastered the art of waking up at the crack of dawn, when the rising bell went off, and dealing with the activities of a new school day. She now understood that the most important procedure of the day was that of getting ready for school in the morning, and after several coach sessions from Zika, Carlotta learned to use her time effectively.

When the rising bell goes off, she would snap out of sleep, unlock her overhead locker and pull out toothpaste, toothbrush, and plastic cup. She would then jump down from her bunk without disturbing her bunkmate who would still be asleep, and fill the plastic cup with water. She would squeeze the right amount of paste on her toothbrush, recap the tube, and march to the bathroom sinks laden with the loaded brush and cup of water.

She would brush her teeth, reserve a turn at the bathroom stalls, return quickly to the dormitory and change into her bath towel, place sponge and wash cloth into her bucket of water, and pick up her soap dish. She would carry the bucket of water to the bathroom and bathe quickly. Then return to the dormitory at top speed and dress rapidly in her school uniform.

She would say, "Good morning," to her bunkmate who'd just be awakening, and return her toiletries to her overhead locker. She would retrieve her snacks and any other items needed for the rest of the morning and make her bed impeccably.

Finally, she would pick up her school bag and wet towel, say, "Goodbye," to her bunkmate, and get the heck out of the dormitory as fast as her legs could carry her, before the prefect barked "Leave the dormitory!" simultaneously with the ringing bell.

Carlotta knew that to deviate from the procedure meant trouble. She had gotten in several squabbles with Anita, her dormitory prefect, each time she thought she could outsmart the system or save time by skipping one or two steps. Problem was, something always went wrong, which ended up escalating into much bigger problems.

Apart from her first morning when she had fallen off her bunk and squashed toothpaste all over her bunkmate's locker, Carlotta had tried deviating from the proved procedure and had landed herself into several unfortunate incidents as a result.

There was the time when she thought she would take a bath before brushing her teeth. By the time she was bathed and dressed and ready to go brush her teeth, the SS1 students responsible for cleaning the bathroom sinks as their morning duties had already begun their work and wouldn't let her use the sinks—no matter how much she pleaded. She had ended-up brushing her teeth behind the dormitories. But, that was a big mistake because she had been discovered and was reported to the house prefect, who in turn had meted out a befitting punishment for the crime. Chidi had ordered Carlotta to clean the gutters in the tap area during breakfast. However, Zika had intervened and managed to extricate a pardon for her bunkmate.

Another incident occurred when Carlotta decided to make her bed first before taking a bath and getting dressed. The irony was after spending precious time making the bed, she kept remembering certain things she needed from her locker and had to climb back on the already made bed to retrieve them. And to make matters worse, she had foolishly remade the bed each time she disturbed it. By the time she was ready to go take a bath, the senior girls had risen and were all over the place. Had Zika not intervened and snuck her into an empty bathroom stall before the SS1 girl who was supposed to use it arrived, Carlotta would never had bathed and dressed in time to leave the dormitory just one minute after the bell for morning duty went off. Still, Anita had almost punished her for tardiness, but Zika had pleaded and gotten her off the hook as usual.

Apart from these few incidents, Carlotta was adapting nicely to the strict rigors of boarding school life. It's not as if she really had a choice. Survival in a boarding school like FGGC Uddah required serious and mandatory discipline—even from the most self-willed or headstrong of students.

The weekends were a bit less regulated than the school days. Apart from the rising bell, dining times, night prep, and lights out, the students were pretty much allowed to do as they wished on Saturdays and Sundays. Fun activities such as Visiting Day, social nights, and school club functions were reserved for the weekends. Some dreary functions also took place on the weekends. Preeminent among these were the Saturday morning inspections and the once-a-month Manual Labor.

No matter how hectic a weekend was going to be, it still wasn't mandatory to get up on the sound of the rising bell on these days. Saturday morning duties were done after breakfast, so there wasn't really any need to get up at the crack of dawn.

Breakfast on Sunday was served at 10:00 AM so most students just slept in late on those days.

Just a few weeks into boarding life at FGGC Uddah, Carlotta realized that one mistake had a way of producing repercussions that escalated and lasted the whole day, or even several days if one were unlucky.

Getting punished for not leaving the dormitory on time in the morning meant arriving late or not showing up at all at one's place of morning duty. This in turn leads to being punished by the prefect on-duty and punishments like these were tackled after lunch.

Because of serving duty punishments, one might fail to be present for the siesta inspection. This leads to another punishment from the dormitory prefect that is due after siesta, causing one to be absent from afternoon prep.

Not being in class for prep roll call, results to punishment from the prep prefects. If one were lucky, the duration of the prep punishments would be contained within the recreation or miscellaneous periods.

However, in an unlucky situation, which was usually the case, the prep punishment draws out till dinnertime, whereby one falls to either get one's laundry done, or fetch one's water for the following day, or both. This dereliction then gets one in trouble with one's bunkmate, who then demands that one should stay up after lights out and beg for extra buckets of water from other students.

Missing the lights out inspection then results to another round of punishment that is servable the next day. Also, one could get punished for going to class in dirty uniforms because of the inability to get the laundry done the day before.

The best way for junior students to stay out of trouble, therefore, was by learning to get things done as efficiently as possible within the allotted time. Or by perfecting one's zapping ability— methods of which included, hiding in the bush, taking-off at top speed when an unfamiliar senior girl is calling for junior students, sneaking out of mass-punishments without detection, sucking-up to influential senior girls or prefects, and plainly pretending to be asthmatic, anemic, or prone to migraines. Another effective way, as in Carlotta's case, was having a nice bunkmate who is willing to get one out of sticky situations whenever possible.

Fate had dealt Carlotta an incredible stroke of good fortune when she was paired with Zika as a bunkmate. Every week, she watched in horror as Anita and other senior students, for one reason or the other, sent their bunkmates and other junior girls on errands and punished them for every little mishap.

"Kneel down there and fly your hands," the senior girls would command.

To make the words have more impact, many senior students would say, "Decrease your height immediately."

To be even more creative, some senior girls would go the extra step. "Just take your position!" Or, "Show me your bald spot!"

And the witchy senior girls could always be trusted to go overboard with it. "Kiss the floor with your knees, extend your arms at right-angles, hide your eyeballs, and stick-out your tongue!"

The prefects would usually add some kind of manual punishment as well. "Go and sweep three classrooms in the SS3 Block," they'd order, after making a culprit kneel on the hard cold floor for more than an hour.

Carlotta recalled several occasions when Zika, having not been successful in convincing Anita to let Carlotta off a well-deserved punishment, had actually taken it upon herself to perform Carlotta's morning duty, so as to prevent Carlotta from getting into further trouble with the Sapphire-One dormitory prefect.

Also, Zika would always accompany Carlotta to the taps to fetch their water and when indisposed would delegate a JS2 or JS3 student the responsibility of making sure Carlotta got water from the taps. Often times, Zika would give her bunkmate a break by having another junior student fetch the water entirely.

Sandra and Uche, on the other hand, rarely enjoyed this kind of luxury from their bunkmates.

In effect, Carlotta came to rely more and more on Zika's defense and assistance, and they became very good friends.

The role of being a junior girl, though underrated, was one of the toughest at FGGC Uddah. Junior girls were expected to do all the necessary work for their bunkmates, including fetching water, making beds, doing laundry, cleaning sandals, and generally being at their bunkmates' service and making life easy for them.

For this reason, JS1 students usually bunked SS2 students, since they were relatively new to the boarding school life and could be patiently grounded-in by the SS2 students.

SS3 students, on the other hand, were always bunked by JS2 students. In this case, SS3 was an examination class, and the students in this grade were expected to be preparing for their West African Senior School Certificate Examination (WASSCE) and the standardized tests from the National Examination Council (NECO). SS3 students, therefore, had no time to take care of themselves or train junior students to do them the honors.

It therefore follows that SS3 students at FGGC Uddah expected everything to be done for them by their bunkmates and gave very little in return. Since the JS2 students had already been well-grounded in matters of bunkmate care-giving from their experiences the year before, they usually tackled this role of dealing with selfish and demanding SS3 students with expertise.

JS3 students always bunked SS1 students. JS3, like SS3, was an examination class and students in this set were also required to spend time studying for their junior level examinations. Since there was only a class difference between JS3 and SS1, the JS3 students were not mandated or required to do anything at all for their SS1 bunkmates.

This is not to say that there was always bunkmate harmony between these groups of students. Sometimes, the very fact that an SS1 girl, though a senior student, had no authority over her

JS3 bunkmate, would be the reason for a fall-out between bunk-mates in this category.

In addition to their bunkmate duties, junior girls were also expected to be at the service of any qualified senior girl who requested it. By default, at FGGC Uddah, a senior student had general authority over any student that was more than one class level below them. This meant that an SS1 student only had authority over the JS1 and JS2 students, and so on with SS2 and SS3.

The unusual situation whereby SS3 girls regarded SS1 girls as junior students may also arise. These occasions, though rare, were due to the more than one class difference between SS3 and SS1.

On the other hand, although JS3 students were more than one class removed from JS1 students, they had no authority over the younger students. This fact was because JS3 and JS1 were both junior classes, and students in this group had no authority or say, whatsoever, in the rulings of boarding life.

Carlotta couldn't have cared less about the lack of jurisdiction of JS3 students over JS1 girls. In her opinion, the fewer the sets of students she had to respect and obey, the better.

Paramount to all positions of authority in boarding life at FGGC Uddah was the school bell. Its ringing was viewed as the highest level of discipline and authority that had to be obeyed at all times. The bell dictated when to wake up, eat, study, hang out, relax, and go to bed.

Therefore, life at FGGC Uddah was governed largely by the metallic sound of the school bell, which had no sympathy for students—prefects and SS3 girls included. Not to obey the summons of the school bell could result in punishment for an SS3 student from a prefect—WASSCE/NECO examinations or not.

The activities of boarding life relied heavily on the chiming of the bell. As a result, whoever wielded the bell had the highest position of authority. Ironically, this glorified responsibility was customarily bestowed on an SS1 student, with an SS3 prefect acting as the assistant bell bearer.

The only time the bell bearer relinquishes the bell to a prefect was during meal times. At these times, the school bell is handed over to the dining hall prefect, who then conducts the dining process with it. Afterward, the bell is solemnly returned to the Honored School Bell Bearer. The only other situation where the bell bearer relinquishes the school bell is when she is sick. Otherwise, nobody else is granted the right to wield the FGGC Uddah school bell.

Why an SS1 student had to be made the Honored School Bell Bearer, was totally lost on Carlotta. She imagined that Senior Kemi, the Honored School Bell Bearer for the school year, must be a very organized student, who either never slept or slept little. Senior Kemi was basically the last student to go to bed at night and the first to get up in the morning—even on weekends.

On several occasions, Carlotta couldn't help thinking how hilarious it would be if the honored school bell bearer somehow lost her mettle and rang the rising bell at 2:00 AM! *The whole school will totally go topsy-turvy, and I, for one, would love to see the horrific look that would be on Senior Chee-dee's witchy face.*

It was the custom at FGGC Uddah for senior students to relegate errands to junior girls if they so desire. Sometimes the senior girls would just sit in their corners and yell, "I need a junior girl!" whereupon, every student in the dormitory who is at least two classes below that senior girl, would be required to respond to the call. The senior girl would then choose a junior student from the lot to attend to the errand and dismiss the others.

When the call goes, "I need a ju-girl—last one to get here!" it means the last junior girl to rush to the caller will automatically attend to the caller's needs.

Carlotta's all-time favorite was Senior Bisi, the SS3 student in her dormitory that always called, "A ju-girl!" instead of the standard five-word *I need a junior girl* request.

Also, sometimes, Anita would just yell, "Who wants to go on my errand?" *Yeah, right! We all are totally dying to attend to your every need, Senior Anita.*

Fortunately for her, Carlotta was almost never chosen to go on an errand, even if there were no other JS1 or JS2 student in the dormitory. Being a Feddie Girl, Carlotta realized, had its own advantages if one were willing to be nice to others.

Most senior girls would rather send a JS3 student to attend to a trivial issue than send Carlotta. A good reason was Carlotta was a total disaster with Nigerian native names.

Another reason was, more often than not, the senior girls had to make not less than two repetitions of their request before Carlotta could understand exactly what they wanted.

Exchanges of this type were always accompanied by serious laughter from the other girls, who would tease their mates for not being fluent enough in the English language to make a Feddie Girl understand their intent.

The same happens the other way round. Many of the students had to make Carlotta repeat everything she said at least twice, before they were able to comprehend.

Sometimes, mischievous senior students would send Carlotta to their friends in other houses, on a prank-errand, just so they could get later feedback on how their friends fared with her American accent. Carlotta could usually tell these prank-errands from the real ones because another junior girl was always delegated to accompany her and provide details on the whole encounter.

Also, for these pranks, the senior students always request specifically for her by saying, "Feddie Girl, come here," instead of just making the standard call for a junior girl.

However, those pranks were played only when Zika was not around. The Sapphire House students knew that Zika would never allow her bunkmate to go on prank-errands if she could help it.

Nevertheless, Carlotta learned to always do what she was told, so as not to get herself in trouble with prefects or senior girls alike. After all, Zika could not follow her everywhere. Carlotta also knew that not obeying the orders of a qualified senior student usually resulted in cruel punishment for junior girls.

In addition to Zika always coming to her bunkmate's aid, the other students loved her and adored her American accent. They were always happy to assist her in any way they could. Carlotta worked hard at maintaining a very sweet disposition, and had a way of making everyone feel at ease in her presence. This attitude, in turn, earned her the trust and friendship of her dormitory girls.

In effect, one could say that Carlotta had it easier than most other junior girls at FGGC Uddah. Everyone was friendly to her.

Everyone, that is, except Chidi and Sandra.

The Sapphire House prefect never passed up an opportunity to taunt and humiliate Carlotta, and often resorted to punishing her for the smallest offences. Most of the time, Zika intervened and successfully got Carlotta off the hook for trivial issues. But occasionally, out of pure malice, Chidi would not indulge Zika and would resort to meting out arduous punishments for Carlotta's smallest offences.

Sandra, on the other hand, just concentrated on giving Carlotta a hard time. She ridiculed Carlotta, called her names behind her back, and told tall tales about her family and background to her friends and classmates. Twice, Carlotta almost lost her temper with Sandra, but fortunately, Onyedi had always been there to calm her down.

Carlotta didn't know what she would have done without Onyedi. Though two years younger, Onyedi was mentally mature for her age. Carlotta met Onyedi's mother on several occasions, and made plans to visit Onyedi's home during the school Outing Day.

As the days went by, Carlotta became very close to Onyedi, and they grew attached to one another. Not only did they do almost everything together, they also went everywhere together. They were like two halves of the same bean. Carlotta loved and trusted Onyedi and always sought her opinion on all matters.

If there were a complex situation she couldn't deal with on her own, Carlotta would go to Zika for assistance but only if

Onyedi agreed it was wise to do so.

Onyedi never judged Carlotta on her past or race, and had a special ability to instill a sense of tranquility and contentment within her best friend.

In time, Carlotta began to understand the difference between friendships like the one she had with Sasha and the one she enjoyed with Onyedi. While Sasha was only interested in material things and saw Carlotta as an accomplice in obtaining such things, Onyedi, on the other hand, gave a deeper and soul-searching meaning to friendship. She was quiet, peaceful, kind, honest, patient, and enduring. She was a true friend indeed, both to Carlotta and to other members of their study group—including Emeh.

At first, Emeh had been jealous and miffed that Carlotta preferred to spend time alone with Onyedi than with her. She had sulked for a few days and was quite curt with Onyedi. But, after a while, she got over her disappointment and contented herself with just being a distant friend and a member of the study group.

Ossie and Amanda, on the other hand, did not seem to mind at all that Carlotta spent more time with Onyedi than she did with the rest of them. They appeared to take the special bond between the two in their stride.

Carlotta was thankful she had her study group members. She counted herself lucky to have Zika as a bunkmate. Above all, she regarded the friendship she had with Onyedi as the best thing that had ever happened to her.

Chapter 10
Jika & Anita

Her arm reached over to explore the side of the bed before Shelley fully awoke. She was alone. Then it came crashing back.

Richard is gone...

Sharp pangs of betrayal sliced through her heart. But underneath all the pain was something else. A feeling she couldn't ignore. It seeped through the bed covers and chilled her bones.

Loneliness...

Shelley shut her eyes and tried to bury the feeling deep inside.

✻ ✻ ✻

After inspection on Saturday morning, Carlotta was on her way to her classroom to study with Onyedi when Joke ran up to them. She took Carlotta aside and whispered, "Grace is looking for you. She said that you should please come to the Sapphire House taps, right now. It's very urgent."

Carlotta looked concerned. Grace was one of her favorite girls in the dormitory. Besides, Carlotta had real respect for the JS2 and JS3 students in Sapphire-Six.

"Is she in some kind of trouble?" Carlotta asked.

"I don't know." Joke replied. "Please just follow me."

Nona David

Carlotta bade Onyedi farewell and promised to catch up with her later. Then she followed Joke down the winding path toward the dormitories.

Back at the Sapphire-House tap area, a panic-stricken Grace met with them. "Thank God you came," she said to Carlotta. "I want you to help me. Please."

Carlotta studied Grace. The girl had tears in her eyes and looked as though she were ready to bawl her heart out. "Hey, *whatsa* matter?" Why do you look so hysterical?"

Grace swallowed before speaking. "I think I've entered trouble. I broke my bunkie's bucket." She began to sob.

"*Awww,* that sucks." Carlotta's heart went out to Grace and she placed a consoling hand on her shoulder. "Anything I can do? How can I help?" The girl looked miserable and her pathetic sobbing could have extricated sympathy from any heart—even those made of stone.

Grace wiped the tears from her face. "Please, do you think you can come with me to my bunkie's corner? I want you to tell her you're the one who broke her bucket." Grace heaved and a fresh bout of tears rolled down her cheeks.

"You're totally kidding me, right?" Carlotta replied, sounding a little addled. This was yet the craziest favor the two JS2 students had asked of her. "Why would I *wanna* do that?"

Before answering, Grace produced what was formerly a gray bucket that now looked like five plastic shards joined together at the base. She placed the plastic disaster on the ground in front of Carlotta. "If my bunkie finds out I was the one who broke her bucket, she will so deal with me."

"You got that right," Carlotta said, imagining the look on Anita's face when she sees the fate her favorite bucket had undergone. She poked the ruined bucket with the toe of her fluffy pink flip-flop and raised an eyebrow. "This definitely looks like someone went over it with a steam roller."

Grace sniffed and wiped her eyes. "The thing is that my bunkie warned me the last time when I misplaced her jerry can.

214

If she sees this bucket, I will be so done for. Please now, you have to help me."

"Yeah, that's all good for you, but what about me?" Carlotta pointed an index finger at her heart. "Don't you think I'll also get into serious trouble with Senior Anita if I admit to breaking her bucket for no good reason?" She crossed her arms over her chest. "Well?"

Joke had an idea. Her voice took on a pleading note. "Just tell Senior Anita you were helping Grace carry the bucket of water then you slipped and fell and the bucket broke."

Carlotta chuckled. "Yeah right, like anyone's actually *gonna* believe that." She saw the look on Joke's face and determined the JS2 students were quite serious. "And how do you suppose I'd get away with this?" she asked, wrinkling her nose with displeasure. "I really don't care to serve one of Senor Anita's punishments." Carlotta shrugged and rolled her eyes. "It seems like there really isn't much I can do to help you out. Sorry."

Joke cut in, "But you're forgetting that Senior Zika is your bunkie. You know she won't let anyone punish you."

"Yes oh," Grace added. "Your bunkie is always saving you from punishment in the dorm. Please, help me now." She sniffed and wiped more tears off her face.

Carlotta considered the JS2 students for a while, her mouth bunched-up to one side. "Oh, all right!" She picked-up the shattered bucket and stared dubiously at it. "I'll do it, but just this once. And if for some reason my bunkie fails to get me out of this mess, you're both so *gonna* owe me big time."

Grace let out a sigh of relief. "Okay, but don't even worry. Trust me, your bunkie *shakwall represent* you. Thank you for agreeing to do this."

Joke snickered. "You can't imagine the kind of *gbe se* that would obtain Grace if her bunkie finds out about this thing."

Carlotta got the message. "Hey, relax. I'm not *gonna* snitch on you two." She eyed the broken bucket again and couldn't stop herself from painting a mental picture of Anita's would-be shocked face.

The JS2 students drenched Carlotta's skirt then doused her legs and feet with water. They even added a few mud smudges on her face, knees, and calves for good measure. When they were done, Carlotta really did look like she'd had a nasty accident with a bucket of water.

Having considered her job done, Joke left Carlotta and Grace to it and went about her business.

The two girls made their way to Sapphire House, Grace struggling under the weight of a blue, medium-sized, plastic jerry can filled with water; Carlotta lugging the damaged, plastic bucket and trying to muster-up a look of sorrow and remorse.

They got to the double doors.

Why do I always let myself be talked into these situations? Carlotta wondered. Suddenly, she turned on Grace. "Wait a minute. How on earth did you manage to blow-up this bucket anyway?"

Now she knew she wasn't going to take the heat for the crime she committed, Grace had no compunction about telling Carlotta the truth. "My bunkie punished me for a tiny margarine smudge she found on her locker, and made me miss my food this morning," she said with a smirk.

Carlotta almost laughed out loud. "What a befitting revenge, huh? I don't blame you, I'd have totally done the same."

Ten seconds later, Carlotta, accompanied by Grace, marched bravely into Sapphire-Six and prepared to meet her fate.

❋ ❋ ❋

*A*nita took one look at the ruined mess in Carlotta's hands and shrieked, "What happened to my bucket?"

Carlotta held-on to the shreds of plastic with both hands, bowed her head, and summoned a remorseful attitude. "I'm sorry Senior Anita, I think I broke it." Her act was perfect. Anyone watching would actually think she was responsible for what happened to the bucket.

Anita was none the wiser. "You think?" she belted out, rearing up from her bed and springing to her feet. The multi-colored piece of cloth wrapped loosely around her body almost fell off but she caught it just in time and tucked the end firmly under her left arm. Lacey-white bra straps originated beneath the top of the wrapper and disappeared over her shoulders. Her long hair, which she had loosened from their corn-rows earlier that day, was puffed at the top and sticking out at the sides from her having lain on her back with her head on a pillow.

Anita looked Carlotta over. Her face clouded with irritation. "That bucket wasn't even mine, I borrowed it from Chinyelu at the beginning of term." She turned and addressed Grace, "Bunkie, why did you let her touch my bucket?"

Grace thought it best not to answer and, instead, busied herself with pushing the blue jerry can under the bunk and rear-ranging a few odds and ends while she was at it.

"I'm totally sorry—" Carlotta began.

Anita cut her off. "I don't need to hear your apology. You have to go and report yourself to the real owner of the bucket—Chinyelu Obiekwe in Emerald House."

Carlotta was aghast. Things weren't turning out as she hoped. She glanced at Grace, who shrugged and shook her head then promptly disappeared under the bunk again. Carlotta glanced sideways at Zika's bed. She gasped. *Shoot! Senior Zicker is not here. Why didn't we cover this major part of the plan before carrying it out? Oh boy! I'm totally screwed!*

Carlotta turned to Anita. "Um, Senior Anita? Is it okay if I do what you suggested later? I mean, I totally didn't know the bucket wasn't yours and I *sorta wanna* think about the whole *reporting myself* part for a while."

"See me see this Feddie Girl oh!" Anita clapped her hands twice in exaggerated surprise. Other senior girls started to take an interest in what was going on.

"Anita, what did the Feddie Girl do now?" Bisi asked.

"Can you imagine her?" Anita turned to lament to Bisi. "I borrowed a bucket from someone, and she broke it. Now she has come here to yarn me rubbish! That she should go and report herself to the correct owner of the bucket, and she's refusing to go!"

"Hmm, the girl has guts oh," Bisi declared.

"*O di kwa* serious!" Maryanne agreed.

Anita turned back to berate Carlotta. "You didn't know the bucket wasn't mine, so what? So I should start vibrating? That actually means you broke the bucket on purpose because you thought it was mine, *shey*? So you broke it deliberately?"

"No!" Carlotta couldn't believe the unforeseen outcome of the situation. "It really was an accident!" *Oh boy! Am I gonna hear it now.*

"Hmm, you should be very happy it's not even my personal bucket." Anita shook her head and her lips curled in a derisive manner. "Please, before I close and open my eyes, start marching to Emerald-Two and go report yourself to Chinyelu." As she spoke, the wrapper came loose again, and this time successfully slipped down her chest to her waist.

Anita ignored her exposed white-bra-encased breasts and went on admonishing Carlotta. "Don't even bother coming back to the dorm without reporting yourself to Chinyelu. Meanwhile, you have to find me an extra bucket of *warrer*, I *gats* to have my night bath, *abeg*. Now, start going." She waved Carlotta away. "Bunkie, come and oil my hair!"

Grace scrambled out from under the bunk. She spared Carlotta a sorry glance as she made her way out of Sapphire-Six to Emerald House, in search of whoever Chinyelu Obiekwe was.

Unknown to Carlotta, she would spend two very miserable hours kneeling on the hard cold floor of Emerald-Two, both arms extended high up above her head.

$\mathcal{T}$hat evening, Carlotta lay on Zika's bed sulking and looking very pitiable. She had damp towels wrapped around her red, swollen knees.

Zika was furious about what happened and made no bones about showing it. She'd learned of the incident from the bespectacled Maryanne, and couldn't believe that Anita had sent Carlotta to Emerald House to be punished. "Anita, you knew Chinyelu was going to punish my bunkie," Zika fumed. "Why did you send her there?"

"Before *nko?*" Anita retorted, her tone suggesting she wasn't in the least bit sorry. "The bucket she broke belonged to Chinyelu. What else did you want me to do? Besides, she's neither the first nor the last junior girl that had to kneel down. What will not kill her will only make her stronger. *Biko,* your bunkie should stop feeling sorry for herself and get used to it."

Teary-eyed, Carlotta watched her bunkmate bicker with her dormitory prefect.

"You should have just informed me that my bunkie broke the bucket you were using," Zika remarked in a stiff voice. "I would have just replaced the bucket for you, or even given you two extra buckets for dash."

Anita sighed. "You've seen me now, your information officer. Zika, *abeg,* your bunkie is just a ju-girl. Why are you being so annoying?"

"You think I'm annoying, *shey?*" Zika yelled from her corner. "Carlotta might just be a ju-girl to you but she's my bunkie, and I have all the right in the world to protect her from harm." Although Zika was angry, she knew better than to step out of her corner and challenge Anita head-on. Anita was an SS3 student, one class above Zika, and a dormitory prefect to boot. Therefore, Zika knew her place and remained within the confines of her corner as she directed words across the room.

"You're not the only one who has a bunkie. *Biko,* allow the girl to learn on her own and stop following her around and perching on her like a fly." Anita rolled her eyes and smacked her lips. *Mscheew!*

Several girls tittered.

But Zika would not be out-done. She poked her head above her bunk to get a full view of Anita's face. "And what about you that are always looking for ways to *she-kpe* my bunkie? If you're jealous of her, please say so and let us know!"

Carlotta understood that *she-kpe* was slang for *dealing with someone.*

Anita stood and positioned herself in such a way that the front part of her body directly faced Zika's corner. "Me? You think I'm jealous of your bunkie? As if I've never seen a Feddie Girl before?" She sneered, drawing back her head and raising her eyes in mock surprise. "Just for your information, when I was a ju-girl, my SS3 bunkie was a Feddie Girl." Her whole attitude showed she regarded what Zika just said to be absolutely ridiculous.

"In that case, please stop picking on my bunkie!"

Anita's tone became unpleasant. "You that you're protecting your bunkie, what are you trying to feel?" She placed one hand on her hip and used the other to gesticulate and add weight to her words. "Or, you think the Feddie Girl will take you with her to America for Christmas?" She forced the upper part of her body to undulate with each syllable of the next words she spat. "*Shioor!* In-short, Zika, you just need to wake-up from your slumber and smell the coffee!"

Zika rolled her eyes and hissed. "Keep your advice to yourself, *abeg!*" Her right hand swept the air, palm-out, in the famous *I don't need your opinion* style. Turning to Carlotta, she said in a loud voice so everyone in the dormitory including Anita could hear, "Bunkie, please gather your things, we're going to my friends corner in Sapphire-Four to chill. There just seems to be too many witchy individuals flying around in this dorm."

"Who are you calling witchy?"

"The guilty are afraid," Zika retorted. Seconds later, she ushered Carlotta out of the dormitory.

So began the long-standing feud between Zika and Anita in Sapphire-Six.

❋ ❋ ❋

*A*fter spending several weeks at FGGC Uddah, and thanks to her study group members, Carlotta was fairing well in her classes. She earned average results in the first tests of the semester. Her study group members were very studious and did their best to ground her on the basic history and current affairs of Nigeria, which she needed to know in order to make the passing grade in JS1 level social studies class. They also made sure she was kept abreast of the lessons in the native language classes.

Carlotta, like the rest of her study group mates, was taking Yoruba as a beginner's language and Igbo as a native language.

Like Carlotta, Emeh was also suffering in Igbo classes for she originated from the south and spoke Efik as a native language. Since Efik wasn't one of the languages offered, Igbo was the closest option. The rest of the study group members were Igbos and spoke Igbo fluently. They helped Carlotta and Emeh with their study of the language.

On the other hand, Emeh was excellent in French and pulled her study mates along in the class.

Ossie, having been born and bred in Lagos, was fluent in Yoruba as well as Igbo. She happily offered her group members assistance with this subject.

Although Amanda also lived in Lagos, she unfortunately hadn't picked up the Yoruba language like Ossie had, and so needed help with it as well. However, she was a natural in Fine Arts and was quick to produce fine sketches and drawings. She was also a favorite of the Fine Arts teacher because of her artistic skills.

Onyedi proved to be a whiz not only in math but also in most subjects. Her only weakness was fine arts. She couldn't draw to save herself.

Much to her amazement, Carlotta found she was quite good in literature, music, and physical education. However, she knew she couldn't have gotten this far without her friends. She also knew that if she kept working hard, she would do well enough by the end of the school year to earn her return to the United States.

Some of the subjects that were new to members of the study group were home economics, agriculture, business studies, and introductory technology. They studied these subjects together and helped one another out where they could.

With the encouraging results of her first tests in mind, Carlotta rushed off to the computer room the next Saturday morning to send e-mails to her parents.

The students at FGGC Uddah were allowed to use the school computers periodically for academic research and home-work. Students who wanted to surf the Internet during the weekend for personal reasons, had to sign up with their house prefects from Monday to Thursday. By Friday evening, the schedule for the use of the computer room was posted on the notice board in each house.

Since they weren't on good terms, Carlotta tried hard to avoid encounters with Chidi as much as possible, and refrained from signing up with her to surf the web.

Finally, Onyedi, who was a member of the Computer Club, came to her rescue and gave up one of her practice session slots, so that Carlotta could surf the web in her place.

The computer room was large, spacious, and equipped with three or four-dozen computers. A big picture of the school administrative building hung on the wall beside the windows, which had been flung open in an unsuccessful bid to dissipate some of the heat from the room.

Several ceiling fans churned the warm air but did very little to coax cooler air through the open windows. A few portraits of the principal and academic staff decorated the walls of the room. Carlotta made out the grinning faces of the computer club members staring down from their framed group photographs arranged in chronological order from 1998 to the present.

Sitting in front of a system, Carlotta logged on to the school cyberspace as Onyedi, and signed into her mailbox. There was one message from her dad asking how she was doing and how she liked Nigeria. She had a few messages from her mom asking about school life and how she was coping, and informing her that Uncle Daniel would be in to see her on the student Visiting Day, which would be the next Sunday. *Oh my God, it will be awesome to get a visitor.*

Everything back home seemed normal, but one thing worried Carlotta. Her parents had e mailed her separately and didn't mention each other in their mails. Something about that seemed odd, Carlotta thought, but decided to pay no further attention to it. Her parents were always in some kind of squabble or another that usually sorted itself out with time. *Oh, what the heck? Let them totally deal with their own stuff. I have my own problems to take care of.*

One message from her cousin, Ada, asked how she was doing and how she was finding boarding life.

Carlotta saw she also had a message from Sasha. She clicked on it.

Hi Carly,

Hope u r having a gr8 time in Nigeria. Seventh grade is a pain, lots of homework and stuff. Guess whom I ran into the other day? Nick! OMG isn't he like the cutest guy? I haven't seen him since we started middle school last year. That was right about the time u moved to OK with ur folks. He asked me to go sk8ing with him this afternoon and I said yes! Wow, that's so like a d8 right? Lol.

Anyway, I want to hear all about boarding school and about Nigeria. I'm in the cheerleading squad now (isn't that so cool!). Please write and tell me whatz up with you and how u r liking ur new school. I take it ur cell phone doesn't work there, cos I've tried calling u like a thousand times already, and sent you like a million text messages. I posted new pics and

some cool stuff about the Hannah Montana concert I
went to during the summer on Facebook. You should
totally check them out.

My mom said to say hi to u. We miss u so much.
Hope u can come to CA to visit us during ur holidays. I g2g now, my mom's calling 4 me.

Ttyl.

Love,

Sasha.

A wave of nostalgia washed over Carlotta as she read Sasha's
e-mail. She closed her eyes for a moment and imagined Sasha
skating all over their old neighborhood with the cute Nick in tow.
Then she could see them eating ice cream after burgers and fries,
and sipping iced soda from big paper cups. She sighed. *Gosh!*
What I wouldn't give to have a Big Mac right now.

Carlotta missed eating ice cream, and longed to go skating
or swimming with Sasha. Most of all, she missed her parents and
wished she could go home. *I'm so homesick.*

Swallowing back the lump in her throat, Carlotta typed out
replies to her parents' mails and sent them. *I guess I'm not mad at*
them anymore for sending me to school here. However, she planned
to bide her time and do the best she could in her studies, so they
would get her out of boarding school as fast as possible.

Carlotta clicked on Sasha's e-mail and read it through again.
How'd Sasha managed to sign-up for another Facebook account? The
last time we like, tried it, some old dude ratted us out and we were
totally blocked for being underage. She hit the reply button and
started typing:

Hi Sasha,

Sup? Ur e-mail made me realize how much I miss
being in Frisco. I could really go for a super-sized
double cheeseburger right now. Lol. I hope you had

a nice time with Nick. And yes, u r right, he's so cute. Have fun!

Cell phones, PCs, Ipods and like a gazillion other electronics r not allowed in this school. I left all my cool stuff with my mom when we got here. There r no air-conditioned rooms or vending machines or water fountains or running showers. There is a tuck-shop, though, where we can buy snacks and cold drinks during classroom breaks. There isn't any hot water for baths either. We have to fetch our bath water in plastic buckets, and drink warm water all day. This place is worse than the stories you hear about summer camp. It totally sucks! Well, just some of the time.

I'm in JS1 here. That is Junior Secondary One. It is the same as sixth grade, I guess. Anyway, I am taking lots of classes this year, like fifteen different subjects and they r all compulsory. I have made a few friends in my class, and we totally formed a study group. The group helps me a lot with most of the subjects especially the native languages.

Do u know we have to study like, 3 other languages in addition to English? A lot of English words r spelled differently and the native languages r very difficult to master. There r like 25 alphabets in the Yoruba language and the other one has like 36 alphabets! Luckily, they both use the English letters but with markings and such on or beneath them. Some of the alphabets have two letters joined to form one alphabet and r like very hard to say, like the gb, gh, gw, kp, kw, nw, and ny, consonants of the Igbo language! Totally scary, right?

Also, the money here is counted in Naira, symbol-ized by the letter N in caps crossed with two horizontal lines. I think one dollar equals a hundred-and-fifty naira.

The teachers here are very strict. The worst of them is the science teacher. He totally calls everyone animal names and sent me out of class on my first day! Crazy huh? My favorite teacher is Ms. Nora. She thinks I have like a real talent for drama. She totally made me join the Drama Club. There is an international drama competition starting this term. For the regional competition, my school will compete against several schools from different countries in West Africa. The Drama Club auditions for the contest is next week. I hope I make it, it's so gonna be exciting!

We get to sleep on bunks in the dormitories. My bunkmate is really nice and I like her. She gets me out of trouble most times. The students here can be very funny. They have slang for, like, everything you can think of. Witchy means being very mean, famous students r called Bubble girls, rich students r Barbie dolls, everyone here is a Feddy student but non-Nigerians and half-castes like me r called Feddie Girls, the religion fanatics r Kabashers, a dormitory prefect is a Subsidy, non prefects in SS3 r Floor-members, students who have been to foreign countries like America and England r Been-tos, students who are repeating a class r Meant-tos, students who transferred from a different school r Transits, someone who talks too much is a Yacker, bunkmates r called Bunkies, clueless students r Floaters, the school principal is known as Princy, and so on. There r just too many to keep track of.

The food here is interesting…

A prefect came into the computer room to remind the students they have only five minutes before their time was up. Carlotta quickly completed her mail to Sasha and sent it. She also sent a quick reply to Ada's e-mail, then logged-off and left the computer room, feeling a bit forlorn.

Carlotta stepped out of the computer building into the bright warmth of the mid-day sun, its rays warming her face. The sparkling gravels crunched as she stepped hard on them in a haste to get back to the cool shade of a building—any building at all.

Since the classroom blocks were the most accessible from the computer building, Carlotta headed toward the JS1 block.

"Carlotta, wait!" a voice screeched.

"Jeez! You must be kidding me." Carlotta rolled her eyes and halted. She knew the owner of the voice. Her whole body became bathed in irritation. Her jaw tightened and her eyes narrowed. She set her face in a cold mask and turned to face Sandra. *What does the little brat want now?* She watched Sandra draw nearer. *Is she here again to tell me how totally dysfunctional my family is?* Carlotta curled her hands into fists and waited.

Sandra ran up the winding path at full speed. "Carlotta, I've been looking for you everywhere," she panted, coming to a complete stop about two feet away, puffing and gasping as though she had just completed a hundred meters dash. She even had her hands supported by her knees, keeling over and managing to portray that the very act of drawing breath was too much for her over-worked lungs. Actually, she had only run a few dozen feet.

"What do you want?" Carlotta asked in a cold voice. Her face was devoid of expression, her eyes calculating.

"Senior Rema Yang came looking for you in dorm." Sandra made a sudden remarkable recovery. She drew herself up straight and deposited herself squarely in front of Carlotta, her eyes flashing with malice. "She said you should come to her dorm. Pearl-Four."

"Just get outta my face." Carlotta made to walk around Sandra. But her attempt was thwarted as Sandra quickly blocked her off.

"She said I should come with you." Sandra took a stance that was much like that of a boxer preparing to defend himself from a dauntless opponent. It didn't matter to her that the subject of her defensive manner was several inches taller than she was.

Carlotta hesitated. *I don't wanna start anything.*

"You have to follow me to her dorm right now," Sandra advised, grinning in a determined away. Her white teeth were in sharp contrast to the dark complexion of her skin.

If placed in a really dim room, Carlotta had no doubt all that would be seen of Sandra would be her eyeballs and white teeth.

"Senior Rema said I should make sure I find you and gather you to her dorm before afternoon dining, or she will punish me and make me miss my food."

"You can miss your food all year for all I care," Carlotta spat. "Actually, you can do us all a favor and starve to death." She looked in the cold marbles of Sandra's eyes and shuddered. "Just move aside."

Sandra did not budge. She grinned. And inched closer. She was clearly looking for a fight.

"Oh, great!" Carlotta let out her breath, goose bumps jumping out on her arms. The girl gave her the creeps. After a few seconds, her shoulders sagged in defeat. "All right, let's go see what Senior Rema wants this time." Carlotta had been avoiding this particular senior girl since she received the first of the purple envelopes, with the sprawling writing on them, several weeks earlier. Since then, she'd dreaded everything purple that came her way.

Her heart pumping rapidly, sweat beads erupting on her brow, Carlotta turned and headed down the winding pathway, toward the dormitories, Sandra following closely behind.

Carlotta knew there was no running off into the bush to get out of the situation, as she'd already done on two different occasions, and resigned herself to meeting with the one person she dreaded most in FGGC Uddah.

Chapter 11
Drama Club Auditions

Rema Yang was seated in her corner reading a novel when Carlotta walked into Pearl-Four with Sandra.

Rema was a conceited, obnoxious, Nigerian-Hong Kong half-caste with an exaggerated sense of self-importance and regal bearing. She was in SS2 and thought herself to be the Queen of the student body.

She always made it a point to let others know she had some English blood, since her dad was of mixed English-Hong Kong descent. Almost all the students at FGGC Uddah despised her because she was self-absorbed and snobbish, and always categorized other students into two groups: Feddie Girls and nobodies.

Rema watched Carlotta enter her corner with Sandra and took her time marking her place in the novel. She put the book away as if it was a valuable piece of china. A tiny wave of her hand dismissed Sandra.

The girl left at once.

Judging from her sycophantic attitude, Carlotta almost expected Sandra to bow before leaving.

Rema smiled and invited Carlotta to take a seat. "Did you receive my invitation last night?" Her tone was low but distinct, her eyes staring down the bridge of her nose. Contrary to what one might expect, there wasn't the slightest trace of a Chinese accent in Rema's voice. Instead, she spoke through her nose like a true Brit.

When Carlotta did not answer immediately, Rema flapped her eyelids in a high and mighty way and raised her brows expectantly, undeniably sending across the message that she was still waiting for a reply.

"I don't think so." Carlotta shook her head and stared at Rema, wondering how long it must have taken her to cultivate the British accent. *Three years?* "I didn't receive an invitation from you or anyone else." She imagined Rema spending endless nights in front of the mirror, honing her haughty look and imbibing the perfect condescending smile. *How do you do govnoh? She was appallingly in a very bad temper. The rain in Spain falls mainly on the plains.* It had probably taken her somewhere in the vicinity of five years or even longer, Carlotta decided. *She's less British than I am Nigerian, yet she forces herself to appear so—English! Gosh, she's so pathetic.*

Rema shook her head ever so slightly, her elegant neck seeming to elongate as she stared down her nose at Carlotta. "Pardon me, what was that?"

"I didn't get an invitation," Carlotta denied, and felt her ears become warm. She had thrashed the purple envelope the moment she saw it sitting on her bed after returning to the dormitory the evening before. She hadn't even bothered to open and read the invitation, but she wasn't going to tell Miss High-and-mighty that. Ever since the first invitation she had received to join the Feddie Girls Club several weeks earlier, Carlotta had started dreading all manner of purple objects.

"Alas, I instructed my bunkmate to place the invitation on your bed if she was unable to reach you at your humble abode." Rema flicked her delicate fingers in a way that suggested she would give Carlotta the benefit of the doubt. "Perhaps, my bunkmate misunderstood my orders?" she remarked, and smoothed her long, straight dark hair over her shoulders in a striking imitation of Ashley Tisdale in 'High School Musical.'

Rema continued, "That not withstanding, I have here a special invitation I wish to present to you myself." She reached under her pillow and pulled out a purple envelope trimmed in red and gold, holding on to it by the tips of her fingers, and offered it to Carlotta.

Carlotta hesitated, then took the beautifully embroidered envelope and tore it open with unnecessary force.

Rema winced.

Carlotta stalled the twitching in her lips and hid a smile. She reached in and extracted the equally purple card within the envelope and read:

Your presence at the next Feddie Girls Club
social event is highly requested.
4:00 PM on October Twenty-Seventh,
at the Club Patrons Residence, FGGC Uddah.

Signed:
Rema Yang, Club President.

"This time, you will have no reason to claim you did not receive an invitation," Rema sneered. The condescending look on her face matched the tone of her voice

The beginnings of a smirk froze on Carlotta's lips. She did a double take and read the time and date for the event again. With determination, she regarded the senior student in front of her, who was watching her with a sweet smile that didn't get anywhere near her eyes. "I can't make this event. It's the same time as my Drama Club auditions next week."

"That can't be helped, now can it?" Rema was still smiling but her chilly eyes betrayed her true feelings.

Carlotta was incredulous. "But, Senior Rema, you totally don't understand. I have to audition next week for the school play. The drama competition we are preparing for is a big one and it's supposed to take place in Ghana!"

Students in the dormitory were starting to take an interest in the conversation.

Carlotta lowered her voice. "I simply can't make it to your event. I'm not even a member of your club." She made an apologetic face and raised a shoulder. "Sorry."

Rema examined her nails. She took her time, lips pursed, eyebrows raised, eyelids fluttering. "No, my dear," she finally replied. "I am afraid it is you who do not quite understand." She pinned Carlotta with slanted eyes the color of young grass and continued in a voice barbed with scorn, "You are a *Feddie Girl* and so a member of the Feddie Girls Club by default. However, you *are* in order to be sorry, for that is exactly what *you* will be if you fail to show your presence at this event."

"No way—" Carlotta couldn't believe the cheek of the self-proclaimed queen-bee seated opposite her. She considered the green knobs of Rema's eyes, which were her only claim to Caucasian blood, and stalled.

With a negative air of expectation, Rema blinked. "What did you say?" She pinned Carlotta with daring green eyes.

Carlotta swallowed down her fear and injected an ounce of bravado into her voice. "Senior Rema, with all due respect, may I totally remind you that extra curricular activities are optional? I have the right to choose to be in any school club I want and totally reject whichever I choose." Her heart raced. "You can't, like, force me to join your club. It's against the school regulations!"

Green eyes scrutinized Carlotta.

Carlotta wished Rema would stop pointing those jade daggers in her direction and go back to examining her nails or something.

Rema was not fazed by Carlotta's heated tone. She kept her voice even but icy-cold. "You will do well to remember that the Feddie Girls Club is the most important, and by far, the most powerful club in the history of this school." She crossed her long, golden legs slowly—almost deliberately. "Our patron, Mr. Adetunji, who incidentally is also the VP Academics of this school and a half-caste of German origin, was a co-founder of the club."

Rema stared Carlotta down and continued in a regal tone, "Why, only a few years ago, a parent of one of the members of the club had his company donate one hundred computers to this school. Those are the same computers being used by the Computer Club now."

Rema drew a long breath and batted her eyelids. In a voice that was dripping with pride she remarked, "Also, last year, another parent donated a concert piano to the Music Club. This is just to name a few examples.

"Because of the powerful connections we have with people of affluence and importance in foreign countries, officers of the other school clubs come to us with their needs. Benevolently, we grant their favors and request other favors from them in return."

Rema removed a colorful, Chinese hand fan from her locker, spread it out, and fanned herself with it. "You have no idea how far and wide our influence extends, and underestimating us is a grave mistake."

Carlotta watched Rema fan herself in silence for a while. The dormitory wasn't warm, and the overhead fans were rotating at full speed. The British wanna-be couldn't possibly be in need of extra air-current. Each stroke of her hand was a premeditated action aimed at producing the desired regal effect.

Carlotta began to despise all Brits in general. She said to Rema, "Still, I wouldn't *wanna* miss the Drama Club auditions. If you can, like, move your club event to a different date, I might consider attending."

Rema stopped and placed the fan on her pillow. "My event cannot be moved. Some very important personalities were invited and many are coming all the way from Lagos, Port Harcourt, and Abuja." Her green eyes narrowed. Listening to her, one would think Rema was addressing the national assembly. "Several are also taking the trouble to fly all the way in from London, New York, and Paris."

Carlotta noticed she pronounced *Paris* the French way, with the rolled *r* and silent *s*. "I totally don't see what all that has got to do with me."

Rema leaned close to Carlotta and whispered in a steely voice, "This event is in your honor, so you will see that you have no choice but to attend, my dear. It is in your best interest. No other club can match the power and prestige of the Feddie Girls Club." Her voice took on an ominous quality. "Always—remember—that."

Rema's last three words sent chills up Carlotta's spine. She didn't dare breathe, or speak, or move, but remained in her perched position, drowning in the green pools of her intimidator's eyes.

Finally, Rema sat back and picked up her fan. "I am done with you. You may leave." She broke eye contact.

Carlotta took in a sharp breath to keep calm and dispel the chills that were creeping up her neck. She got up slowly and departed. At the door, she stopped and looked over her shoulder. Rema was already absorbed in her novel and appeared to have forgotten that Carlotta even existed.

Her anger threatening to explode, Carlotta walked out of Pearl-Four. She closed the door and leaned back against it, hating Rema and wondering what on earth she should do.

✳ ✳ ✳

Back at Sapphire-Six, Carlotta recounted her conversation with Rema to Zika, Nneka, and Shade.

"Can you imagine?" Zika fumed. "That stuck-up Feddie Girl has guts. She doesn't have the right to force anyone to join her club—no club president has that kind of power."

"Maybe she was just joking," Shade reasoned.

"And what kind of a stupid joke is that?" Zika was working up a considerable head of indignation. She shook her head and pronounced in a raised voice, "Rema threatened my bunkie. She told Carlotta that she has no other choice but to join her manipulative club. I don't know why Princy won't dissolve that club. They are worse than the Bubble Girls."

Nneka guffawed. "Zika, we all know that Princy needs the Feddie Girls Club and would never vote to dissolve it. Didn't you hear the rumor that Rema's mother donated a large sum of money to the school last term? She said it was a gift from The Chinese Sisters of Consolation, her charity organization." Nneka shook her head and grimaced. "Her mother is not even Chinese, she's from Benin!"

"Ah-ah," Shade remarked, "Nneka, *na* you go know. How are you so sure that Rema's mumsie is a *Beni* woman?" Shade's lips were pursed and pointed as she spoke. "*Abeg*, who told you?" She nodded once as she came to the end of her sentence, managing to convey the notion that Nneka might just be fibbing.

Nneka rose to the challenge. "What's your own?" she threw at Shade. "Everyone except floaters knows the whole story." The look on Nneka's face suggested she would regard Shade as one of the floaters if she maintains her ignorance on Rema's mother's place of origin.

Shade admitted defeat. No one relished being labeled a floater at FGGC Uddah.

Turning away, Nneka placed a sympathetic hand on Zika's shoulder. "Standing here and shouting won't do anything and wouldn't stop Carlotta from getting punished if she doesn't attend the so-called social event."

"Maybe we should just go and talk to her," Zika suggested. "Nneka you are an officer in Drama Club, you should go and confront Rema about this. That Chinese Feddie Girl has to be reminded that she doesn't own all the Feddie Girls in this school."

"No oh! Please hold it there," Nneka replied in a hurried voice, frowning. "Why should it be me who will go and talk to that snob?"

"Ah-ah, what's your own? She's in your class, *shey?*" Zika asked, nodding at Nneka.

"*Abi o.*" Shade agreed. "And if no one complains, Rema will just keep doing this. Remember how she bullied Sharon into joining the club? That was three years ago—we were in JS2 then."

"Yes oh. And last year, she did the same thing," Nneka supplied. She went on to tell how Rema, then in SS1 but president of the Feddie Girls Club all the same, had forced a new student whose father was British to join the club. The girl had reluctantly done so, but the rumors were she complained to her parents about the happenings in the club, and her folks had promptly whisked her away from the school during her second term.

"No, no that's not true," Zika interrupted before Nneka had quite finished with her story. "Lisa did not leave the school because she was forced to join the club. She left for other reasons. I think her parents were about to get a divorce or something like that."

"That's exactly what the school authorities wanted everyone to think," Nneka scoffed, her lips twisted to one side of her mouth. She rolled her eyes. "Let me tell you girls the truth, it was the Feddie Girls Club that drove Lisa away from school. Yes now!" Her voice dropped conspiratorially, as if she wanted to share a secret with the others. "A friend of her best friend's cousin personally told me so."

"Grabber!" Shade giggled. "Nneka, *na* you-you!"

"Anyway, that has nothing to do with the problem we have here." Zika wrinkled her nose and dismissed Nneka's story with an impatient wave of her hand.

Nneka looked a little miffed but did not pursue the matter further. She shrugged and bit her lip, assuming an air of nonchalance.

"Nneka, but you're the secretary of the Drama Club and Rema is in your class," Zika maintained. "I think you should be the one to talk to her."

Carlotta caught both Zika and Shade staring at Nneka with hope in their eyes. Their looks spoke volumes.

"I don't know—" Nneka said. "Wouldn't it be better for a school prefect or even a subsidy to do it?"

"Which prefect or subsidy do we know that is an official member of the Drama Club and would be willing to take Rema on for size?" Shade asked.

"Well, Anita is a member, but she's not an officer. Maybe we should ask her," Nneka suggested. "What do you girls think?" She shrugged a careless shoulder.

Carlotta saw Zika frown. She knew there was no way Zika would go for that option. Zika had been having problems with Anita for some time now. They always seemed to be at each other's throats over some petty matter. Carlotta suspected the real reason for their quarrels was Zika's protective attitude toward her. She had tried to get better at avoiding trouble with her dorm prefect. *Seriously, I've been trying.*

Carlotta spoke up. "Um, wouldn't it be a good idea to just report the whole incident to the school authorities? I mean, they can totally take care of it, right?"

"Please, no!" The SS2 students replied in unison.

"Okay—okay." Carlotta was surprised by the conviction in their voices.

Zika looked impatient. She said to Nneka. "You remember how good Carlotta is with plays and music and things like that? So her auditioning for a part in the play will be good for your Drama Club." Shoulders hunched, she spread her hands in front of her, palms up. "If you people want to win the competition in Ghana, shouldn't you take all the talented students you can find?"

"But Carlotta is just in JS1—" Nneka started to protest, but changed her mind when she saw the disappointed look on Zika's face. "Okay, I will talk to Rema, if you think it's the best thing." She glanced sideways at Carlotta and added a little too quickly, "You can audition for the play if you really want." She shrugged and rolled her eyes.

"Fine, it's settled." Zika heaved a sigh of relief. She turned to Carlotta. "Bunkie, please go and start practicing for your audition. Mrs. China will not disturb you anymore."

"Great!" Carlotta beamed. "Thanks. It means a whole lot to me to be able to audition. I've been totally looking forward to it, like, forever." She pumped her fists in the air. "Yes!" she exclaimed, and did a small wiggling dance. "Thank you all so much," she said in an excited voice. "Right now, I really need to go find *On-yeh-dee*, so I'll catch up with you guys later. Bye, and thanks again!"

The three senior girls watched Carlotta run out of the dormitory, her footfalls echoing the sound of her voice whooping with relief down the hallway.

✳ ✳ ✳

$\mathcal{S}$helley's hand shook as she maneuvered the mouse of the computer that controlled the projector in the classroom. She was trying to pull up the folder that held the presentation she needed for her grammar lecture. The good-looking male student seated in the front row was irritating her with his stares. She had noticed him during the last lecture, but would swear he hadn't been with the class from the beginning of the semester. However, that wasn't what bothered her about him.

Shelley found the folder she needed and clicked on it. As she waited for the file to load, she glanced again at the student. She saw him wink and smile in that special way of handsome twenty-something year olds.

Shelley swallowed. Her palms suddenly became damp. *Did I imagine it or did he just leer at me?*

Mustering up a great deal of effort, she ignored the student and began to teach the class about the various functions of the comma in essay writing.

Forty minutes later, the lecture was over. Shelley stayed to answer students' questions and offer academic advice to those who requested it. Before long, almost everyone was gone except the young man.

"Excuse me, Professor?"

"Yes?" Shelley tried not to look into his smiling eyes, though she couldn't help but notice his perfect teeth. She looked away and busied herself with packing up her teaching materials.

"I was wondering if you could help me?"

Shelley looked at him. The cocky attitude was in place. Her mouth went dry. "Are you registered for this class?" She licked her lips. "This is ENGL 2010. Perhaps, you are in the wrong classroom?"

"Yes. No, I mean, my major Professor advised me to take this class as a remedial course. This is the second lecture I've attended and I'm hopelessly lost. Maybe I can come in for extra lessons in your office?" The boy smiled and this time, there was no mistaking the suggestion behind the wink.

"That will not be necessary," Shelley said in a voice that sounded strained, even to her own ears. "See the teaching assistant if you need extra help with this course." She scooped up her heap of teaching materials and without looking at the student again, flounced out of the classroom, almost careening into a desk on her way out.

Back in her office, Shelley slumped into her chair and tried to calm her nerves. Looking down at her shaking hands, she wished desperately for a drink. "This is absurd," she said aloud. "It is only nine in the morning and, already, I crave alcohol like a lunatic. I need to do something about my drinking."

Fifteen minutes later, Shelley peeled her mind away from thoughts of sexy male students and tried to concentrate on the manuscript she was editing. The words swam before her eyes and the headings and page numbers danced on the pages. She slapped the manuscript down. *I need to find myself a boyfriend, or a companion, or any man at all!*

Her mind wandered. This time, Shelley saw well-toned muscles plastered on young male bodies. The muscles rippled, and became sleek with sweat. She imagined—

"Damn it!" Shelley groaned. She was falling apart and she knew it. The amount of booze she consumed every day was obviously making matters worse.

Since Richard left, Shelley's drinking had worsened. She no longer tried to hide it at home—there was no reason to. Every evening she came home and drank herself into oblivion.

What a joke her life had become, Shelley thought. Here she was, posing as a distinguished academic professor while her personal life was down the tubes. Her teenage daughter smoked marijuana and had been packed off to a boarding school in Nigeria; her husband was a cheating bastard of a physician who couldn't keep his hands off pretty women to save his life; she was a raging alcoholic who sought solace from the bottle for every little misgiving.

Shelley pinched the bridge of her nose with her thumb and forefinger and tried hard to dismiss the thoughts that threatened her sanity.

There was a knock at the door.

"Come in," Shelley invited, not bothering to look up.

"You don't have to run away from me, Professor. I don't bite," a male voice drawled.

Shelley's head snapped upward. Her eyes focused on the student standing just inside the door of her office. She stared at him for a while, her face devoid of expression. "You again," she finally said with a sigh. "I did not catch your name." She studied the student's appearance.

Like Richard, the guy was tall and clean-shaven. However, he wore his hair in the long shaggy style of most young adults. Blue jeans hung smugly from lean hips; unbuttoned flannel shirt spanned the width of his shoulders, revealing a thin, gray tee shirt underneath. Taken separately, his clothes looked scraggly and careless. But pooled together and capped with the charming smile and undaunted manner with which he leaned against the wall, the student's appearance was dashing and classy in a weird sort of way.

"Joshua Greinbach," the student drawled. "You can call me Josh," he invited, tossing back his hair. He placed his backpack on the floor, sauntered into the office and took the seat opposite Shelley.

"Well, Mr. Greinbach," Shelley stated, clearly ignoring the invitation to use his first name. "I believe I informed you to see the TA if you need extra help with my course?"

"I understand that, Professor," Josh intoned. "But, I didn't come here for study advice."

"Excuse me?"

"I came to see *you*, Professor." Josh's eyes drilled into hers. Casually, he reached out and covered her hand with his. He raised the imprisoned hand to his lips and placed a tender kiss on the back then flipped it over and traced his tongue along the lines in the palm.

Hot flames trailed up Shelley's arm at the feel of his pulsating tongue. She withdrew her hand and jerked to her feet. "Now, look here, Mr. Greinbach. I will not tolerate this kind of behavior from students. You will please leave my office at once, or I will have a word with the Dean of Students about your untoward conduct."

"Hey, hey, no need to be rash. I was only paying a beautiful lady a well-deserved compliment." Josh chuckled. "I didn't mean any harm, Professor." He planted himself on his feet and picked up his backpack. Still keeping cool green eyes on Shelley, he flicked-back a lock of hair. "If I offended you in any way, I apologize." He sucked in his lower lip, his eyes boring into hers. "However, should you change your mind..." he winked, then bowed and left.

Shelley stared after him in wonder. "That is a strange student," she said to herself. *A young, handsome, and assertive guy but a student all the same. I will do well to remember that.* She shook her head and lowered herself into her seat.

Without meaning to, Shelley imagined the way it would feel to kiss Josh, or have him hold her. *Oh my goodness, I could use a guy right now. A good-looking Greinbach of a guy, who will—*

Suddenly Shelley picked up the manuscript on her desk and flung it at the chair where Josh had been seated just minutes before. *Damn you young students who think it acceptable to seduce your professors, damn the whole lot of you!*

✳ ✳ ✳

*A*t 4:00 PM on Saturday evening, exactly one week after Carlotta's conversation with Rema, about sixty students were gathered in the FGGC Uddah dining hall for the Drama Club auditions.

Carlotta was one of them.

The Drama Club officials assembled in front of the students and silence fell over them all. After the initial protocols, Georgina Ubong, the president of the Drama Club, addressed everyone.

"As you girls know, our school has qualified to compete at the West African Regionals of the All African College Drama Competition (AACDC). We are one of the three qualifying schools in Nigeria that are to compete against forty other West African schools for the regional title."

The girls clapped and cheered.

Georgina waited for the noise to die down then continued, "The competition will take place in Accra, Ghana, and is scheduled for the beginning of second term. Only the top five schools from this regional division shall be allowed to continue to the last stage and compete for the final All-African Title. The finals will take place in South Africa during the third term."

The students murmured in excited tones.

The club president put up her hand and silence fell again. She continued, "We have just been informed that the play chosen for English-speaking schools in the competition will be," she paused, "*Wedlock of the Gods*, by Zulu Sofola."

The students' voices went up in a roar.

Carlotta closed her eyes and pressed her hands to her chest in relief. It was the same play they had already studied in literature class. *How lucky was that?*

Georgina resumed speaking. "I know most of you studied the play in class during your junior days." She smiled. "So, that should be a plus for us." She looked down at her notes. "Right now, we are going to have the general screening. Those who make the cut will then audition for the lead roles of Odibei, Uloko, and Ogwoma. Then, you'll be expected to read actual excerpts from the play."

A round of applause greeted her comment.

Georgina indulged the students for a while then put up her hand for silence. "We will soon start with the auditions. Before we do, I want you girls to think of which character you want to portray. We will choose the best two students for each character: one as the main, the other as the understudy. All other good actresses would then be cast in the secondary roles on merit."

The students murmured, but fell silent when the club president raised her hand.

"Needless to say, it will be easier for the masculine students amongst you to audition for the character of Uloko. This will make disguises and costumes easier to manage when the time comes."

The students cheered and whistled.

"Any officer who wishes to be cast in the play will also have to audition," Georgina continued, "because the auditioning process will be kept fair and firm. So, too, will the casting process." She paused and took a deep breath. "This year, we have appointed two reputable student members, in addition to the club matron and myself, to act as judges."

The students protested, "No! No! No!"

"Don't worry," the club president reassured them, "the judges are not permitted to audition." She looked around at the students and smiled. "As soon as the club matron arrives, which should be in a few minutes, we shall begin. Good luck to you all!"

A round of applause erupted from the girls. The crowd scattered all over the dining hall, and friends psyched one another up for the auditions.

Carlotta looked at the sixty plus members of the Drama Club preparing for their ninety seconds of glory before the judges and her mouth went dry. *Where do I get off thinking I have anything on any of these students?* She wished Onyedi and the rest of her study group were there to offer encouragement. But the audition was a closed one, so friends and well-wishers were not allowed to sit in and observe the proceedings.

A few minutes later, Ms. Nora, the Drama Club matron, walked into the dining hall, her sharp heels clicking, as always, amidst hearty cheers from the students.

Seats had been arranged in front of a small clearing at one corner. The students gave their character preference to the club president and seated themselves behind the judges.

When everyone was seated, Georgina read a prepared synopsis of each character: "Uloko is a young warrior that is in love with the recently widowed Ogwoma, his childhood sweetheart. He is ecstatic that the love of his life has been freed from the bondage of a loveless marriage and wastes no time in rekindling their romance—to the chagrin of Ogwoma's mother-in-law, Odibei." Georgina stopped and smiled.

The students clapped and cheered.

Georgina silenced them and continued, "Odibei is Ogwoma's mother-in-law. She is enraged that her son had only been dead a short while and already his lecherous widow is planning on getting remarried. She plans to do everything in her power to salvage her dead son's dignity, and punish Ogwoma and Uloko for their betrayal."

"Witchy!" someone yelled, and the students cheered.

When they quieted down, the club president concluded, "Ogwoma, the village beauty, was forced by her parents to marry a man she did not love so as to raise money to save the life of her dying brother. She sees her husband's death as an opportunity to reunite with her first love, Uloko. Despite the fact that her late husband had a brother that she should marry, as was the village custom, she is adamant to be together with Uloko, whose child she is secretly carrying."

The students clapped, and the club president took her seat. The general screening began.

First were the candidates auditioning for the male character Uloko.

The first name was called.

A senior student stood and walked to the center of the clearing and faced the crowd. She was dark and muscular with angular facial features.

Georgina addressed her, "Assume you are a man who has been married for two years. You come home and your wife tells you she's pregnant and the man responsible is your best friend. How will you react to this news?"

The onlookers became silent and watched with growing tension.

The muscular student stiffened and her facial muscles slowly arranged themselves into a frown. She stood still as a rock for a few moments and then bellowed, "What? Are you crazy?" Her voice resonated around the dining hall.

Ms. Nora covered her ears and almost ducked under her table. Clearly, she hadn't been expecting that sort of loud reaction from a stiff character.

The students applauded. A few girls howled, and yelled catcalls to the muscular girl, who was now smiling and looking very pleased.

"Thank you, thank you," the recovered Ms. Nora said. "You may please take your seat now. Call the next candidate."

The muscular girl returned to her seat and a gangly senior student took her place in the clearing.

The club president spoke, "You are a taxi driver struggling to raise money for your family of seven. Your wife is in labor and you are in the hospital waiting room praying for her safety and safe delivery. The doctor comes up to you and tells you your wife has just delivered four bouncing baby boys. How will you react?"

With a piercing cry, the gangly student collapsed on the floor like a heap of laundry. "*Wetin* I do *dis* world *wey dem wan* dash me three extra *pikin* make I manage?" she wailed. "Ha, *wetin* I suppose do now?" Her shoulders heaved and she placed her head in her hands, her whole body shuddering with the weight of her sorrow.

Although the girl didn't look much like the cab driver she encountered that fateful night in Lagos, Carlotta felt like going to console the student. Her acting was that good.

"Okay, okay. Thank you. Next please," Ms. Nora called.

And so the auditions continued until the list of students for the Uloko character was exhausted.

Carlotta thought some of the acts were quite good, while others were deplorable. Two of them had been total disasters. One student had removed one of her flip-flops and holding it aloft like a matchet, proceeded to chase an imaginary promiscuous wife with it. The students had laughed and applauded with gusto. The matchet-wielding girl's act had been more funny than menacing.

The next character was Odibei.

Then Ogwoma.

First student on the list to audition for Ogwoma was Nneka. She gave a marvelous performance, Carlotta thought. The students clapped long and hard for her. Thirteen candidates later, it was Carlotta's turn. She delivered herself on shaky legs to the clearing. Willing her mind to ignore her nervousness, she faced the judges.

Georgina cleared her throat. "You walk into your backyard and discover a dead body. You realize it's that of your only son. How will you react?"

Carlotta closed her eyes and focused all her senses inward. In her mind's eye, she saw her two-year-old son Bobby lying out in the yard, a few feet away from where she stood. He was bleeding... dying...

A heart-rending cry ensued from somewhere deep within. Carlotta pried her eyes open and beheld the still and bloody form of her son. Her mouth gaped, her hands shook, her whole body trembled. She closed the distance between them and sank to her knees. Tears stung her eyes and her shoulders shook with the depth of her emotion. She cradled his head to her chest.

"Someone call an ambulance!"

Her eyes grew wild.

"Somebody help me. Please!"

The whole left side of Bobby's head was a bloody mush, blown away by a bullet shot at close range. Carlotta bent so low she could almost kiss his head. Her whole body was wracked with sobs as she said to the dying boy in her arms, "Oh God! Bobby, Bobby, please—" But she knew it was hopeless.

"God! Noooo!" she screamed. "No! Bobby—you can't just go like this." Her shaking voice made it difficult to speak. She looked sideways. "Call 911. I need an ambulance!"

She placed her head on his, and rocking him from side to side, she cried, "Bobby—Bobby! No—no!" She held his lifeless body tight and sobbed like her heart was breaking. Her back arched. Her arms tensed. She held her eyes tightly shut, as if by succeeding to stem the flow of tears, she would be able to bring her son back to life.

She did not succeed.

"No!" she wailed, and her heart broke.

The sound of clapping brought Carlotta back to the present. She got up and wiped the tears off her face.

Most of the students stared at her in awe as they clapped. Several dabbed at their eyes. A few sniffled.

"My God, she was wonderful," Ms. Nora said.

Thunderous applause filled the dining hall. The girls cheered and cheered.

Carlotta could not believe her ears. Pleased, she went back and took her seat.

"That was simply wonderful," Ms. Nora repeated in a thick voice, and blew her nose on a white handkerchief. "Call the next student, please."

The screening continued and finally came to a conclusion. Apart from a dozen girls who Carlotta thought had seriously sucked, and three or four who had bailed out at the last minute, all the students were recalled to do a scene reading. The Club president thanked them all for their performances and assured them the closed readings would be scheduled individually for each contestant and would be completed within the next few days.

"The results of the reading will be posted on the notice board of every house by next weekend," Georgina finished, and took her seat.

Ms. Nora was in the middle of giving last minute instructions to the club members, when a junior student burst into the hall, screaming as she ran.

"What is she saying?" a student beside Carlotta asked.

"I think she said that girls are fighting in Sapphire House," one girl replied, and turned back to the screaming student, who was now being calmed down by Ms. Nora and a few senior girls.

Another girl countered, "No, she said a floor member slapped a subsidy in Sapphire House and they are fighting."

"No, that's not true," a third girl volunteered. "She said the house prefect slapped a subsidy then choked a floor member in Sapphire-Six."

"No, please! That's not what she said," someone else intervened.

"Original *amebo*. Who even asked you?" the first girl argued.

"You girls are just floating. What she said is—"

"*Biko*, stop yacking. The real gist is—"

"It's a lie, I heard her say—"

"No. The truth is—"

"Listen to me—"

"No oh—"

A shouting match broke out.

Carlotta did not wait to hear anymore. The mere mention of Sapphire-Six was all that was needed to galvanize her brain into action and make her conclude that Zika was somehow in trouble.

Pushing the arguing girls aside, Carlotta jumped to her feet and bolted out of the dining hall, closely followed by Nneka.

Chapter 12

Dated!

"Thanks for dinner, Doctor." Maria said and smiled.

Richard placed his hand on her shoulder. She stiffened and turned her back to him. He didn't know why she kept insisting on calling him "Doctor" but wished she would stop with the formality. *I would have much preferred something more personal, like Rick, for instance, Dick, Rich, Richie, or Ricky. Oh hell, even Richard would do nicely, thank you.* Instead, Maria stuck doggedly to her use of *Doctor*. It made him feel old and feeble, not at all like the sexy hunk he regarded himself to be.

They were seated in a rental car parked in front of the hotel in Ontario, Canada, where they were to spend the next several nights. They'd arrived in the city a few hours earlier, and had just returned from having dinner. It had been a long flight from Tulsa, but Richard was determined to score before turning in for the night.

Maria reached for the door handle.

"Not so fast," Richard muttered, stopping her hand. "A little extra appreciation wouldn't hurt now, would it?" He drew her closer and put his arms around her.

Damn!

Maria did things to his emotions that he couldn't describe. He twirled her long black stresses around his fingers, pecked her on the cheek and breathed in her scent. She smelled like flowers—pretty, blossoming flowers with intoxicating scents, making him want to do things that would drive them both crazy.

He sighed and angled her body toward him. He took her face in his hands and kissed her lips, lingering on the lower lip, drawing it tenderly into his mouth and massaging its soft fullness with the tip of his tongue.

She kissed him back.

"Oh Maria," he breathed, nuzzling her neck. "I want you so much." He maneuvered her so she sat with the small of her back against the hand brake. Then bent his head and kissed her again, more insistently this time. *Boy, do I want you!*

Maria twined her arms around his shoulders, holding on to him, kissing him back—matching his sense of urgency.

His hand found her knee and caressed the exposed flesh, coaxing her tight black skirt to ride a little higher up her thighs.

She moaned.

"Come back to my room with me," he whispered, tone husky, body on fire, heart threatening to explode.

"I'm sorry, Doctor, I can't."

Disappointment washed over Richard in hot waves. "Why not?" he asked, not letting himself be daunted for a second. If anything, he was more aroused. *Nothing like a good old 'I don't wanna' to keep the 'little guy' interested.* He reached for her lips.

"We can't do this," Maria protested, and pushed him away.

Richard felt himself straining against the thick material of the khaki pants he had on, and sighed with desire. He bent his head and started kissing her again. He ignored her protest and pushed his tongue between her parted lips—teasing, urging, and willing her to melt in his arms.

His right hand traveled over the smooth plane of her flat stomach, and moved upward, underneath the flimsy material of the blouse she had on, to cup her breast.

He met no resistance. No bra.

Maria shifted.

Oh yes, baby! He started to knead her breast, his thumb rubbing against the nipple that strained to escape the light cotton blouse that encased it.

"It's not right, Doctor," Maria mumbled. "We shouldn't get romantically involved."

Richard barely heard. *It's a little too late for regrets.* His heart pounded with the force of his need. The nipple under his thumb hardened and he felt himself stir, wanting very much to close his mouth over its hard knob and tease it till she cried out for mercy.

Suddenly, her lips stiffened. Maria stopped kissing him and pushed away, trying to sit up.

"What's the matter?" Richard's voice was edged with hurt and disappointment.

"I'm sorry, Doctor. It's not you—we, we can't do this. I need to get back to my room right away." Maria was agitated. Moving away from him, she started arranging her hair and straightening her clothes.

"Why not?" Richard demanded. He sounded like a spoiled child whose favorite toy had been taken away. "Why the hell can't we do *this*? You can't deny you want me as much as I want you."

"We just can't. I'm so sorry, Doctor, but I can't explain." She pushed the door open and stepped out.

"What the hell—?"

Maria shut the door with just enough force to ensure it was firmly closed, cutting him off. She sighed, leaned against the door, and closed her eyes.

Richard scrambled out from behind the wheel to confront her from the opposite side of the car. His emotions were in turmoil; he couldn't understand why she kept holding back on him.

This isn't fair, he thought. He wanted her so much; his wife had even thrown him out of their home on her account.

He regarded Maria over the top of the car but she wasn't even looking back at him, she had her eyes closed. Her face looked serene, as she stood there—like a face in a perfect oil painting. The ebony hair that had been piled up at the beginning of the evening was now loose and framing her head, accentuating the softness of her facial features. A red dot resided on the left side of her temple.

That's odd, Richard thought, *I didn't notice that pimple there before.* Then his eyes widened as he saw the dot shift on Maria's forehead. It shimmered.

Realization hit Richard. In a split second, his brain stopped. His heart followed suit. He opened his mouth to shout a warning to Maria. Before any sound escaped his lips, the top of Maria's head dissolved in a silent explosion, showering blood, gray matter, and tiny skull fragments.

Richard jerked back in horror, his mouth now screaming its useless warning to an equally useless corpse.

Out of nowhere, a heavy hand clamped a damp cloth over Richard's nose and mouth and snuffed-out his frantic screams. He twisted and tried to free himself.

The hand wouldn't let go.

Richard ceased struggling against the massive body that held him captive. He took a deep breath and braced himself for his assailant's attack. Hot, searing fumes filled his lungs. His head enlarged and floated away. His legs weakened and melted from under him. His panic ebbed.

Ether!

That was the last thought on Richard's mind as he lost consciousness and slipped into blackness.

✳ ✳ ✳

The staff and students of FGGC Uddah were gathered in the school hall for the Friday morning principal's assembly. Two student representatives from the Music Club stood beside the school piano, deposited on the raised dais in front of the hall, and prepared to lead the rest of the school in the national anthem, as was the practice every Friday morning. The pianist gave the key tunes, the two students signaled, and all the students started to sing:

Arise, O compatriots;
Nigeria's call obey.
To serve our fatherland;
With love and strength and faith.
The labor of our heroes past;
Shall never be in vain.
To serve with heart and might;
One nation bound in freedom, peace, and unity.

The students waited for the signal then joined in the second stanza:

O God of creation;
Direct our noble cause.
Guide our leaders right;
Help our youths the truth to know.
In love and honesty to grow;
And living just and true.
Great lofty heights attain;
To build a nation where peace, and justice shall reign.

Thereafter, all staff and students placed their right hands on their chest and on cue, recited the Nigerian National Pledge:

I pledge to Nigeria my country;
To be faithful, loyal, and honest.
To serve Nigeria with all my strength;
To defend her unity, and uphold her honor and Glory.
So help me God.

The students took their seats and the assembly commenced. Carlotta's mind was whirling. She had a foreboding about what the principal's decision on Zika's fate was going to be. Actually, nobody really knew exactly what happened between Zika and Anita. The story had been told and retold so many times even the few students who'd witnessed it could no longer agree on what had transpired.

Some said Anita was choking a junior girl, and Zika had slapped Anita to make her stop. Another version was that it was Zika who had slapped and choked Anita. A few maintained that both Zika and Anita had been choking each other, and a junior girl had tried to stop them. A more disturbing version was that Anita tried to strangle Zika and had received a dazing slap as a result.

It didn't really matter anymore what actually happened or in what order it occurred. The fact remained that Ms. Nora had taken up the case and Zika was in trouble for daring to raise a hand against a prefect. Apparently, that was a serious offence at FGGC Uddah.

The students sat quietly while the principal went through the whole routine of Friday morning addresses: news, academic encouragement, instructions, and advice. Finally, she brought up the topic they were all waiting for.

"Head girl, approach the stage," the principal announced in her clipped tone. "Please call the student who needs discipline and the prefect she attacked."

Marietta Adams, the head girl, stood and walked briskly to the dais. She looked over to the section of the hall where the senior students were seated. "Anita Desouza and Zika Makanna, please come up to the stage."

The students cheered as Zika stood and simply walked over, her face devoid of emotion. Anita, on the other hand, marched up to the dais in defiance. The students jeered. Some called her mean names.

"Silence!" the principal ordered, and the students became quiet.

"Thank you," the principal said to Marietta. Then she addressed Zika in a voice that carried throughout the hall. "Now, please tell us why you decided to attack a school prefect."

Zika looked at her feet. "I acted out of turn. I apologize to the school for my misconduct."

The principal waited a few moments then addressed the students, "I will not tolerate fighting in my school. More importantly, I will not tolerate students attacking a school-appointed prefect."

Carlotta's heart was beating very fast. She dreaded what might come next. "Princy is not known for her leniency," Onyedi had informed her the day before.

Carlotta looked at her bunkmate, who was still staring at her feet in remorse, and felt her pain. She didn't know what exactly happened that fateful Saturday afternoon—the day of her auditions. By the time she had made it to the dormitory, both students were restrained by a number of students, in their respective corners.

The dormitory had looked like a madhouse and everyone had been talking at the same time. The junior girls who'd witnessed the show from their bunks had dazed looks on their faces, as if they'd just seen a gory boxing match. It was then the distorted versions of the incident began to materialize.

"You are supposed to be respectable students, and not fighting dogs," the principal admonished the entire student body. "I am not running a school for mad girls."

Carlotta knew deep in her heart that Zika was not the kind of person easily provoked to violence. She had a sweet disposition and was one of the nicest senior students at FGGC Uddah. Whatever reason Zika might have had for slapping Anita—if in fact she did—must have been a serious one. However, she had not asked Zika for her version of the incident, nor had Zika volunteered an explanation.

Anita, on the other hand, had been acting really weird since that day. *It's as if the incident had turned her into more of a bitch, and she seems to worsen with each passing day.* It had been a tense week for the dormitory-mates of Sapphire-Six.

Right then, standing on the dais, Anita had a smirk on her face, which deepened with each word the principal spat at Zika.

Dear God, don't let Princy expel my bunkie. Carlotta laced her fingers together and sandwiched them between her knees, holding them in place with sheer force. *I'll start fetching my own buckets of water from now on. Anything but total expulsion—please!*

"Because you are a student with excellent academic records," the principal directed at Zika, "I shall let you off lightly. However, should a case like this repeat itself, I shall bring a heavy hand down upon you."

Here it comes, Carlotta thought, and cringed. *Please, God!*

"For your punishment," the principal continued, "you will be gated for the rest of the term."

The students gasped.

Carlotta was perplexed. *Gated? What does that mean?*

"Quiet!" the principal ordered, and silence prevailed. "I hope this will teach you all to compose yourselves like young ladies at all times no matter how badly you are provoked." She said to Zika, "Now, you will please apologize to your dormitory prefect."

"I am sorry, Anita," Zika said.

The students sighed and clapped.

The principal dismissed Zika and Anita, then ordered the students to be quiet. Soon after that, the assembly was concluded with the FGGC Uddah school anthem and the students filed out of the hall by order of classes.

Carlotta said hello to Onyedi's mother, left Onyedi with her, and waited around the school hall for a while. Finally, she headed back toward the JS1 classroom block with Ossie. Many of their classmates, who were also heading toward the classroom, were all around them.

Someone sneezed.

Carlotta turned and spotted Onyedi a few feet behind, wiping her nose with a piece of bath tissue. She waited for her to catch up.

Carlotta looked at Onyedi, her eyes narrowing with concern. "I didn't think you'd be finished so soon. Are you okay?"

Onyedi nodded. "Mother has a class." She sneezed again.

"You don't look good well at all. You sound like you have a bad cold." Carlotta put an arm around Onyedi's shoulders and winced at the heat emanating from her friend's skin. "You should totally go to the medical clinic, I think you're running a slight temperature."

Onyedi shook her head. "I'm okay. Thanks."

"Let us take her to class," Ossie suggested. "She will feel better inside."

The three girls began making their way to the JS1 block, Carlotta and Ossie on either side of Onyedi.

"What does it mean to be gated?" Carlotta asked.

"I'm not sure..." Ossie started to answer.

Onyedi sniffed. "No outing privileges." She adjusted her glasses and grimaced.

"It is true," Ossie agreed. "It means that your bunkie cannot leave the school until end of term."

Onyedi shrugged. "Just eight weeks left."

"So, being gated is the boarding school equivalent of being grounded, huh?" Carlotta asked, her eyes on Onyedi.

"I think so," Ossie answered carefully.

Onyedi was sniffling and rubbing her nose. Carlotta squeezed her shoulder and gave her a cheerful look. *Probably not a serious cold,* she thought, as Onyedi returned the look with a wan smile.

Carlotta glanced at Ossie. "But how does being gated count as punishment? Seeing as we are in a boarding school and don't get to go anywhere anyway?" She guided Onyedi around the corner of the JS1 building, narrowly missing bumping into a group of junior girls going the other way.

"Being gated also means that your bunkie cannot go to club outings, excursions, or any other social event that is taking place outside school." Ossie nodded to Onyedi as if to affirm what she had just said. Onyedi nodded back. "She cannot even leave the school premises at all, no matter what."

Carlotta made a face. "So, big deal." She rolled her eyes then shut them for a second. *Thank you, God!*

"Yes, so your bunkie is not going to be allowed to go for the SS2 outing," Ossie said, nodding ruefully.

Carlotta recalled that Zika had mentioned the SS2 outing to her about two weeks back. The first term of every year at FGGC Uddah, the SS2 students were allowed to take their new JS1 bunkmates out of the school grounds into the town beyond. This was a practical way to help the new students learn about their new environment. Zika had been quite excited about the outing and was planning to show Carlotta a few fun places in the city of Onitsha. *Now, she won't be able to. Poor Senior Zicker! But at least she totally didn't get expelled.*

Onyedi sniffled again.

"*On-yeh-dee*, are you okay?" Carlotta asked in a small voice.

"Yes, fine," Onyedi said and visibly suppressed a sneeze. Her voice sounded like she was speaking into a balloon. She sniffed and wiped her nose. She appeared weak.

"I suppose you *oughta* go to the clinic," Carlotta said in a worried voice. She rubbed the palm of her hand against Onyedi's forehead. The skin still felt a little warm. "Come on, I'll take you."

Onyedi shook her head. "No need."

She is so self-assured and independent, Carlotta thought. *I should be more like her.*

They got to their classroom and went to their seats. Emeh and Amanda came over to Carlotta and expressed sympathy for Zika's plight. Some of their other classmates did likewise.

Ndidi sneered. "Serves her right for trying to kill a prefect. She should have been suspended, or even expelled!"

Carlotta was not surprised. After spending several weeks in the same class with the sharp-mouthed Ndidi, she had come to expect barbed remarks from her and no less.

But many girls thought differently. They pounced on Ndidi at once.

"Shut up and sit down you big-headed Omata babe," Joyce retorted.

"Who are you calling an Omata babe?" Ndidi returned in a flash.

Carlotta knew the term *Omata babe* was used to refer to students who lived in Onitsha, the largest city in Anambra State and east of the Niger. She didn't understand why living in Onitsha was considered derogatory by some FGGC Uddah students, even though Ossie had explained that most people who lived in Onitsha were businessmen and commercial traders. *Why the heck is that such a big deal?* New York City and Chicago were full of corporate workers and small business owners, Carlotta reasoned. And still, both cities were regarded as the height of social status in the United States. Or at least New York City was. *No one in her right minds would ridicule anyone for living in New York, Las Vegas, or California. Why then Onitsha? I just don't get it.*

"You!" Nelly challenged Ndidi, getting to her feet. She placed both hands on her desk and leaned forward. "Are you going to deny that you live in Onitsha?" Her attitude showed she was ready to pounce the moment Ndidi came back with anything short of the truth.

"*Sharrap* there!" Ndidi spat, eyes closed, nose in the air, neck extended, head spinning from side to side so fast Carlotta feared it might break free. "Just because you managed to live in Lagos, you think you're better than everyone else?" Her hiss reverberated all over the classroom. *Mscheew!*

"Don't you dare *sharrap* me," Nelly raged. "You stupid, bombastic, *jabajantic*, nonsensical Ikeregbe!" Nelly finally ran out of adjectives. For her, the likening of Ndidi to Ikeregbe, the comical character of a dwarf, was just apt.

Many girls tittered.

"Why shouldn't I tell you to *sharrap*? You think because you live in Lagos, everyone should bow down and start worshiping you? *Biko* just *gerrout!* As if it's your father that owns Lagos. *Afo-anu!*" Animal offal!

"At least she takes pride in living in Festac and being called a Lagos babe." Joyce was quick to come to her friend's aid. "What about you, you witchy rat? How come you're not proud of living in Onitsha?"

"What is it with you girls *sef* and where people live, *ehn?*" Bukola asked in her deep Yoruba accent. "What does it matter if somebody lives in Ijebu-Ode? Or in *ehn...* Asaba? Or even Enugu? It is the same Nigeria, *abi?*"

For a well-seasoned Yoruba student like Bukola, peppering her sentences with pidgin words and exclamations was not uncommon. In this case, she used the word *abi* to reaffirm that what she said was in order. It would be the same way one would ask, "right?" at the end of one's sentence in an attempt to draw a positive response from the person to whom one was addressing.

"How would you know if some places are better than others, when you've lived your whole life in a place like Ogun State?" Joyce turned on Bukola. "Do you even know where Lagos is?"

"*Yeh!* See this one oh!" Bukola exclaimed, pointing a *you're so ridiculous* finger at Joyce. "What do you mean by that? You—You—" she launched into the Yoruba-expletives-yelling mode, as she always did in situations like this, when she found it difficult to express herself properly in English.

Soon, the whole class was in an uproar.

Ndidi had managed to scramble onto her locker and was now poised, legs a few feet apart, school skirt hitched up about two inches above the knees—in a bid to give her legs more spreading room. She was waving her arms above her head and verbally battling with Nelly, Joyce, and a few other Lagos babes.

Some other students had climbed on their lockers as well and were arguing amongst themselves about which city was better: Lagos or Enugu? Port Harcourt or Abuja?

A few others began crooning old nursery rhymes. *"Solomon Grundy: Born on Monday, christened on Tuesday...!"*

Two *Kabashers* were standing and praying loudly, their arms spread out in front of them, in a desperate attempt to cast the demons of noisemaking from their boisterous peers. "In Jesus' name! Amen!"

Bukola was still yelling curses in Yoruba.

The nursery rhymes increased in tempo. *"This old man, he played one, he played nicknames on my thumb…!"*

As expected, Rosemary started banging on her locker with one of her school sandals, intent on bringing the rowdy class back to order.

The old-timers missed no beat. *"John Bull my son, I sent you to school…!"*

From her seat, Carlotta watched them. "This never gets old," she shouted to Ossie and sighed. "Very soon the whole class will totally get punished for making such a racket."

"My Grandfather's clock was too tall for the shelf, so it stood ninety years on the floor…!"

Carlotta wasn't disappointed for a few moments later, loud knocks were coming from the classroom door.

❈ ❈ ❈

"*Mary had a little lamb, little la—!*"
The rhymes screeched to a halt.

The rest of the class stopped yelling and looked to the source of interruption.

Framed by the door was the darkest and largest man Carlotta had seen since she left the United States. The man's total weight could be estimated at a hundred and eighty pounds.

Girls dismounted from the top of their lockers and sat down. Others rushed back to their seats. A few opened their books and pretended to be reading.

"Kneel down, all of you," the man ordered. He ambled into the classroom and stood facing the students who hadn't moved an inch. This time, he shouted. "I said, kneel down!"

The students scrambled to obey.

"Kneel down! And raise your hands!" The man surveyed the class. He demanded, "Who's your class monitor?"

Rosemary stood.

"I did not ask you to stand up!" The man's eyes shot fire.

Rosemary dropped back to her knees at once, and raised her hands.

"So, why were you disturbing the whole school?" The man scanned the class with stern, calculating eyes. "You!" He pointed to Chikor, who had her hands resting on her head. "Raise your hands up straight!"

Chikodili hastily obeyed.

Satisfied, the man turned his attention back to Rosemary. "Yes?"

"Excuse me, sir." Rosemary was in tears. "They started it, I was telling them to stop making noise and—"

The man interrupted. "Who started what?"

"Ndidi and Nelly," Rosemary said. "They started the noise."

Ndidi made a clucking sound with her tongue. But the man heard.

"You! Come here!" He bounded into the row of desks, reached out and grabbed Ndidi by her shirt collar. Ndidi's feet entirely left the ground as the man dragged her outside. He made her lie facedown, with arms stretched forward, on the concrete floor surrounding the classroom, all the while swearing and hurling insults her way.

Despite the grave situation they were in, a few girls giggled. The man's insults at Ndidi were more hilarious than scary and many of the tiny girl's detractors reveled in her discomfort and humiliation.

The man returned and wagged a forefinger at the class. "I don't ever want to hear a noise from this class again." He turned to Rosemary. "What lesson are you supposed to be having?"

"Social studies," the class prefect answered. "But, Mr. Okenwa is not coming to class today. He told us to do the exercises in our textbooks during his period."

"In that case, remain kneeling until your next teacher arrives. If I ever hear you making noise again…" He left the threat hanging and shook his head from side to side. Then he walked through the door and disappeared as quickly as he had come.

"Please, who was that?" someone whispered.

No one knew.

"Mr. Abass. SS1 physics," Onyedi supplied. She sneezed and wiped her nose.

"How do you know?" Joyce asked.

"Joyce, please, hold your own there," Amanda intervened. "You should better not pick on Onyedi."

"That what?" Nelly sneered. "Since when did you become her spokeswoman?"

Several girls giggled.

"Are you going to say something?" Ossie whispered to Carlotta.

"I've learned to pick my battles," Carlotta replied. But she kept a keen eye on Onyedi. She was still worried that the cold might be serious.

"You girls, please don't start again," Rosemary wailed. "We are already serving punishment for making noise."

"Go and tell that to the little rat lying outside." Joyce sniggered. The girls giggled again.

Carlotta looked at Ossie who gave her a defeated look in return. Her arms were beginning to hurt. She closed her eyes and wished she were someplace else. Anywhere at all but where she was at the moment kneeling on the hard floor with her arms extended above her head. "Great," she whispered. "Don't you just love it when this happens?"

Onyedi sneezed. Several girls reacted. Onyedi sneezed again, three times in quick succession.

"Are you sure you are okay?" Carlotta called.

"Fine," Onyedi replied. "Thanks." She sniffled and blew her nose.

"Please oh, spare us the germs," someone said.

"*Biko,* show some sympathy, the girl is not feeling well," Onyedi's neighbor admonished.

"Oh! *O kwa* miserable sympathizer."

"Since when did sneezing become a sickness?" another girl asked.

"You girls should just close your smelly mouths and stop spreading tuberculosis," someone else advised.

"Which kind tuberculosis?" one girl directed at the student who'd spoken. "You that you're insulting people don't let thunder strike your cholera-infested mouth there!"

"You *nko?*" the first girl returned. "It's kwashiorkor that will obtain your head."

"All of you that are talking, may you acquire beriberi!"

"May *ojuju* catch the eyes of the next person that opens her mouth!"

"And you, may your left hand turn into leprosy!"

"That what? In short, may all of you turn into Ijebu monkeys!"

"Please, you girls should just shut your rotting traps *joor!*"

"Shut your own dirty mouth. Zebu cattle like you!"

"Who are you calling a Zebu cattle? You Muturu! Better mind your gossiping mouth there!"

"N'dama! Sokoto Gudali! Red Bororo! You are all cattle-rearers."

"*Sharrap dia,* all of you!"

"Okay, time out," Carlotta declared, and jumped to her feet. She was genuinely worried now and could not take it anymore. She would get Onyedi some help even if it meant tilting the girl over her shoulder and carting her off to the medical clinic.

"Feddie Girl! Get back on your knees!" Joyce snapped.

"Screw you," Carlotta hissed. She jumped over legs and avoided stepping on feet as she made her way to where Onyedi knelt—hunched into a small, pitiable lump.

"*Carrottah,* go back to *yah* position!" an irritated voice said. "You are going to put us in *tlouble.*"

"*Duh!* You all are already in deep shit."

"*Oya*, return to your corner with immediate effect!" another ordered.

Come make me. Carlotta ignored the girl. "Get up," she said to Onyedi, pulling her to her feet. "We're *gonna* go get you some help. You need medication for that cold." She wrapped her arms around her friend, supporting her as she walked to the door.

Onyedi's body felt really warm.

"It's probably only a virus," Carlotta whispered, praying she was right. "I'm sure they'll have something for it at the clinic."

"Look me look trouble with this Feddie Girl oh! *Biko*, just rewind to your position with automatic alacrity!"

"To kneel *hia* no be beans oh! I *shakwall* seek revenge if she take style manufacture extra punishment for us oh!"

"*Abi o!* Class monitor, *abeg* use remote control to wire her back to her position!"

Not heeding the protests of the kneeling class, Carlotta bundled Onyedi through the door and away from the classroom. *You all deserve to be punished anyway.*

When Carlotta returned twenty minutes later, her classmates were still kneeling with their arms above their heads.

"How's she?" Ossie whispered.

"She'll be okay." Carlotta nodded, reassuring the questioning looks of Amanda and Emeh. "The nurse said it was a viral infection, and she totally needed medication and bed rest."

A few minutes later, and to the utter relief of the class, the bell rang.

"It's time for business studies," Rosemary announced.

Groaning, the girls scrambled to their feet and dug in their lockers for their textbooks.

As they left the classroom, Carlotta noticed Ndidi still lying on the floor. She nudged Ossie and indicated with an angle of her head.

Ossie called, "Ndidi, get up! It's time for business studies."

Ndidi did not move a muscle. She had fallen asleep right there on the floor, her head supported by her hands, which were bunched into fists. She continued to lay there, a lone figure high-lighted by the warm rays of the morning sun.

Carlotta stooped before Ndidi and shook her. "Hey! Get up! You don't totally plan on laying here all day, do you?"

Ndidi woke with a start. "What? What's happening?" She looked dazed. "Where is everybody?"

"They've gone to the Business Building," Ossie informed the perplexed looking girl. "We have business studies now."

Ndidi jumped to her feet. "How come they didn't wake me up?" She ran into the class and began rummaging through her locker for her textbook. "You girls, please wait for me," she called to Ossie and Carlotta, who were about to continue on after the rest of the class.

"Hello?" Carlotta said. "Wait for *you*? Are you kidding me?" Then she raised her voice so that Ndidi could hear, "Why on earth should we wait for *you*? You are a witchy student, remember?"

Carlotta walked away with Ossie, leaving the agitated Ndidi by herself in the classroom trying to locate her textbook.

✳ ✳ ✳

That afternoon, as the students left the Dining Hall and headed back toward their houses, Emeh sidled up to Carlotta.

She grinned. "Guess what?"

"Oh, I don't know. What?" Carlotta was tired; she was in no mood to play games.

"The list is out. The students for the school play. It's on the notice board, in the house lobby." Emeh beamed.

"No way." Carlotta's heart missed a beat. "Did I make it?"

Emeh's smile faltered. "*Ah non, mon amie*, you have to go and see for yourself." Oh no, my friend.

Carlotta did not need another invitation. She sprinted off to Sapphire House. There were several students in front of the notice board when she got to the lobby. She stood on tiptoe and quickly scanned the list of names of the chosen few—those that would represent FGGC Uddah in the school play.

There it was. She was in! She got the part of the main character Ogwoma. Nneka was her understudy. *Great!*

"You got in! You got the part!" Emeh was behind Carlotta, jumping and clapping. Carlotta joined in. The two girls whooped with excitement.

"Isn't it wonderful?" Carlotta thought she would burst with happiness.

"Yes, very wonderful indeed," a sarcastic voice replied.

Carlotta stopped jumping. She had not seen Nneka enter the lobby.

"Congratulations. You did very well at the auditions," Nneka said in an acid tone, and left.

"You don't think she's mad at me for getting the part, do you?" Carlotta asked Emeh.

"Who cares," Emeh said in a singsong voice. She resumed jumping. "The important thing is that you auditioned and got the part. Full stop."

"I guess you're right." Carlotta no longer felt like celebrating. "Thanks again for letting me know the results were in. Listen, I gotta go."

"Where are you going?" Emeh asked, still smiling. "We're supposed to celebrate."

"Sorry, *A-mer*, but I need to go check on *On-yeh-dee*."

Emeh's face fell. She opened her mouth to say something. But the bell rang. It was time for siesta.

In the next instant, Carlotta was out the door.

❋ ❋ ❋

The Drama Club practices for the school play began the following week. Carlotta put a great deal of effort into mastering her part in the play. She memorized a few lines for her part every day, and practiced with her study group mates during her free time. Members of the Drama Club thought she was doing a good job. Even Nneka thought so.

Carlotta was relieved Nneka appeared to be over the disappointment of being passed over for the lead role in the play.

Zika, on the other hand, seemed to withdraw further into her shell with each passing day. It appeared the incident with Anita had affected her more deeply than Carlotta first realized.

Although Zika was stiffly polite to Anita, and would not speak much to the other girls in the dormitory—except for Shade and Nneka—she remained good friends with Carlotta. Zika continued to protect and assist her bunkmate whenever she could. She even implored Onyedi's bunkmate to take Carlotta on the SS2 outing instead, since Onyedi was taken ill and couldn't make it.

Despite her commitments to the Drama Club, Carlotta continued to work hard in class and, with the help of her study group, her grades went from average to good. She was delighted.

Onyedi made a full recovery from her cold. She rejoined the group in time to study for the second tests.

Everything was going very well for Carlotta and the group of students that were her friends.

All was well for Carlotta indeed.

✻ ✻ ✻

Prone, Shelley maneuvered him on top of her.

She ran her hands up his back and buried them in his hair. She pulled his head down, and planted a deep kiss on his lips, reluctant to let go.

I want you so much.

His hands were everywhere, kneading, exploring, probing. Then they settled on her breasts.

Shelley moaned.

Kiss me, she said.

He did.

She held him tight and rolled over so she was on top—straddling him. She began to move. He responded by thrusting upward to match her rhythm.

Faster! Shelley's mind screamed. Her hips followed the order. A warm sensation originated from her center and fanned out, enveloping her, drowning her senses, seeking release.

My goodness!

She couldn't hold on…

Oh…!

She let go…

Josh…!

Shelley woke. She jerked into a sitting position. She was in bed. Her pulse was racing. The sheets were tangled about her legs.

"Oh God! It was a dream."

It had felt almost real. And she'd woken a few seconds too early.

With a cry of anguish, she fell back against the pillow and crushed it beneath her head.

Chapter 13
Horror, Horror, Horror!

"The inspectors are here!" A Sapphire House subsidy yelled.

"You have five seconds to return to your dormitories and stand by your beds!" Chidi ordered.

Pandemonium broke out in Sapphire House as everyone raced to stand at attention by their bunks.

The whole place gleamed. All the dormitories, bathrooms, laundry rooms, and the lobby had been scrubbed and mopped clean. The windows had all been washed and polished to perfection. All the students' personal belongings were either stuffed into their owner's lockers, or stowed away in the boxes, bags, and suitcases that were neatly stashed in the large luggage room next to the lobby. All beds were impeccably made in the official sky-blue bed sheets of Sapphire House.

The students were dressed in their day uniforms, complete with white socks and brown sandals. Senior girls had their hair either woven into cornrows or combed and tied back behind their heads.

Saturday morning inspection routine at FGGC Uddah was a serious business. Basically, the students had breakfast at 9:00 AM then labored hard at their places of duty to get the whole school whipped into shape for the routine.

The inspectors consisted of the school matron, two members of staff, Marietta Adams—the head girl, and Lola Ajayi—the senior boarding house prefect. The house prefect of the house under scrutiny was also expected to join in the inspection train.

The routine inspection usually commenced at Ruby House, after which the train would proceed to Sapphire House, followed by Emerald House, then Pearl House before Gold House. Crystal House was always the last to be inspected.

Points were awarded to each house for level of cleanliness of the house exterior, interior, and facilities, while special points were given for each student that exceeded a pre-determined level of neatness.

On this particular Saturday, however, exactly five minutes before the inspectors were due, everything and everyone in Sapphire House was in place, except for the area to the north of the building—some pranksters had littered the place with discarded peanut shells.

Chidi Anayo was furious.

As was her duty, and the duty of the subsidies of Sapphire House, Chidi devoted her Saturday mornings to making sure every nook and cranny of Sapphire House was spick and span. Not a strand of hair or grain of sand was to be out of place.

Therefore, for the house prefect, discovering the peanut shells rudely scattered behind the building barely a few minutes before the inspectors were due, was like a serious slap in the face.

Chidi had assembled all the students of Sapphire House, from JS1 to SS2, and ordered them to stand outside the house double doors, while she tried to ascertain which students were stupid enough to attempt something that disrespectful.

"The students responsible for the groundnut shells had better come forward right now!" Chidi had yelled.

When no one came forth to take the blame for the prank, the house prefect had threatened to punish everyone until someone confessed.

However, the timely arrival of the inspectors saved the Sapphire House students from further berating.

Carlotta fumed. *Punishing everyone is just so wrong on so many levels. What makes her think the prank wasn't carried out by SS3 students, or students from another house, or even by her stuck-up subsidies?*

Carlotta was not one to take lightly to being punished for something she didn't do. There was no love lost between her and the Sapphire House prefect. And in spite of having to be mass punished with the other students of Sapphire House, Carlotta thought Chidi deserved all the silly pranks that could be dropped in her lap.

Back in her corner at Sapphire-Six, Carlotta stood behind her bunkmate. She hated inspections. In her opinion, the grand total of ten minutes it took for the inspection train to look-over the whole of Sapphire House was a complete waste of time. As far as she was concerned, the ten minutes of scrutiny wasn't worth the whole morning it took the students to prepare for the inspection.

She hated the way the inspectors strutted up and down the concrete floors. She was sure that no one ever apprised them of just how backbreaking the job of flooding the concrete floors with soapy water and using brooms to scrape and scrub them clean, could be. This was in addition to mopping and polishing the floors with absorbent materials till they glistened.

The inspection train probably will never know how hard some JS1 students worked to sweep the areas immediately surrounding the building, free of debris, and how tasking it was to hand-pull weeds from the ground to meet Chidi Anayo's specifications.

They also wouldn't have any idea what the SS1 students had to endure to get the toilet bowls sparkling and the bathroom stalls in the state required for inspection.

Carlotta was convinced the SS1 students had the worst end of the deal. She honestly didn't want to think about how the poor students managed to get the toilets clean, twice every day, especially since there was no running water in the bathrooms.

Ugh! Gross! I can totally wait to get to SS1. I definitely shouldn't be here long enough for that to happen anyway.

Several minutes later, when the inspectors were finally done with their, "Why couldn't the stain on that wall be removed?" and "Why is the mattress on that bed crooked?" they checked-off Sapphire House as inspected and passed for the week, and proceeded to the next house in line.

Carlotta breathed a sigh of relief.

But the feeling was short-lived for Anita immediately announced, "All JS1 to SS2 students should march back to the front of the house and wait there for Chidi Anayo!"

No one dared give an audible groan—not even the SS2 students. Only the SS3 girls could be heard heaving sighs of relief that the inspection ordeal was finally over for another week.

Carlotta followed her dormitory girls out of Sapphire-Six.

Two minutes later, she was kneeling on the rough ground with eighty percent of the inhabitants of Sapphire House, enduring the house prefect's threats and show of power in silence.

✳ ✳ ✳

The mass-punishment of the students of Sapphire House had been going on for about fifteen minutes when Chidi Anayo turned her back on the kneeling students for a moment.

All at once, a movement caught Carlotta's eye. She turned her head. To her surprise, she found that one of the two JS2 students that had been kneeling on her left had disappeared.

That's odd. I could have sworn—

A movement took place on Carlotta's right. Another disappearance—this time a JS3 student.

Wow! How do they do that?

Carlotta felt a tapping sensation on her heel. Discreetly, she looked back. Joke and Grace were making subtle signals with their heads.

She immediately knew what they meant.

Glancing forward to make sure Chidi Anayo still had her back to them, Carlotta inched her way, with Joke and Grace, to the edge of the kneeling mass of students. Once clear, she jumped to her feet, doubled-over, and quickly stole-away, flanked by the JS2 students.

They scurried a few feet then dived behind a large shrub. Peering through leaves and branches to make sure the coast was still clear, the three girls skirted around the shrub and sprang their way to the back of Sapphire House. They ignored the winding path, headed straight for the bushes to the side of the dining hall, and began thrashing their way to freedom.

Oh God! I totally hope we don't get caught.

Carlotta's heart beat wildly as she cut through shoulder-length grass blades and dodged low-hanging branches of untended trees. She'd just been maneuvered through the classic zapping action—one that was the most difficult to pull-off owing to the number of witnesses involved and what was at stake if discovered.

The JS2 students with Carlotta were not afraid of being ratted-out. Carlotta learned form them that one of the unspoken rules of zapping was never selling-out a fellow zapper. She was made to understand that no student would admit to ever seeing her get up and depart from the group of kneeling students.

That was just the way things worked.

Yeah right. That's if the witchy Senior Chee-dee doesn't realize that one out of the three Feddie Girls she punished has totally vanished. But then, who cares?

Carlotta couldn't have cared less what Chidi would do when she discovered her gone. As she thrashed through the bushes of the unfamiliar and unused terrain leading to the general direction of the classroom blocks, all she could think of was *we only have an hour till the dreaded Manual Labor. I need to find myself something to eat. Fast!*

✳ ✳ ✳

Manual Labor was every bit as labor-intense as the name suggested.

The whole student body of FGGC Uddah was first summoned to the school hall with the chiming of the school bell. Thereafter, the labor prefect—a pudgy student who looked like she could easily bench-press a hundred and fifty pounds—addressed them.

The students formed a single line per class and cutlasses were handed out as they exited the school hall. Work was assigned by class and the prep-prefects acted as supervisors. Much to Carlotta's horror, her class was assigned to cut the grass behind the Arts and Music Building.

Jeez! What on earth are they thinking? We are not cattle ranchers, for Pete's sake. Carlotta kicked at a tuft of over-grown grass with the toe of her sandal. She cried in dismay, "Making human beings work like bulldozers is totally wrong on all levels."

"*Ssh!*" someone hushed Carlotta. "Senior Patricia might hear you."

"Who cares?" Carlotta was just about ready to throw in the towel and return to her dormitory regardless of the dire consequences. The air was stifling and filled with the sickening scent of fresh grass. She was sweating and her shirt stuck to her back. She dropped the cutlass she'd been trying in vain to use, and stared at the palm of her right hand. "Shoot! Get a load of this. I've totally developed another blister!"

Ossie, who'd been attacking her portion of grassland with gusto, stopped and straightened. "Neighbor," she called to Carlotta, "don't worry. When I finish with my portion, I'll come and help you with your own."

"Thanks," Carlotta muttered. Using Ossie's promise to help as a perk, she summoned up the enthusiasm to try cutting the over-grown grass on her assigned portion again. Raising the cutlass, she succeeded in leveling off two or three blows before the weapon flew-off her hands and landed out of sight some ten feet away.

"*Kai!* Who threw her cutlass on my head?" an irritated voice demanded.

"Sorry! Are you okay?" Carlotta asked, hoping she hadn't dismembered one of her classmates. *Christ! Where to dial 911?*

Nelly straightened, rubbing the back of her neck with one earth-stained hand. "Feddie Girl, please take it easy. You almost beheaded somebody just now." She retrieved the run-away cutlass and threw it back to Carlotta.

"I'm really sorry," Carlotta said, flashing Nelly an apologetic grin. "It was an accident." She eyed the cutlass that was now within reach, but was reluctant to pick it up. "I'm totally beat. I doubt if I can keep going."

"Then just pack-up and go," Nelly advised. "It's not as if Senior Patricia will even notice if you spend ten whole hours cutting your grass." She shook her head sadly at Carlotta. "Your portion looks like someone let a pack of monkeys loose on it." She cackled. "Do you see all those rat-chops you made there? It would have been better if you didn't even touch the grass at all. At least, the grass would still be even."

Carlotta considered the work she'd done so far, her head cocked to one side.

In comparison to Ossie's meticulously half-done portion, hers looked just like Nelly described. Small patches of freshly dug up earth showed areas where she had lost her temper with the unmanageable cutlass and pulled-out the stubborn grass with her bare hands. On other parts, she'd only succeeded in bending the grass blades.

Carlotta found she was a total disaster when it came to grass cutting.

She sighed, and said to Nelly, "Well, much as I'd love to do just like you suggested, I can't just get out of here and leave my work undone."

Joyce joined in from her squatting position, where she was busily raking up butchered grass blades with her fingers. "Yes you can. It's easy if you know how to do it."

"Neighbor, please don't listen to Joyce. She'll only lead you into trouble," Ossie advised Carlotta before turning on Joyce. "If it's that easy to boycott Manual Labor, why don't you go and do it first?"

Joyce pulled herself to her full height of five feet nine inches. "Are you double-daring me?"

"No," Ossie challenged, "I'm triple-daring you."

"Okay, fine." Joyce nodded. She wiped her grass-stained hands on her skirt. "Wait oh! What will you give me if I succeed?"

Ossie considered the proposition for a while. She dropped her cutlass and wiped her sweaty brow with a dirty wrist. "How about you collect my meat for one whole week if you succeed. And if you fail, I will collect yours?"

"Done!" Joyce cracked her knuckles, stretched, and looked around. When she was satisfied none of the prefects was within earshot, she raised her voice. "Mr. Ikenna, I'm dead oh!"

"What's she doing?" Carlotta whispered. She tugged at her shirt to get it unstuck from her sweaty back.

"I think she's calling on Mr. Ikenna, the music lab attendant, to come release her." Ossie had laughter in her voice.

"Is that possible?" Carlotta ran her tongue over the roof of her mouth. She felt sure she detected a grain or two of sand in there somewhere. "Can a non-academic staff let you off from Manual Labor?"

"I don't know, but this Joyce has guts," Ossie said in awe.

Carlotta brightened. "Sounds like a brilliant idea to me. Why didn't I totally think of it first?" *Gosh! I'm so dumb.*

Several girls stopped working and stood to watch.

Ossie wiped her eye with a corner of her blouse and fluttered her eyelids. "I think there's sand in my eye," she said.

"That totally sucks. I've got sand under my tongue. *Eeuw!*"

Joyce tried again. "Mr. Ikenna, I am dying here oh!"

Mr. Ikenna was a short, light-skinned, middle-aged man whose uncanny gift for making people laugh endeared him to the students. Though he worked as the music laboratory attendant, he had no real talent with musical instruments and sounded like an enraged elephant whenever he tried to sing. Senior students had nicknamed him Macbeth because of his habit of speaking like he was reciting poetry.

Joyce continued to call and wave her arms. Finally, Macbeth took notice and appeared from the music laboratory.

He approached Joyce. "What troubles you, my dear one?"

Carlotta stifled a giggle. Ossie hid a smile.

Straight-faced, Joyce complained, "Sir, I'm not well and my prep prefect is still making me cut grass. Please, can you give me an excuse?"

Macbeth considered Joyce for a second, his eyes half-closed. "All right, you are excused. One who is laden with pain; shall not be made to labor in vain."

Joyce beamed. "Thank you, sir! Please remember to tell my prep prefect that you released me oh." She turned and winked at Ossie and Carlotta. Then she started to walk away, making sure to take small, sickly steps for the benefit of all who were watching.

After a few steps, when she thought Macbeth wasn't looking, Joyce quickly recovered and took to her heels.

But Macbeth saw. And understood.

He yelled, "Oh, horror, horror, horror! How can a disabled fly? Is it in a dream or in reality? Come back here! Come back here!"

The next thing anyone knew, Macbeth was after Joyce in a flash.

Carlotta couldn't hold back her mirth. Quite forgetting about her fatigue, she leaned her hands on her knees and gave herself up to gales of laughter. It was just too funny to behold the short Macbeth chasing after Joyce at full speed.

You go, Joyce!

Still laughing, Carlotta didn't notice her prep prefect's approach. She was only aware of the prefect's presence when Patricia struck her on the head with a stick.

"*Ouch!*" The laughter died in Carlotta's throat at once.

"Get back to work," Patricia hissed. With one thin leg, she kicked Carlotta's cutlass back to her and marched out of the way of flying blades.

✳ ✳ ✳

He was always there—same seat, cocky attitude, knowing look.

I do not need this from a student. But Shelley knew the truth— she was attracted to him. And she was in need of male attention.

But she had a responsibility as a professor.

He is my student.

From his seat, Josh winked, and smiled. Shelley looked away and pretended not to notice.

This is absurd. I should not think of him in that way.

But she did. And the dreams made it easy. His open admiration helped, too.

Enough! I shall have a word with the Dean of Students right after this class.

By the time the forty-minute lecture was over, Shelley had given herself several reasons not to go see the Dean—none of them had anything to do with professional etiquette.

✳ ✳ ✳

On the Saturday following the SS2 weekday outing, Carlotta rushed off to the computer building after lunch. She had several new e-mails; most were from her parents and cousins. One was from Sasha.

Hi Carlotta,

Sup? Sounds like u r totally having fun at ur new school. Nick & I went on another d8 last nite. Thought I'd let u know. When r u coming back? Mail me when u get a chance. Facebook rocks. You should totally join again.

Freddie Oyel

Ttyl.

Sasha

Carlotta stared in surprise at Sasha's e-mail. She expected longer mails from her friend. Maybe Sasha was just very busy or going through rough times with the middle school cheerleading squad. She would probably write another e-mail soon with news of the happenings in San Francisco, like she always did. All the same, Carlotta decided to reply and give Sasha details about the goings on at FGGC Uddah.

Sup, Sasha.

I didn't expect to get one or two lines from u, and I mean that literally. I'm glad you and Nick are still a couple.

My Drama Club auditions went very well and I was offered a main part in the school play. Isn't that awesome? The drama competition would take place in Ghana, next term. I am pretty much excited and I really look forward to visiting another West African country. Did you know Ghana is famous for its gold? I learned all about that in social studies.

Anyway, we've started practicing for the play and everyone thinks I'm totally doing a good job on my part.

Yesterday, my bunkmate's friend took me on an outing into the city of Onitsha. My bunkmate could not take me cos she had been gated (more like grounded) for the term.

There are a lot of people in Onitsha and the streets are mostly untidy. There are some pretty neighbor-hoods in the city as well, but I love the Holy Trinity Cathedral the most.

Well, the outing was fun. I got to see the Main Market, some grocery stores and a few other fun places.

281

I was also taken to a fast food restaurant. Mmm! My first good meal in, like, forever. The stores are not exactly like what you'd expect to see in San Francisco. Did you know that all sodas here are sold in glass bottles?

I am learning to speak a few words in Igbo and Yoruba languages. Bia means 'come', and Kedu means 'how are you' in Igbo. The Yoruba's say Wa and Baoni. I still find most of the native words difficult to pronounce though. French, on the other hand, is a little easier to learn, probably because one of my friends is like totally fluent in French and she helps me out a lot. I can now write simple sentences in French and I can conjugate a few verbs, too. Isn't that, like, totally awesome?

I wish you'd tell me more about what's going on in San Francisco and how you're handling middle school this fall. I am still doing a good job of keeping my grades up, and hopefully, by the end of the school year, I will be back in the US.

Well, take care and keep me posted.

Lotta luv,

Carlotta

Carlotta sent off her reply to Sasha and replied to her parents' and cousin's e-mails, too. Her mother was currently in Boston attending an annual editors conference. Her dad was busy with hospital stuff as usual. Carlotta was still a little confused about why her parents kept e-mailing her separately without mentioning each other in their mails. *Something fishy is so going on.* She put the thought out of her mind, and left the computer building.

When Carlotta returned to Sapphire-Six that afternoon, there was a gold-and-red trimmed purple envelope on her bed.

Chapter 14
The Purple Envelope

Carlotta drifted up to her bunk and reached out for the purple envelope. Her hand shook as her fingers closed around it. She dreaded what she feared it might contain.

Carlotta's mind raced.

Did Nneka forget to talk to Rema like she promised? Or did the pompous Feddie Girls Club president, despite Nneka's intervention, decide to go ahead with her threat anyway?

Rema doesn't seem like the sort of person who made empty threats. Now I'm totally in a crappy situation. What a major bummer!

Carlotta let out a heavy sigh as she glanced at the envelope, her thoughts jumping in different directions.

Just what exactly am I to do about this?

She clenched her shaking hand to keep the envelope still. It was addressed in a neat handwriting.

This is definitely odd.

Carlotta had come to associate the purple envelopes with Rema's sprawling style of writing. Maybe another member of the Feddie Girls Club had addressed the envelope this time, she reasoned.

Why?

Carlotta looked around the dormitory, suspicion sharpening her senses. Zika wasn't present, and neither was Nneka. Shade, on the other hand, was on her bed, fast asleep. Anita was reading a book. Bisi was talking with a friend of hers from Gold House. Uche was nowhere to be seen. Sandra was watching Carlotta's every move from her bed across the room. Joke and Grace weren't—

Carlotta turned back. Sandra was still watching, trying hard to make eye contact.

What now? Did Senior Rema order you to yank me to her dorm again?

Carlotta glared. Sandra scowled back. Carlotta turned her back on the nosy girl.

"A ju-girl!" Bisi yelled.

Carlotta, Sandra, and two JS3 students immediately jumped into action and hastened to Bisi's corner. Carlotta looked around for the JS2 students; they were not in the dormitory—probably off studying or something of that sort. Bisi chose to send Sandra on her errand and dismissed the remaining three girls.

I need to get out of here before Sandra returns and drags me to Rema's dorm.

Carlotta placed the unopened purple envelope in her school bag and left the dormitory, in her haste forgetting to close the door. All she wanted at that particular moment was to read the contents of the envelope with a little privacy, somewhere away from Sandra's prying eyes. If Rema was going to reprimand her, then it should be best done in private.

At least it's so not gonna be a 'howler' like the mail Ron got in 'Harry Potter.'

Carlotta exited Sapphire House and hurried toward the Mystical Mangy standing majestically in its strategic position. The area under the tree was deserted, not a soul sought solace from the bright rays of the sun.

Just as well, Carlotta thought. *I can really use a little alone time.*

She stepped over the cement blocks that demarcated the grassy lawn under the tree from the looped graveled path, and flopped herself down on one of the small benches under the tree. From her sitting position, the walkway to Ruby House was clearly visible, while Sapphire House was directly behind. She was completely shaded from the mild November sun, and was partially concealed by the wide, sweeping branches of the tree.

"The Mystical Mangy never sheds its leaves," she remembered being told. Most of the students at FGGC Uddah found that creepy but Carlotta didn't give a hoot.

The weather was already cooling-off with the advent of the harmattan season. Ossie and Onyedi had informed Carlotta that the season signified relatively cold and dry weather, which usually started in November, peaked in January, and dissipated in March.

The weather was definitely getting drier, Carlotta figured. *As for how cold it's gonna get, that surely remains to be seen.* She removed the purple envelope from her school bag and studied the writing on it for a minute. Then she tore it open.

Carlotta stared in surprise.

There was no matching card in the envelope as was usually the case. Instead, a folded, white sheet of paper peeked out. Carlotta removed the sheet; spread it open and read what was written on it.

Her jaw dropped.

She read the message again.

Written on the sheet in the same style of writing as the address on the envelope were the words:

My Darling Carlotta,
I have admired you since the first day I saw you. Being with you always puts a smile on my face. I miss you very much, and I hope as each day goes by, that we become more intimate than we already are.
I love you.
Me, xxx.

Carlotta could not believe her eyes.

Is this some kind of sick practical joke? Who the heck is 'Me, xxx'?
She looked around in confusion. No one was paying any particular attention. A few Ruby House junior girls were carrying buckets of water up their walkway. Several other girls, mostly senior students, were strolling aimlessly about the dormitory area, talking and laughing. None of them looked suspicious.

Her mind in a whirl, Carlotta wondered who would write such a note.

Rema? *No, definitely not.* The British queen-bee was too snobbish to even think of bringing herself down in that way.

Maybe it was one of the students of Sapphire-Six.

Which one?

Zika? *No way,* Carlotta decided.

Who then is it?

Sandra? Probably. *After all, she was staring at me, when I discovered the envelope.* But Carlotta knew that Sandra despised her and had no reason on earth to write her a love note. *Or hadn't she?*

But, what if the note is so not from Sandra?

Emeh? *Maybe it is A-mer.* But Emeh wouldn't resort to writing a love note—Carlotta was sure of that. Emeh would have sought her out and told her what she had to say plain and simple, or maybe said what was on her mind in French. But a love note? She doubted it was Emeh.

Carlotta was at a dead end. She decided not to tell Zika about the note. Her bunkmate already had enough on her plate without having to deal with this latest development. She closed her eyes and thought for a while.

A few minutes later, Carlotta knew exactly who to confide in. She leaped to her feet and made straight for Sapphire-One, where she found Onyedi lying on her bed, reading.

Onyedi accompanied Carlotta back to the tree. When she was done reading the message on the sheet of paper, Carlotta asked, "So, what do you think? Totally creepy, right?"

Onyedi did not reply at first, and chewed on her lower lip. "Your bunkie knows?"

"Nope. I haven't shown this to anyone else." Carlotta thought for a moment then added, "There's this JS3 girl in my dorm, though. Ursula. She was watching me in a totally freaky way last night. You think she might have something to do with this?"

"Maybe." Onyedi's face screwed up in thought. "But why *purple?*"

"You think it's from Senior Rema?" Carlotta asked in a worried voice. She totally communicates events of the Feddie Girls Club with purple envelopes. You know about the club invitations, right?"

Onyedi sighed and adjusted her glasses. "Hmm." She handed the note back to Carlotta. "Good."

Carlotta looked at Onyedi, wondering if perhaps the cold she'd had several days back had affected her head in some way. "Good? What do you mean *good?* Some gay girl writes me a love note and you say it's good? Okay, I'm officially freaked out!"

"Don't think that," Onyedi advised.

Carlotta had just about had it. "What the hell else am I supposed to think?" She rounded on her best friend. "I'm only *thirteen*, for Pete's sake, and obviously, someone believes it's worth her while to make me the target of some twisted lesbian joke. Just for the record, I don't know what the hell else to *think!*"

Onyedi was speechless.

"I'm sorry." Carlotta sighed. "I guess I'm freaking out a little."

After a few moments of deep thought, Onyedi spoke, "Keep this quiet."

Carlotta watched Onyedi with keen eyes.

Onyedi appeared deeply concerned.

"Any ideas as to who might have written this? Or why?" Carlotta asked, waving the white sheet of paper, producing sounds somewhere between crunching and crackling.

"Not yet," Onyedi replied. She put out a hand and made the paper-waving action stop.

Carlotta knew that if she could trust anyone to discreetly find who was responsible for the note, it would be Onyedi. She might be very taciturn but she was also very smart.

"You know what?" Carlotta suggested. "Why don't you keep the note? Maybe you could get some clues from the hand-writing."

"Bad idea."

Carlotta stared sharply at her best friend. Then the meaning of the words sunk in and her shoulders sagged. "Okay," she said in a resigned voice. "Whatever you say. I guess everyone might totally see us in a bad way if they thought you wrote me a note like this, huh?"

Onyedi nodded. "I'm a suspect," she admitted.

"But you didn't write it though, did you?" Carlotta's voice was little above a whisper.

Onyedi looked deep into Carlotta's eyes. "Do I need to?" she asked in a pointed way.

Carlotta's cheeks colored. "I'm sorry, I shouldn't have said that." She reached out and squeezed Onyedi's shoulder. "I guess I'm just a little confused right now, and I don't know anything anymore." She passed a hand through her short curls. "Hell, I'm just thirteen! Whoever said I'm supposed to know anything about these things?"

"You know how I feel." Onyedi took Carlotta's hand in hers. Her gaze did not waver. "And I'm eleven."

A surge of resolve went through Carlotta. She smiled and studied Onyedi's face. Time seemed to stand still for just the two of them. "Yeah," she said softly, lacing her fingers through Onyedi's thin ones. "I know how you feel, 'cause I totally feel the same way, too. Whoever wrote this note, we're so *gonna* find her, right?"

Onyedi nodded a silent promise.

The two girls gazed into each other's eyes for a moment. There was no need for words.

Suddenly, Carlotta cocked her head. "Did you hear that?"

"What?"

"Never mind."

Strange, Carlotta thought. She glanced at the branches high above their heads. She could have sworn she'd heard whispers coming from somewhere up there. *But leaves don't talk, do they?*

Onyedi shrugged and got to her feet, drawing Carlotta up with her. She put an arm around her friend's shoulders, and together, they walked back to Sapphire House, their footsteps blending in perfect harmony with the rapid beats of their hearts.

Once they cleared the walkway of Sapphire House, Carlotta turned back to stare at the sweeping branches of the Mystical Mangy. Onyedi stopped and followed her gaze.

"Leaves totally don't whisper, right?"

"I wonder," was all Onyedi said in reply.

The two girls turned and disappeared through the entrance doors.

✳ ✳ ✳

Shelley pried out the pink paper that was jammed between the doorknob and wooden frame of her front door, her fingers holding on to it like pincers. She didn't need to read the message to know it was a request from the homeowners association in the district, reminding her to *take care of her home and its surroundings.*

This was the third note she'd received from them in the past two weeks. Basically, they were politely informing her to either mow her overgrown lawn, or pay someone to do the dirty work.

What nerve!

Such courage they had telling her how and when to take care of her own surroundings. Shelley looked around and sighed. They were right of course; her lawn did look tacky with its overgrown weeds and grass poking out of everywhere.

Since Richard left, the lawn hadn't been mowed a single time. Shelley just couldn't seem to find the strength to mow the acre of overgrown grass engulfing the immediate vicinity of her home.

She crumpled the pink note and aimed at a large bush that had sprung up in front of the porch.

She missed.

The paper ball landed sluggishly in front of the bush, just one foot short.

She ignored it and went inside.

Kicking the front door shut with one perfectly aimed thrust of her right foot, Shelley grabbed the phone book from the table in the hallway and flipped open the pages as she walked to the kitchen. She found the page she sought and laid the heavy book on the counter. She snatched the phone and dialed the number advertised in bold black letters.

"Yes, I need someone to come over and mow my lawn, please," she said briskly into the mouth receiver, in answer to the cheerful greeting on the other end.

"Only personal checks? That is fine. When is your earliest availability?" She listened for a moment, and then nodded vigorously as she said, "Sure, that will be great. I shall be expecting someone in thirty minutes." She gave the receptionist her name and address and hung up.

She heaved a sigh of relief.

It had been a particularly hard day at school and she was exhausted. Surprisingly, many college students couldn't properly punctuate a sentence even if they had a grammar handbook under their noses.

Students of today—what do they learn in high school? In addition to the punctuation mistakes, many of them simply cannot spell!

Shelley poured herself a half glass of orange juice from the refrigerator then shrugged and topped it with vodka from the bottle in the freezer. She sipped the drink and satisfied with the strength, went to sit in the living room and flipped on the television. She skimmed the channels as she sipped her drink, not particularly interested in any of the featured programs.

Twenty-five minutes later, the doorbell chimed.

Shelley picked herself up from the sofa and went to the door. As she pulled it open, she started to instruct the guy from the lawn mowing company on what she needed done. She took one look at him and her voice froze in her throat.

Lolling against the doorframe and grinning in that cocky way of his, was an amused Josh Greinbach.

* * *

Richard slowly came to. His eyes were unfocused. Images danced around before him. He was prone in bed, and his head felt like a watermelon that had been split with a sledge-hammer. He tried to sit up but winced at the blinding flash of pain that seared through his skull. He collapsed on the pillows and clamped his eyes shut, biting his lip, steeling himself against the painful bolts of thunder exploding in his brain.

"Glad to see you're awake, Doc," a familiar voice greeted.

Richard started, and yanked himself upright. He immediately regretted the abrupt movement as another clap of thunder ripped through his skull. He dumped his head back on the pillows and bit his lip hard to prevent himself from crying out. His mouth filled with the coppery taste of blood. Tears escaped his eyes and rolled into the lobes of his ears.

Richard's breathing was sporadic, puffing out of his chest like black smoke from a coal-fired steam engine. Beads of sweat formed at his hairline and on his upper lip. His tongue felt and tasted like a lead-copper alloy. He waited for the pain to subside, then sat up slowly and wrenched his eyes open, wincing with the effort.

There were two men in the room with Richard. One was mean and burly. The other was tall and wiry—he featured tattoos on every inch of skin on his arms, and owned a head that was bald and so clean-shaven it resembled a giant egg sitting on his neck.

The burly guy sucked air between his teeth as his dark eyes scrutinized Richard.

"Bruno?" Richard ventured. His voice sounded like the scrape of a chair against a concrete floor.

"Bingo! Nice to see you again, Doc," Bruno leered. His pasty face widened and his squat nose looked flatter than Richard remembered.

"What do you want?" Richard croaked. He gritted his teeth against the pain in his head. *What in hell's name did they take to my skull—a crow bar?*

"We are your benefactors," Bruno replied.

"What do you mean? Wait a minute, what's going on here?" Richard wished the throbbing in his head would subside so he could think. Maria was murdered; he was drugged—that was all he remembered. Now, he was lying in a strange bed, with Bruno and his side for company. It didn't make sense.

"Let's just say you owe us big, Doc."

"I don't understand." Richard's eyes widened. The pain jabbed at him.

"That's not important." Bruno took a step forward. Richard cringed. "What's important is the shit we saved your sorry ass from."

"You shot her?" Richard was incredulous. It was more a statement of fact than a question.

Bruno shrugged. "Who said anything about shooting anyone?"

"Why Maria?" The intensity of the pain in his head made it impossible to concentrate. "Why did you blow her away?"

"You own your mouth, Doc. My business is to reason with you." Bruno sat on the bed, which sagged heavily under his weight.

Mr. Egg-head just stood his ground and said nothing. Somehow, his silence was even more menacing than Bruno's intimidating voice.

"You check out of here tomorrow and return to the US. We will be in touch." Bruno's lips drew back to reveal large, tobacco-stained teeth.

Watching Bruno's dental particulars, Richard couldn't help thinking about an alligator. "Go screw yourself, fat ass. You can't tell me what to do."

"Like I said, Doc, you own your mouth." Bruno reached inside his jacket and produced a large envelope. "I'm sure the press will have a slight interest in photos of your rental car decorated with the brains of your secret lover." He leaned in so his face was a few inches from Richard's. "Let's not forget the murder weapon with your prints all over it. The cops will piss their pants with joy."

"I didn't kill her," Richard stressed.

"All a matter of opinion, Doc. We will be in touch." He gave Richard a pat on the shoulder. "See you in America."

"And if I refuse? Or go to the police?" Richard threw back at him.

"There, there, Doc. I think you're a smart guy." Bruno shook his thick head in mock disappointment. "You do what you want." He stared meaningfully into Richard's eyes and sucked on his teeth.

Richard cringed.

In a low voice, Bruno asked, "You know what happens to birds who go singing?" He tossed the envelope across Richard's knees and got to his feet. "See you in America."

"Screw you," Richard said with all the vehemence his throbbing skull would let him muster. "Screw you and the shit-ass Palorizzi Family."

"You own your mouth, Doc," Bruno wheezed. He lumbered out of the room; the silent Mr. Egg-head close behind.

Chapter 15
You Have A Visitor!

The excitement in the air was palpable.

It was a Sunday morning and all the students were preparing for visiting hours. Everyone was in a cheerful mood. There was a smile on every face.

The students were filled with high hopes of getting a visitor from home. Just the prospect of seeing a familiar face that didn't belong in FGGC Uddah was euphoric. Not to mention all the edible goodies that would be available during the course of the day.

Carlotta was learning fast. She now understood that Visiting Day was the only day that junior students could literally get away with not doing any work for their bunkmates. Not that she cared—Zika never let her do any work—but, still, it was exhilarating to see Joke, Grace, and even Uche bounce around the dormitories with gleeful smiles.

Visiting Days at FGGC Uddah were almost as important as Christmas Eve itself. The dormitories, classrooms, and surrounding environs were polished the day before, which was a Saturday, and on the Visiting Day eve, the head girl addressed the students during dinner, reminding them to behave properly in the face of their visitors.

The school rules were not enforced on Visiting Days. The only special rule for the day was for students to dress in their school uniforms—complete with the ubiquitous white socks and brown sandals. Meals in the dining hall were optional. In fact,

---

on Visiting Day, one could actually get away with consuming ten plates of food in the dining hall, if one desired.

No one would be there to complain.

Everyone would be too busy preparing to meet with their visitors, and afterward, would be engaged in sharing and enjoying whatever home-cooked meals the visitors had brought with them. There was always surplus home food being passed around. So even if one wasn't expecting a visitor, like Carlotta wasn't on her first official Visiting Day at FGGC Uddah, one could still stock up on food from friends' visitors.

On the prior Visiting Day, which had been four Sundays earlier, Carlotta had been presented with more food than she desired. First, Onyedi's parents had come to visit, and Onyedi had insisted Carlotta go with her to meet her parents. Onyedi's family lived nearby, since her mom was a teacher in the school, and was always one of the first visitors to arrive on Visiting Day. They'd brought fried rice, fried chicken, stewed beef, fried plantains, vegetable salad, and cold bottles of soda.

After that, Emeh's parents had arrived. Carlotta had enjoyed another plate of rice—this time white with tasty red stew, and garnished with seasoned beef and sautéed vegetables. There'd also been chicken soup, moin-moin, bread buns, and cold drinks.

By 2:00 PM, when Zika's people arrived, Carlotta was already too stuffed to move. She'd managed to go say hello to Zika's parents and afterward, she'd been rewarded with a large plate of Jellof rice, hard-boiled eggs, and fried chicken, plus a bowl of spicy goat-meat pepper soup, and several bottles of malt drink. She hadn't been the least bit hungry, but still managed to swallow every last morsel. It had taken her almost two hours to eat all that was on her plate, and Zika still had a great deal left over.

Later that day, Shade had also had food to share and so had Nneka. Joke, Grace, and Uche had presented Carlotta with plates of food, too. Even Bisi wanted to know if Carlotta wanted something to eat. By 6:00 PM that day, Carlotta had more than eight different types of rice dishes sitting on Zika's locker awaiting her attention. *Why don't we totally have refrigerators for days like these?* she'd wondered, her senses dulled from all the carbohydrates her body was digesting.

Looking back on the last visiting day, Carlotta couldn't help but feel a real sense of excitement now. This time, Uncle Daniel had informed her he was coming to visit. And to cap it all, he was bringing Ada with him. *That will be so awesome. I just can't wait for them to get here already!*

At 10:00 AM, the gates of FGGC Uddah were opened and the visiting day officially began.

Junior girls piled out of their dormitories and went to wait in their classrooms, where they could see and scan the in-coming cars for any trace of familiarity.

After greeting Onyedi's parents, and enjoying a hot plate of home-cooked food, Carlotta joined her classmates by the windows of their classroom. She kept craning her neck to see beyond Nelly's shoulders.

While the JS1D girls waited, they chatted distractedly, their minds full of expectation.

"I think they've come for me!" a light-skinned girl called Onyinye suddenly announced. "That looks like our blue Mercedes-Benz."

Immediately, the rest of the girls took up the chant. "You girls, they've come for Onyinye! You girls, they've come for Onyinye!"

Onyinye's face was piqued and shiny with excitement. She held her breath and waited impatiently for the blue vehicle to draw closer so she could ascertain if it truly was her parents' car or not.

Exercising a little patience was a wise decision on Onyinye's part. It was not uncommon for overzealous junior girls to run from their classrooms screaming, "Yay! They've come for me!" only to approach the vehicle in the parking lot and realize in dismay that they don't know the strange couple emerging from it.

Carlotta had heard the funny story where one girl actually flung herself into a couple's arms assuming they were her parents, and the duo had hugged and kissed her in return thinking she was their daughter. Only when the couple addressed the girl by an unfamiliar name did both parties realize their mistake.

Carlotta chuckled. She imagined what would have transpired in such a situation.

"Dad! Mom!" the student would yell, and throw herself at her parents.

"Hey, Irene! It's so wonderful to see you again!" the couple would reply, faces wreathed in smiles. "See how much you've grown!"

"Whoa! Hold on! My name's not Irene. I'm Brenda. And now I can see you closely, it seems you guys are totally not my parents. Sorry about that!"

"Yeah, all right. You little girls all look the same. Please, can you tell Irene her parents are here?"

"Sure. Whatever."

Carlotta almost laughed out loud. *Now, I'd like to see my mom totally mistake me for someone else! How hilarious will that be?*

The blue Mercedes-Benz turned out to actually be Onyinye's folks.

"It's our car! They've come for me!" Onyinye took off to the sound of cheers.

The rest of the girls settled back to continue waiting.

Soon, Joyce yelled and rushed out. Thunderous cheers.

Then Chikor. More cheers.

Amanda. Cheers!

Fifteen minutes later, it was Ndidi's turn. Carlotta didn't think anyone could yell louder than the tiny student. Her already over-sized head seemed to expand as she rushed for the classroom door.

One girl, whose eyes were red with tears from the frustration of being made to wait so long, screeched and closely followed Ndidi. The class sighed. The crying girl's case was so pitiable. She was still wailing and shedding tears as she surged out of the classroom.

The rest of the class waited. One by one, the girls shrieked and rushed out.

When the clock struck 3:00 PM, only a handful of girls were left in the JS1D classroom.

A seed of doubt began to germinate in Carlotta's mind. *Maybe Uncle Daniel changed his mind. He's probably too busy to make the long drive from Lagos. Maybe Ada took ill or something.*

The day drew close to 4:00 PM. The number of visitors and their wards in the parking lot thinned out. When vehicles left this time, none arrived to take their place. The excitement began to wane.

The rest of us should probably just give-up and go enjoy the food other parents brought for their kids. Carlotta decided to give it one more hour.

Soon, two other girls shrieked and rushed out of the classroom. Another girl followed barely ten minutes later.

The countdown continued.

Please God, let them get here already.

By 4:42 PM, Carlotta was sitting alone, with just one other student, in the JS1D classroom. The student lived in one of the northern states and wasn't really expecting to get a visitor anyway. She'd only been in the classroom for the laughs.

At 4:50 PM, the northern student shook her head in silent apology and quietly left the room.

They're not coming. What a bummer.

Carlotta closed her eyes and wiped tears off her cheek.

Several minutes later, she gave up waiting and returned to Sapphire House with a heavy heart. She planned on drowning her sorrow and disappointment in the rice dishes she knew would be waiting for her on Zika's locker.

Way to go, Uncle Daniel. Thanks for nothing.

* * *

Back in Sapphire-Six, Carlotta was seated on Zika's bed. She had just finished consuming her fourth plate of rice, and felt very sure she wouldn't be able to eat another mouthful without bursting, when Lola Ajayi walk into her corner, teeth flashing.

"Carlotta, you have a visitor," Lola announced.

Carlotta looked up in disbelief. Her heart skipped a beat. *Please, please, please!*

Lola stepped aside. Right behind her was a beaming and stunning Ada Ikedi.

"Carlotta! How are you?" Ada rushed forward.

Oh my God! Carlotta was at a loss for words. She'd lost all hopes of getting a visitor. Without uttering a word, she jumped to her feet and launched herself into her cousin's arms.

✳ ✳ ✳

Shelley's eyes raked over Josh's disheveled appearance and came to rest on his face. "You seem to take delight in disturbing people," she remarked.

"I don't reckon so." Josh's eyes were guileless. He shook his head. "The company sent me over. You need help with your lawn?" The smile vanished and was replaced with a speculative look. "Right?"

Shelley held on to the doorknob, her body blocking any kind of access into the house. "I absolutely do not allow personal visits from students."

"I'm not here on a personal visit." He dislodged the rivulet of hair that had fallen over his eye with one casual flick of his hand. His voiced mocked, "Right now, Professor, I'm here on business—to mow your lawn and get paid for it." He pursed his lips, eyebrows raised in a knowing arch. "Sometimes, students need part-time jobs to keep them going. Mind if I come in, Professor?"

Shelley frowned. She crossed her arms over her breasts and assumed an assertive stance. "My lawn is outside, not in my kitchen, Mr. Greinbach." She made to slam the door in his face.

His foot shot-out and thwarted the attempt. Eyes intent, he nodded—giving the impression he understood perfectly what was going on in her mind.

Shelley's nose flared and she gave the offending foot a pointed look. "Do you mind?" *Why does he keep getting under my skin?* "The lawn is *outside.*"

"Yes, of course, Professor. That's quite obvious." Josh's eyes taunted. "May I use your bathroom?"

"I would rather you do not," Shelley retorted. "But then again, I do not want you messing-up my lawn, either." She stepped away from the door. "The bathroom is to your left."

Josh grinned. "Makes sense, I suppose." He walked past her, his right shoulder almost brushing her chest. "And thanks, Professor." He turned on his heels and flashed her an appreciative smile before disappearing into the guest bathroom.

Shelley leaned against the wall, her heart pounding. Josh Greinbach affected her more than she would care to admit. The very maleness of him, his brown wavy hair, cocky smile, warm green eyes, and subtle masculinity combined to make him seem more than just a student. When he exited the bathroom, she swallowed hard and felt her knees weaken. *All I want is for him to—*

"What do you need done?" Josh drawled. *"Professor?"*

"Oh, er—" Shelley was thrown by the question. There was so much she wanted him to do—*needed* him to do. "Just the front lawn should be sufficient for now."

Josh closed the distance between them. "Is that all?" He placed his hands on her shoulders and gazed deep into her eyes. When he pulled her toward him, Shelley didn't resist.

Her arms circled his neck and she hugged him fiercely, hanging on to prevent her knees from giving way entirely. He smelled like a mixture of aftershave and masculinity. She felt his heartbeat and hugged him close. A thrilling sensation snaked down her spine when he hardened against her thigh.

He squeezed her closer.

What on earth am I doing? All thoughts of lawn mowing were gone from Shelley's head. She sighed and parted her lips to receive his kiss, one slim leg finding its way around his calves. Her senses reeled with the soft stroke of his tongue darting slowly in and out of her mouth. His fingers traced the length of her spine.

Just like in my dreams. Shelley shivered.

She hadn't experienced the touch of a man in a long time, and wanted to melt in his arms and lose herself in the pleasure of her desire. She took his hand and led him down the hallway, into the living room, and onto the couch.

"Oh, my God, you are so beautiful," Josh whispered against her lips. "Like the sunrise in the valley of fantasies." He laid her gently on the couch and positioned himself above her, his mouth never leaving hers.

Shelley shivered. Her hands tugged at his tee shirt, pulling it free of his pants. She ran her palms down the solid muscle of his back and arched her body, bringing her chest closer to his.

He slid his hand up her thigh, taking the hem of her skirt with it. She reciprocated by pulling his shirt out of the way. He found her breast and bent his head to kiss her again. The tip of his thumb caressed her nipple through the lacy fabric of her bra.

"You're so sexy," he whispered. "I could just—"

The phone rang.

Shelley crashed back to earth. Josh bolted off her and lunged for the phone.

"No! Do not answer it." Shelley's warning came too late. Josh had already picked up the phone.

"Yeah?" Josh growled into the receiver. "Can I help you?" He listened for a moment then lowered the receiver and stared at it for a second. "Yeah, right back at *ya*," he muttered, and hung up.

"Who was that?"

"I don't know. The line went dead." He gave a one-shouldered shrug. "Whoever it is will call back if it's important enough, I guess."

"Sure, right." Shelley hastened to set her clothes right and correct her appearance. She pushed her bra back in place and pulled down her blouse. Her hands fluttered to her hair and neck. "Listen—"

Josh sprang for the couch. He placed a hushing finger on Shelley's lips and took her in his arms. He gazed into her eyes—making her drown in the depths of his. "Now, where were we?" His fingers stroked her hair. He kissed her again, drawing her lower lip into his mouth.

All words of protest went flying out of Shelley's mind. She kissed him back, pinning herself to his chest. "Let us get you out of these clothes," she said, smiling. She lifted his shirt over his head and pulled it free. The sight of his bare chest, a few inches from her face, made her giddy with excitement.

Josh relieved Shelley of the black, button-down blouse she had on, and flung it over the couch.

She giggled.

He reached for her bra straps, and tugged at them, intending to slide them down her shoulders.

Shelley placed her hands on his, stalling him. "I have a better idea," she said, looking at him from underneath her lashes. Her tongue traced the length of her upper lip. "Come with me." She slid to her feet, pulling him up with her.

He held her from behind, and caressed her breasts and the flat wall of her stomach. "I want you so much." He breathed in the scent of her hair then bent his head and touched his lips to the nape of her neck.

Shelley trembled. She folded her arms over his, drifting forward, toward the stairs. Josh's footsteps fell in synch with hers and they moved as one, up the stairs and into the master bedroom. He released her, and advanced to the middle of the room—his eyes questioning.

"Are you sure?"

"I hope *you* are ready for this." Shelley kicked the door shut and leaped, pushing him down with her on the bed.

✳ ✳ ✳

Richard unlocked the door to his apartment and stepped into the semi-darkness. He secured the door, ignored the light switch, and turned around.

A movement caught his eye and he jumped in alarm. His heart collided with the walls of his chest and began to pump at a rapid pace. His senses sharpened. He tasted his own fear.

Silhouetted in the dark living room to his right, were two human figures.

Swallowing the initial wave of panic, Richard flicked on the light. The menacing forms of Bruno and his egg-headed companion became discernible.

The hairs on Richard's arms stood on end. His pulse ticked. "How did you get in here?" he asked, trying to keep the apprehension out of his voice.

"Easy enough. We picked your lock." Bruno shrugged and sucked on his teeth.

Mr. Egg-head gave no perceptible reaction. Richard wondered if he was even breathing.

He took a step back. "What do you want?"

"We are here to see you," Bruno replied, angling his head. "Have a seat, Doc."

"Like hell you're *gonna* order me around in my own home." Anger, hot and searing, ran through the base of Richard's skull. "What the hell do you want?" He took a few belligerent steps into the room then stopped, obviously realizing it was a bad idea to get too close.

"Sit down, Doc, we need to talk business," Bruno instructed. When Richard made no move to comply, Bruno's voice dropped a notch. "Sit down, Doc, or Whacko here will knock your ass into a chair."

Richard took one glance at the egg-headed guy called Whacko, and threw himself into a chair at once. Whacko snarled, his teeth looked sharp and pointed, like they'd been filed to precise points.

"Glad to see you got some sense left in you, Doc."

"What do you want from me?" Richard whispered, keeping a wary eye on Whacko. He thought it would be a bad idea to let those fangs get within inches of his person—a very bad idea indeed.

"Now he's a good lad." Bruno's eyes gleamed. They reminded Richard of cartoon drawings of jackals. "You owe us a favor, Doc." He turned the gleaming eyes on Richard. "We want a small favor for the trouble of cleaning up your mistake."

Richard waited.

"I want you to reopen your connection with the Palorizzi Family."

The blood drained from Richard's face as he processed Bruno's demand. He jumped to his feet, staggered, and checked himself. He took a deep breath. "What? You must be kidding!"

"Not on your life, Doc."

"But, it's impossible. I can't do what you ask."

"You better find a way to do it, Doc. You only have three months." The sucking sound came again.

Richard wished Bruno would stop doing that—the sound grated on his nerves. "How do you suggest I get that done? Are you freaking out of your mind?" His shock was fast receding, but his anger was rising.

Bruno shrugged. "That's your problem now, isn't it, Doc?" He sucked air through his teeth. "My job is to keep the contents of the package I left with you away from the cops and the press." A sly look came into his eyes. He reached inside his jacket and tugged a yellow envelope free. "We also think your wife will be happy to see a *coupla* pictures of you and your ex-lover." He tossed the envelope in Richards lap. "You *stab* 'em, then blow their brains out. How's that for a psychopathic physician?"

Richard winced and made no attempt to pick up the envelope. "You didn't involve my wife in this? And who the hell gave you the authority to blackmail me?" He stared Bruno down for a second, trying to compose himself. When he spoke, his voice was low and threatening. "Does The Family know about this?"

"It's really up to you if you wish to inform them, Doc. And remember, you never saw me or spoke to me. Understand?" Bruno's fat stomach shook as he spoke. "You gain back that connection in three months, or the cops learn how you murdered your assistant, and the university learn about your wife's affair."

Richard started. "What affair—?"

Bruno ignored him. "We figure the divorce rap will make a nasty mess, but who knows?" He sucked on his teeth and shook his head slowly from side to side. "Last I heard, you rejected your birthright as heir to the Palorizzi Family. You can claim it back if you get what I mean."

"What about Maria?" Richard wailed. "She will be reported missing and the cops are bound to come fishing around. Sooner or later, they will sniff out your trail." A stab of pain went through Richard at the thought of Maria. *What a total waste of a pretty assistant.*

"Maria is replaceable." Bruno chuckled. He sounded like a distressed turkey being slaughtered for Thanksgiving dinner. "As a matter of fact, her replacement will be waiting for you at your office tomorrow morning." Bruno sucked on his teeth and bobbed his fat head up and down. "You see, Doc, we think of everything. So you take care of your end, an and let us handle Maria." Having said that, he hauled himself out of the seat.

"Oh, one more thing, Doc. Anyone ever mention you look like Barack Obama on steroids?"

At Richard's scowl, Bruno shook his head in amusement and lumbered out of the apartment, Whacko slinking along behind him.

As soon as the door closed behind the two men, Richard sprang to his feet and grabbed the phone. The envelope shot-off his lap and landed on the floor with a loud thunk. He paid it no heed and started to dial. Suddenly, he hesitated, his finger resting on the second digit.

Richard's heart thumped. His breath came in short bursts. Beads of sweat formed on his forehead and above his upper lip. His mind raced.

He knew their type. Calling the cops will do no good.

They always get what they want and will kill for it.

Poor Maria was just a warning, a pawn in the game. These people were very ruthless; he had no choice but to deal with them. What would he tell the cops anyway? Would the pigs believe him? Can he afford to take the heat and dish-out thousands of dollars for a high-powered defense lawyer?

I only have three months.

The phone began to beep, letting out sharp, frantic sounds, as if irked with having to bear the burden of an incomplete dial. Richard hung up. He changed his mind and picked the phone up again. This time, he called Shelley.

Please pick-up!

The line connected.

"Yeah? Can I help you?" A gruff voice—not Shelley's. Male. Young. Self-assured. Pissed.

What the—? Richard did a double take and slammed down the phone.

Masculine, male, assertive—like he owned the place. Male! A guy answered!

His brow creased and his mouth curled into a snarl.

The drunken bitch is cheating on me!

A cry of anger and pain ripped from his throat as he yanked the phone off the wall and hurled it across the room. The phone hit the far wall and shattered into three distinct fragments connected together in a mess of multicolored wires.

How dare her?

Like an enraged bull, Richard charged up to the fragments and began to stomp on them. Only when they were reduced to a hundred tiny pieces did he stop and catch his breath.

Reeling from the discovery of his wife's betrayal, Richard turned his attention to the heavy envelope lying on the floor.

Chapter 16
Tales Beneath The Sea

The students of FGGC Uddah began to prepare for the first term final exams.

During the weeks preceding the finals, Carlotta received several more love notes, delivered in red-and-gold-trimmed purple envelopes, from the secret admirer who always signed off as *Me, xxx*. She kept Zika in the dark, only showing them to Onyedi. No one else, not even Ossie and the other members of the study group, knew about the notes.

Carlotta couldn't comprehend why the notes came in the signature envelopes of the Feddie Girls Club, unless the culprit was a member of the club.

Onyedi thought differently. She doubted a Feddie Girl would draw more attention to herself in that way. So far, they'd ruled out junior students as possible perpetrators. None would blatantly write a love letter to a fellow student, Onyedi had explained, especially since lesbianism was regarded as a serious crime at FGGC Uddah.

Meanwhile, Onyedi advised Carlotta to pay particular attention to overly friendly students. Carlotta couldn't think of anyone, except Zika, who was nice to her in any special way. She was quite friendly with Nneka and Shade but only because they were Zika's friends.

As for the SS3 students Anita and Bisi, Carlotta avoided them like the plague. Still, she doubted if anyone in Sapphire-

Six had a reason to write her a love note. None of them expressed lesbianism tendencies, not even Ursula, who seemed shy and never said much in the dormitory.

I'm not an expert in the subject, but having lived most of my life in 'Frisco, I can at least spot a lesbian.

By the time the first term final exams were over, Carlotta had accumulated five or six love notes. She and Onyedi had also tried to match the handwritings of students to the style on the notes but were unsuccessful. Onyedi kept advising patience, for such situations usually unraveled themselves.

Apart from the offending notes, the rest of the term continued without a hitch. The results of the first term exams were released, and Carlotta couldn't be happier with her performance. She still had room for improvement in the indigenous languages, but she thought she had done well so far. At least, for a student who four months ago, didn't even know that languages like Igbo and Yoruba existed.

After final exams, several days before the Christmas holidays, school rules were relaxed and the students took to spending more time in their house lobbies. Most evenings, the students watched movies or played board games with their friends. Carlotta enjoyed seeing her favorite Nollywood artists on screen. She adored their accents and colorful traditional attire. Their hair-dos were attractive, many of them favoring the long braids that were very becoming on women of color. They all seemed at home on screen, and Carlotta learned a great deal about Nigerian culture from watching their movies.

The practice sessions for the school play intensified and were more frequent since the students were no longer under the pressures of examinations. Once the second term resumed, the cast of the play would be leaving for Ghana.

Carlotta was excited. She had worked hard, grinding long hours into her role. She had become everybody's favorite and could be counted on to do exactly as expected, while taking corrections and critiques in her stride.

In effect, Carlotta believed her little world was perfect and nothing could go wrong.

Three days till the end of the term, Carlotta was in the house lobby finishing up a board game with Onyedi when Zika came looking for her. Several students were glued to the screen, watching Funke Akindele in the movie 'Jenifa.'

Onyedi excused herself and went to bed.

"Bunkie, I'm afraid I have some very disturbing news," Zika said. Her eyes were downcast. Something about her attitude sent Carlotta's pulse racing.

"Okay?" Carlotta attempted, but her mouth felt dry. She'd never heard Zika sound so grave.

Zika took Carlotta to one side of the room where they couldn't be overheard. She looked her bunkmate straight in the eye and said, "You remember that Uche's bunkie is a *Kabasher*?"

"Yeah?" Carlotta wasn't sure where Zika was going with that. *Kabash* was the school slang for religious fanaticism. The group of students called *Kabashers* claimed to be born-again Christians and had the annoying habit of praying loudly whenever they found themselves in challenging situations. Shade was definitely one of them and everyone in Sapphire House knew it.

"After dining this evening, Shade told to me that a girl in their prayer meeting had a vision last night." Zika would no longer look Carlotta in the eye. "The girl told them that according to her vision, there are possessed students in Sapphire House." Zika paused and chanced a glance at Carlotta, confirming that she understood what's been said so far.

"Right…" Carlotta said, not knowing what Zika had in mind.

"Well, the girl accused you of being one of them. She said that you are possessed by evil spirits, and that you are an *Ogbanje*."

"I see," Carlotta said automatically. She stared at Zika with confused eyes. "Sorry? What was that again?"

Zika explained, "*Ogbanje*, is an Igbo word used to refer to people that possess spiritual forces. It is like the *Mammy-water* phenomenon, but I doubt if you know about that one, either. *Mammy-water* generally refers to mermaids." She paused and took a deep breath. "To be an *Ogbanje* or *Mammy-water* does not mean you are evil but—"

"It's not a good thing to be possessed by spirits anyhow?" Carlotta finished.

Zika simply nodded and bit her lip.

"So, that's it? That's what you literally came here to tell me? That I'm a water spirit or whatever the heck you called it?" Carlotta shook her head. "Seriously?" She was surprised at how steady her voice was, even though her mind was beginning to whirl.

"No no no, I didn't say that," Zika said quickly. She placed a hand on Carlotta's arm. "I'm just telling you what Shade told me that a girl said in their—"

"Yes! I get it." Carlotta interrupted.

"Anyway," Zika continued, letting out a deep breath, "I don't believe that the girl knows what she's saying. I think she's just joking. You are not possessed, are you?"

Carlotta shrugged Zika's hand off. "How the heck would I know if I'm possessed or not?" she yelled. "Shouldn't there be some kind of mysterious birth-mark or tattoo on my skin or something?" she demanded in a high voice. She was beginning to freak out. "Shouldn't I totally be able to jinx people or make things fly if I were a witch, or water spirit, or whatever?"

"Actually, it's quite complicated," Zika said, avoiding Carlotta's eyes. She glanced around the room.

No one in the room was paying them any attention. Their eyes were drinking in the image of Funke Akindele parading around campus in pajamas and red, ankle boots.

Zika lowered her voice. "Most *Mammy-waters* usually dream of swimming under water, that's how they know they're possessed. The gist is that *Mammy-waters* always have a second home beneath the sea." She took a deep breath and placed a hand on

Carlotta's shoulder. "*Ogbanjes* are a different matter altogether but I know you are not one. I am sure you are not possessed at all."

Carlotta felt the weight of Zika's consoling hand. "I'm allowed to totally freak out, right?" She wasn't exactly sure what she should be freaking out about, though. "Okay, let's say I'm one of those people who, like, live under the sea, and that I dream of scuba diving every night. Big deal, right?"

"Actually, it is a big deal around here." Zika appeared sympathetic. "People hate *Ogbanjes* and are scared of them because they have special powers. Anyone accused of being an *Ogbanje* gets ostracized, even if the accusation finally ends up being a false one."

"I don't get it. Why are people allowed to make false accusations? They should be sued for slander or better still, get locked up for it, right?"

Zika shook her head.

A ripple of giggles went through the lobby. Carlotta glanced at the screen. Jennifer had been discovered camping outside her friend's hostel.

Zika bade her overwhelmed bunkmate goodnight and left the lobby.

Standing alone, and not in the mood to see the rest of *Jenifa* with the other girls, Carlotta was at a loss of what to do. She took a seat in the back of the room and tried to make sense of what Zika had said. She certainly didn't believe she was possessed by anything or anybody, and she definitely didn't have a second home in the sea. Actually, the longest she had ever held her breath under water, during swimming lessons in her former school, was thirty seconds. FGGC Uddah did not even have a swimming pool and offered no swimming classes. How then could someone accuse her of living under water?

Water-spirit. Seriously?

Carlotta didn't know if she believed in people claiming to have visions about others.

Like, what planet are they from?

Zika's information just didn't make sense, Carlotta decided, and dismissed the bogus accusations as unimportant.

Phew!

✻ ✻ ✻

By the next morning, Zika's information began to make sense to Carlotta.

Every student she passed in the hallway avoided making eye contact with her. Some of them even shrank away when she approached them. The girls became unusually quiet each time she entered the dormitory. Groups of girls pointed at her and whispered whenever she walked by.

Totally weird!

Carlotta had the spooky feeling that everyone was talking about her all the time. In the dining hall, nobody would sit beside her. Vivian even preferred to stand rather than sit anywhere near Carlotta.

Great!

By the time the day was over, Carlotta believed the whole school was convinced she was possessed. The only students still speaking to her were Onyedi, her study group members, and Zika. Even Nneka and Shade seemed to be avoiding her. Sandra was having a field day. She went about spreading the rumors and defaming Carlotta's name to anyone who cared to listen.

What's so going on?

Fortunately, the school play practices had ended for the term so that Carlotta had no reason to go by the classroom buildings. She couldn't bear being snubbed by the other students in the play or even being kicked out of the play altogether.

Most of all, Carlotta avoided the classrooms because she absolutely loathed to chance a meeting with the big-headed Ndidi, which would entail enduring her snide remarks, especially if Nelly and Joyce wouldn't be inclined to shield her from the tiny student's sharp tongue.

On the day before the students were to vacate the school, Carlotta could take the cold shoulders no more. She complained to her study group members after the principal's last assembly.

The five girls sat in the empty classroom, around Carlotta's desk.

"Maybe you should tell your parents so that they can take you out of this wretched school," Emeh suggested. "It will probably be better for you in America, *n'est-ce pas?*" Is it not?

"*Uh-uh*, no way." Carlotta shook her head. "If I breathe a word of this to my parents, my mom's so *gonna* freak out. She will probably get on the next flight out and bundle me back home. That means I'll totally miss out on going to Ghana for the drama competition next term." Carlotta didn't even want to consider not being in the competition as an option. Not after what she had gone through to master her role.

"And you've worked so hard on your part in the play," Amanda said.

"There you go! My point exactly," Carlotta agreed.

"You girls should remember that we are going home tomorrow oh." Ossie shrugged. "By the time we come back for the second term, I think everybody would have forgotten about the whole thing."

"Seriously?" Carlotta asked in a doubtful tone. The image of Vivian standing behind the table instead of sitting by her side was still fresh in her mind. "What is the deal with you guys and totally weird beliefs anyway?"

Ossie sighed and gave Carlotta a pitiable look. "Okay, let me tell you," she said. "There have been many stories about *Ogbanjes* in secondary schools. Nobody knows if it is true, but they still believe the stories. My elder sister told me about the one that happened in her school last year."

Ossie went on to recount to the group how the girls in her sister's school had observed one student walking toward them during a rainy night. Her feet were not touching the ground, and she'd appeared to glide along as she advanced. The students had freaked out, and the girl was apprehended and questioned. She had confessed to being a mermaid and could only communicate with her kind when wet, hence the gliding in the rain.

Amanda reported she'd read in a book about a school where students went to bed with scarves tied around their heads and secured to their chests. This practice was due to the belief that every night, the *Ogbanjes* in their school gathered for a game of handball in the dormitories. If somehow they lost their ball during the game, they substituted a student's head. So the action of girls securing their heads to their chests when they went to bed ensured their skulls wouldn't be tossed around as handballs during the night.

And what happens if the spirit-players lose a girl's head? Or fail to catch a head-ball? Or even return the wrong heads to the wrong owners? Carlotta thought, but didn't ask. She imagined waking up to discover Sandra's skull—cracked and decorated with bits of flapping flesh—sitting on her neck. She shuddered. *No, we'd probably have to look under bunks to find our heads. That's if the overzealous players don't toss them right outta the window!*

Emeh told the story of *Ogbanje* kids having up to nine lives in her village. The belief was that such youngsters usually died shortly after birth only to be reborn the next time their parents conceived. The *Ogbanje* children died in this manner to punish their parents for some wrong-doing that occurred in their past lives. Some of them were also purported to have the ability to transform themselves into animals of choice. After puberty, the child loses this transformational power. The parents usually bury a stone in the ground upon the birth of their babies. If the young one dies, they dig up the stone, disfigure the corpse and bury it with the dug-up stone so the dead child is prevented from being reborn.

Amanda told another story of a pupil in the primary school she attended. The boy liked to sit and play by himself all the time. He had been observed conversing and playing with invisible play-mates on several occasions. At one time, he had been caught transforming into a dog.

A boy-dog. Whaddya know?

"Sometimes, when you annoy them," Ossie supplied, "*Ogbanjes* will use their powers to harm their enemies."

Onyedi, who had remained silent up till then, simply said, "They are all made-up stories," and shook her head from side to side.

"No, some of the stories are true oh!" Ossie disagreed. "What about *Madam Koi-koi*? Is that one a lie, too?"

Carlotta shot her class neighbor a wary glance. She'd heard stories about the dreaded lady who went about in high-heels harassing studious students burning the late night candles. She implored Onyedi, "All that's not true, right?"

"Myths and legends," Onyedi said.

Emeh maintained that the existence of *Ogbanjes* was still a strong superstitious belief among many ethnic groups.

Amanda and Ossie concurred.

Onyedi insisted that if properly investigated, there would be a scientific explanation for most phenomena seemingly beyond human comprehension. In her opinion, it was the nature of Nigerians to take the easy way out of difficult situations by blaming supernatural forces for all their problems.

If their child dies of malnutrition or from some strange disease, they blame it on *Ogbanjes*.

People who get fired from their jobs point fingers at their neighbors, accusing them of having supernatural powers.

A family member has a car accident—people say evil forces are at work.

A person falls down a flight of stairs—the spouse automatically gets labeled as an *Ogbanje*.

A bat flies into a house—the inhabitants claim they saw it change into an old witch.

Onyedi sighed and shook her head.

Carlotta felt dazed. She didn't think it were possible for such things as the girls described to exist. The only time she had come across magic and supernatural powers was in fairy tales, movies,

317

and novels like 'Harry Potter.' But all that was fiction, she reassured herself. No human being could actually change into an animal or live under water or play games with a human skull.

She imagined the *Oklahoma Sooners* scoring a touchdown with a severed head, and cringed.

This is so creepy!

Then again, Carlotta acknowledged she was in a foreign land that had its own special way of doing things.

Maybe I should totally start wearing helmets and life jackets to bed.

Nevertheless, the problem still remained that someone had accused her of being something she wasn't, and most students were avoiding her because of it. She couldn't even pronounce the term *Ogbanje* properly, but she definitely would not be intimidated into running back to America with her tail between her legs.

The only good thing that came out of the accusation was the love note stopped coming.

Apparently, even lesbians are totally scared of the water people. What a joke!

However brave she considered herself to be, Carlotta was thankful she would be leaving the school the next morning for the Christmas holidays. She'd had quite enough of FGGC Uddah for the time being and looked forward to an exciting time with her uncle's family in Lagos. Hopefully, the whole bogus story would blow over by the time school resumed in January.

Water spirits indeed, whatever will they think of next?

Carlotta rolled her eyes to high heavens.

Chapter 17
X-mas Hols

It was 8:30 AM on a Friday morning, the last day of term at FGGC Uddah and Carlotta was still within the confines of Sapphire-Six. Senior girls were hijacking junior students and ordering them to lug their bags and suitcases from the dormitories to the school parking lot.

Glad she escaped being used as a mule, Carlotta recalled waking up at 2:00 AM and observing Joke and Grace getting up to take their bath, get dressed, and transfer their luggage out of the dormitory. She'd wondered what they were up to and if they were actually sane. After convincing herself the JS2 students were definitely out of their minds, Carlotta had closed her eyes and gone back to sleep.

Zika had finally woken Carlotta at 6:00 AM, and by 8:00 AM, she was dressed and seated on Zika's bed eating breakfast.

While munching on bread smeared with the last bit of jam from the jar in Zika's locker, Carlotta watched as Sandra and Uche were made to lug most of their bunkmates' baggage out of the dormitory and up to the school parking lot.

Between them, the two girls transferred a total of two suitcases and five travel bags, and the figures didn't even include their own luggage.

As soon as their bunkmates left for the bathrooms, Sandra and Uche bailed-out on the luggage carting and didn't come back for the fourth and final round.

When Nneka returned from her bath, she realized her bunk-mate was nowhere to be found. She still needed someone to carry the last of her things, including the empty bucket she'd brought back from the bathroom, and was irked that Sandra had not returned to complete the task.

Nneka looked around the dormitory and brightened when she spotted five junior students standing at attention by Bisi's corner.

"Bisi, are you going to make use of all five of the ju-girls you gathered?" Nneka tugged off the towel wrapped around her torso and began to dry her body with it.

"Yes oh!" Bisi answered. "I have a lot of things for them to carry."

"I only need one ju-girl," Nneka pleaded. She rolled the towel into a thick string and seesawed it across her back. "Just one girl to carry my—"

Anita cut her off. "Nneka, *biko*, don't even bother. I've already told Bisi I'll use the ju-girls after her, so save your breath."

Shade joined in. She was clad in just a bra, the tips of her loose long hair dripping whitish drops of water on her shoulders. "But Bisi can still spare one of the ju-girls now." She retrieved a pair of black panties from the pile of clothes on her bed and stepped into them, pulling the thin fabric up her legs as she spoke. "Bisi, you don't need all five ju-girls, *abeg*. Moreover, you can always find another later on."

Bisi stopped struggling to zip her suitcase closed. She straightened and faced Shade. "Hmm, if only you know how much trouble I went through to even find these ones, you wouldn't be asking me why I gathered five of them." Her tone mocked, "Do you know I had to search through the bush to find them? And this one here," she pointed to a rebellious looking girl, "was even trying to run away and climb up a tree. If not for the ants that made her fall off, I wouldn't have gathered her, too."

Jeez! These senior girls are all messed-up. Carlotta conjured an image of the poor junior girl plummeting to the ground, creepy-crawlies scurrying all over her skin.

Yikes! Carlotta yanked her feet off the ground. Then admonishing herself for being so squeamish, she returned them to the floor.

The girl's at least twenty feet away, for Christ's sake. And it's not like she's harboring any leftover bugs. Nevertheless, she kept a keen eye out for anything not on two legs, or without legs at all. *Worms! Eeuw!*

An SS3 student from Sapphire-Five poked her head through the door. "Bisi, is anyone going to use your ju-girls after you?"

"Yes oh!" Bisi declared. "Anita has already asked me." She finished zipping the suitcase and instructed two of the junior girls to lift it.

They promptly obeyed.

"Take that to my class, SS3A," Bisi instructed. "Drop it by the second desk closest to the door and come right back." She'd collected a personal belonging from each of the students to ensure their return.

The SS3 student at the door made way for the two students to labor through, laden with Bisi's suitcase. "Okay," she propositioned, "if Anita isn't ready, may I use the ju-girls? My driver is supposed to be here to pick me up soon and I'm running late."

Bisi hesitated for a second, her eyes scanning the rest of her stuff. "Emily, I can only lend you one ju-girl, but you'll have to return her in the next fifteen minutes," she compromised.

"Okay, thanks!" Emily was visibly relieved. "You, the one with the punk hair," she called, and signaled to one of the three remaining junior girls standing by Bisi's corner. "Come with me."

A stocky junior girl walked up to Emily.

"*Ehn-ehn*, no oh!" Bisi protested. "*Abeg*, not the strong ju-girl. You can take one of the lanky ones, but please, leave this one here. I'm saving her for something heavy." Bisi pushed a lean girl toward Emily and called back the stocky student.

Emily frowned. Her eye raked over the junior girl Bisi was willing to lend her. "Ah-ah, Bisi! This ju-girl looks like she hasn't *chowed* in two days."

"*Ehwo,*" Anita smirked. "Wonders shall never end. Emily, *na wa* for you oh! Someone managed to *allow* you to borrow one of her ju-girls and you're now seeking *allowance.*" She started laughing. "*Biko-godu,* provide the girl with chow!"

"But the ju-girl Bisi's giving me is really thin," Emily complained. "I don't know if she'll be able to carry my things."

"Beggars shall not be choosers." Bisi retorted, referring to Emily. "You've seen me now, Mother Christmas. Please, if you don't like the ju-girl, just go and jump into the bush and gather your own. Everyone knows that ju-girls are always scarce on vacation days, and you *gats* to collect the ones you can find without question."

Nneka, Shade, and Anita burst out laughing.

Carlotta was perplexed. *Boy! Have they all lost it?* She shook her head in disgust. *Hello? The junior girls are standing right there! And in case you've all forgotten, they are human beings, too!*

"Make *una dey dia dey* laugh, which one concern me?" Emily chided, and left Sapphire-Six with her newly acquired beast of burden.

Carlotta shut her eyes in pity. *Who would totally believe what junior girls go through in this school? And why on earth aren't they allowed to say "no" to such treatment? How come no one else thinks this is totally unfair?*

As she watched Bisi load her travel bag on a junior student's head, Carlotta finally understood why Joke and Grace bailed from the dormitory hours before dawn.

When the time came to transfer her luggage to the parking lot, Zika offered to get help but Carlotta would not hear of it. She insisted on carrying everything herself.

Thirty minutes later, a sweaty Carlotta succeeded in moving all her personal stuff from Sapphire-Six to the school parking lot. When she finally put the last of her three bags down beside the rest of her luggage, her shoulders felt like they had been torn from their sockets.

She was ecstatic. *I did it! Yes!*

✳ ✳ ✳

The FGGC Uddah parking lot was rowdy and packed full with students, buses, taxis, and private cars. An erected signpost stated that the five large buses standing to the left of the clearing were headed to Lagos State. Two other identical buses just like them were going to Rivers State. One solitary bus, at the far end of the parking lot, was headed for Abuja. Several minibuses were to go to Enugu State. Students milled around each of the buses, their luggage on the floor around their feet.

Carlotta knew she was to go with one of the Lagos buses. When Daniel and Ada had visited several weeks earlier, they'd presented her with a pre-paid bus ticket for the journey to the bus park in Lagos State.

Ticket in hand, Carlotta moved her things close to the second bus in line and waited with the other students. Ossie and Amanda came over and stood with her. Onyedi had already said her goodbye, minutes earlier, and departed with her mom. Emeh was at another side of the parking lot standing with students headed to Port Harcourt, Rivers State.

Carlotta's eyes were drawn to the solitary large bus meant to transport students to the northern part of Nigeria. The gleaming bus was more modern than any of the others. Dainty, blue curtains hung from tinted windows. The exterior was sleek and shaped like an elongated oval. Despite the inviting look of the bus, Carlotta couldn't envy the students standing around it. She knew it would take them many hours to get to their destination. *If they leave right away, they probably won't get where they're going until tomorrow. Total bummer!*

Soon the students were allowed to board the bus and find their seats. Carlotta couldn't wait. She wanted to be outside the school gates and be free as a bird. She imagined it would be nice to do as she pleased once again, without having to wonder if Anita or Chidi was watching and waiting for a slip-up.

By 9:45 AM, the five Lagos buses were completely loaded with students and their luggage. The final warning horns beeped and everyone cheered. The bus engines whirred to life and the drivers addressed the passengers through inbuilt systems. At exactly 10:00 AM, the buses nosed their way out of the FGGC Uddah parking lot.

The passengers cheered.

Content, Carlotta sat back and sighed. The Christmas holidays had officially begun.

* * *

Carlotta woke with a smile. She was nestled under the covers in Ada's large bed. It was the first day of the Christmas holidays, and she was back in Ikoyi, Lagos state, with her uncle's family. She realized it was already 11:00 AM and grinned. She couldn't remember when last she'd slept in that late. Ada was no longer in bed and Carlotta hugged the second pillow to herself. She stretched and yawned.

Hmm, it feels so good sleeping in a real bed again.

There was barely four weeks for the Christmas holidays, and although Carlotta wasn't going to be spending any of it in the United States with her parents, she planned on having a swell time in Lagos with her cousins. At least the power generator in her uncle's house had been fixed, and there was no real reason to fret over mosquitoes or power outages, as was the case the first time she'd stayed with them.

As Christmas day drew near, the whole city visibly took on a festive atmosphere. Store windows displayed inflated Santa Claus balloons and other Christmas decorations. Corporate buildings had holiday banners strung up on the outside. Hotels and private businesses displayed holiday messages spreading joy and cheer. Christmas carols blared from car radios, and speakers mounted in fast food restaurants and market stalls.

It was all so familiar to Carlotta, and yet so different.

Unlike her last Christmas in Oklahoma, where they'd put up with snow and sleet, the weather in Lagos was warm and cozy. There was no need for winter jackets, snow boots, hats, mufflers, and gloves. They didn't even need to wear thermal underwear. Instead, everyone went about the streets in scanty clothes like it was the height of summer.

Apparently, the northeast trade winds responsible for the harmattan season in Nigeria didn't make it to Lagos. Bare midriffs, sandals, and slip-ons were the order of the day for young females.

Wide-eyed with wonder and excitement, Carlotta found she was beginning to appreciate the beauty of Lagos.

Oh wow! I totally love it here.

By the time her four-week Christmas holiday was over, Carlotta would realize she had grossly misjudged the city based on her past experience. When she'd first arrived in Nigeria from the States, Carlotta had been horrified at the look and feel of Lagos, and was only attuned to the negative aspects of the city.

However, after spending a few months in boarding school, and having learned a thing or two about Nigerian culture, Lagos now seemed like a different place to Carlotta. She found it exciting and intriguing.

Carlotta soon realized that Lagos was a place like no other, a city no one should take for granted. She was made to understand that Lagosians proudly refer to the city as Eko, and as far as they were concerned, no other city in the world could offer what Lagos does.

Having spent hours with Ada scouring the city and visiting places and friends, Carlotta began to acknowledge the beauty of Lagos. The exciting nightlife, the hardworking people, the exotic and mouth-watering foods, the language, the rowdy markets, the parties and ceremonies, the music, and the beautiful skyscrapers. It was too much to take in at first glance. But before long, she was absorbed by the city and began to feel right at home.

❋ ❋ ❋

hristmas Eve was nothing short of exciting. From dusk till dawn, the air was rendered with the smells of food being fried, grilled, and smoked. The unmistakable scent of hairs being singed from the carcasses of slaughtered animals also hung in the air.

The day before, Carlotta's uncle provided several plump chickens, a turkey, and goat quarters for the holiday celebration.

Aunt Nkem ordered holiday cakes from a special bakery. Early that day, she set up a Christmas tree at a central location in the house. Ada's brothers had a great time decorating the tree, and stringing holiday lights on the walls of the living room.

Carlotta helped Ada make pastries and snacks. They baked meat-pies and rolls, and fried heaps of chin-chins. These were small lumps of deep-fried dough prepared from wheat flour, sugar, milk, and eggs. When cool, the chin-chins were crunchy and tasted like cookies. Carlotta couldn't get enough of them— *they are so addictive. I'm totally gonna weigh a ton by the time the new year rolls around.*

They went to church at 10:00 PM that evening and long before the religious service was over, the boom of firecrackers could be heard in the distance.

Carlotta was excited. *Christmas in Lagos is totally like Christmas Eve, Thanksgiving, and Fourth of July rolled into one. Totally awesome!*

Carlotta spent the whole of Christmas day gorging herself with all kinds of food. Aunt Nkem had prepared the standard holiday meals of Jellof rice, fried rice, and white rice with stew. There was also fried chicken, braised beef, fried goat-meat, and broiled, spicy fresh-fish.

Nkem also prepared okro and egusi soups with pounded yam to go with them. The soups had pieces of goat tripe—called *shaki*, offals, stockfish, and periwinkles in addition to goat meat and goatskin—known as *pomo*.

Nkem's goat-meat pepper soup was out of this world. It contained pieces of well-seasoned goat meat, skin, and offals, and was hot and mouthwatering.

The last dish Nkem prepared was a local delicacy called *Ngwo-ngwo*. Basically, she boiled the goat head to tenderness, then chopped-up the tongue, ears, and skin surrounding the skull. To these she added palm oil, spices, seasoning, and bitter herbs.

Carlotta thought the dish was excellent if only one didn't look too hard at what went into its creation. The delicacy had been Daniel's favorite meal of the day. He'd wolfed down several bowls while quaffing cold beer.

Despite her misgivings about consuming animal tongue, brain, and eyeballs, Carlotta thoroughly enjoyed a few mouthfuls of the delicacy before the heat stopped her. But she really didn't mind because the refrigerator was packed full with bottles of soda and juice boxes.

Visitors came and were entertained with food, drinks, and snacks. In the evening, the whole family gathered together to watch movies.

Carlotta was so stuffed she could hardly keep her eyes open. But once in bed, she just couldn't wait for the next day to come, for Ada had promised an exciting excursion into town.

Chapter 18
This Is Lagos!

"Hurry up, Carlotta!" Ada called. She poked her head through the bedroom door. "Are you ready?"

"I'll be just a minute," Carlotta mumbled. "It took me more time than I thought to blow-dry my hair." She zipped-up her pants and tossed the shimmering-red bodice Ada had lent her for the night, over her head. The top had almost non-existent sleeves and the bottom came down to somewhere above her navel, revealing a great deal of cleavage, mid-riff, arms, and shoulders.

"Temi and Danny are already here." Ada cocked her head to one side. "Do you need help with that top?"

"No, I got it, thanks!"

"Well hurry-up! We don't want to keep them waiting. The concert will start in about two hours and we still have to fight our way through the crazy traffic to get to Ikeja." Ada withdrew her head and pulled the bedroom door closed. "Please, I want you downstairs in five minutes!" she called as she walked away to go join her friends in the parlor.

Carlotta sucked in a deep breath. Twisting her neck one way, and arching her back in the opposite direction, she strained one arm above her shoulders and down her back to reach the back-zipper for the blouse. Her other arm held the shiny top down as she worked the zipper upward.

It was getting quite frustrating. Each time her fingers grasped the zipper and pulled, it got stuck. She had to let go and take the blouse off to get it unstuck. *Oh, come-on already! I don't have all night.*

She tried again. And again. Same result. Stuck zipper.

Finally, Carlotta lost patience. In annoyance, she yanked the top over her head and flung it into a corner of the room.

That's it! I'm done with that little torture of a party blouse. She let out a pent-up breath and stamped one stiletto-clad foot. *Ada and her friends can go on without me. Stupid zipper!*

Carlotta stomped to the edge of the bed and dumped her one-hundred-and-fifteen-pound self on it with chagrin. Hot tears washed her carefully applied mascara down her cheeks and marred her face. It had taken close to forty minutes to get her hair and face to look right. Now everything was ruined.

I don't fit in. I'll never look like my cousin. I'm just a fat, miserable, teenage wannabe. She kicked the black stiletto sandals off her feet, and hugged her knees to her chest. Ever since the day Carlotta found out she'd put on ten pounds, she'd constantly beaten herself up.

Carlotta sat there, wallowing in self-doubt, until an impatient Ada poked her head through the door.

"You must be the slowest dresser I've ever met, Carlotta. Come-on, the others are waiting for—" Ada's eyes widened. She scanned Carlotta's half-dressed form huddled on the bed. "What? Don't tell me you're planning on going into town wearing just jeans and a strapless bra?"

Carlotta sulked even more. "I've got nothing to wear, so I'm totally not coming with you guys." She shrugged and made a stubborn face. She'd rather stay home than go to the concert dressed in less than acceptable attire. Ada had previously gone through Carlotta's clothes and decided she had nothing suitable to wear to Motherland in Ikeja, where they had tickets to see Lagbaja, the famous masked saxophonist, perform live.

"What do you mean you don't have anything to wear? What about the red top I gave you?" Ada looked resplendent in a white tube top and dark-blue jeans. Her full dark hair was piled up to the top of her head like a tiara, leaving her long, graceful neck bare except for a black and white choker with a black onyx nestled at the base of her throat.

"The top doesn't fit." Carlotta sniffed. "I'm too fat."

"That's total rubbish, Cuz, and you know it." Ada had taken to calling Carlotta *Cuz* as short for *cousin*. Sighing, She glanced around the room.

She'd gone down the *I'm too fat* lane twice with Carlotta and it seemed she was about to take a third trip. She located the discarded top where it lay, huddled in an untidy heap, in one corner of the room. In a trice, she'd retrieved it. She presented it to Carlotta with a flourish. "Here you go!"

Carlotta frowned and squeezed her mouth to one side. She raised stubborn eyes to Ada. "No way. I couldn't zip it up. I must have put on a hundred pounds. I totally hate myself."

Ada let out a deep breath and sat beside her cousin. "So that's it? You were having trouble with the top then decided not to go to the concert? You could have just asked me to zip you up. Cuz, *na wa* for you oh!" She smiled and shook her head, jabbing Carlotta playfully on the shoulder.

"Well," Carlotta admitted in a small voice, "I guess that's not all." She pulled a sulky face. "I just don't like the way I look. I'm too fat, and next to you and Temi, I seem so pathetic."

Ada took Carlotta by the shoulders and looked her straight in the eye. "Now, you listen to me! You are not fat. Rather, you're one of the most beautiful girls I've ever seen."

Carlotta frowned.

Ada shook her head. "What's your problem? You are only thirteen, and already, guys break their necks just to get a glimpse of you."

"You're just saying that," Carlotta replied. "I know I've put on a ton of weight since I've been here."

Ada shrugged. "Okay. So you added a little. So what? You still look marvelous." She eyed Carlotta's frame. "Gosh! Your complexion and accent alone are to die for. And don't even get me started on your figure, the shape of your nose, and the texture of your hair."

Carlotta smiled.

Ada continued, "Girl! You should wake up every morning, kneel down, and thank the Lord for creating you as you are. I wish I had your legs and face."

Carlotta beamed.

"Oh," Ada said, "and that American accent of yours?" She paused and kissed the tips of her fingers with a smacking sound. "Hmm, that is just the best thing about you."

"You really mean all that?" Carlotta asked. "You aren't just saying them to make me feel better, right?"

"I mean every word. Now, hurry up and put on this top so we can leave. If I miss seeing 'Konko-Below' tonight, I'm going to strangle you."

Within seconds, Ada had Carlotta bundled into the red blouse. She swiveled her around and zipped up the garment without much trouble. "There!" she announced with pride. "You're good to go." She turned Carlotta around again and fussed with her now messy hair. "Forget about your ruined make-up. We can fix that in the car." She gave Carlotta's hair a final pat and pushed her toward the door.

Carlotta grinned. "Thanks, Ada. You totally rock."

Ada raised an eyebrow. "Trust me, Cuz, you look good enough to eat. Now, off we go or Temi and Danny will get impatient and leave us behind!"

❋ ❋ ❋

After thirty-five minutes on the road, Temi's boyfriend, Danny, maneuvered the blue Volkswagen Jetta through the streets of Surulere, and found a parking space close to the suya spot at the intersection of Akerele and James Robertson streets. They were on their way to Ikeja, but Danny had insisted on stopping in Surulere for suya.

"How did I know this was the place you had in mind?" Ada teased with laughter in her voice.

"Trust Danny and his Surulere suya," Temi replied. "He just can't get enough of it." She slapped Danny lightly on the thigh with one perfectly manicured hand. "See? His mouth is beginning to look like ram suya *sef.*"

Danny laughed. "A brother has got to have his treat on Friday night. And this is one of the best places in Lagos to get great suya. Plus, it would be a good opportunity to give our American friend here her first taste of authentic Naija cuisine." He turned to Carlotta. "So, have you had good mainland suya? I'm not talking about the leather they serve you guys on the islands."

Carlotta nodded. "Yeah, sure. I've tried *sew-yeah* on several occasions."

Danny laughed. "*Sew-yeah?* Now, that's something you don't hear quite often."

"Hey, what did I say?" Carlotta was amused.

Ada rolled her eyes at Danny. She said to Carlotta, "Cuz, don't mind him *joor.* He's just trying to feel like what I don't know." She turned back to Danny. "Suya is suya, *abeg.* It tastes the same no matter where you buy it in Lagos."

Danny disagreed. "That's where you're wrong." He wagged a finger. "A-D-A, if you're of that opinion, it means *you* haven't had good suya, either. And you've lived in Naija all your life." He chuckled, his voice tinged with mischief. "Carlotta's case I can understand. But for you, there is no redemption. What a shame!"

"*Na* you go know which Mallam suya sweet pass." Ada's lips showed the hint of a smile.

"What's so important about the *sew-yeah*, anyway?" Carlotta asked.

"*Abeg*, make *una* wait oh." Temi couldn't help herself. "Which one be *sew-yeah?*" She burst out laughing.

Soon, they were all laughing with her.

* * *

𝒥he suya was smoky-hot. The aroma of caramelized meat proteins accompanied by the flavor of onions and spices provided a mouth-watering and appetite-whetting sensation.

Carlotta's mouth watered. After just two mouthfuls, she had to agree with Danny it was the best suya she'd ever had.

Tender strips of beef—grilled over naked charcoal fires to seal-in the juices, seasonings, and spices, combined with streaks of sizzling marbling to produce a most wonderful sensory experience. The strips of beef, ram, kidney, chicken, and gizzard were grilled in the kebab style, then cut into smaller chunks and served straight off the grill with raw onions, cabbage, and tomatoes on plastic platters covered with layers of newspapers.

They ate with their fingers. The meat was juicy, with a hint of wood smoke, peppers, peanut powder, caramelized onions, and several other smoky spices.

Carlotta chewed and chewed, then swallowed down mouthful after mouthful of savory, spicy goodness. She licked her fingertips and rolled her eyes.

Mmm! This is utterly delicious. I had no idea grilled meat could be this tasty. It's so aah-mazing!

But no matter how finger-licking good she found the suya, Carlotta had enough sense to stay away from the fresh hot peppers served on the side with the grilled meat.

She watched in fascination as Ada, Temi, and Danny guzzled down the hot peppers like their tongues were made out of rubber. The heat didn't faze them in the least bit. Though they had cold drinks handy with which to wash the fiery sensations down, the trio hardly sought relief until they hit bottom platter.

Wow! It will totally take me years to learn to eat hot peppers like that.

When they were done, they piled back into Danny's car and continued on their way to Motherland, Ikeja, and to the promise of a wonderful evening filled with music and excitement.

* * *

ew Year day came and went.
For the remainder of the holidays, Carlotta went to the theater, up-scale restaurants, the beach, museums, and exclusive clubs with her uncle's family. She also went swimming and shopping with Ada. They attended several birthday parties, two baby showers, and a wedding. Carlotta thoroughly enjoyed the experience, and relished the attention afforded her by Ada's friends. She acquired some colorful traditional outfits and pieces of jewelry, which she wore to appropriate occasions.

Soon it was the last week of the holidays. The date for school resumption drew near.

Carlotta knew she was going to miss Lagos. She was drawn to the exhilarating life of the city. The pull of the crowds, the chant of street-hawkers, the energy of party-goers, the self-abandon of religious worshippers, the excitement of church services, the exotic foods, the lavish ceremonies, and the never ending Lagos night life all gave her a sense of belonging.

Carlotta now knew better than to go out alone. She wouldn't step out of her uncle's house after 7:00 PM, unless she was in the company of an adult. Even then, she would be wide-eyed in the open streets and dread all manners of crowds and altercations. She'd truly learned the hard way.

She became one with the city. She learned how to jump onto moving commercial buses. She proved adept at jaywalking on busy streets heavy with traffic. She mastered the art of haggling with market traders. She learned to differentiate authentic goods from knock-offs. She understood the exchange rates between Naira and US Dollars. She yelled in excitement with her cousins when the power came on, and moaned with them when black-outs occurred.

She appreciated the television broadcasts and featured domestic movies. She enjoyed watching her favorite Nollywood stars on screen, especially Joke Silva, Rita Dominic, Chioma Akpotha, Genevieve Nnaji, Stephanie Okereke, and Omotola Jolade-Ekeinde. She also had respect for the acting talents of Richard Mofe Damijo, Van Vicker, and Ramsey Noah. She understood why Ada and her female friends shrieked each time one of these male superstars came on screen. The actors definitely had something going, and teenage girls couldn't help but respond to their masculinity.

In addition to loving the Nigerian way of life depicted in the Nollywood movies, Carlotta acquired the taste for High-Life music and Afro beats, and even mastered a few specific dance steps. By the time the Christmas holidays came to an end, she'd begun to appreciate the legendary music of the late Fela Aniku-lapo Kuti and to understand why his music was so important to Nigerians.

Carlotta was surprised to find that she'd developed a taste for Nigerian ethnic foods. Among her favorites were suya; Jellof rice; white rice with stew; okro, Egusi, and vegetable soups; pounded yam; and dodo.

Although she loved moin-moin with boiled eggs and learned to appreciate akara, she hated boiled beans and wouldn't consume it for the life of her. She also hated boiled yam and when mixed into porridge with beans, the meal became her worst nightmare. She still didn't care much for bitter-leaf soup—the pungent flavor always affected her in a bad way.

Finally, Carlotta began to differentiate between the Yoruba, Igbo, and Hausa languages. She could neither speak nor under-stand any of the three languages, but she could at least tell them apart given the tone and inflexions of the speaker.

Carlotta loved being part of her uncle's family. She couldn't imagine why she ever tried to run away the first time she visited with them. The few months she spent in boarding school had caused her to see her uncle's family in a new light. She was begin-ning to understand why things were so different from what she was accustomed to in the United States.

She no longer thought her cousins' respectful behavior toward their parents was weird. She sincerely began to admire the way they behaved and did her best to imitate them. She saw Ada as a role model and tried to emulate her actions. By so doing, her insecurities diminished and she felt more comfortable with herself in the presence of Ada's friends.

Carlotta began to realize that the whole world didn't revolve around her. She began to understand that there was more to life and existence than just trying to be cool, acquiring material things, and always getting her way. She felt at peace with herself and was content with just being alive.

In the second week of January, Carlotta found herself seated in a commercial bus with many other students heading back to FGGC Uddah.

Chapter 19

Kabashers!

Second term at FGGC Uddah kicked-off in January with preparations for the AACDC Regionals.

The Drama Club members had to present their play to the staff and students of the school before leaving for the competition the following week. It was a busy time full of hustle and bustle for Carlotta. As predicted, most students took no notice of the *Kabasher's* accusation of the term before.

Carlotta was glad things were normal. However, she kept mainly to herself, for she had learned not to trust anyone except her bunkmate and close friends.

Finally, the day for their departure arrived. Fifty students accompanied by four staff members including Ms. Nora were to travel to Ghana by bus. They would go from Anambra State, which was in the eastern part of Nigeria, to the western states. They would then cross the border into the Republic of Benin. Thereafter, they would head for Togo, and finally alight in Accra, the capital of Ghana. At a leisurely pace, the whole journey would take nearly three days.

Many students gathered at the parking lot to see the competitors off. They shouted encouraging words:

"You girls should show them what we're made of!"

"Don't come back without making the finals!"

"Bring back souvenirs from Ghana!"

"Remember to do your best and make them sweat!"

"Give them something to talk about!"

Someone in the crowd started the FGGC Uddah school anthem and the girls sang along.

Carlotta threw her backpack on her shoulders and hugged her friends and well-wishers goodbye.

Several minutes later, the students were shepherded into the bus and they were off. The crowd cheered as the bus made its way from the parking lot up the wide driveway to the school gates.

To Carlotta's surprise, the bus interior was posh, air-conditioned, and comfy. She sat back, closed her eyes, and drew several deep breaths. Relaxed in the deep cushioned seat of the bus, she tried to recall all that the Drama Club officials had advised. Also, she called to mind the private practice sessions she had with her study group members. They had been most helpful and had assisted her with the practice of several plays including 'The gods are not to blame' by Ola Rotimi.

The group members had made her rehearse the parts of every character in each of the plays, so as to ground her on how Nigerian actors should behave. 'Wedlock of the Gods' was set in the Eastern part of Nigeria, so Carlotta needed to be conversant with the ways of the Igbos. The group members had kept reminding her of important points as she worked through the scenes:

"You should be more active than that; Igbos overreact when they are angry."

"Don't just stand in one place, dance about like a warrior."

"Make your face look mean, you are supposed to be a witchy mother-in-law."

Often times, they showed her the proper way to act in unusual circumstances, like when Odibei, the mean mother-in-law, chanted evil incantations in Igbo. Carlotta had tried hard to mimic the girls' accent. It had all been fun.

Sitting in the huge bus on her way to Ghana, Carlotta felt nervous and scared. She wished she still had her iPod. Better still, she wished Onyedi were with her. Shaking her head resolutely, she willed herself to relax and endure the multi-day ride to Ghana.

* * *

he AACDC West African Regional competition lasted for two weeks. Once all the schools had presented their version of the chosen play, it took the judges six hours to deliberate and announce the winning schools that would move on to the final round of the competition. FGGC Uddah won second place among the five top schools. The students were ecstatic.

Carlotta was thrilled. *We made it! We're gonna compete in South Africa next term!*

For the finals, FGGC Uddah, along with four other schools in West Africa, would compete with five schools each from the northern, southern, and eastern parts of the continent.

The FGGC Uddah students sang most of the way back to their school. It was a great moment for them, for they had excelled amongst forty schools, and had earned the sole opportunity to represent their country in the AACDC finals. In the ensuing excitement, the three-day journey back to their school went by in a flash.

Just a few days after the return of the Drama Club members, life at FGGC Uddah was back to the ordinary.

School rules and regulations were re-established. The school bell rang punctually. Marietta Adams resumed her duties as the head girl, Chidi Anayo as the Sapphire House prefect, and Anita Desouza as the Sapphire-Six dormitory prefect.

Dining time became regular. The quality of food served in the dining hall at first peaked then stabilized. Students late to the dining hall were locked out, punished, and made to go without their meals.

Classes commenced with full force. The homework and assignments piled up. Snipes maintained his fast pace of teaching,

Mr. Ndubuisi perpetually likened dumb students to animals, Ms. Nora wore dark glasses and clicking heels to class, and Mr. Dubem, the form master, handled the complaints of his students during the form period on Fridays and still started every other sentence with 'Ahah'.

The JS1D students continued to bicker over small incidents. Ndidi became more obnoxious, and Nelly and Joyce picked on her more often. As a result, Bukola's Yoruba tirade came more frequently. Rosemary, the class prefect, continued to work herself into a frenzy over noisemakers, and the class got punished more often during school hours.

Oge, the fat JS1D prep prefect, became more liberal and continued to nap during afternoon prep, while Patricia, her skinny counterpart, became more skeptical of students with detention excuses.

The study group resumed their study sessions. Ossie remained a perfectionist, Onyedi was as taciturn as ever, Emeh remained a whiz in French, Amanda continued producing clever sketches, and Carlotta worked as hard as she could on her studies and in drama practice.

The school clubs resumed their usual functions. Drama Club continued with play practice and other club events. The Feddie Girls Club left Carlotta alone, but Rema maintained her delusions of grandeur.

In the Sapphire-Six dormitory, Zika persisted in protecting and assisting Carlotta. Anita and her punishments became more unbearable. Joke and the other junior students resumed helping Carlotta with her chores. Sandra remained a royal pain. Ursula got punished more often for tardiness.

The animosity between Carlotta and the Sapphire House prefect took a turn for the worse. There was no love lost between those two. Chidi wouldn't give up an opportunity to deal out punishment to Carlotta no matter how much Zika pleaded. And Carlotta wouldn't suck-up to Chidi, irrespective of how often she got punished.

Almost everything at FGGC Uddah was back to normal.

One thing that wasn't quite the same was Shade and Nneka's attitude toward Carlotta.

In light of the vision from a fellow *Kabasher* the term before, Shade kept badgering Zika to force Carlotta into attending one of their meetings so she could be prayed for.

Zika refused. Then Nneka threatened to involve the Sapphire House matron in the matter. She argued that the rest of the Sapphire-Six students should not be subjected to residing in the same dormitory with an *Ogbanje* suspect, especially not if a prayer group could do something about it. Zika remained adamant.

After many arguments of this kind, several others at Sapphire-Six, including the SS3 student Bisi and the dormitory prefect Anita, backed Shade and Nneka on the matter.

Finally, one fateful Thursday afternoon, Zika was forced to give in to their demands. They arranged for Carlotta to attend the next prayer meeting taking place in an empty classroom after dinner the following Saturday night.

When Carlotta arrived with Zika, the determined-looking *Kabashers* were already in place, waiting solemnly. To Carlotta, they seemed more like vultures anticipating animal carcasses. She didn't know if she should be brave or scared.

Whatever! I'm not a water spirit no matter what anyone says or dreams. However, the *Kabashers* didn't look all too kind.

Carlotta moved closer to Zika and was reassured when Zika's arm sought her shoulders.

The prayer meeting commenced.

First, they held hands and sang:

> *Praise God alleluia, praise God amen;*
> *Praise God alleluia, praise God amen.*

They switched songs:

> *We are here again;*

Nona David

We are here again.
Father we are here again;
Holy Ghost we are here again.

Then:

Holy Ghost fire pursue them,
Holy Ghost fire pursue them;
Wherever demons are gathered,
Holy Ghost fire pursue them;
Wherever spirits may be oh,
Holy Ghost fire pursue them.

They went on for a while then slowed to a stop.

In a low voice, the leader thanked God for all His mercies and kindness. Then she introduced Carlotta and the reason for her presence in their midst. The other *Kabashers* nodded gravely, their fervent stares pinned on Carlotta.

The prayer tempo increased; the voice got louder.

Before long, the speed with which the words tumbled out the leader's mouth was such that Carlotta could hardly decipher one word from the next. After a short time, Carlotta wasn't even sure the words were still in English. Just as she convinced herself that what she was hearing definitely had no place in the English language, the leader yelled.

"Prayer!"

The prayers poured forth.

Carlotta thought she was in a mad house. The thirteen or so *Kabashers* strode around, screeching words Carlotta had never heard in her life, their right arms extended, all traces of dignity abandoned.

You must be kidding me. These girls are insane! Perplexed, Carlotta glanced at Zika. Her bunkmate's face was tightly drawn.

Carlotta turned her gaze on Shade. The girl's eyes were tightly shut and she was screaming so loudly and so fast it was a wonder

344

she could breathe. She reckoned the senior student would turn blue in the face and collapse from asphyxiation. *Jeez! What's she doing?*

Suddenly, the leader yelled, "Fire!"

Alarmed, Carlotta quickly glanced around. She expected to see thick smoke and red flames bellowing out of somewhere.

But taking the cue from their leader, the *Kabashers* were now jumping up and down in one spot, yelling, "Fire!" while simultaneously pointing their right arms toward Carlotta.

Carlotta stared at them, her eyes widening. *Oh no! They've totally lost it!*

The sound made by the *Kabashers'* feet reconnecting with the hard floor as they jumped punctuated each scream of *Fire!* in such a way that if one were to close one's eyes, what one would hear would be:

"Fire!" *Thud!*

"Fire!" *Thud!*

"Fire!" *Thud!*

The ground shook with the impact of the jumps.

The scene was bizarre. And ridiculous.

Despite her fear, Carlotta almost laughed out loud but stopped herself just in time. She looked sideways and saw the beginnings of a smile tug at the corner of Zika's lips. *Okay, I'm definitely not the only one who thinks these girls look totally funny.*

Carlotta didn't get how yelling *Fire!* was supposed to help any possessed person get better. She shook her head in exasperation. *This whole thing is getting really weird!*

Finally, Carlotta could take it no more. She tugged on Zika's hand and signaled with her head. Zika nodded. Quietly, the two girls crept out of the classroom, leaving the yelling *Kabashers,* who still had their eyes closed, by themselves.

Staggering down the classroom corridors, laughing, Carlotta could still hear the *Kabashers* screaming their heads away.

"Fire!" *Thud!*

Seriously? They are still jumping?

"Fire!" *Thud!*

Both girls couldn't hold back. They supported one another and laughed long and hard as they made for the dormitories, two bemused figures enveloped by the cool blackness of the night.

* * *

Carlotta savored the smooth feel of the water against the length of her body as she swam to the bottom of the ocean. She went past shoals of fishes and other sea creatures, her arms sweeping the clear water, her naked form gliding downward. The lower part of her body had somehow transformed into a long solid piece of scaly muscle, tapering downward and flaring out into fins at the point where her toes should be.

She got to the ocean bed and swam directly to the group of mermaids in the far distance. A solemn meeting was in progress. Carlotta swam to an empty sea rock and sat on it. The rock turned out to be a turtle, but she wasn't alarmed. It was as if she had expected to find herself where she was.

Carlotta studied the other mermaids. Their long black hair were swept away from their faces and suspended in the slowly rippling water, like the spiral doodles of a five year old. They seemed too beautiful to be real.

The mermaid leader said something and raised her eyes. She had a sea-green pitchfork pointed at Carlotta—straight at her heart.

A feeling of trepidation washed over Carlotta. *What the—?*

The other mermaids caught hold of Carlotta and laid her flat on her back. They grinned. Their faces no longer looked beautiful.

Eeuw! Disgusting!

The feeling of trepidation within Carlotta deepened, then turned into sheer terror. Her eyes zeroed in on black spikes of teeth protruding, like rusty nails, from the open mouths of the mermaids poised above her body. Forked, red tongues darted to and fro between the black spikes as greenish eyes glared. The mermaids' scaly fish tails wobbled and twisted underneath them.

Carlotta understood what they meant to do. *Jesus Christ! They are going to kill and eat me!* She struggled to free herself, heart pounding, breathing labored as she wriggled in vain.

The mermaid leader approached. She progressively aged as she drew nearer. The wrinkles made the skin of her face seem like the surface of a worn-out leather shoe. The other mermaids made way.

Carlotta squirmed. *Jesus! Save me!*

The leader advanced. She chanted in a guttural voice that made the scales on the lower part of Carlotta's body stand on end. She placed her gnarled hand on Carlotta's neck, raised the pitchfork and prepared to strike.

A cold hand of fear gripped Carlotta's heart. She struggled harder, her eyes on the deadly weapon suspended above her heart.

Jesus, please!

She watched in horror as the pitchfork descended, and opened her mouth to scream.

But no sound came.

Just as prongs made contact with her skin, blackness descended. Carlotta felt herself floating rapidly upward, weightless as the smoke rising from the tip of a burning cigarette. She continued to scream. Silently.

Jesus! Jesus! Jesus!

The weight returned to Carlotta's body with a sudden jolt and she was wide-awake. Her mouth opened and she let out another soundless scream.

Jesus!

Terrified, Carlotta glanced around, her mind reeling with fear from the visions of her dream. She was sitting on her bed in Sapphire-Six, cold sweat popping on her forehead and dripping down the sides of her face. Her arms felt hot and clammy; moisture trickled down her back. Her breathing was ragged as if she'd just run a mile in one minute.

Carlotta's teeth chattered. The nightmare had been very vivid and seemed so real.

Oh God, no!

Carlotta shuddered. She clenched her jaw to stop her teeth from chattering. All her dorm girls were still fast asleep. She looked out the window, at the pitch-blackness beyond, and her fear increased. She imagined she saw a pair of unblinking yellow eyes and became smothered in terror. She shrank back.

Someone let out a loud snore.

Carlotta screamed.

✻ ✻ ✻

Carlotta's blood-curdling shriek woke Zika. She leaped out of bed and beheld her bunkmate, perched on her mattress with her knees up to her chin, shaking like a leaf caught in a raging harmattan wind.

"Bunkie, what is the matter? Why are you screaming?" Zika sounded concerned.

At first, Carlotta could not answer. She was shivering so hard she thought she heard her bones rattling around underneath her skin.

Zika reached out and helped her bunkmate down from the bunk. She put her arms about Carlotta's shoulders and tried to calm her down.

"I, I—" Carlotta was shaking so badly she couldn't get past the first word.

Zika fished out a dressing gown and placed it around Carlotta's shaking shoulders. The air was chilly from the cool harmattan breeze.

"Did you have a bad dream?" Zika asked. She mopped Carlotta's wet brow with a face towel.

Carlotta nodded. Tears cascaded down her eyes. She swallowed the lump in her throat and tried to explain. "I was a mer—A mer—" she shuddered. She couldn't put the nightmare into words. She broke down and started to sob.

A few girls stirred in their sleep. Someone mumbled something intelligible. Shade rolled over on her bed.

Zika quickly pulled on a sweater, then with an arm around Carlotta's shoulders, led the way out of the dormitory and into the deserted house lobby. She didn't bother with the lights for she didn't want to attract the attention of a prefect. Though the lobby was dark and bathed in shadows, enough light filtered through the windows to enable them see where they were going.

Zika avoided an overturned armchair and stepped over an empty soda bottle. She dusted peanut shells off a chair and made Carlotta sit and take a few deep breaths.

Carlotta wiped the tears off her eyes and tried to compose herself. She began to hiccup.

"I will go get you a cup of water," Zika said, and made for the lobby door.

"No!" Carlotta screeched.

"Shush! You don't want to wake the whole house," Zika whispered, and returned to sit beside her bunkmate.

"Please don't go anywhere," Carlotta pleaded in a shaky voice. "I'm so scared. I had a most horrible dream."

"Okay. What happened in your dream? Can you remember?" Zika asked.

Carlotta nodded. She trusted the look of concern in Zika's eyes. She told her bunkmate all that happened in the dream, and then added, "Do you think they were right? Am I a water spirit after all?" Carlotta couldn't remember the word for what she'd been accused of the term before. She broke down again and wept.

Zika pulled Carlotta into her arms and tried to reassure her. "No," she replied. "Dreaming about being a mermaid doesn't automatically make you one. And it doesn't make you an *Ogbanje* either." She sighed and said in a low voice, "If anything, I will say the prayer meeting we attended last night probably triggered the nightmare. It could have happened to anyone."

"Honestly?" Carlotta was a little doubtful.

"Yes, of course. Those *Kabashers* can be very scary with their prayers and speaking in tongues. They scared you, too, right?"

"Yeah, totally," Carlotta agreed, her voice full of tears.

"I understand. Had it been my first time to come in contact with such manner of praying, I, too, would have had nightmares," Zika assured her bunkmate. "Moreover, *Ogbanjes* and *Mammy-waters* are different things."

"You think?" Carlotta sniffed and wiped her eyes.

Zika drew her closer. "Bunkie, I don't think you're a mermaid; you only had a bad dream." She rubbed Carlotta's tears off with the back of her hand.

"I'm sorry I made so much noise and disturbed your sleep." Carlotta apologized. She felt an immense sense of relief.

"I'm sorry I gave in to their threats," Zika apologized, too. "I should never have let you attend that prayer meeting." Then she continued after Carlotta nodded her acceptance, "However, it would be best if you told no one about this. Things are already bad as they are and we don't need the *Ogbanje* rumors to start again."

They sat in silence for a while till Carlotta was nodding off to sleep. Zika stood and led the way back to the dormitory. Carlotta was still too scared to sleep alone, so Zika let her climb into bed beside her.

Minutes later, Carlotta's breathing slowed and she fell fast asleep with Zika's arms wrapped reassuringly around her shoulders.

Chapter 20
The Press Club Cartoon

*A*round 9:30 AM on Sunday morning, approximately two weeks after the night of Carlotta's nightmare, Bisi strode into Sapphire-Six looking agitated.

"You girls need to go and see what's on the general notice board in front of the dining hall." She brushed her palms together, making a sound that sounded very much like shuffling feet. "Hmm, wonders shall never end."

At these words, the bespectacled senior girl and several senior students scurried out of the dormitory, obviously in the mood for some juicy school gossip. Bisi stopped for a second beside Zika's bunk to throw Carlotta a scathing look before striding off to her own corner.

Carlotta shrugged and returned to the tepid cup of cocoa she was making. There was another thirty minutes before dining time and she was hungry. Sunday breakfast was usually delayed till 10:00 AM to give students ample time to return from their places of worship and complete their morning duties.

"Feddie girl! Come here," Bisi ordered. It had only been a minute since the scathing look.

Carlotta put down her cup and approached Bisi's corner. "Yeah? You *so*, like, called for me?"

Bisi ignored the attitude. "What is it with you and Zika?" she asked in a rough voice.

"Excuse me?" Carlotta shook her head in confusion. "I'm so not following. What exactly do you mean?"

"Better mind the way you speak to me, you *Durrelle*," Bisi hurled at Carlotta, her words barbed with scorn.

Carlotta had no idea what Bisi was talking about. "I'm totally sorry, Senior *Bee-see*, but I really, like, don't know what you're getting at."

"I said, what is it with you and your bunkie? What's going on between the two of you?" Bisi was no longer speaking quietly.

The dormitory door crashed open and the bespectacled senior girl darted in.

"I saw the Press Club poster," she yelled. "It's about Zika and her bunkie." She covered her face with her fat hands and declared, "They were cartooned as bunkie-*durrelles*. Oh my God, this is bad." She ran to her bunk and collapsed on her bed, her hands still covering her face. The giggles ensuing from her mouth belied the fact that she thought of the situation as anything but funny.

The rest of the girls, who hadn't taken Bisi for her word the first time, bounded out to go see the cartoon for themselves.

On her way back to her corner, after Bisi released her, Carlotta saw Onyedi poke her head through the doorway and beckon with a sense of urgency.

Onyedi took Carlotta by the hand and led her away from Sapphire-Six, away from Sapphire House, past the Mystical Mangy, up the winding pathway, and far away from the sight and earshot of other students. Onyedi did not stop until they were close to the classroom blocks. Then she strode off the graveled path, onto the carpet grass beyond, and alighted under a small tree.

Carlotta followed suit. The green grass felt soft and spongy beneath her feet. It was the first week in March and the rainy season was beginning to revive the brittle ruins left behind by the dry harmattan winds.

"Seen the cartoon?" Onyedi asked. She hunched and sat on a young patch of grass.

"I don't get it. What is so interesting about this cartoon everyone's totally harping about?" Carlotta was beginning to get very irritable. "I haven't left the dorm since I got up this morning. What's going on?"

"Press Club posters." Onyedi indicated for Carlotta to sit. Carlotta ignored her.

Onyedi shrugged. "Lesbianism cartoons."

"What?" The blood drained from Carlotta's face as comprehension dawned. "Oh—my—God." Her hand flew to her mouth and she looked down at Onyedi. "No way—" she whispered, her eyes narrowing with disbelief. "You mean—?"

"No, not us," Onyedi replied, shaking her head. "Your bunkie." She sighed and bit her lip. She could no longer meet Carlotta's gaze so she looked down at the ground and pretended to play with the damp grass. "And you."

"Hold on," Carlotta sounded shocked. "You don't mean to tell me the Press Club made a *waaay* suggestive cartoon about Senior *Zicker* and me being lesbians?" She seemed incredulous. "And they put these posters up on the general notice board, where the whole school can, like, totally gawk at them?"

Onyedi nodded.

"Oh my God! What a bummer!" Carlotta was visibly appalled.

Onyedi indicated again for Carlotta to sit down. This time, Carlotta obliged and dropped down on the grass beside her best friend.

"How can they totally do that?" Carlotta asked. "Tell me, why would they even, like, think of such a thing?" Her eyes welled with tears. "And, why me? Why Senior *Zicker*?" She covered her face with her hands and let out a long groan.

Onyedi remained silent for a while. "It's a serious crime," she said finally. "Punishable by expulsion."

"Gee! Thanks a lot for totally pointing that out! What an awesome friend you are!"

"I'm just saying—"

"Damn it, *On-yeh-dee*! I'm so not a lesbian!" Then Carlotta added in a quiet voice, "You know I wouldn't do a thing like that though. Right?" She looked Onyedi in the eye, "You do believe me, don't you?"

"Yes." Onyedi let out a deep sigh and hugged Carlotta. "Senior Zika?" she whispered in Carlotta's ear. "Does she know?"

Carlotta shook her head. "I doubt it. She left way early this morning for church service, and hasn't returned to the dorm yet." *Oh boy! Is my bunkie gonna be so bummed out!* Carlotta looked like she was going to cry. "This is such a bummer. Honestly, what should I do?"

Onyedi took Carlotta's face in both her hands, looked into Carlotta's eyes and said, "Nothing you can do." She got up and dusted off the seat of her skirt then stood there and gazed down at Carlotta for a while. "Too much trouble." Her voice sounded thick, like she was about to break into tears. She swallowed and remained silent for a moment. "I'm sorry," she finally said, then turned and walked away in the direction of the dormitories.

"Hey, *On-yeh-dee*?"

Onyedi did not stop. She didn't even look back.

Yeah, that's right! Just get up and walk away. No one wants to be totally associated with the lesbian suspect. Not even my best friend. What ever happened to us being best friends forever?

Several minutes after Carlotta watched Onyedi walk away, the school bell rang. It was time for breakfast.

Carlotta ignored the summons of the bell. She wasn't hungry and didn't care if she missed her food or got punished for boycotting mealtime. Actually, she thought of not eating anything ever again.

Sitting there by herself, poor Carlotta was very desolate. She didn't know which hurt more: being accused of lesbianism or being rejected by her best friend.

You can totally go to hell, On-yeh-dee! Who needs a friend anyway?

Carlotta put her hands to her face and began to cry.

* * *

*few hours later, when Carlotta returned to the dormitory, Zika was sitting on her bed looking very forlorn. Nneka and Shade were on either side of her, consoling and offering sympathy. When Carlotta walked in, both girls stood and returned to their own corners.

Carlotta sat beside her bunkmate. She now understood the word *Durrelle* was slang for a student with lesbian tendencies, while bunkie-*durrelles* meant bunkmates who indulge in lesbian acts together.

"What's so *gonna* happen now?" Carlotta asked. "Are we, like, *gonna* get suspended for something that's totally not true?"

"No." Zika sighed and shook her head. "A student panel will be set up to investigate the allegations. If they find some truth to the matter, they will then take it up to the school authorities."

How awesome! Carlotta rolled her eyes. "Seriously?"

Zika nodded. "My case will be much worse because of the incident that happened with Anita last term."

"Wait, I don't get it. You mean anyone can just stand up and, like, make up stories about us, and we totally get punished for it?" Carlotta was trying to keep her voice down. "We are *so* not lesbians. We didn't do anything wrong. Why should we even be investigated?"

Zika almost smiled at Carlotta's naivety. "You are forgetting that the Press Club is a reputable school club. They already have evidence for the accusation. Otherwise, they wouldn't dare make suggestive cartoons like that."

"But, that's so not fair!"

Zika tried to be comforting despite her own obvious misery. "The problem is that even though you and I know what they are suggesting is not true, everyone else, except maybe our close friends, will want to believe that we are lesbians. The girls here love juicy gossip and, in situations like this, will believe anything.

So instead of just sitting here and feeling sorry for ourselves, we better start thinking of ways to counteract the accusations."

"In that case," Carlotta snapped, "let them go right ahead and do their stupid investigation. We are not lesbians, and we've totally got nothing to hide."

* * *

A few days later, the members of the student investigation panel met to discuss their findings and query the students charged with lesbianism. The panel consisted of Marietta Adams, the head girl; Lola Ajayi, the senior house prefect; Chidi Anayo, the Sapphire House prefect; Anita Desouza, the Sapphire-Six dormitory prefect; Nnedinma Chileta, the press club president; and two randomly chosen SS2 students from Sapphire House.

Throughout the investigation, Zika and Carlotta maintained their claim of innocence. When Anita asked why it was they were found sleeping together on the same bed several weeks before, Zika told the truth about what happened that night, but wouldn't divulge the details of Carlotta's nightmare.

Twenty minutes into the investigation, most of the panel members were ready to vote for a dismissal of the accusation when Chidi produced a red-and-gold-trimmed purple envelope that she claimed was sent to her by an anonymous student.

Carlotta gasped.

As usual, the purple envelope was addressed to Carlotta, and contained a love note from the elusive student that always signed off as *Me xxx*. The content of the note was read aloud.

Zika and the others stared in astonishment.

Carlotta was surprised. No one else knew about those envelopes and the love notes but herself, Onyedi, and whoever sent them. *How did this witchy house prefect come about one?*

When questioned, Carlotta denied vehemently that Zika had anything to do with it. "It's so not my bunkie's fault," she tried to assure the panel. "Senior *Zicker* totally had nothing to do with those envelopes."

In light of the new evidence, however, the panel had no choice but to hand the matter over to the school authorities.

❊ ❊ ❊

The following night, as Carlotta got ready for bed, she noticed the edge of a purple envelope sticking out under her pillow.
That's odd, I haven't received one of these since last term.

Sighing, she retrieved the envelope and tore it open, expecting to see another love note written on plain white paper. She was surprised to find the official gold-and-red-trimmed card of the Feddie Girls Club nestled within.

Please God; don't tell me this is another invitation to a snobbish event. I thought we were so over with this stuff.

Inside the card, and written in Rema's untidy sprawl, were the words:

I can help you. But you'll owe me one in return.

~Rema Yang

Carlotta stuffed the card back into its envelope and threw the whole thing in her backpack. She climbed into bed, buried her head under her pillow, and gave herself up to her misery.

❊ ❊ ❊

Shelley walked Josh to the front door. Her strides were long and languid, like that of a cat that had just finished a good meal. Easing open the door, she kissed him goodbye. "See you in class tomorrow," she said.

"You *betcha*, Professor," Josh replied, and laughed. He had visited several times in the past weeks and was settling quite nicely into the role of having his professor as a mistress. He squeezed Shelley's shoulders, nodded, and walked out.

He watched her close the door behind him then walked down the driveway and to the sidewalk.

The day had already turned into night.

"What a sweet tigress she is," he said to himself as he walked to where his truck was parked.

Suddenly, a black car materialized and almost flattened him.

Panicking, Josh dived and plastered himself to the hood of his truck.

Tires screeched to a halt.

Josh ducked. His heart raced.

No gunshots. Heavy, padded footfalls instead.

Josh jumped to his feet. A strong hand planted itself over his mouth and nose.

Josh kicked out backward. His heel connected with nothing. He quickly retracted his foot and prepared to jack-knife his shoulder into his assailant. But the chilly blade of a knife, pressed dangerously close to his jugular vein, cut him short.

"I wouldn't do that if I were you," a cold voice threatened, close to his ear. "Not if you want to keep your *friggin'* head on your shoulders."

Josh hesitated. His heart hammered. Air puffed out of his lungs at a rapid pace. Sweat trickled down the sides of his face.

The blade pressure increased.

"Don't move a muscle," the cold voice instructed. "Just come with me. Nice and quiet."

Josh smelled alcohol on the man's breath and tensed.

He waited.

They moved slowly backward to the black car.

The man kicked the trunk open. At that same instant, Josh felt the hold on his face slacken.

"To hell with you!" Josh whipped his elbow backward, connecting with his assailant's ribs.

Bones crunched.

The man growled. His knife clattered to the pavement.

Josh kicked the knife away and whirled around, slamming his foot into the man's stomach.

The man's face contorted in pain. He clutched his side with both hands and sank to his knees. His shaved head shone like an oiled egg.

Quickly, Josh drew his knee upward. He aimed for the man's chin. The weight of his body drove the movement. *Crack!*

The man groaned.

Josh threw his fist forward. But the blow never connected with its target, for a crushing force caught Josh at the back of the head. The fist sailed wide.

Several more bangs to the skull threw Josh out of control. He doubled over in pain. He never saw the second assailant. He didn't realize he had been attacked with a shovel pulled from the back of his own truck.

A blow crashed into the back of his neck.

Josh felt himself falling...

His head smashed the asphalt.

Everything went blank.

❋ ❋ ❋

During math period the following Monday morning, Carlotta was yanked out of Snipes' class and marched straight to the principal's office.

Upon her arrival, she was surprised to behold a stricken Zika being berated by the principal and a few teachers. Carlotta watched in horror as Zika, tears cascading down her cheeks, stuck to her story of innocence about the lesbianism accusation.

When questioned, Carlotta backed Zika up. But the school authorities still needed an explanation for the love note now residing on the principal's desk.

Feeling sick to her stomach and hating herself for what she was about to do, Carlotta declared, "The letters were written by my house prefect. She sent them as a way of enticing me to become her lesbian partner."

"*Ehwo! Chineke m eh!*" One teacher exclaimed. Oh! My God!

The principal's eyes bulged and she almost swooned. "What are you talking about?"

Feeling so much like a she-devil, Carlotta recounted the prepared story exactly as Rema had instructed.

The declaration by Carlotta started off a chain reaction leading to major consequences.

Chidi was summoned and questioned, but though she kept shooting malevolent looks at Carlotta, she did not deny the allegation. As a result, she was demoted from her post as a school prefect and transferred from Sapphire House to Gold House.

Vivian's sister, Agnes, was transferred from Gold House to Sapphire House to take Chidi's place as the house prefect.

Zika, on the other hand, was pardoned and transferred to Ruby House and forbidden to come in contact with Carlotta in any way.

An SS2 student, Felicia Ebere, was sent from Ruby House to Sapphire-Six, to take Zika's place as Carlotta's bunkmate.

Just two hours after the students were dismissed from the principal's office, the news that Chidi Anayo was a *Durrelle* and had been demoted to a floor member permeated the whole school.

A few days later, the full implications of not having Zika as a bunkmate hit Carlotta. For the first time since she set foot in FGGC Uddah, she knew exactly what it meant to be an ordinary junior student in a Nigerian boarding school.

Felicia yelled at Carlotta and punished her all the time. She made her fetch and carry buckets of water, do laundry and other menial tasks, and also sent her on odd errands around the school. The new bunkmate had no interest, whatsoever, in helping Carlotta, or protecting her in any form or manner.

Carlotta found she lacked the necessary skills required for independent survival as a junior student, and began to wish that

Zika had not protected and pampered her nearly as much. Without Zika, she was right back at where she started as a new student.

So, while other JS1 girls had learned to tolerate their bunk-mates and bear the life that came with living in a boarding house, Carlotta was at a loss of how to handle the situation with her new bunkmate. Before long, she began to despise Felicia as much as she did Chidi.

After Carlotta realized she had no one to depend on now but herself, she put in more time and effort into doing and completing menial tasks to the best of her ability. But her best was never enough for Felicia.

To make matters worse, Agnes Gussoh, the new Sapphire House prefect, was everything Vivian had made her out to be. She ruled the house with an iron hand, and as a result, all the junior students and the SS1 bathroom workers of Sapphire House suffered.

As the long weeks of the term dragged by, the laughter grad-ually died in Carlotta's eyes.

The Sapphire House students slowly turned into unthinking automatons that woke up each morning and went about their duties without a ray of hope.

During the weeks of sorrow and hardship that followed Zika's transfer to Ruby House, Carlotta became best friends again with Onyedi, spent less and less time in her dormitory, and sought solace in her drama practices and her study group. She was lucky not to have been banned from the Drama Club. The principal had allowed her to continue as a member of the club only because of her outstanding performance in the school play.

Carlotta became stressed and miserable, and stopped eating. She lost weight and looked like a shadow of her former self. Anyone who saw her couldn't believe she was once a vibrant Feddie Girl with a gracious smile for all and sundry. Many felt sorry for her.

In effect, Carlotta realized her glory days at FGGC Uddah were over.

✳ ✳ ✳

On a Saturday morning in April, one week before the end of term, Carlotta logged on to her e-mail box. In addition to the usual mails from her parents, there was a mail from a username she did not recognize. The subject of the mail alone was enough to make her break out in a cold sweat. She clicked on it. The message was precise:

I know your secret. Zika can no longer save you.

Carlotta quickly logged out of her mailbox and ran out of the computer building, straight to Sapphire-One to find Onyedi.

That evening, right after dinner, and upon Onyedi's insistence, Carlotta recounted the contents of the e-mail to her study group members. The five girls sat huddled in the empty JS1D classroom and Carlotta sat in their midst, nervously twisting her fingers together in her lap. The girls seemed unusually quiet, Carlotta thought. *Aren't you all gonna say something?*

Finally, it was Onyedi who spoke. "Why Senior Chidi?"

Carlotta opened her mouth to reply, but no sound came. She could tell from the expression on their faces that the other students didn't understand what Onyedi meant by her question.

But Carlotta knew. Onyedi wanted to know why she had implicated Chidi in the lesbianism incident, when she knew the former house prefect might be innocent.

In fact, Carlotta had asked herself that same question several times. But how could she begin to explain to the four students who had trusted and helped her through two semesters of academic toil, that she implicated an innocent prefect to save her bunkmate from suspension?

How could she tell them that after all that was said and done, she had visited Pearl-Four once more to meet with the dreaded Rema Yang?

Blaming the whole incident on Chidi had been Rema's idea. She had promised the plan would work like a charm—and she'd been right.

The only hitch was Carlotta wasn't allowed to spill her guts to anyone about their little chat. Not even to her best friend.

Sitting there, watching her study-group mates argue the reason for her behavior, Carlotta felt goose bumps erupt on her skin. She shuddered.

She had known right then, in the principal's office, that Rema was right. Implicating Chidi was the only way to save Zika from an undeserved punishment. She also knew that the principal would be far more lenient with Chidi as a school prefect than she would with Zika, who already had one count against her from the previous term.

As a result of Rema's plan, instead of suspension, Zika had gotten off with just a house transfer. Chidi, on the other hand, had been officially demoted from her prestigious post as a school prefect. It was sort of a win-win situation for all concerned—not counting the humiliation and embarrassment Chidi had to endure for a crime she did not commit.

What bothered Carlotta, though, and nagged at her since then, was the fact that Chidi had not denied the accusation. She had just nodded and accepted her fate without offering a word in her own defense. It was as if she'd opted to be the sacrificial lamb.

Totally weird. And creepy!

"So why did Senior Chidi write you those love letters?" Amanda asked.

Carlotta stared at her friends for a while and suddenly she couldn't take it anymore. "Oh God! What have I done?" she wailed. *Has Senior Rema spun a web to trap us all?* She shuddered.

"Neighbor, what is it? What did you do?" Ossie asked, her voice full of trepidation.

Carlotta had tears in her eyes. "It's a long story," she said, and looked at Onyedi. "Where should I start?"

"The beginning," Onyedi prompted with a knowing smile, her eyes huge behind the twin lens of her glasses.

"You're totally right," Carlotta agreed. "I should tell the whole story from the very beginning." She wiped tears off her eyes. *The guilt has bothered me, like, forever.*

Without saying another word, Carlotta reached up and snatched the Italian wig she had been wearing for two terms off her head.

Chapter 21
Carlotta's Confession

Maria poked through the door of Richard's office without knocking. She snaked in and placed a folder on his desk.

Richard frowned and dismissed her with an irate flick of his hand.

"Sure, Rick, anything you say," she said, chuckling. She gave him a one-eyed gesture and leaving the door wide open, sashayed out and back to her desk.

This girl is a royal pain in the butt. Richard got up and slammed the door. The physical similarity between her and the murdered Maria was so remarkable nobody in the office guessed they were different girls. Had he not witnessed Maria's head being blown off, he might not have seen through the switch, either.

Richard shuddered.

The thugs had replaced his Maria with this demon from hell—a brunette of the same age, height, and weight as his Maria. Hell, she even had the same hazel eyes. It was like they were both made from the same mold. *Maybe they have factories that make and store them in warehouses. Shoot one and replace her with another, no one would ever be the wiser.*

The replacement also came with Maria's date of birth and social security number. *Not surprising, since The Family has far-reaching tentacles with which they obtain anything they need. Anything! Including human replacements.*

On the other hand, Richard had other ways to tell them apart. While his Maria had always called him *Doctor*, the replacement insisted on calling him *Rick*. Richard hated that. Also, he loved the hint of shyness in the old Maria but hated the attitude of her replacement. And yes, she reciprocated the feeling.

The irony!

But they had to keep up appearances—they were professionals after all. And it would be disastrous for anyone to discover the truth: the big-shot physician from San Francisco involved with a shady Las Vegas Family. *No way. Wouldn't do for my reputation. A scandal like that would definitely bring down my career and wipe me out for good.*

Richard sighed. *Who said life always dealt a fair hand?*

The phone rang. He picked up. "Doctor Ikedi."

"Hello, Doc, this is Bruno."

Richard frowned. "Yeah?" He imagined the burly man sneering on the other end of the line.

"It's almost payday, Doc."

"I'm still trying to get a final verdict from the decision-makers in Vegas. It doesn't help that my father is long dead and buried, but I guess you're already aware of how succession works." Richard was chagrinned by the sound of air being sucked through teeth. "Cut me some slack here. Give me more time."

Silence came from the other end of the line. Then, "What was that?"

"I need more time!" At that moment, Richard hated Bruno with every fiber of his being.

Bruno chuckled. "Tell me Doc, how's your daughter making out in Nigeria?"

An icy fist encased Richard's heart. "Leave my family out of this shit!" *How on earth did they find out about Carlotta? You would think Nigeria would be the last place they'd look. Lord, please, they shouldn't harm my little girl.* He took a deep breath and combed his fingers through his hair.

"Now, don't be getting all smart on me, Doc. I have a deal for you. Why don't you persuade your *li'l* daughter to join the family business? You know, make things move along a little faster? What was this idea of you sending her to Nigeria—a just in case factor? The deal you made with the Palorizzi Family only covers you and not your offspring. *Capisce?*" Understand?

Richard let out a deep breath. "I said to leave my daughter out of this," he replied in a cold voice.

Bruno laughed. "Think about it, Doc, you can spend the rest of your life in jail, or you can speed things up by having your daughter join the family business. Either way, the choice is yours. You've only got three weeks, then you and your family are toast, starting with your li'l girl." Bruno made the sucking sound again.

"Go to hell, you bastard!"

"You talking to me, Doc?"

That's it! I've had it!

Maybe it was the detested sucking sound, or the fact that he wouldn't stand to being told how to handle his family, or the simple fact that he was plain tired of being jerked around by a man who greatly resembled humpty-dumpty; but something in Richard snapped and he decided he'd had enough.

Richard clenched the phone with both hands and held it directly in front of his face, the receiver inches from his lips. "Listen to me, you god-forsaken piece of shit," he snarled, his voice taking on a maniacal quality. "I will get you what you want, but don't expect me to give it up that easily. In exchange for my birthright with the Palorizzi Family, I want five million dollars. You got that, Fatso? Five million big ones!"

A stunned silence followed. Finally, when Bruno found his voice, he didn't sound as self-assured as before. "What did you say?"

"You heard me. Five million. And make no mistake about this. If you as much as touch a hair on the head of any member of my private family, the deal is off and I will come after you with everything I have."

For the first time in his entire organized-crime career, Bruno was at a loss for words. "Are you black-mailing me, Doc?" he asked, after a few seconds. His voice sounded wary, very cautious.

"You got that right, you fat bastard! This is the price you absolutely pay for daring to lay an eye on my immediate family." Richard paused. "And one more thing. Tell your good-for-nothing replacement of a Maria to start addressing me as *Doctor Ikedi*. I'm done taking crap from either of you!"

Bruno started to say something but he might well have saved his breath. The phone connection was dead.

✳ ✳ ✳

Shelley stared in open-mouthed horror at Josh. "Are you out of your mind?" She pushed the glossy photo prints off her desk and covered her face with her hands. It sickened her to see intimate details of her evening romps in the sack with a student captured in a dozen photo printouts.

Josh sighed. "I'm sorry, Professor, I had no idea they had your home planted with microphones and cameras."

Shelley shook her head, attempting to clear her jumbled thoughts. "What is this nonsense?" She pinched the bridge of her nose and closed her mind against the possibility of sleazy, wide-eyed men leering over the image of her naked body riding that of her young student, in her own bedroom, in her own home. *Why do they not brandish a gun and shoot me instead? Oh God!*

"Shelley—"

She cut him short. "Are you saying some thugs tapped my phone lines and installed hidden cameras in my home?" Her voice shook and her fingers tapped out a nervous rhythm on her desk. "Why on earth did you not tell me this before?" *I am finished as a professor. I need a large drink!*

Josh sighed and rubbed his temple. "Shelley, to be honest, I had no idea they were after me again until I was captured in front of your house three days ago."

"We are certainly in serious—" Shelley stopped. Her voice hardened. "Again? Did you say *again*?" She glared, looking like she was ready to hurl her desk in his face. "Why did you not tell me you had a past hanging over your head in the first place?" Her breath swooshed out at a rapid pace, chest heaving with the effort.

"I'm sorry. I've been in the custody of some very dangerous men for the last three days." Josh rubbed the swollen and raw spot on his wrists where the thin wires with which he'd been bound had bitten into his flesh. "Why else do you think I missed our last date? I was only allowed to leave this morning on the condition that I come straight here and show you these photos."

Shelley's eyes were wide with concern and she forgot her anger for a moment. "In that case, we should go to the police."

"No!" Josh's voice dropped to a desperate whisper. "We can't go to the cops." He glanced fearfully at the door. "They are watching us. They will be following us everywhere. You don't know these people and how ruthless they can be. If we as much as breathe a word of this to anyone, we'll disappear in an instant and probably end up in the depths of the Nevada desert as vulture bait."

Shelley shrieked and almost wet herself. "You are crazy." Her eyes darted around the room as if trying to locate a hidden camera. Abruptly, she reached for the phone. "I am calling the police."

"Don't!" Josh scrambled to stop her. "Listen to me! Shelley—"

"It is *Doctor Ikedi*," Shelley snapped.

"Whatever you say, but listen to me!" Josh covered the telephone's push buttons with one hand, the other still holding on to Shelley's wrist. "They threatened to kill me. Worse still, if we go to the cops, they will send copies of these compromising pictures to the Dean and expose us to the faculty. I don't mind sacrificing my life, but you could lose your faculty position or any possibility of making tenure if that happens. That is, if they don't do away with you first!"

"And my family." Shelley dropped the receiver back on its cradle.

"Yeah. Them, too." Josh released her and bent to retrieve the pictures from the floor. He stuffed them back in their envelope and looked apologetically at Shelley.

"But, they are asking for five million dollars." Shelley raised her hands for Josh to see and counted out the numbers on her fingers. "Not one, not two, not three, not even four, but *five million dollars?*" Her eyes were huge. She shook her head and stared Josh in the face, her eyes doubling in diameter. "I have a hundred thousand, do you have four-point-nine million?"

Josh did not answer.

Shelley sighed.

Finally, Josh said, "There must be a way out of this. We've got three weeks to come up with a plan."

"Three weeks? Who earns five million dollars within that space of time? Bill Gates? Oprah? What about Donald Trump? Are we supposed to steal it? Maybe we should rob a bank? How about we win the lottery? Surely, you are out of your mind. Your brain is malfunctioning. Either that or—" Shelley realized she was rambling and shut up. Her hands were shaking badly and she needed a drink. She slapped her hands on her desk and bolted to her feet.

Josh watched her with wary eyes. "Actually, I can raise the money in Vegas. But I'll need an advance."

"How much of *an advance?*" Shelley queried, towering over Josh's seated frame.

"Two hundred grand."

Shelley flinched. "How do you suppose I could come up with two hundred thousand dollars in cash without raising suspicion? And how on earth do you hope to turn that into five million?"

Josh shrugged. "If you can provide me with the advance in a few weeks, I assure you, I'm good for it. And in the worst case scenario, I will return from Vegas with a little bit more than the advance." Josh stared at the raw flesh around his wrists and said, "I didn't tell you this before but I'm rather good at poker and blackjack."

"Is that all you are not telling me? Why do you not tell how you happened to get yourself involved with phone-tapping shylocks and camera-clicking black-mailers?" Shelley twisted her fingers in her hair, and for a minute, looked like she was going to yank a fist-full right off her head.

"It's a long story, Professor, one I can't go into right now. Believe me, I don't know most of it myself, something to do with amnesia and the really bad accident I told you happened in Paris a while back."

Shelley stared doubtfully at him. She'd thought he was kidding when he told her some enemies had tried to kill him. He'd also said he spent a few years in France before returning to the United States to commence his college education.

Though Josh's story accounted for his impeccable French and charming attitude, Shelley had thought he made the whole thing up to seek attention. Especially the part where he said he had been fortunate enough to catch a bullet with his head and live to tell the tale.

But standing right there in her office, Shelley believed him. And became really scared of him. *God help me, I sure do know how to pick them.*

Without saying a word, she plucked her car keys off her desk.

Josh hurried. "Listen, Professor, I'm sorry I wasn't completely honest with you from the beginning. But, right now, I need you to trust me. Bruno and his gang aren't kidding around. They are *gonna* kill me if we don't come up with that money—fast."

Shelley stared at him. "I think you are insane. I am going home." She crossed to the door. "I need a large drink. And if I were you, I would get myself drunk, then head straight out of town." She scampered out of her office then poked her head back in. "When you leave, please close the door after you. And if you do leave town, please do not bother sending me a post card."

Shelley arrived home and went straight to her stash of liquor. She grabbed a bottle at random, uncapped and stuck it in her mouth. She emptied a quarter of its contents in one gulp.

God help me. I am finished as a professor. She chugged down another mouthful of the drink and staggered to the living room, vodka bottle in hand. She flumped herself down on the couch and groaned. Her head hurt, and her brain screamed *five million dollars* every so often. She tipped back her head and poured another generous amount of the fiery drink down her throat. She burped and opened her mouth, expecting a cloud of smoke to bellow out.

After a few moments, Shelley emptied the last of the drink and threw the bottle at the wall behind the fireplace. The bottle fell short of the target and landed with a plunk on the heavy rug.

"Bashtard," she yelled, and belched. She wrestled one shoe off her foot and held it by the spike of its heel.

"You *bashtarrrd shon* of a *beessh!*" She flung the shoe at the empty bottle with all the strength her drunken arm could muster, and then started to sob.

All at once, Shelley stopped sobbing and heaved, disgorging a third of the fiery contents of her stomach onto her lap. She lurched, closed her eyes and collapsed on the couch.

Two seconds later, she was unconscious, and soaked in her own reeking vomit.

❋ ❋ ❋

"Ι did not cut my hair," Carlotta admitted and shook her mass of brown curls loose from the tight bun behind her head.

Onyedi nodded. Ossie, Amanda, and Emeh stared in shock.

"Jesus Christ," Ossie screamed. "Why on earth would you put yourself in this kind of trouble?"

"Oh la la!" Emeh exclaimed.

"How come you didn't tell us about this before?" Amanda screeched.

"You deceived everyone, you deceived the whole school, *c'est terrible!*" Emeh chirped. It is terrible!

"I really didn't *wanna* do it. No, I mean it wasn't totally my decision, but it seemed like a way awesome idea then," Carlotta admitted in a heavy voice.

"Hmm, it is really a bad decision. Just wait till they find out." Ossie pointed toward the dormitories as she said this. "What do you think will happen to you then?"

"I think someone has already found out," Emeh said. She dropped her voice to a whisper. "That's what the e-mail was referring to? The secret—*n'est-ce pas?*" Is it not?

"Yes," Onyedi simply replied.

"I would definitely think so," Carlotta added. "Look, I totally need your help. We need to, like, figure out a way to get me outta this mess."

"Are you mad?" Amanda queried. "You have long hair—it's against the school rules. And somebody knows and is causing trouble for you. What do you expect us to do about it? Chop your hair off with our teeth?"

Ossie shook her head. "We are only in JS1. We can't just drag you out of a big pot of hot okro soup. Especially since you were the one who jumped into the pot with your two eyes wide open."

Ossie folded her arms across her chest. She looked not quite pissed off. No, definitely pissed off, Carlotta thought.

Carlotta also knew that not cutting her hair was the least of her problems. She took a deep breath and told the rest of the story: about the love notes, how she implicated Chidi to save Zika. Everything. She only left out the bit about Rema Yang.

Then Carlotta said, "I know there isn't much that we can do. But we can totally do something, right?" She stared at the four girls.

Onyedi examined her nails. Ossie, Amanda, and Emeh stared back at Carlotta, their eyes challenging her to come up with a plan. They had never looked more pissed.

Carlotta sighed. "Okay," she said. "I screwed up real bad and I'm totally sorry. But, right now, there's absolutely nothing I can do to change the past." She spread her arms in a helpless manner.

Onyedi stood. "Let's just focus."

"What do you mean?" Emeh asked, her eyes wide.

"It's not a coincidence," Onyedi explained. "Who gains?"

"Oh, I think I understand what Onyedi is trying to say." Ossie's eyes were bright and shinning as she explained, "Somebody knows that my neighbor is carrying her long hair. That same person also knows what Carlotta's e-mail address is so that she would be able to send that e-mail."

"And she may be the person who wrote all the love notes, too," Amanda said.

Carlotta cringed.

"But, why would anyone do all that?" Emeh asked.

"It's easy. To make Carlotta give up and leave school, and maybe go back to America," Ossie said. She looked dazed.

"But who would want you to leave?" Amanda asked Carlotta. "You haven't done anything wrong to anybody we don't know about, or have you?"

"No, I don't think so—" Carlotta started to say.

Amanda declared, "Wait oh! Hold on a minute! What about Senior Rema, the president of the Feddie Girls Club? Didn't she threaten you last term when you refused to join her club?"

Carlotta's heart fell.

"You mean that Senior Rema is the person doing all these things?" Ossie asked. "*Ehn-hehn*... Hmm..." She clapped her hands in disbelief. "Well, *sha*, that would explain about the purple envelopes."

"Yes and the love notes started coming right after you turned her club down. See?" Amanda was beginning to get excited.

"We need proof," Onyedi cautioned. "We may be wrong."

"Then let us go and prove it!" Emeh quipped. "What can we do? How do we catch her red handed?"

Carlotta squirmed inwardly. Rema hadn't written the notes, that much she knew. But there was no way she could call the attention of her friends to that fact without giving the whole game away. *There's nothing I can do but play along and hope we totally catch-on to the guilty person before any serious damage is done.*

"There is one way," Onyedi said. She explained there was a way to trace e-mails back to their origin. Being in the computer club, she could gain access to data logs that would match students to their on-line names if they had signed up through the school network. It was very likely that whoever sent the e-mail to Carlotta had signed up for an e-mail address through the school network and, therefore, the e-mail could be traced.

Carlotta asked, "But how do we get into the computer room? The Computer Building is closed for the term."

Onyedi devised a plan. "The club president has the keys," she whispered. "Pearl House."

"I know who she is. She is in the dorm next to mine," Ossie added. "Tonight, Amanda and I can get the key from her corner without her knowledge. We can all meet at midnight and sneak into the computer building." Ossie looked at Onyedi. "Will you know what to do after that?"

Onyedi nodded.

"What about the guards?" Emeh asked. "Won't they catch us?"

Ossie solved the issue. "Emeh, you and Amanda will have to be our lookouts while Carlotta, Onyedi, and myself go into the building. If you see the guards coming, just run inside and warn us. Okay?"

They all nodded. The plan was complete. They would meet again at midnight to carry it out.

✻ ✻ ✻

*A*t midnight, Carlotta slid down her bunk and pulled on her dressing gown. She tiptoed out of the dormitory without making any sound and shut the door. She inched up the long, lighted hallway to the Sapphire House doors where Onyedi and Emeh were already waiting. They both had flashlights. Carlotta realized she had forgotten to grab her flashlight. *Great!*

Onyedi and Emeh stood aside while Carlotta reached up to unlock the heavy bolts. After a minor struggle, the double doors creaked open. The three girls stepped out into the inky blackness of the night.

The air was cool but heavy with moisture, typical of any tropical night during the rainy season. There was hardly any breeze ruffling the damp leaves of the Mystical Mangy that loomed silently ahead of them.

Emeh found a heavy stone and held the Sapphire House doors closed with it. It wouldn't do for a prefect to get up in the middle of the night only to discover that the entrance doors were wide open. The three girls hastened to the neck of the pathway loop, where they'd agreed to meet up with Ossie and Amanda.

Minutes later, the five girls stole up the winding pathway toward the classroom buildings. They huddled together and crouched low, as if afraid to lose sight of one another.

A tinkling sound startled them. Instinctively, they halted and became very quiet, straining to listen.

The sound got nearer.

They tensed.

"What is that?" Amanda asked. Her voice shook.

"I don't know," Ossie replied. She was equally afraid.

Actually, they were all afraid now. They didn't know what was making the tinkling sound.

It got even nearer.

Louder.

Pattering footfalls followed.

"*Ehwo!* It's *Ekuke!*" Ossie bolted for the classroom buildings, the four other girls very close behind her.

Carlotta didn't know what *Ekuke* was, but she trusted that if the others were running at top speed, she ought to run like hell, too. Before long, the girls leaped onto the SS3 block pavement and stopped to catch their breath. They were panting furiously.

"That was close," Amanda whispered.

"*Oui.* We are very lucky," Emeh agreed, her breath coming in heavy puffs. Yes.

"Oh my God!" Carlotta exclaimed, her eyes wide with fear. "What on earth were we running from?"

"It was *Ekuke*, a mad dog," Ossie replied. "You will catch rabies if it bites you."

Onyedi nodded, biting her lip, looking apprehensively around.

Carlotta looked back at the winding path. Whatever that dog was, she was glad it hadn't come running after them.

The five girls continued with their journey to the Computer Building. When they got there, Ossie produced the key ring she had filched and unlocked the doors. Emeh and Amanda quickly crouched out of sight behind a hedge.

Carlotta snuck into the building with Ossie and Onyedi. Using the light from the flashlights, the three girls made their way through the corridors, until they found the door to the computer lab. Ossie selected a key from the bunch and inserted it into the lock but it would not turn. She tried another and another but the lock would not budge. Her hands began to shake so badly she could hardly hold the key ring steady. She cursed and stamped her foot.

"Let me try," Carlotta offered, and took the keys from Ossie's shaking hands. "Hold the light up," she instructed Onyedi.

Carlotta carefully tried each key until one of them made the clicking sound she hoped for. She turned the lock and shoved. The door opened with a tired creak, revealing the empty room within.

The three girls headed straight for the computers. Onyedi immediately turned one on and it began to boot. They sat and waited.

Onyedi logged on to the computer with a special password then launched the Internet browser. Carlotta logged on to her mailbox and provided the username for the e-mail in question.

Thereafter, the rest was left to Onyedi. She launched some software and accessed the data within. She started going through some files.

Just then, Amanda and Emeh came flying into the room.

"The guards are coming," they whispered, their wide, fearful eyes and flailing hands conveying a need for urgency. "We have to run away from here, right now."

"Where are they now?" Ossie asked. Her voice was shaking again.

"In the Home Economics Building," Emeh said. "They will check this building next. We have to go now. We will enter into serious trouble if they catch us." Emeh was almost in tears.

Carlotta glanced at Onyedi. The girl's hands were flying over the keyboard as she sought the information she needed.

"You girls go," Onyedi said breathlessly, and hit the escape button. The computer screen went blank. "The keys." She motioned to Carlotta to hand them over. Then she pushed the girls toward the door. "Go, now!" she insisted when Carlotta hesitated. "Wait in the house lobby."

The girls didn't have much of a choice. They either leave, or risk getting into serious trouble if caught by the guards. They hurried back through the waiting room, down the corridors, and out of the Computer Building.

"Please, be careful," Carlotta whispered, and gave Onyedi a brief hug. Onyedi nodded then ushered her out and closed the door. Carlotta heard the front door click shut as Onyedi turned the key in the lock from the other side.

"Bend down," Emeh whispered, tugging on Carlotta's arm.

Carlotta crouched next to the three girls, adrenaline dumping into her blood stream.

Making sure they were in the clear, the girls scurried from the Computer Building. When they were several yards away, they looked back to make sure they couldn't be discovered by the guards. Then they stood and ran down the winding pathway to the dormitories, moving as fast as their legs would allow.

Back at Sapphire House, the four girls crouched low on the front pavement and waited for Onyedi's return.

Minutes dragged by. They waited in fidgety silence.

Then they saw Onyedi's thin form making its way down the pathway toward them. Ossie stood and pressed her hands to her chest. Carlotta heaved a sigh of relief. She didn't realize how tense she was until then.

Onyedi handed the keys back to Ossie. She hadn't been caught. They were safe.

The two Pearl House girls whispered goodbye to the Sapphire girls and promised to meet up with them the next morning to discuss Onyedi's findings. They needed to get back to Pearl House and return the keys.

In the hallway, Carlotta locked the double doors behind them. The heavy bolts slid home without much difficulty.

"Meet you in the lobby," Onyedi whispered, and disappeared through the door of Sapphire-One.

Carlotta and Amanda went on to the house lobby to await Onyedi's return. From the light of Emeh's flashlight, Carlotta looked around the room. The lobby was very untidy. Chairs lay around haphazardly, empty soda bottles littered the tables, banana and orange peels were all over the floor, discarded peanut shells were everywhere, and there was a big puddle of something that looked suspiciously like orange juice in the middle of the room. The lobby looked like a group of students had a party and not bothered to clean up after themselves.

Carlotta sighed and stepped gingerly around the puddle. She found a clean chair close to the back of the room and sat down. Emeh sat beside her, and together, they waited in the darkness.

A few minutes later, they heard Onyedi coming in through the door.

"Interesting discovery," Onyedi said as she walked up to them. She had her flashlight in one hand and some sheets of computer paper in the other. But Onyedi was not paying attention to the scene her flashlight illuminated, for she never made it to where Carlotta and Emeh sat.

In slow motion, just like in the movies, Carlotta watched in horror as Onyedi skidded on the puddle of orange juice and struggled in vain to regain her balance. Then she must have stepped on a banana peel because, the next thing Carlotta knew, Onyedi was flying up in the air. Then she descended, and landed with a resounding crash on the hard floor. The flashlight flew out of her hand as she landed, ending up somewhere under a table in shattered pieces.

Carlotta screamed. She ran to where Onyedi lay and sank to her knees. Emeh must have been screaming, too, because Carlotta could hear her but her voice sounded far, far, away.

"*Nooo!*" Carlotta yelled, staring down at Onyedi who was whimpering but wasn't moving. Onyedi raised a weak hand toward Carlotta. Her head was bent in an odd angle. Just as Carlotta reached out to take her friend's hand, the lobby lights snapped on. Framed in the door way was Anita.

A red puddle began to widen around Onyedi's head.

"*On-yeh-dee! Nooo!*" Carlotta strung out in a stricken voice.

Her body went rigid.

Her vision blurred.

Her head lolled.

Carlotta lost all consciousness and collapsed on the still form of her friend.

Chapter 22
An End, And A Beginning

"Professor, may I have a word with you?"

Shelley turned and her face fell. Josh was hurrying toward her.

"What do you want?" she hissed from the corner of her mouth. "Can this wait until later? You know it is a bad idea for us to be seen together in the department." She had been avoiding him since the photo incident in her office. He had already jeopardized her career enough.

Josh bit his lip and blinked away his hurt. "I'm sorry, Professor, but this can't wait. We only have a few weeks till the deadline."

Shelley stopped. She glanced around to make sure no one was within earshot. "I am doing my best to raise the cash you need. What is it this time?"

"I received a call from Bruno last night. They're willing to cut us a deal."

"What could they possibly want?"

"They want you to persuade your daughter to join a certain family organization your husband once belonged to."

Shelley's heart ground to a halt. *Oh my God, please not that.* Her face first showed fear then the muscles stiffened into a stone mask. "My— My daughter?" she asked when she could speak. "How did my daughter get into this?"

"I honestly don't know. I'm just relaying the information I was given. Bruno said you'd get the message."

Shelley's eyes narrowed in suspicion. *Bruno? So this is what it has all been about? Richard and that Family of his? He swore he was out of organized crime for good.* Looking directly at Josh, Shelley shook her head and said in a firm voice, "Not a chance. I am not going to have my daughter involved in any of this."

"But, Professor—" Josh began.

Shelley cut him off. "No, Joshua. I do not care about the consequences. There is no way I will have my daughter involved with these thugs." She shook her head and took a deep breath. "I will get you the money you need for Las Vegas, even if it means I have to sell all I own."

"Professor, please think about this. A lot is at stake. My life is on the line here—"

"I understand, Joshua, and I am sorry about the whole situation. However, my daughter is only thirteen. My first priority is to keep her safe."

Josh's face fell.

"We have to go with the first plan. You said you are a professional high-stakes card player and I believe in your prowess. I will press my brokers to sell more stocks and raise the second hundred thousand in a few days. I should have it to you by Friday."

"Professor..."

"No, Listen." Shelley's voice became stern. "You have to go to Las Vegas and win five million dollars." She shook her head sadly at Josh. "I know it is a lot of pressure, but my daughter being a part of organized crime is out of the question. You got us into this situation, so *you* are to get us out of it." She closed her eyes just for a second. When she opened them, they were blue stones. "This is my final decision. Good day, Mr. Greinbach." *And I hope you live long enough to get to Vegas and win the money.*

Shelley strode off. Josh's eyes bored into her back but Shelley did not look back. When she got to her office, the phone was ringing. She reached it just in time.

"Yes? Dr. Ikedi."

She listened to the heavy Nigerian-accented voice on the line describing a situation involving Carlotta.

Shelley's jaw dropped.

The phone slipped and crashed to the floor.

She jerked herself into action then grabbed her purse and rushed out of the office.

"*Madam? Are you there? Can you hear me? Hello? Madam?*" the voice at the end of the line prompted from Nigeria.

But Shelley was already out of the building and on her way to the international airport in Tulsa.

Overcoming her panic, she paused just long enough to call her banker and have him ready two hundred thousand dollars in cash.

Then Shelley called Josh and coldly gave him instructions on how to pick up the dough.

✳ ✳ ✳

When Carlotta came to, she was lying in a hospital bed. Her mom was bending over her, looking very concerned.

"Honey, are you okay?" Shelley asked, looking down at Carlotta's face.

Carlotta nodded. "Where am I? What happened?" She realized she was in a ward, dressed in a hospital gown, a long IV-tube connecting a needle stuck in her left arm to a pouch suspended high above her head.

Carlotta winced. She hated needles.

"Oh, honey." Shelley sat on the bed beside her daughter and laid a hand on her forehead. "You are in a private hospital in Onitsha. You have been unconscious for three days." She had undisguised sorrow in her eyes. "The school called me and I came over as soon as I could. Try and get some rest, honey, the doctor will come by any minute. You will be okay."

Carlotta closed her eyes and tried to remember how she came to be at the hospital in the first place. She remembered being in the Computer Building with Ossie and Onyedi. Then she was running back to Sapphire House, then she was sitting in the dark in the house lobby, then Onyedi was falling—

Carlotta sat up. "*On-yeh-dee*," she said. "Where is she? How is she? Is she okay? I must see her!" She made to get out of bed but Shelley placed a hand on her arm.

Carlotta looked up at her mom's face. She read the message in her mom's eyes even before her mother spoke.

"Honey, I am afraid your friend did not make it," Shelley said, her voice laced with sadness. "She died the morning after the accident. The school told me what happened."

Oh God, no! Tears welled in Carlotta's eyes and fell unbidden down her cheeks. Her chest constricted. Her throat felt dry.

Nooo!

Carlotta wept. She let herself be cradled in her mother's arms as she sobbed and sobbed.

It's my fault. I caused the whole thing.

Bereft, Carlotta believed she was never going to be happy again.

"Take me away from here," Carlotta begged. "Just take me away from this wretched place, right this minute." She sobbed harder. "I don't ever want to set foot in this place again. Please get me out of here." She buried her face in her mom's shoulder and cried like she hadn't done before.

On-yeh-dee is gone? It just can't be true. This can't be happening.

In her mind, Carlotta saw Onyedi's face; glasses perched on her nose, thin lips stretched into that knowing smile. Then she saw her falling... falling...

A few days later, Carlotta boarded a plane headed back to the United States with her mother. Shortly after they arrived home, she was curled on her bed in her old bedroom and crying herself to sleep.

* * *

*O*phone message was waiting for Shelley when she returned home from Nigeria with Carlotta. It was from Josh:

"Still in Vegas. Have the dough. Awaiting instructions for the drop-off. When can I see you?"

Shelley heaved a big sigh of relief. Josh had held up his side of the bargain and for that, she was grateful. Her few nights of indiscretion had cost her two hundred thousand dollars.

Better my savings than my life or my daughter's innocence.

She stood silent for a minute, contemplative. Then she raised a finger and depressed the button to delete Josh's message.

Goodbye, Mr. Greinbach.

Seconds later, Shelley picked up the phone and held it to her chest. Carlotta had been too upset to ask about her dad. But soon, she would, and Shelley wanted to make sure she was spared any more misery. She loved her daughter with all her heart, and for her baby's sake, she was willing to let by-gones be by-gones.

Drawing in a deep breath, she dialed Richard's number.

He answered on the first ring. "Shelley…"

Pain knifed through her at the sound of his voice.

"Carlotta is here," Shelley said, ignoring Richard's surprised greeting. "She needs you. We both need you."

She hung up before he could reply.

* * *

*T*hirty minutes after receiving Shelley's call, Richard drove up and parked in the driveway.

Shelley was at the door to greet him. He held her in a tight embrace and shut his eyes.

They had both made mistakes and were sorry. There was no need for words or apologies. After all, they were life partners and were destined to remain that way.

The following day, Richard called his lawyer and had him cancel the divorce proceedings. Then he packed out of his rented apartment and moved back in with his family.

✳ ✳ ✳

The weeks after her return to Oklahoma, Carlotta walked around in a daze.

She could not think straight; she had no appetite for food or for any of the things that usually amused her. She didn't try to contact her old childhood friend Sasha and let her know she was back. She didn't bother to get dressed in the morning. She didn't go downstairs for meals. She didn't watch TV or see any movies.

Carlotta just spent her time alone, curled up on her bed, wishing she could turn back the clock.

It's so not fair. On-yeh-dee shouldn't have died. It was really all my fault.

She refused all attempts by her parents to get her back to her usual self. She turned down invitations to go shopping or to the hairdresser's or out for a meal.

Her parents enrolled her in a different middle school in Owasso.

Carlotta did not care.

She ignored her cell phone. She didn't log on to the Internet. She was very desolate and was determined to stay that way. She mourned the death of her best friend and cried herself to sleep each night.

Then one evening, exactly four days before school was to resume in May, Carlotta mustered up the courage to go through the suitcase she had brought back with her from boarding school.

She vaguely remembered Ossie, Amanda, and Emeh helping her put her things together and packing up her stuff on the afternoon she was discharged from the hospital. She had insisted she wanted to leave, and the school authorities had let her go. It had been just a few days to the end of term anyway.

Now, she just wanted to get rid of everything in the trunk that reminded her of the two terms she had spent in boarding school.

She zipped open the suitcase and lifted the lid. Several sheets of folded computer paper fell out the top to the floor of her bedroom.

Carlotta picked up the papers and unfolded them.

One look had her gasping. Her eyes widened. She sat down hard on the floor in astonishment. They were the same sheets Onyedi had on the fateful night of the accident.

On-yeh-dee, I'm so sorry... Carlotta's throat constricted and a fresh bout of tears rolled down her cheeks. She'd forgotten all about the incident that led to that night's adventure. She looked at the sheets again. There were a lot of html codes and computer language stuff she couldn't understand printed on them, but Onyedi had also penciled in some paragraphs in her own handwriting.

Stunned, Carlotta dried her eyes and read what Onyedi had written.

Oh my God!

They had been suspecting the wrong person all along. The real culprit was someone who had wanted Carlotta out of school since the first term. She was someone who was close to both Carlotta and Zika and had access to Rema's purple envelopes at the same time. She was someone who had nothing to lose but everything to gain from Zika striking out at Anita, from Carlotta being accused of being a water spirit and being implicated as a lesbian, and from Carlotta's secret of keeping her long hair being made public and reported to the school authorities. The culprit had only one ulterior motive. She wanted Carlotta's part in the school play!

No other person fitted the description like a glove but Nneka.

Of course! How could I have been so dense? I didn't even see this coming. And she had pretended to be my friend!

It had been Nneka all along. It made perfect sense. There were some e-mail printouts to prove it.

First, Nneka had tried to get Carlotta in serious trouble by tipping off Anita that Carlotta was lying about cutting her hair and that Zika was helping her with the cover up. When Anita had tried to confront Zika, they had gotten into a fight, which had resulted in Zika being gated. But, Carlotta had remained safe.

Then Nneka had tried to get rid of Carlotta by sending her all those love notes. She had expected Carlotta to freak out and decide to go back to the United Sates. When Carlotta kept the notes quiet and didn't react, as Onyedi advised, Nneka's plan had failed. Carlotta remained in the school play and gained enormous fame due to her natural acting talent.

After their success in the competition at Ghana, Nneka had gotten quite desperate. She'd concocted the story about Carlotta being possessed by water spirits and passed that on to her friend Shade. But even that didn't get Carlotta fired from the play.

Then came the press club and the lesbianism accusations. Nneka had tipped them off, too. Anonymously, Nneka had also sent a replica of one of the love notes she'd written to Carlotta under the disguise of *Me xxx*, to Chidi Anayo, who then presented that to the student panel during the investigation. However, Carlotta still managed to slip through that one with Rema Yang's help by implicating Chidi as the writer of the love notes, thereby saving Zika and herself from probable expulsion.

Nneka's final stunt had then been to threaten to make known the secret about Carlotta's long hair. She had hoped Carlotta would freak out and report herself, thereby earning a much-deserved suspension for her deceit and for breaking a serious school rule. That might have worked, had Carlotta not gone to her study group members for help. However, when things turned sour and Onyedi ended up paying for all the trouble with her life, Carlotta had given up entirely and left the school, thereby handing Nneka exactly what she wanted on a platter of gold!

Oh my God! The conniving bitch! Technically, it's her fault that On-yeh-dee died. She basically implicated my bunkie and killed my best friend!

Mind whirling, heart racing, Carlotta got off the floor of her bedroom and sat on her bed. She couldn't believe Nneka could do all these mean things and hurt so many people, just so she could take her place in the drama competition. As her understudy, if for some reason Carlotta got indisposed, Nneka would take her place as the leading actress in the school play. Now that Carlotta had left the school, Nneka would get to act in the play and compete with the drama club in South Africa that coming term!

Good thing On-yeh-dee figured the whole thing out. The murdering bitch! She can't just go free. She so has to pay!

And what about Chidi? Why had she accepted the harsh hand fate dealt her and borne the brunt of a crime she did not commit, without complaints?

All of a sudden, it dawned on Carlotta.

Senior Rema Yang must have something on Senior Chee-dee. Of course! That must be it! Why else would Chidi give up her prestigious status as a prefect without a fight?

It made complete sense now.

Carlotta sat on her bed and thought for a long time without moving. The sunrays seeping through the blinds of her bedroom windows got weaker and weaker then faded altogether. By the time the room got completely dark, Carlotta had decided on what to do. She slipped off her bed and turned on her bedroom lights. Then she found a plain letter envelope and addressed it:

To: *Rema Yang*
        President, Feddie Girls Club,
        FGGC Uddah.

Then Carlotta booted her computer and began to compose a letter in Microsoft word.

Several minutes later, she was finished. The final piece of the puzzle was in place.

It is time the Feddie Girls Club earns a new member. Senior Necker has to pay dearly for her sins!

$\mathcal{T}$he next morning, Carlotta came down for breakfast, cheery faced and fully dressed, to the surprise of her mom, who was bustling about in the kitchen.

Richard had already left for the hospital.

"Mom, I need a big favor from you," Carlotta said, staring her mother in the eyes.

Shelley nodded and wiped her hands on a dishtowel hanging by the stove, and then waited for Carlotta to continue.

"Please, I need you to take me to the hairdresser's on your way in to school. I will take a cab back when I'm done," Carlotta said in a serious voice. "And may I borrow your credit card? There are a few things I need."

Shelley regarded her daughter for a moment. "All right," she said, handing over an American Express Gold card. "You know the rules. And you have to promise to be very careful, and to come straight home as soon as you are finished."

"Okay, Mom, I promise," Carlotta said. When she saw her mom turn her back, Carlotta smiled and added under her breath, "That won't be a problem. That totally won't be a problem at all."

$\mathcal{T}$wenty minutes away, right about the time when Shelley handed Carlotta a credit card, Richard picked up the phone and dialed the number of the police station in Tulsa.

Here goes, Bruno.

390

He listened to the ringing signal on the phone, waiting for the call to get through. *My daughter is safely home, and my wife took me back, so you and The Family can do your worst.*

Unknown to Richard, while he was waiting to spill his guts to the cops over the phone, Bruno was halfway to Switzerland, where five million dollars was waiting for him in a Swiss account. Richard had no idea Bruno never planned on paying him a cent and was actually saying to himself at that very moment, *"Screw you, Doc, and your shit-ass Family. Who the hell needs you guys when he's discovered a free ticket to big bucks? That horny kid is a freaking genius. He is a true poker legend!"*

Within thirty seconds of Richard's call to the police, Shelley was marching down to the office of the Dean of Arts and Languages. *I may not be perfect, nor even be a very good professor, but what I can be is a good wife and mother, and an honest woman who has willingly made a very terrible mistake with an equally willing male student.*

Unknown to Shelley, while she was self-righteously thinking of punching a hole in the bag of her indiscretion, Josh had just exited a plane in Paris, France. In addition to the five million he'd wired to Bruno's Swiss account, he'd also wired thirteen-point-seven million dollars to a private account in Paris registered to a Mathieu Devoir.

What Josh didn't know was that Whacko had flown coach in the same plane and was now shadowing him as he made his way through customs.

Nora David

✳ ✳ ✳

ust as her mom walked into the Dean's office, Carlotta
settled in a high, low-backed, swiveling, leather chair facing
a huge mirror. She watched as the hairdresser wrapped a white
sheet about her shoulders then picked up the scissors and went
to work on her hair.

Carlotta watched without an ounce of regret as her long
brown curls fell to the dark marble floor, around the hairdresser's
feet.

Carlotta gave a rueful smile.

Eyes closed, she leaned back against the black seat and
contented herself with listening to the *snip-snip* made by the scissors being worked by the hairdresser's practiced hand.

Nestled in Carlotta's purse was a newly purchased one-way
flight ticket to Lagos, Nigeria.

Coming Soon
to
Bernard Books Publishing

FICTION

The Poker Legend
(By Mundy Mill)

✻

Partial Insanity
(By Mitch Brandon)

✻

Hole in My Plate
(By Koj Kopeck)

www.bernardbooks.com

How much is your life worth?

THE POKER LEGEND

By

Mundy Mill

Josh Greinbach has two vices: Poker and Women. One perfect hand at the formidable Las Vegas Moritz Hotel's casino brings Josh's dreams of fame and success to life—in an unexpected way.

Josh gets involved with the wrong woman and his existence takes on a new meaning.

Seduced by the irresistible Maria Ryczek, shadowed by the ruthless Bruno, and wanted dead by the most dangerous organized crime family in Vegas; Josh's world takes on a sizzling, toe-curling tempo.

To salvage the honor of his secret lover, Josh stakes his most-priced possession in the deadliest card game of all time…

This gut-wrenching, adrenaline-pumping parallel story to *FEDDIE GIRL* will take you on a thrilling ride from Atlanta to Las Vegas to Paris and beyond.

**Coming to Bernard Books Publishing
in November 2010**

QUICK ORDER FORM

Fax orders: (513) 662-5201

Telephone orders: (513) 662-5200 (All major credit cards accepted.)

Email orders: mail@bernardbooks.com

Web orders: http://bernardbooks.com/form.html

Postal orders: Bernard Books Publishing, P.O. Box 11010, Cincinnati Ohio, 45211 USA

Please send the following number of books. I understand that I may return any defective book within 14 days of purchase for a replacement copy.

Book Title: _____

Quantity: _____

Customer information:

Name: _____

Address:

_____

City: _____ State: _____ Zip: _____

Email Address: _____

Telephone: _____

Sales tax: Please add 6.45% for books shipped to Ohio addresses.

Shipping* by air: US: Add $3.99 per book; Canada: Add $5.99 per book; UK: Add 6.99 per book; Nigeria: Add N1899 per book.

*No shipping cost for single orders of FEDDIE GIRL placed before June 2010.

Bulk orders: Email James Downer (james.downer@bernardbooks.com) for more information.